THE

CUP

OF THE

WORLD

THE
CUP
OF THE
WORLD

John Dickinson

Published by Laurel-Leaf
an imprint of Random House Children's Books
a division of Random House, Inc.
New York

Originally published in hardcover in Great Britain by David Fickling Books, London,
in 2004. This edition published by arrangement with David Fickling Books.

www.randomhouse.com/teens
Educators and librarians, for a variety of teaching tools,
visit us at www.randomhouse.com/teachers

RL: 5.9
ISBN: 978-0-553-49489-1
April 2007
Printed in the United States of America
10 9 8 7 6 5 4 3 2 1
First Laurel-Leaf Edition

For Robin

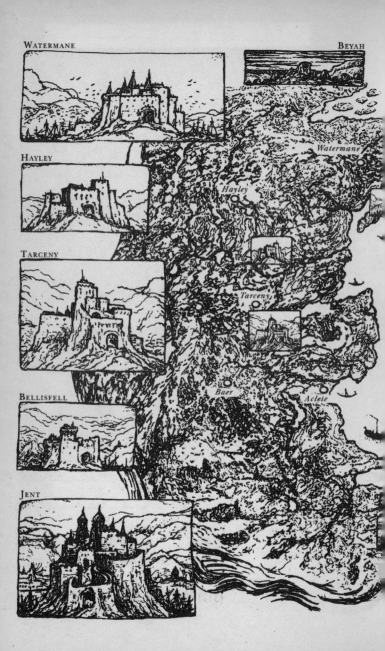

WATERMANE

BEYAH

Watermane

HAYLEY

Hayley

TARCENY

Tarceny

BELLISFELL

Baer

Aclete

JENT

Contents

Part III: The Traitress   329

PART I

THE MAN IN THE DREAM

I

The Courts of the King

haedra did not know the way, in the unlit corridors of the King's house. She was following the older girls through the shadowy passages, going by their whispers, the scuff of their feet and the sounds of their suppressed excitement. The noises led her to the left, and then to the right, past storerooms and scroll rooms and rooms for purposes that she could not guess. The shutters on the windows were all closed. No one had thought to bring a light, because it had been bright day outside when they had hatched this plan between them. She supposed that someone up at the front must be leading.

There was a pause ahead. The girls had reached a door. From beyond it there rose a great babble: the sound of a crowd in a large room.

Phaedra had imagined that the royal court was a silent place, like a service in chapel where people only spoke when necessary. She had not expected this unruly noise. Perhaps it would make it easier for them to get into the throne hall without being noticed. She had no idea what would happen after that. She had never seen a witch trial before.

A trumpet sounded from ahead of them. The girls had the door open. Phaedra saw the shapes of their heads and shoulders against the light beyond as they stepped one by one through the doorway. She made her way out after the others onto a narrow wooden gallery that ran along the wall of a huge vaulted hall. The babble she had heard was dying. Somewhere below her, a voice had begun to speak. She found a place at the rail, and drew breath. She knew she should not be where she was, looking down at the throne hall of the King.

It was hard to see.

From the high windows the sun shot, barring the hall with rays. Torches glowed feebly. Gold threads gleamed upon banners that swayed in the columns of heat. Below her was the crowd – knights and barons and nobles, packed against either wall so that the long aisle was clear. Where the sun fell the men stood lit in white silver, every detail plain from the badge of a house to the blink of an eye. Their faces were tense, bearded, craning for a view. Between the light beams was a mass of shapes and silhouettes, in deeper and deeper shadows up the hall to the throne. The air pricked with the sweat of two hundred men in heavy cloth. Little noises washed around the walls: clinks, shifting feet, the squeak of leather, and half-sentences murmured into neighbours' ears. The men spoke like hunters, a-tiptoe in the forests. And the beast that stalked the thickets was the imminence of Death.

She looked at once for her father, down among the mass of unknown men. He must be there – but had he seen her? If he had seen her, he might be angry that she had come when she should not have done. If she was going to have to face that later, it would be better to know now. But she could not pick him out, because she was a stranger to the court and did not know where to look for him. She did not know where he would stand among all these nobles: high, surely, but how near to the King?

She could see the King – that white-bearded figure upon the High Throne. Above him the sun of his house blazoned the wall with dull gold. In the shadow to his right sat a younger man – Prince Barius, upon the Throne Ochre, bolt upright with a sword across his knees. And the younger man to the King's left must be Prince Septimus, who was to be knighted that evening at the same feast during which she was to be presented.

To one side of the thrones stood a small group of bishops, robed and capped with gold, and their tonsured priests. On the other were the chosen officers of the court – a rank of serious faces, with gold chains around their necks. There were guards before the dais. Their helms and axes and polished shoulder-pieces flickered with reflected torch fire.

A baron stood in the aisle, in the last streak of sun before the throne. His black beard and doublet paled in the glare, and the skin of his face was dead white, except for the solid little shadow below the tip of his nose. He was facing full into the light. Surely he could see very little; but every soul in the hall could see him: his heavy brow; his face strong. He must have placed himself deliberately in that ray of sun the moment the trumpets had died. The voice she had heard came from a figure in the gloom beside the baron: a man in a cap and robe who was reading aloud from a scroll.

'. . . *Didst consort with fell spirits . . . didst conspire with rebels . . . didst most foully plot violence by magic, against us a baron of the realm . . . we call on our liege for justice and an end to evil . . . that thou shalt suffer death under the law of this land . . .*'

Somebody else was standing in the expanse of gloomy flagstones. It was a woman, alone. Her head was bowed a little. And it seemed to Phaedra that not a face in the crowd changed as the charges poured on over this creature. Their frown ran from the steps of the King to the gates of the hall.

Phaedra had not known what a witch would look like. If she had expected anything, it was some cackling nightmare, caged like a beast to thrill a fair. She had not been prepared for a plain woman, only a few years older than herself. So this was the one on whom the baron wanted revenge. This was the woman who would lie in an unshriven grave, buried headless with a stake through her heart. Phaedra drew another long breath, and wondered if her limbs were really trembling in that stifling air.

The reading ended. The accused woman was replying, in a voice too low for the watchers to hear. Her speech did not take long. The space that followed was filled with coughs and the murmur of a crowd shifting its feet.

From the shadows the King spoke: a question. The baron was nodding. The King beckoned. Six retainers came forward carrying long swords. They laid them in a row on the floor between the baron and the woman, alternating hilt and blade so that three pointed each way. A herald bellowed down the hall.

'*The King yields judgement to the eyes of Heaven. Let any that feel the right of this cause come forward before the third trumpet. I*

6

say, let them come forward who are ready to prove the truth with their body!'

The King raised his hand, and a trumpet blew.

The watchers jumped. Sudden, shattering, the tongue of the brass was far more powerful than the voices preceding it. At once two knights stepped forward from the crowd. They took their places side by side at the hilts of swords before the baron. Somewhere in the gallery someone was whispering their names, as if these were well-known fighters. A moment later the baron himself took a pace forward to stand by the hilt of the third sword on his side. Again he placed his feet carefully, so that the light bathed him from head to toe for everyone to see.

Then nothing happened. People whispered to one another on the balcony and down below. No one moved from their place. Phaedra stared down at the woman, standing alone with her back to the gallery.

Come on. Come on. Why did they not blow? Had the herald fallen asleep on his feet? Beyond the hall the sun had already shifted. A patch of shadow had crawled over the baron's foot. He had not noticed.

There was movement in the lower hall. Someone had emerged from the crowd down there, and was standing in the empty aisle. He was looking around, looking back, like a little boy who had been told to step up by a parent, and had forgotten at once what it was he was supposed to do.

Now he had begun to walk up towards the throne. He crossed a shaft of light, and appeared as a plain-looking knight in mail. His head was bare, but his face, and his device, were obscure for long seconds more until he

7

stepped through the last sunbeam and threw his shadow for a moment across the baron's knees. A heavy, stubbly cheek showed briefly under lank hair. A red hound danced on his surplice. In the gloom before the throne the man bowed to the King. Then he sidled to his right and, without appearing even to look at the woman behind him, stood at the hilt of a sword on her side. As he did so the trumpets sounded at last.

Now the whispering increased. The change was palpable. Without a champion the woman would have been a witch. Her sentence would have been passed and done before nightfall. One man had thrown the matter open. Men would die to close it.

The dazzle of the light was fading; high above the hall thin clouds veiled the sun. The contrasts blended into detail that became clearer to the eye. The baron and his knights were looking woodenly at their opponent. The newcomer wore the gear of a poor manor lord – one of the 'dog-knights' of the Kingdom, who owned no master but the King and no follower but some faithful hound. He was looking at his feet, at the throne, to the woman at his back. Perhaps the full implications of what he was doing had only just come to him. The woman too was no longer fixed by the row of armed men before her. Her eyes moved from her feet to the crowd, and then up to the gallery. She was slender, and wore a simple blue dress. Her long hair shone a deep brown, and was adorned with a few sparse yellow gems. For a moment Phaedra looked down into a pale, triangular face, with large eyes and a pronounced nose: an expression bewildered and alone. Phaedra saw she was afraid.

8

'They'll kill them both, now,' muttered a voice in the gallery. 'Him, then her.'

It was like a dream – worse than a dream, for Phaedra felt that in her dreams she was never as helpless as here. She wanted to turn away, leave the hall, and not see how it ended. But she did not know her way through the dark of the King's house.

And, just as in a dream, she could suddenly see her father's face clearly. He stood among the nobles in the opposite aisle. He had not looked up. His big, bearded face was frowning at the scene before him. He did not like what he saw. What could he do? Phaedra felt sure he wanted to do something. He was quick enough to say what he thought was right and wrong at home. Would he tell the King, in front of all these people, that this trial was wrong? Surely not. The King had said that it should take place.

Would he come out and be a champion?

But then he would have to fight! Fight men who wanted to kill him, one after another, with none of his soldiers to help! She did not dare think what might happen.

Near where Father stood, a young man stepped out from his place and stared down the hall. He must be thinking that if someone else would take up the second sword for the witch, then he would take the third. The third man would fight last, and would have the best chance of surviving. But no one else moved, and the hand of an older knight pulled the young man back. The sibilants of fierce whispers carried across the floor. And Father had not moved, either.

She wanted to look away. Somehow she would find her way down the back corridors and out of this place.

Still she did not move. Neither did the three fighters, the woman, or the man of the Dancing Hound.

Come on. Come on. Come on.

The knights looked to the trumpeter, who looked to the King. The King did not sign for the last trumpet. He had turned in his throne and was talking with a herald and a counsellor. The point of his finger moved gently as he spoke. The princes were leaning from their seats to hear. For a moment all the hall strained to catch the King's words. The herald and the courtier were looking doubtful. The King seemed to repeat a short phrase, twice, and again. He turned back to meet the gaze of the baron. The herald was coming forward to stand beside the trumpeter at the lip of the dais.

'Men have declared themselves willing to die for the right.

'But before blood is shed, the King will consider this further. The justice day is ended. The subjects of the King will depart.'

At once the crowd broke into sound. They were surprised – even alarmed. The thing was incomplete. If it wasn't settled one way or another, what then? The long dismissal fanfare began, raggedly, as though the trumpeters had been caught unawares. Now the door guards understood that the audience was over. The doors were thrown open. The packed ranks of the knights and courtiers dissolved from their places into a milling, talking, shouting mass. Phaedra saw the baron standing stock-still in his place. She could not see his expression, for he was staring away from her up at the throne. The white-bearded King looked back at him, unmoved.

The woman had disappeared somewhere, presumably under guard. Courtiers were arguing with the knight of the hound. A marshal looked up and saw the gallery was occupied, and by whom. He waved them away with the back of his hand, frowning, as though there had been something obscene or improper that the onlookers should not have seen. A guard joined him, repeated his gestures, and called for a comrade. The girls fled.

They ran down the ill-lit corridors and stairways that wove in rigid tangents around the royal kitchens and storerooms. Hands rattled latches that stuck and gave way. Their feet clattered and voices called to one another in the dark and hurry. There was alarm and laughter in them, which rose more loudly and with more laughter as they drew further from the hall and dropped to the level of the little courtyard from which they had gained entrance an hour before. The door was ajar, as they had left it. It swung under the hand of the leader to admit the heat and glare of the day. They poured into the courtyard, blinking, breathing hard.

'Oh!' said one. 'Was any of them more handsome than Barius?'

They were a half-dozen young ladies of the court. Phaedra, at fifteen, was the youngest. None was older than twenty. Like Phaedra, they were children of important men who had come for the great banquet the King would hold that night to mark the final victories over the rebel barons, the end of summer and the knighthood of his second son. With all the fighting around the Kingdom, it was years since there had been an occasion like it. Phaedra was not the only one who had never been to court before. Most of them had only met the previous day.

They were dressed informally, for they had no ceremony

11

until the feast that evening (and certainly no business attending the King's justice). Even so their long, lightly woven gowns in blue and green and yellow made them a gay party in that stony little courtyard with the well and the stunted olive tree.

'Do you think he saw us?'

'Who?'

'Prince Barius, of course—'

'Why didn't they fight? What will they do?'

'I'll swear they were going to drag her up and cut her head off on the steps – right in front of us . . .'

'. . . I *waved* to him. I'm sure he looked up at me.'

'Someone put that dog-knight up to it. I wonder who?'

'Maybe he fell in love with her – then and there!'

'Dibourche was gobbling, wasn't he? Like a turkey. He nearly had us seized. If he saw me he'll speak to my father and I'll be packed off to the city convent for the rest of our stay.'

'If you are lucky. He's looking for a wife, I hear. Maybe he'll ask your father—'

'No, no! Amanthys, don't say that . . .'

'Gobble, gobble . . .'

More laughter. The sun beat upon the courtyard with the full force of early afternoon. Two or three of the girls were sitting on the rim of the well, catching their breath in the shade of the tree.

'I suppose a prince can't just step down from his throne and defend an accused woman. But I'm sure he wanted to . . .'

'Perhaps we should all commit witchcraft . . .'

'Oh!'

'. . . or *say* we had, tonight. Then we would be tried one by one before the throne until he chose which of us to rescue!'

The air was hot in the little well-court, and very still. Nothing stirred the shadows of the olive boughs, or the dry leaves upon the cobbles.

'That is the silliest idea I have heard since Hallows,' said the girl called Amanthys.

'You'd be killed—'

'You might be rescued by some dog-knight from the back of nowhere who would throw you over his carthorse and lump you off to a flea-ridden two-roomed manor house to stone olives for the rest of your life. And good riddance.'

'Do you know,' said the oldest girl, whose name was Maria, 'that because some dog-knight from the back of nowhere is ready to fight, that woman may be innocent? But if none of them had been prepared to fight those cut-throats Baron Seguin had with him, we'd have known she was guilty and had her killed? And now the King says he's going to think about it. Why didn't they think before? They can't just leave it like that—'

'It was a show,' Phaedra broke in. 'The King had agreed with the baron what was going to happen. All justice is a show, like that.'

The others looked down at her, half-strangers.

'You've made a study of these things, I suppose.' said Amanthys.

Phaedra was from a lonely house. She was not used to company like this, as well-born as she, and a little older.

'All justice-giving is a play,' she told them. 'If a man

13

is good at the play, and settles the quarrels in ways that stay settled, the people he judges are happier to be ruled by him. And then they don't fight. When Father holds court at Trant he tries to fix or agree the outcome beforehand. Then he summons everybody to his court, where he puts the King's keys of the castle on the table in front of him, to remind everyone that the King has chosen him to be Warden. He makes Brother David – our priest – stand behind his chair, to show that justice comes from Heaven. And they try the case and decide what he's already decided.'

'Trant?'

'Yes. My father is Ambrose, Warden of Trant Castle. Our badge is the Sun and Oak Leaf . . .'

Now Phaedra realized that she was being led on. The others were waiting, for . . .

Amanthys frowned lightly, as if with an effort of memory. 'Trant? Oh, yes . . . Fat and noisy. That one.'

Someone shrieked, and put her hand to her mouth. Others giggled. Phaedra felt herself going red.

Of course Father was big (and loud); and she would not be surprised if people chose to dislike him. But – but to insult him – and at the same time pretend they barely knew who he was . . .

And *noisy* had not been aimed only at Father.

'My father's fat,' said Maria. 'He says it's so he can stand a proper siege.'

'*Your* father has all the burghers of Pemini paying dues to him,' said someone else. 'Unlike some. Warden of Trant! Oh, dear girl. If your father doesn't even own his own roof – then who will want to marry you?'

'Is that all you think about?' asked Phaedra, with her cheeks hot.

'Fat as a pig,' another girl murmured. 'Do all the Trant horses have bowed legs? I wouldn't like to be your mother.'

That was easy.

'My mother's dead.'

And it was easier still to walk away.

The King's castle of Tuscolo was a complex of courtyards and walled enclosures, some vast, others just pockets of stone buildings like the well-court where the girls chattered on about the princes. A short climb up a cobbled ramp and under an archway brought Phaedra, seething with hurt, to the main upper courtyard. The huge space before her was scattered with straw and mess, and busy with many people. To her right the tall keep punched upwards to the sky. To her left was the royal chapel, with its bell towers and long windows. Carved figures massed in their stone niches about and above the chapel doors. A party of monks glided down the broad steps as she approached it. They wore brown robes, with the Lantern badge of their order, and walked in silence through the bustle of the King's house.

She had seen so many monks in her short stay here. At home there was only Brother David to lift his hands to Heaven and bring its blessing upon the people of Trant. But here the castle and the city beyond it swarmed with monks of all orders. At first she had assumed that Tuscolo was a very holy place. Now she thought that the royal capital must need this many priests because it was really very wicked. She was certainly finding it so.

The doors of the chapel stood open. In the blue light of the windows statues brooded on the holiness within. Phaedra walked boldly up the long, paved aisle. She bowed to the altar on which stood the Flame of Heaven: the sign of Godhead, bright, formless and unknowable in a world of shadows.

On this altar the Flame was a great, four-armed thing, far larger than the simple gilt candlestick in the chapel of Trant. Each of its arms was cast in the shape of one of the angels that the Godhead had sent into the world to struggle for souls. And above the altar the same angels reared in four stained-glass windows that dominated the chapel. Michael the Warrior swung his huge sword and grinned, his mouth square in battle-frenzy. Beside him Gabriel the Messenger bent from Heaven with flame upon his wings. Raphael trod an endless road with his staff in hand, and Umbriel looked down with seven eyes and wrote in the book in which all things were written. They were bigger, more garish and less human than in the hangings of home; but Phaedra knew them. She did not feel that she should be shy of them, even here. Under their gaze she felt her anger settle within her, not fading, but going deeper, to places where it would be remembered and yet would no longer tie her tongue.

After a little she found her way to a bench and sat down.

People drifted by and glanced at her, but she ignored them and they passed on. Voices rose behind her, coming her way. Men were talking heatedly. She felt no surprise when Prince Barius, dark and angry, stalked past in the aisle with his brother and a half-dozen others at his heel.

The party halted barely six feet from her, at a doorway that led to the King's cloisters. No one seemed to notice her.

'In that case, my lord, my father is forsworn whatever course he chooses,' said Barius. 'You shall say that to him from me. And say he must now choose either wisely, or well. Many, no doubt, would have him choose wisely. I for one would have him choose well!'

A chamberlain bowed, and looked to Prince Septimus as if to ask whether he wished to add to his brother's advice. The prince simply nodded, and the men bowed again before hurrying back the way they had come, on the track of some fast-moving matter of state. Barius had already disappeared through the low doorway to the chapel cloisters. Septimus, a man barely older than she was, hesitated for a moment. He had seen her, an unknown girl who must have overheard what the men had been saying. Then he smiled, as if sharing with her the absurdity of what was happening, and followed his brother through the low doorway.

Footsteps receded, and the chapel was still.

What was that about? asked Phaedra of the unseen figure on the bench beside her.

The knight stirred.

The King is in a dilemma. He must choose between breaking a promise to someone who has influence, and doing the same to someone who has less, but to whom, in the prince's mind, it would be more honourable to stay faithful.

There was a case in the court this morning, Phaedra told him. *They were going to settle it by combat. The King stopped it and said he was going to think.*

No doubt it is that. How do you like the court?

Not at all. I thought I had found friends, but when I told them what you said about justice they laughed at me.

You told them the truth. You should not be ashamed of that. How they treat it is their affair.

Phaedra knew that she was awake, and therefore if she turned to face him he would not be there. But if she looked in front of her, up at the faces of the Angels, she could sense from the corner of her eye the shadowy folds of the black cloak, his dark hair and pale skin, and the huge stone cup that he nursed upon his knees. She knew they were there, for she saw them in her dreams.

There must be power before there is law, said the knight. *And all laws bend to it.*

'When shall I see you again?'

The sound of her own voice startled her. She had not meant to speak aloud. And there was no reply, for now he had gone.

That night she swept out onto the floor of the throne hall, where the witch had stood alone a few hours before. Again the walls were crowded with people: the knights and nobles of the Kingdom. But this time their women were among them, and this time the eyes were fixed upon her.

Father paced at her side. Tall, big-bearded, barrel-chested, he trod the aisle towards the throne, and in her heavy brocaded dress she moved in his shadow. Ahead of her, Amanthys and her father were already making their curtsy and bow to the King. Behind her, the voice of the herald was calling the name of the next knight and daughter to come forward. The ceremonies had been underway

18

for more than an hour, beginning with the long rigmarole of the knighting of Septimus, and then of three other young squires. But now, and for a few moments more, it was her turn. The eyes were on her and the whispers were about her, the child of Trant upon her father's arm, with her father's jewels in her hair. She knew that they liked what they saw. She wished that they did not.

They approached the trio of thrones, and the broad steps that led to them. The King was robed in gold in his place, just as if he had not moved since the morning. The princes, the same courtiers – they were there too. A few paces more: the last yards seemed also to be the slowest. The slightest tug from Father's arm halted her a moment before she expected it. He was bowing. She dropped slowly into her curtsy – long and low, Father had said, and the more of both the better. Now Father was speaking to the King the ritual phrases of introduction that he had repeated to her during their rehearsals. She must stay down.

Had the witch made a curtsy that morning, before the eyes that had been planning to kill her?

'Greetings, Trant,' said the soft voice from the High Throne. 'We have loved your house for its valour in our service. Now we may love it for its beauty as well.'

And now she could rise and look up into the King's face, which was nothing more than an old man's face framed between a gold robe and a heavy crown. The white hair and beard were thin. She could see the pink of old skin beneath them. She looked into the pale eyes, and saw one eyebrow lifted slightly, as if he was surprised by something he saw.

19

'And has the beauty of Trant words that it would wish us to hear?' said the King, after a moment.

Words? Her?

Father had not warned her about this!

She felt his arm tense. He had not been expecting it, either. And surely Amanthys had not been asked to say anything when it was her turn.

Why her?

There was only one thing she could say. And she must curtsy again.

'Only my obedience, Your Majesty,' she said, keeping her eyes down.

'Obedience?' said the soft, old voice. 'Obedience is good. We know we may look to Trant for that.'

He must have given some sign then, for as she rose for the second time Father's arm was pulling at hers, drawing her away from the thrones. She looked back. The eyes of Barius still followed her, from the Throne Ochre. Septimus, with his bright gold spurs on his heels, was staring after her, and so were some of the counsellors. But the King was already looking down the hall at the next man and girl to approach him – and the next, and the next. Phaedra was gone from his mind.

They joined Amanthys and her father, waiting a little to one side of the steps to the thrones. Amanthys was ignoring her, so Phaedra did the same. She looked around the long hall and drew deep breaths to steady her heartbeat, which had been going like a hammer without her being aware of it.

The walls were lit with the light of the low sun, pouring through the windows. It must be a wonderful, calm evening out there, away from all this throng of people. Up in the gallery where she had been that morning, a group of minstrels were sidling into their places. Below them the court watched the father-and-daughter couples, approaching the thrones in their turn to announce that another girl, and yet another, had crossed the threshold to womanhood. She watched closely to see if the King spoke to any of the daughters. He did not. Why had he spoken to her?

Septimus was still looking her way. She dropped her eyes quickly.

The murmurs of the crowd were rising more loudly. Phaedra realized that much of the talk had nothing to do with the formal procession. The faces in the first rank – mainly women – were following the walkers intently, looking for matches for their sons. But behind them men were standing in twos and threes, whispering among themselves. Some were not even pretending to watch. Phaedra saw one man gesturing across the aisle to another, whom she could not see, but who must have been standing in the crowd not far from her. They were arranging to meet. Did they want to discuss marriages already? More likely it was to do with the hearings that had run for days, and must run a day or two yet before all the vanquished rebels had been judged and the loyal men rewarded. They would be talking over the outcomes – perhaps even trying to fix them, as someone had tried so murderously to fix the outcome of the case that afternoon.

She could sense Father beside her, watching the hall as she was doing. He too seemed to have forgotten the exchange at the thrones. He was itching to be out intriguing among his fellows.

Now the fifth and last of the couples was joining them, and beyond them the singer of the King had taken his place in the centre of the hall. The strings of the minstrels began to flow with their notes from the gallery overhead. In a high voice the singer began the well-worn opening phrases of *The Tale of Kings*, which related the coming of Wulfram and his seven sons over the sea to found the Kingdom. Around her, the group of fathers and daughters had begun to break up. Father was already bending to hear what some baron was whispering in his ear. She did not want to talk with anyone. She did not want to stand there, watching the court seethe with politics while the King carried on as if the ceremony was the only business, and all the land was at peace. There was a small door in the wall behind her – half-ajar, because someone had already gone down it. She hesitated. No one was looking at her.

She knew it would be improper to leave the hall before it was time for the procession to the banquet. Father at least would be angry, if he realized what she had done. But the singer was telling a long version of *The Tale*, running through the deeds of generation after generation of kings, because the King on the throne wanted to remind everyone how important kingship was. So she would be a prisoner here for an hour or more before the procession began. Others had slipped out, quietly. She would go also, because she dared to.

Obedience!

A short passage led to an archway lit by the evening sun. The sound of the ceremonies diminished behind her. She found herself in a little paved court surrounded by

22

old, white colonnades. Low fruit trees grew within its walls. There was a fountain here, its waters lying still in its wide bowl. Phaedra leaned her arms upon it.

She remembered another fountain, very like this one, in the ruined court outside the walls of her home. She wished that they had never left Trant. She wished that they could be like some other families – including one or two of the greatest – which still held themselves aloof from the court. Why come just to grovel before the King? But Father was a king's appointed warden, and a king's man to his very heart.

A voice spoke at her elbow.

'Is it that you prefer Wulfram's stones to Wulfram's songs, Phaedra?'

It was the oldest of the girls who had gone with her to the witch trial, standing alone beside her. She was wearing court dress, so she must have followed Phaedra out of the hall.

'What do you mean?'

'I saw you leave. I wondered why.'

Phaedra remembered that her name was Maria. She had a pleasing, oval face, with big eyes and heavy cheeks framed with light-brown hair. Perhaps she had hung back when the others had teased Phaedra that morning. But Phaedra was suspicious, and did not want to risk being laughed at again.

'I like it here,' she said, as if she had been coming to this fountain for centuries.

'So do I. I thought it could be my private little place in Tuscolo. But of course everybody knows about it. I heard someone say it is the centre of the world.'

'Why?'

'I imagine they meant that it is the centre of Tuscolo, and therefore of the Kingdom. If that means it's the centre of the world, well . . . I suppose there must be lands beyond the wild Marches, but nothing comes from them. And Father says there are kingdoms over the sea, but only the mariners of Velis know how to get there, and they will not give away their secrets. Whatever the truth of that, it is certain that this court and fountain were built by Wulfram's sons. So they are as old as the world we know, at least.'

She was not teasing Phaedra for leaving the ceremony. Indeed, she seemed happy to play truant with her. Perhaps she too had been bored and disgusted in there. But Phaedra did not want to be easily won back. So she observed a dark silence, to show how much she had been hurt by the others that afternoon.

'And the world knows you are a woman now,' said Maria. 'Or at least, all of the world that matters. Presented before the King and princes themselves. No one did as much for me. You made an impression up there, I could see. What was it they said to you?'

Silence did not seem to work as well as Phaedra felt it should.

'I – I was remembering that woman we saw today, on trial,' she said. 'I think I must have frowned at the King. He wanted to know why.'

Frowned? She had been scowling, she realized: at the King, who was supposed to be the Fount of the Law!

'Oh, Angels!' Maria laughed. 'And what did you say?'

Phaedra shrugged. She felt ashamed of what she had said.

'The others will have fits when I tell them—'

'Please don't,' Phaedra said firmly.

'Oh dear. Well, I shall not then. And I'm sorry if we upset you, Phaedra. I thought it was all nonsense, too.'

'They said we weren't good enough,' Phaedra said, hoping she would be told at once how high and noble Trant was and that its wardens were respected throughout the Kingdom (although Father's grandfather had himself been a dog-knight, of course).

'Good enough for what? If they meant marrying a prince, you've no less chance than the rest of them. You have looks. And Trant is a big name: one of the seven, even if it is not your father's of right. Whatever you did back there, I'd say Septimus was quite struck with you. He was looking your way just now, all the while that they were presenting those other girls.'

'I didn't notice,' said Phaedra, who had.

'I did, and I doubt that I was the only one. But in truth, it is only the most powerful families who can count the odds of an alliance with the crown. They keep their daughters and cousins and nieces muffled away behind lace and locked doors against the prospect – poor things. Prince Barius is an impressive man, but he thinks of little beyond his devotions. He would much rather have been a monk, you know . . .

'Of course marrying princes is a dream, Phaedra. We have to dream. We have to put a face on tomorrow. You should be sorry for us, not angry. And sorry for yourself, too. Do you know what – or rather who – will be waiting for you when you return home?'

'No one. I'm not going to marry.'

She heard Maria sigh, softly.

The last sunlight played on the waters at the centre of the world. In the branches of the fruit trees, doves cooed loudly at the coming dusk.

'I've a cousin almost the same age as you,' Maria said, in a dreamy tone as if she was talking to herself. 'She has just passed her fifteenth birthday. She was a lovely, happy girl until this summer. Now she is shut up in a room at home, fed thinly and beaten each day, because she says she will not wed the man my aunt thinks it good that she should. And wed him she will, unless he tires of waiting for her spirit to be broken and seeks elsewhere. I hope my father will not use me so, in my turn. But he has ambitions and is waiting for a good chance. And when he has made up his mind, my fortune, rights, purpose, will be my husband's . . .

'We all marry, Phaedra. Nothing works if we do not. But who? Amanthys already knows whose home it is she will be going to. If she is sharp with us sometimes, maybe she has reason. The rest of us – who knows? We may be scattered widely. I have made good friends here, and it hurts to think that we may not meet again. Some of the others have promised to write to me. I hope you will too.'

Phaedra looked down at her fingers, which gripped the rim of the bowl. The knuckles were white. Father won't make me marry, she thought. He can't.

Maria was watching her. 'When you said that about your mother – was that in childbirth?'

'Yes,' said Phaedra.

'I see.' She understood, now.

'I'm sorry,' Maria said. 'So did mine.'

26

Neither of them spoke again for a while.

'I found out what happened after the witch trial,' said Maria at last. 'Do you want to know?'

'Yes, please,' said Phaedra, relieved.

'There was no fight. There was never supposed to be. You were right. The King had agreed to the ordeal to please Baron Seguin, who wanted to do away with that woman, so that he could have her lands. No one was expected to interfere, but of course that dog-knight did. So in the afternoon the King met with Baron Seguin and drove a new bargain. Lady Luguan will keep her life, but will still forfeit her lands to the baron. And diManey is to see that she practises no more magic.'

'Who?'

'The knight with the hound badge. A hound badge for a dog-knight – very right. It's strange. Yesterday, everyone was sure that woman was a witch. Now it seems they don't know. But they are all furious with the dog-knight, and are running around trying to find out if some rival of Seguin's put him up to it. They are saying he deserved to be killed, and he would have been if the King had not gone out of his way to save him. Both Lady Luguan and he are to be free within the realm, but they are banned with the King's displeasure from his court, his lands and roads.'

'And do you know,' Maria went on, 'Barius himself will marry them together! I suppose the bishops and their priests want as little to do with this as possible. But as a royal prince, of course he has the right to perform the office.'

'*They're* to be married?'

'Yes. By order of the King. It was a way of solving the

problem of the woman, and punishing diManey at the same time. Poor diManey! Imagine – you wake up as you do every day, get dressed, go to the court because everyone else is doing so, and a few hours later you're going to your bed in disgrace, lucky to be alive, betrothed to a complete stranger. A complete stranger, Phaedra – someone you've never heard or thought of before today. And she's a rebel – and worse, probably a witch. And all her lands are forfeit so your marriage has gone for nothing . . .

'Still, it was a brave thing he did, whatever his reasons. Perhaps he doesn't even understand them himself. I'm glad Barius has invoked his right to bless them – it isn't much, but it's like him, and more than anything anyone else might have done. I suppose . . . I suppose it's fair to hope, and even dream, if we know there are at least some good men in the world.'

Phaedra was silent. It seemed to her that even Maria was thinking more of the dog-knight – and, of course, Barius – than of the witch. She could well imagine herself as the witch. And she thought that she would rather have died than be married to the dog-knight.

II

The Prisoner

*ah, Trant!*

Ambrose, the Warden, rose in his stirrups in the King's courtyard. The early sun gleamed on his high forehead. His brows clenched. His head jerked this way and that at his followers. His men-at-arms were mounted, checking their horses, looking to him from their saddles. Straps were tight, mail gleamed, swords were hung just *so*. The Sun and Oak Leaf danced on a dozen armoured chests. The servants were lashing the last bundles upon the wagon. His daughter's litter was ready. Phaedra herself stood a little way off, in her travelling gown, waiting for a groom to finish checking the harness of the pony that she would ride when it pleased her.

Around them, the long middle enclosure of the castle of Tuscolo was thronged with wagons and men on horseback. People were moving about with sacks and bales of goods, cursing as they got in each other's way. Dogs barked and children ran among the crowd. The castle and the city beyond it were at last beginning to rid themselves of the travellers that had swarmed within them for days like the indigestion of a vast beast.

Ambrose scowled, and hunted among his people for a victim.

His party watched him. They and their families ate every day because they had been born or been chosen by him to be among those who served him. They knew his loyalties and obsessions, and the thousand little things he thought could be done better. They knew the shout that he was bottling in his guts, ready to rip through the crowd at the man who was a moment behind his fellows. He had been hammering at them since the day began. The big, long-bearded, hard-muscled Warden of Trant would not be dallying when it was time to go.

But this time there was no one for him to shout at. They were ready to the last buckle, all of them.

'Well, good!' Ambrose muttered at last into his beard. Then, as his daughter was helped into her saddle: 'Phaedra, my dear. We will see how our reverend fellow traveller is doing.'

Leaving his party to wait where they were, he nudged his horse into a walk. Phaedra let her mount follow.

Halfway down the courtyard the crowds were at their thickest, outside the long barracks where the Bishop of Jent and his huge following had been quartered. Three standards, each with the bishop's House-of-God badge, hung listlessly from poles in the hands of liveried servants. Three wagons were in various stages of loading. In the middle of the fuss the bishop stood, shouting for haste. He was a round man, round-faced and all adorned with his robe, flat cap, ring and staff. No doubt he was intending to travel by curtained litter to save his fine clothes from the dust. He looked up at them from under furious brows as they approached.

Phaedra knew that Father would not be rude outright, for His Grace stood higher in rank than any warden. But of course Father would not be able to resist scoring his point. *Trant rises early . . .*

'You are ahead of me this morning, Warden. I am grateful that I shall not have to wait for you, at least. Have you eaten, sir?'

'At dawn, Your Grace. Trant rises early, and knows what he must do.'

'There is a tray of pasties and beer at the door to my quarter, if you will. I would offer you more, but I would be on our way as soon as we can. Are you all made up?'

Made and fit, Your Grace. Trant wits no delay . . .

'Made and fit, Your Grace. I wait only for my new charge.'

'That scoundrel? He is at the gate, there.'

Charge? Scoundrel? Looking round, Phaedra saw a party of the king's men on foot at the gate to the upper courtyard. They did not seem to be doing much. But Father was bowing in his saddle to the bishop and wheeling his horse away through the crowd. She watched him ride back up the courtyard, signalling men and horses from his own group to join him. He reached the king's men and bowed again, this time to a short, fair man who stood among the soldiers and bowed in return. A Trant horse was led up. The man mounted, and the king's men withdrew.

'Now your company is made up,' said the bishop, standing beside her stirrup. 'And my fools will be another hour yet. Trant is confident, to travel with so few.'

It dawned on Phaedra that Father had abandoned her

31

in the presence of this unpredictable churchman, whom she knew only from his forceful reputation.

'He might be confident indeed, sir,' she said carefully. 'When he knew we were to travel two-thirds of our way home with you.'

'Ha! His sort are supposed to protect me, and not the other way about. Next time I come to Tuscolo I too will think less of my honour and more on speed. We do not need armies about us this year. Have a pasty, girl. There will be more delay yet.'

Phaedra bowed her head and nudged her pony away. She was thankful to be dismissed. At her knee a bored servant raised a tray of mutton-bones and other breakfast things. She shook her head and returned to the Trant party to wait for things to happen.

It was typical of Father, she thought crossly, both that he should have left her like that in the company of a man he had just needled, and that they should now be faced with this wait. He had roused them all at dawn, and bullied them through packing, not in spite of but *because* of the size of the bishop's party, which would delay them long after every last Trantish strap was tied down. Now they would stand here, perhaps for hours, with their comforts packed away and the sun climbing higher above the dust and heat of the middle courtyard. She wondered why she had not taken more time over her own preparations, to be ready at her convenience, rather than Father's. She could even have made him a fool in front of all the others whom he had harried to be ready.

She might have done it. Now that home beckoned, she could feel herself straining to break out of the mould of the demure daughter that she had worn here, and to live more as she did in her own house. He knew better than to try to punish her if she did not do as he wanted. There had been a moment that morning when he had hung in her doorway as she and her maid Dilly were packing her things – her clothes, her precious book, her cup-and-ball game, candles and candlestick, basin, soap, jewels. He had seen she was going about her part with a will. And there had been relief in his voice as he had turned to bellow at the next man he met upon the stairs.

All the same, this was a victory for Trant. Small in number, they could still start their journey with their heads high among the bishop's great company, for they had shown that Trant knew its business. She was of Trant, no less than Father. And she too was longing to be home.

Horse-steps and harness sounded by her. Father towered over her on his big charger. Beside him was the fair-haired man she had seen at the gate, mounted now, and looking down at her out of the sun. She put up an arm to shield her eyes.

'My daughter and only living child, sir, Phaedra, who will be your hostess at Trant. Phaedra, this is the Baron of Lackmere, Aun, who is to be our guest.'

A guest. And *why* should she endure a stranger at Trant?

This baron was an unsmiling man. He was probably younger than Father – between thirty and forty years – but his lined and unpleasant face, with heavy brows and a pointed chin, made him seem older. He was indeed short – a head below Father as he sat in the saddle, and not much more above Phaedra than the difference between his horse and her pony. He wore his hair shoulder length, and had no beard, after the fashion of the provinces. His surplice was white and blue, and his badge appeared to be a staff held crosswise before a wolf's head. She guessed that he must be one of the lesser barons of the south. He seemed to have no attendants of his own.

'Now Michael guard us, my lady,' said the man, for whom the prayer of fellow travellers was, it seemed, an empty formality.

'And Raphael guide our way, for we are far from home,' Phaedra replied. 'You are to be our guest? Sir, with pleasure. For how long?'

Father's look told her she had said the wrong thing.

'Longer than you or I would wish, I fear,' the baron answered. 'Let us not bear each other ill-will for it.'

Then she realized that he was not carrying a sword. The scabbard that hung at his saddle was empty. Two Trant men-at-arms hovered on their horses close behind him.

They had been travelling for an hour across the sun-hammered plain around Tuscolo before Phaedra could bring her pony alongside her father's mount.

'I regret that I have embarrassed our house, sir.'

'You mean Lackmere? I should not trouble on it. Another time remember that no good hostess asks how long her guests intend to stay.'

'Another time I shall be forearmed, and perhaps fore-warned as well,' she said, to make her point.

He brooded on her words, as he would do for no one else.

'He was wished on me in the last hearings yesterday. By the time I returned to our quarters you were asleep, and rightly so. He remains with us until the King pleases otherwise. He was lucky to escape with so little harm.'

'What has he done?'

'He has been a rogue and a fisher of troubled waters for years. But he was rebel and an ally of rebels when we caught up with him. Good men were lost bringing him down. He might have been blinded and stripped of his lands. The King was moved to grant him clemency, because he would not ask for it. We have to teach him gentility, girl.'

Phaedra looked ahead to where the baron rode bareheaded in the sun. So that small man, riding insolently in advance of the banners, was one of the faceless enemy against whom Father had ridden four times through the wasted fields of the Kingdom. He was not looking back at the long procession that followed him. He would neither acknowledge them, nor pick his way in the dust of the men who were his captors. What might he do? The two Trant men-at-arms rode a short space behind him.

'Will he try to escape?' she asked.

In the distance sun glinted on mail. Outriders of the column were moving slowly along the top of a low rise to the south of their line of march. Phaedra could see the smudge of dust raised by their hooves against the solid blue of the sky. A horn-blast would bring them sweeping in to head off the runaway.

'Who knows? I have his word. And if he runs, he will be outlawed and his lands forfeit. He has a family who will suffer. If he bears the King's sentence he may yet see his home in peace again.'

So he was bound by word, by guard and by the threat of blood. But the very tightness of the grip upon him made him seem dangerous. And he would be fed in her house, and would rise from her table each day, an enemy and a rebel still.

Safe in Trant, Phaedra had been only half aware of the rebellion of the Seabord barons and their southern allies as it had raged around the Kingdom. She still understood little of the complex of disputes and rivalries that had made them league themselves against the crown, or how they had won their early victories over the odds, and so shaken the King's grip upon his throne. For her, the chief effect had been that Trant had been half-empty for months at a time, as Father and his knights answered desperate summons from Tuscolo. But the knights had brought back with them stories of an enemy whose strength was not in numbers but in war-skill and, they had said, witchcraft beyond nature. And in her few weeks at court she had listened to others, who had known a town burned or friends killed, or things so changed that they would never be the same.

Ambrose was also watching the baron, and frowning. He too must be thinking of the King's judgement. Only the King could give justice among the high lords, so that they might do the same among their knights and barons, who in turn might rule the manors and the people who gained their living from the land. But rebellion had to be stamped on. Father, like many, could have lost much if the fighting had gone the wrong way. He must fear that the

King had been too whimsical with this rebel; and maybe, on the evidence of other judgements reached at court, that His Majesty was being altogether less cautious than the times demanded.

'A dismal affair,' said the bishop.

'I am of the same mind, Your Grace.'

They were at supper together at an inn. Baron Lackmere ate with them, at the little round table, carved with saints, that the bishop had carted with him all the way to Tuscolo and back. Phaedra sat with her face glowing from the sun and her limbs aching from twenty miles of bad roads. A part of their joint followings clamoured and drank together in the common room, the length of a corridor away.

'But for another reason, Trant. You are a loyal king's man – no, do not shrug, sir, you are famous for it. So you remember only that the King had to go back on his word to Seguin to save a fool of a knight who didn't know better. Therefore, you think, the trial should not have happened. If the man had not come forward they would have knocked the woman on the head, shared out her lands – and you would have seen no wrong.' He frowned. 'I do not say that someone who attempts murder by whatever means does not deserve death. But witchcraft is no more for men to play their games with than fire is for children.'

At table the bishop wore no cap. It had been a shock to Phaedra to find that he was totally bald. His big, ringed fingers and his fine clothes were stained with food. He hunched in his seat at the end of the table, leaning forward, eyes protruding, his big voice rolling and teasing like one who loved an argument but who loved most of all to win.

'Not just murder,' said Father. 'Rebellion.'

'Hah. As to that, I did not hear this woman was so guilty of it as others. Why does a man rebel against his lord, Lackmere?'

The baron had been taking little part in the talk. Perhaps he was surprised, now, even to have been spoken to.

'Why does a stone fall to earth?' he grumbled. 'Must I own as lord one who would rule over me from afar and perhaps order my living to suit my neighbour rather than myself? And what if my neighbour then pays some bribe to the King or his courtiers before I am aware of it?'

The bishop grinned sourly. 'It is a fallen world, where Good may be no more than the smaller of two Evils. Do not mistake me. I am a churchman, and like my fellows I will bless the King and his Law for what peace they may bring. But I do not suppose either to be perfect. Least of all when men cry witchcraft. I do not like this business— No, Trant, hear me out, sir. Let the King hazard his justice at the edge of a sword if his wits cannot help him better, but scripture tells me nothing of ordeal before Heaven.'

'And what does it tell you of witchcraft?' asked Phaedra suddenly. 'Your Grace,' she added.

She knew at once that she had spoken out of turn. Perhaps that was why the bishop stared at her, blinking, with a chicken leg halfway to his open mouth.

'I mean – why must we be so afraid?'

'Phaedra—' said her father.

'No, Trant,' said the bishop. 'She has seen fit to speak, so speak we shall.'

She suddenly realized how still the other men were, watching him.

'You have spoken an obscenity, child – as you should know. Witchcraft is abomination. I do not mean that a man slain by potion or rune or some such is any more wronged that one whose brain-pan has been opened by a sword. Nor simply, as some of my brethren would say, that the act of witchcraft is damning to the soul. If that woman repents not of her witchcraft, then damned be her soul and good riddance, sir . . .

'But see the world as the Angels see it. See Man, sitting at a table, a round table such as this one. To his right' – the bishop gestured towards the Warden – 'are the virtues: justice, loyalty, honour, and so on brighter and brighter each one until we reach the chairs of Courage, Compassion, Glory and Truth, behind which stand the Angels themselves . . .

'To his left' – the baron grunted a half-laugh as the bishop waved dismissively in his direction – 'war, cruelty, falsehood, and then the little magics – the love-philtres, the potions, the crones who run as lithe hares in the meadow, the words of the dying and of the dead, the images of wax and the blood of cockerels. Beyond them, the dark places where the devils born with us whisper promises that bring the soul to rot.'

He leaned across the table, and his stubby finger pointed at Phaedra's heart.

'And there is a place where truth and witchcraft touch. There may the Angels help us! For we live by truth. Never doubt it. What should justice be, but the exercise of truth? Yet the truth that borders those places is bent. There, the best-kept oath is that which is broken at once. If it is not, it twists the oath-maker to falsehood and treachery. It spreads from doer to the very ones that would bring him to justice. Foul things are done under every day's sun, girl, by men in iron who are held noble. But never more foul than they will do with the scent of witchcraft on the wind.'

He paused for a heartbeat. Then: 'Girl, do you know of anyone who does, or talks of doing, witchcraft?'

She met his look. 'No, Your Grace.'

'As the Angels are my witness,' added Father swiftly. 'She speaks the truth as I know it, Jent.'

The bishop sat back, eyeing them both. He said nothing. Surely he did not doubt Father? Phaedra and the Warden watched him as if he were a bear that might charge.

At last the bishop grinned. 'Did you ever meet that woman, Lackmere? The one they tried?'

The baron looked up from studying his fingers. 'The Luguan? No. I think she was with Calyn of the Moon Rose for a while.'

'Oho! One might say, then, that she had almost invited her trial by the company she kept.'

'Of that I do not know. He was a deep man, but true to his friends, whatever men say of his house or line.'

'And I have already said a few words on truth this evening. Witchcraft or no, a man who is true to rebels such as these may be himself the very worst of all falsehood. What became of him?'

The fire hissed, and the baron did not answer. Perhaps he too was feeling assaulted.

'What became of him, Lackmere?'

40

'He died of a plain fever before Hallows,' growled the baron. 'No witchcraft helped him there.'

The three men sat up long after Phaedra had retired. From where she lay in her room she could hear the rumble of voices rising from the chimney, mingling with the muffled, sentimental chorus from the common room.

South wind, sweeping the waters,
Shaking the sails above . . .

The bishop's voice echoed up through the stonework. 'Fine daughter you've got there, Trant. Credit to you.'

Father said something in reply. Perhaps he was mollified now. Perhaps – battered by the bishop's efforts at tact – he was ready to suggest that the exchange about witchcraft had been her fault after all.

'No! Gabriel's Wings, Trant. Be proud! She thinks. She'll make a handsome woman.'

South wind, sweeping the waters,
Take me back to my love.

'Thinking?' cried the bishop again. 'The greater the merit, the greater the fall – be it man or woman. And the greater the redemption. But a man who looks for a stupid wife is himself a fool. What dowry do you offer for her?'

Three manors and six hundred silver marks, thought Phaedra.

'Small! Ah, you're a clever man, Trant . . .'

'The land stands clear of other claim,' came Father's

41

voice. 'And if I offered not a blade of grass, still the foppoons would be round us . . .'

'As thick as moths! *They* know what will come. And she has looks. Half the Kingdom will be at your door after her. Damn me – I would myself, if I were not a priest.' His laugh rang among the stones. 'And if my other fair acquaintance would let me!'

They would part company with the bishop in the morning, and go their separate ways. (Twenty miles today, thirty tomorrow in the hammering sun. She ached.) She was glad, both because it marked a further stage on their journey home, and because she was in a hurry to get away from this questioning, leering prince of the Church who browbeat men at table and then thought he could flatter them back into friendship with him again. What must the Angels think of such a man in their service!

She turned her head on the pillow. Through the gauzy hangings around her bed she could see her maid Dilly lying by the hearth, a sleeping shadow lit by the last of the embers. From below came the sounds of the priest, the baron and the king's man, wining together into the small hours. Father and the bishop were probably both drunk by now, as they talked on about the misfortunes of the great, and sniffed like dogs at witchcraft on the wind. And the baron – was he quietly drunk too, or was he plotting? Outside, horses shifted and stamped in the long picket lines, disturbed by something in the darkness. Moonlight shone and faded as the clouds passed. Mail clinked under her window where the armed watchmen paced in the night.

Take me back to my love.

Phaedra dreamed.

She was walking in a heavy brown landscape. The light was dim. Around her reared the hills that she knew lay across the lake from Trant. She felt the heavy clod-clod of her boots on the dry stones. She was trying to find her way home.

So the bishop would marry you if he were not a bishop, said the man at her side. *You should be pleased.*

I do not want to marry him, she said.

Then be thankful that he is, after all, a bishop.

He scared me. And Father. He meant to.

You might find he was better than many a younger man they would wed you to indeed.

No!

You are a woman, now. Your father would not have taken you to court if it were not so.

I am going home, she said.

They walked on together, picking their way among the brown rocks. Far away, the horizons rose to the sky, as if all that place lay in a vast circle of mountains. Two great lights, smaller than the moon but larger than any star, hung together on the rim. The air was thick with the rumble of some sound that was too deep to hear.

They had met here before, many times.

She could look at him, because she was dreaming. He was tall, and walked with his head bowed. She could see clearly his lean face and short black hair, despite the dim light. He wore black, and as he went he carried the stone cup before him in both hands. She watched the line of his face against the sky as they walked together. She wanted him to talk, and he did not. She wondered what he was thinking.

At last she said,– *Are we going to drink again?*

He stopped, and did not answer immediately. Then he lifted the cup. *If you wish.*

There was water in the bowl, dark, like jet, like a deep pit. And yet at the same time it was clear. It moved slightly as she watched it. She put her hand to the rim. They held it between them.

You first, she said.

Her fingers rested lightly on his glove.

The secret is not to have fear, he said. *You will be what you will be if you do not fear anything.*

Stones clattered among the rocks to her left. Something eyeless was moving there, grunting, groping its way: a hooded, toad-headed thing. Small rocks broke beneath its feet, and the long claws of its forelimbs trailed as it went. From the corner of her eye she saw it turn its head towards her as she took the stone cup from him. She did not regard it. She did not fear anything.

She drank, turning the cup clumsily so that her lips might touch the same spot as his had done.

Phaedra's pony was a chestnut called Collen. He was friendly and safe, if not very clever. He had plodded through strange, sun-blasted fields and picked his way along the coarse-bouldered roads more competently than some of the grander animals in the cavalcade. Now, as they crawled up the broad slope of Redes Hill in the heat of the late afternoon, he seemed to notice that he was nearing home. Hullo, his ears said as they went up. Haven't I been here before? Let's go and see.

Phaedra let him take her ahead of the party, and on

44

up the slope. The track curved to the right, through olive trees where goats scuffed and nickered at the thin grass. After half a mile it rounded the shoulder of the down, and the world changed.

There, Collen seemed to say as he tossed his head. What did I tell you?

Derewater lay before them. Suddenly, after the days of dry grasslands, the great lake stretched away to left and right until it blended with the sky at the opposite horizons. Its level face wrinkled a deep blue in the late afternoon. Below her, fishing boats crept upon the water, with their sails like little diamonds, curved and pale upon the dark surface. She could see the further shore clearly today. She could make out the shadow of woods and the paleness of grass on the hillsides. Far beyond, the mountains loomed.

It was a relief to be home, after days of strange places and new faces. It was good to see the water after the parched landscapes of the journey and the frenzies of the King's house. Peace, whispered the lake breeze in the branches. The air was a little cooler here among the scented groves than it had been upon the sunbeaten road. The trees were heavy with their small fruits. There would be an olive harvest soon.

Hoofbeats sounded behind her. To her surprise, it was the Baron Lackmere and his two guards. The rest of the party were still out of sight below the curve of the ridge.

'Is this country tame enough that you wander so far ahead without care? I am little use to you myself indeed. But it seemed to me that if I joined you these two fellows would not be far behind, and then we should be better placed if any ill befell.'

'You are good, sir, but it was needless. This is my father's land. Look.' She pointed to the lake.

'I have seen. How far, now?'

'The road follows the lakeside. We should see Trant from the next rise.'

'Let us go, then. Is that a manor?'

Below them, and to their left, she could glimpse between the trunks the familiar roofs of Manor Gowden.

'One of my father's holdings, sir.'

'Rich?'

'I do not know if you would call it so. There is a large house of wood and stone, surrounded by huts and farm buildings, all within a stockade, and outside that strip fields and orchards.'

'But much land?'

'From the ridge to the lake and a half-hour's walk in either direction. There is a fishing hamlet on the shore that is counted part of it.'

The track bore them on round to the right through the olive trees, and ran gently downhill. The baron stooped in his stirrups to peer among the whispering, deep-smelling trees.

'So green, so green,' he said. 'What do you grow here?'

'Why, olives, as you see, sir. And vines, fruits and grain. We have oak woods too, from which we take our badge. For livestock we have mostly sheep and goats. What do you have in Lackmere?'

'The same – where we can. But it is poorer country. A man needs much land to make a fair living – much more than your Gowden. And there are no big towns to bring us wealth or rich goods.'

'Is it very dry? Is that why they call you Lackmere?'

'We have nothing like this,' he said, gesturing to the lake. 'Not one tenth nor one hundredth of the size. Our streams and pools are mostly waterless in summer, and the grass is as yellow as straw. It is not desert, but thorn forest. Many miles of it. Good land for wolves. Hard land for shepherds and goatherds, who must guard their flocks with sometimes no more than a cut-thorn staff.' He touched his badge.

'Wolves? Are they big and fierce?'

He looked at her. His eyes were green. 'Small and scrawny and fierce. And always hungry.'

They came out of the grove and the track rose, keeping the lake on their left. Near the top they halted. Looking back, she could see the rest of their party emerging from the trees.

'Trant is just over this rise.'

'I should like to see it.'

'We should wait here. My father will want us to top the rise together, blowing his horn.'

'Let us go forward and look, all the same. I do not know how long this place will be my prison. I shall feel easier to see it first in your company.'

He kicked his mount forward. She followed reluctantly, for she did not like what she had heard him say. The rise dropped away to show the familiar mass of Trant bulking on the next hillside. It was just the same as it always had been, after all her long journey. Beyond it the lake stretched away to the north and was lost to sight. She was home.

'Hm. Strong,' said the baron.

'It is not so big as the King's.'

Trant was a single compact courtyard, closed in with five huge towers. Below it were other buildings and a wide area surrounded with a dyke that ran down to the lake-side.

'No indeed. But your father has no need to house a thousand men-at-arms in a night, nor to feed and protect a city. My own walls are not so high as these, and yet mine is not the least strong place in the south. What other castles are nearby?'

'There are not many. Tower Bay must be the closest, but it is more than a day.'

'Whose lands are those, then?' He pointed across the lake.

'The mountains you see are beyond the Kingdom. The hill people there are heathen. But the lands on this side of them are the March of Tarceny.'

The baron looked sour. 'The Doubting Moon. I cannot commend you on your neighbours.'

'So they say, sir. Although it has also been said to me that the evil that was done – the harrying of his people and his neighbours – was the work of the old lord there. He died at his hearth some years ago. I have not met the new march-count or his house, and they did not come to Tuscolo for the King's feast. Our sail folk have some dealings with theirs. Otherwise they do not disturb us. Father always left us a strong guard when he was abroad in the recent troubles. But it was not needed.'

'Hm.' The baron was scowling across the lake now.

She should have remembered that he was one of those whom Tarceny could have helped by attacking from across the lake during the uprising. Maybe he and his friends had

48

been begging Tarceny for such a move, as the King's men had closed in on their last strongholds. If it had come, maybe he would not have been a prisoner now. And all this land that he had admired for its greenery would have been black with the trails of war. He would not have cared.

She had to breathe deeply for a moment, and feel the sunlight on her skin, to remind herself that the vultures of Tarceny had stayed at home, and that Trant flourished in its delicate green.

'So,' said the baron. 'No visitors then? No suitors yet?'

'A few.'

'And what do you do here, between waiting for them to come for you?'

'What I please, sir.'

'What? I did not suppose you were a prisoner, like myself!'

'I am my father's daughter, sir!'

'Of course.'

Father was riding up with the rest of his party. She might now just watch him come, and that would be the end of this conversation. But she knew that she would have to spend many hours in this man's company. Once he had understood that she would talk to him as an equal, or not at all, there was no more point in fencing with him. Like it or not, they would know one another better before long.

'I read sometimes,' she said. 'Often I walk and think by myself.'

'You read?'

'Yes, and I have learned arithmetic.'

'This is rare. My own lady can do neither. Nor can I.'

So he had a lady of his own. Of course – Father had

talked of his family. And now Father himself had laboured up the slope and reined in, six yards away.

Suddenly the ridge was milling with horsemen: the whole party, twenty-strong including the wagon, holding their mounts in check and looking to the Warden. He waved an arm. A rider came up, with the big Sun and Oak Leaf banner beginning to lift and blow in the lake-wind. Under the brave device curled the Warden's motto: WATCH FOR WHO COMES. The herald sounded the long flourish of Trant, and the party poured forward from the ridge. Horns, fragmented by distance, sounded from the castle on the far hill.

So Phaedra came home for the last time, under the banner of her father.

III

Suitors and Chessmen

rant wallowed in the harvest.

In the mornings and evenings, when it was cool enough to work, the hillsides swarmed with people among their strips and vines. The grapes were still picking. The grain was in. From every barn came the steady *whack, whack* of flails upon the threshing floor. The thin months were over. The food was here to be gathered, and every day counted. Every man hurried to bring his own crop in before he did his work for the manor, and every manor knight wanted all that was due to him before he thought of what might be owed to Trant. Ambrose was everywhere, riding from one manor to the next to bully the people into giving what they owed to him and to each other. One day he flew into a rage in the middle of a hearing and had three men from the same village put into stocks over their failure to do the labour due. For five days, three women and their children, down to a six-year-old, worked on without the help of their men at the most vital time of the year.

That was at Manor Sevel. Ambrose held court there more often than any of his other manors, because a knight in the service of Tower Bay had once tried to claim the place, and it was still important to be sure that both Bay and Sevel understood who Sevel's lord was.

Phaedra had ridden over with Baron Lackmere for the hearings, but was not present when Father had his temper fit because her guest had wandered away with his guards to the grape presses to sniff at the stew of juice and pulp and twigs (and flies), and to carp at her about the way things were done. Half an hour listening to the Warden's justice had been enough for Lackmere. It was not manor cases that interested him, but the distant possibility of a clash with Bay. Perhaps he imagined that the Warden might give him a sword and let him ride as a knight against Trant's enemies – if only for an hour.

He was often in her company. He was not easy to entertain. For although he was treated with respect and held in comfort, and permitted to go where he would on Trant's lands under escort, he had little to do but brood and wait for orders of release that did not come. She did what she could. She rode with him all over the castle manors, and walked with him on the walls. She tried to read to him, although he had little use for *The Lamentations of Tuchred*, or any of the half-dozen other holy meditations that made up Trant's library. She wrote, at his dictation, a letter to his lady, in which his words and greetings were so stiff that they betrayed his guilt that his family was now protected and his lands held by those he had chosen as enemy.

She wanted him to see Trant as she saw it – a homely place, even to an exile. She wanted him to see beyond the little signs of wealth that he noted, such as the silver plate from which he was served, the numbers of woven hangings or the smooth craftsmanship of the joined tables and benches. She wanted him to show that he understood how lucky he was to have been sent here rather to any other house in the Kingdom: how he might laugh with James the housemaster or Joliper the merryman; or call Sappo the huntsman to take him fowling along the lakeside. She was annoyed when he spoke grudgingly about the dishes the kitchen produced, or complained about some detail. He spoke little with Brother David, the gnarled, greying castle priest, and attended holy service only when duty required.

She took him outside the walls to her favourite place in all Trant, the small oak grove near the lake edge below the castle, where the ruined fountain court stood among the trees with its colonnades open to the sky. She walked with him around the old stonework, thinking that he might be impressed with the deep silence there, under the whispering branches. She told him how she had escaped from the King's feast in Tuscolo to find a little fountain court like this, which reminded her of home. He did not seem very interested.

And one rainy day she walked with him into the chapel to show him the line of stones in the wall cut with the names of her mother, and of her four brothers and sisters, only one of whom had lived past the age of three.

He looked at the stones, and his face was set like stone too. Perhaps he remembered having hopes for children whom he had then had to bury, like these.

'You were the eldest?'

'The second. Guy was the eldest. He is the only one

I remember well. He died of a fever a year before Mother. After me there was a gap, and then . . .' She gestured to the row of stones that ended in her mother's name.

'Why did your father not re-marry?'

Why did people always think that? 'He does not want for wealth, sir.'

'All men want sons.'

'He has sworn he will not. He says the Angels have given him his portion and he will be content with it.'

'Hm. And when one of these fine suitors has carried you off, what will be left of his portion then?'

She hated it when he spoke of things like that. It was like hearing a drunk singing bawdy songs in a cathedral or a quiet street. But, like a drunk, he would not be put off. It seemed there was little else left that he was willing to talk about. She did not want to think of suitors any more than she wanted to think of what Father would do.

'He has sworn he will not.'

A strange oath, said her companion, as they sat together on the brown hillside of her dreams. He fingered the stone cup that he held in his left hand.

Do you remember the first time?

He nodded. *I remember. You were just a child, peeping over the edge of the pool. I saw you very clearly. It was why I spoke to you.*

I thought you were my brother, she said.

It had been not long after Mother died, in that empty time when she had woken each day to find that everything had changed and yet everything was the same. One evening at table, as she sat in Mother's place, Father had begun to list aloud the sisters and daughters of local lords with whom he might make an alliance. He had done it without any great interest, but he would not stop. And she had screamed at him over the table, with her child's voice cracking, that he had killed Mother and would kill her too, if he did this. Then she had gone to her room and refused food. She had refused it for days. The pain had come like grief, and when it had gone she felt her grief had gone with it, and she had begun to dream wonderful, sunlit dreams of watching Mother sewing robes (*Don't come too close, lamb*) or of the lakeside with the ripple, ripple of light from the water on the underside of the leaves and on Mother's skin. And she would wake to find Mother dead, and Guy dead, and Father raging, or begging beside her that she should eat, and she had wanted to sleep again.

But his pride had broken on the twelfth day, and he had wept and vowed he would not marry again, nor would Trant change, so long as Phaedra lived. Then she had closed her eyes, and a dream had come that was not of her mother but of a pool in a deep bowl among the mountains, with the shapes of stones like fists against the sky, and of the man she had thought was her brother, who had moved in the shadow and spoken to her as she paused over the water and the impossible depth beneath it.

She had forgiven her father. She had set aside her fast to sip at the salty gruel they made for her, which stung in her throat like tears. With her legs still trembling from weakness she had come down the stairs to take Mother's place at the table again. So she had sealed her promise with him. No new bride came to their gate, to bury what had been lost beneath the foundations of a new family. And in its long mourning Trant was their home.

She had come to love her later childhood, drifting alone from room to room where the servants were busy, playing quietly with her cup and ball, watching the seasons from the castle walls. She knew all the household, was happy with them, and could rule every one of them if she wanted, because of Father. Once a year she would make him, as Mother had done, a belt or a robe that he might wear at Easter and other high days, to show him that she was being faithful too. And she had never been afraid of his anger again.

Her friend listened to her and said no more that night. She thought that he touched her shoulder lightly as she finished, and the memory of his touch was with her when she woke.

The 'foppoons' were no part of the bargain. Their voices and footfalls were a new sound in Trant, and one she did not like. Young men, gaily clad, they came one after another. The knights from the manors showed themselves more often at the castle as winter drew on. Noblemen and their sons rode by, who had never come before. Word of her looks had spread. The rich and unambitious might have come for that alone, for her dowry was no more than that of many a good knight's daughter. But what they all knew, whether they had laid eyes on her or not, was that she was the only child of a man who held fifteen manors around Trant, where the King had nine, and no one else above three. When Ambrose died her husband would be

56

the King's choice to succeed as warden, holding twenty-four manors for his wife and the crown, and with them one of the great castles of the land. Without knowing it, Phaedra had become one of the finest prizes outside the court at that time. By spring, and her sixteenth birthday, it seemed that not a month passed without some new campaign beginning for her hand.

She knew that marriage was the natural state for a woman (unless she were a nun), and that many married at her age. But she could think of other women who had never married, or who were not married yet. She was not ready to leave her home, where the wind heaved in the oak woods and darkened the water. And she hated the men who might make her do so.

She was cold to them. She rebuffed them. Some – those she thought of as the 'good' ones – accepted it when she asked them not to seek her hand any more. Others did not listen, although they went home quickly enough if Father told them they were unsuitable. The worst were the two or three who believed that they were truly in love and that their love for her was so strong that it must surely triumph in the end. All the popular ballads told of women who refused and refused, testing their suitors in extremes of combat and devotion, until finally yielding with grace. That was how they saw her; and they counted each snub as just another passage of arms in the long siege for her soul.

'My father once said you were beneath me, Phaedra,' said one baron's son, smiling, when she asked him to pursue her no more. 'But oh, he was wrong. You are so far above me, like a lark singing unseen.'

He had no *right* to think like that!

She tried to explain this to Brother David one morning, after they had visited a woman who was sick. The priest nodded agreeably, as if he had understood. Then he said something about taking her time, which showed that he had not. None of them did.

For even in the times she despaired, and began listing to herself the two or three she would be most prepared to marry if she had to, she could not imagine the life she would lead with them in their strange houses, waiting and waiting to come home to a Trant where Father would no longer stalk the floors. She could not imagine her dreams. And she was afraid.

It had been years since the last new baby at Trant. The infants Phaedra remembered had grown to noisy brats that scampered around the stone halls. But she could recall clearly going to peer at them in their cradles and weigh them lightly in her arms. And she remembered the small cold voices that had stirred in her heart, as she clung to those frail things. She thought of the little graves that men would prepare for her children, as they had done for her brothers and sisters. She saw herself burying the children she had borne – even dying herself after birth, watching with her last sight her child being carried crying from her room, never knowing how it might be cared for or whether it would prosper. Some day – most probably – she must run such chances, but she did not know how. In the way that opened before her it could only be wrong. She knew what the end would be.

She refused, and refused, and would not change.

'This is foolish,' said Father in the early summer. 'I'll

not ask you to bear company that is unkind, so that it is in my power to have it otherwise. But marry you must, and I must lose you. Among these men are the best in the Kingdom. So choose and have done, or we shall settle for worse in the end.'

Still he would not order her to marry, and they both knew it. In his heart the demands of his peers and their sons were at war with his desire to keep his daughter for one more year, and with his fear, perhaps, of what she might do if she were wed against her will. But each time that he had to offend the son of a neighbour, or outrage a friend, was a wound to him. After the harvest was in, and the nights began to come early, he sat alone drinking wine in fits of muttering and silence.

I must marry, she said to the knight in her dream.

Do you wish to?

No, she said. *But Father is changing. It cannot go on.*

It seemed to her that they stood in the ruined fountain court under the shadow of the oak trees. There was a light wind blowing, and the trees sighed with it. Before her the bowl of the fountain was full of dark, still water, on which a fallen oak leaf drifted with no power of its own.

It will not be Bay, she said. *If one of Bay became warden after my father's death, they would have most of the east coast of the lake. In peace or war, nothing could cross it, and little move up or down it, without their let. That is too much for the King, or Father, to permit.*

And not Tarceny, either?

Does the hare wed the hell-hawk? Father sent his heralds packing the hour that they arrived.

The old lord of Tarceny is dead, remember.

You have said that to me before. But it makes no odds. One more or less makes no odds. Trant cannot be the same any more. I must choose one of them, and let him take me away. If Baldwin presses his suit, perhaps. He is young, at least, and it will please Father.

They stood side by side in silence. She was wondering what would happen to him when she left Trant for good. He had followed her to Tuscolo a year ago. Could he do so to Baldwin? She could not imagine it. Of all the things in her life, he was the one that had not changed. To lose him might be the deepest loss of all.

He sighed, and put his hands upon the fountain. Under his fingers, it became – it seemed it always had been – the stone cup, which he was lifting to her. A tiny oak leaf still turned in a slow circle upon the surface.

He said: *Shall we drink, now?*

Yes.

There came a terrible day, the eve of All Saints', when Phaedra sat rigid in her seat in the hall of Trant, looking down at the handsome young noble before her, with a score of men in gay cloth and polished armour at his back. She could feel herself trembling as Father rose slowly and told the man that, although his suit was worthy and his gifts generous, although his blood was of the highest and his truth beyond doubt, yet it did not please Trant's daughter to accept him. And Elward, first son of Tower Baldwin and counted among the flower of the land, stared at them both in disbelief. Then, his cheeks flaming, he bowed and led his retinue of twenty knights clashing from the hall.

Shock settled on the castle as they rode from the gates.

People who had greeted the riders of Baldwin with garlands as they came, who had never believed that Phaedra and her father could turn down such a match, stared at her and muttered behind her back. A grown woman must marry. Without marriage there was no future. Phaedra met each glance as it came, but no one spoke to her. Brother David was tight-lipped in the chapel. Father ate in silence that evening and hugged his fur coat around himself like an angry bear. She lay awake in her room with the thoughts circling restlessly for hours in her head, and the taste of water in her mouth.

A letter had arrived from Maria – the third since they had parted in the fountain court at Tuscolo. It exclaimed at the stories that came from Trant to the court, and to Maria at the house of her father in Pemini. She laughed at the discomfort of so many preening knights. Her cousin had now wed the man her parents wanted. But Maria, herself still unmarried, urged Phaedra to go on resisting all until she found the one who was right, regardless of rank or politics. She wrote well, in her own hand, saying so many of the things that Phaedra wanted to hear and that no one would tell her, until now. Reading the letter in the early light, Phaedra felt as if birdsong were twittering to her from somewhere beyond a window in a high wall.

That afternoon she settled in the library to compose her reply. She was staring at a hanging of saints and trying to find words to explain to Maria why, so far as she knew, no man could be 'right', when someone came whistling into the room behind her.

'Good day, Sir Aun.'

'Good day to you. How did you know it was me?'

'There are not many in the house today who sing as they climb the stairs.' And there were none who were that tuneless. She looked over her shoulder. The baron wore the long blue-and-white doublet of Lackmere, and seemed more cheerful than he had in a long time. His guards lounged discreetly in the doorway.

'More fool they,' he said.

'I am to blame.'

'If that is what you think, then you must bear it. I came to ask if you play chess.'

'Why, no. I do not believe there is a set of pieces in all Trant.' There were plenty of knucklebones and jack balls, and even her own cup-and-ball game, but no one played chess that she knew of.

'That was true until a week ago. Will you come to see what I have been at since your father allowed me wood and chisels?'

He was quartered in a room set into the north-west tower, a level above Phaedra's own. His bed was screened by a hanging. The rest of the room was largely taken with a wardrobe and a wooden trestle table, set under the big window that looked along the wall. A neat row of wood tools lay on its surface against the wall, and a set of carved pieces, some stained with dye, stood on a rough chequered board at the near corner. The baron invited her to one of two stools at the table.

Phaedra picked up one of the pieces and looked at it curiously. It was a little wooden statue of a man on horse-back, his head and upper body grotesquely out of propor-tion to the stubby horse he rode, and to his own little legs traced in relief down its sides. The face had a lopsided, staring look, as though the rider were crazed in the saddle.

'I did not know you could carve,' she said.

'Nor could I until these last months. And I have spilt my own blood more than once in cutting these things. Still, I learn slowly, and may replace the worst of them in time. At least these all stand on their feet. Now, pay attention. The game is for two players. Each piece moves differently. The pawn is the simplest – so . . .'

She listened, and realized that his briskness was not, as she had thought, because he did not wish to beg her to entertain him, but because he understood that she herself needed company, and did not know how to offer it without embarrassment. Strange that such a man would want to comfort her. She had not supposed him capable of it before. As time passed, she was learning more about the people she thought she already knew. Perhaps that was part of growing into a woman.

The game was impersonal, and that too was an advantage. She found herself caught by the way in which it moved from ordered rows to a net of staggering complexity, and then to simplicity again as all but the last few pieces were taken from the board. At any other time she would have declined every game after the first, for she lost easily, and did not like to lose. But after that morning at his worktable she played with him daily – sometimes twice a day. It gave them both something they could control. To Phaedra, the mounting pressure of the baron's attack on her position echoed the pressure of the world upon herself, and yet in the game she could develop her defences with pieces that went where they were ordered and did what

63

they were supposed to do. She knew her play was improving, and set herself to hold him as long as possible. And if she ever became frustrated at another defeat, she could tease the baron about the quality of some piece or other, and leave him whetting his chisels to set the fault right.

And they could talk, now, of themselves: of her fears of leaving Trant; of his that he might never do so.

'I had thought of going to Jent, and asking His Grace to let me take the veil.'

'I doubt that your father would give permission. And His Grace would not take you without it. Your move . . . You push her around too much, you know.'

'She's my best piece. Why should I not? You always use the knights whenever you can.'

'Knights are for taking risks with— Ho, what's that?'

A trumpet was blowing somewhere in the castle.

'The gate-horn.' Phaedra stopped with her queen in her hand. When she recovered herself she could not remember where she was moving it to.

'Another suitor?' said Aun. 'I thought they had all been scared off by what happened to young Baldwin.'

Phaedra stared at the board. All the possible squares seemed wrong.

'You're about to lose her, anyway,' said the baron. 'Shall we go and see who it is?'

'If we must.'

Outside the baron's rooms a flight of steps led to the flat roof of the tower. It was a cold, windy day. The Sun and Oak Leaf flapped busily overhead. From the parapet they had a clear view over the hall roof to the gate end of the courtyard. A half-dozen riders had come through the gatehouse arch and were dismounting. Stable hands and men-at-arms milled around them.

'That's a royal banner!'

'Is it, by God!' said the baron, leaning forward and screwing his eyes up to read the device at that distance. She sensed his sudden excitement. Royal messages might well concern him.

'Damn my sight!' he cursed. 'That's the Sun, right enough. But is the field not differenced?'

'It is, sir. The banner tail is vert.'

'Septimus.' He was silent. Phaedra could see his agitation. And she knew he must not allow himself to hope. Nothing from the King's younger son could bring him release. She knew he knew it too; and yet he could not stop himself from hoping. She saw the effort with which he turned from the parapet. 'Septimus, or one of his people. On his way from somewhere to somewhere else. Nothing for either of us, I guess. Come on down, and I'll take that troublesome queen off you.'

He played so badly that she forced her first draw. She took no joy in it.

It was the prince's chamberlain, on his way, as Aun had predicted, from somewhere to somewhere else. He was a funny, round man, bald and bearded, who spoke in an endless wheezy chatter throughout supper. His wit was directed mainly at the Warden, and at Brother David. Some of the time he joked with Phaedra. He seemed not to notice Aun, who sat watching him throughout the meal.

Prince's man or not, he came from the court, and it

was from the court that Aun's release would come. Phaedra watched the baron realize that he was being ignored, saw him sink into himself, eating in silence at the end of the table, drinking, and watching the chamberlain over the rim of his horn. She found, for the first time in almost a year, that she felt real pain on behalf of someone other than herself – pain for the ugly, fierce little man who wore the Wolf Behind the Staff.

She rose as early as she might, and went to her room. Footsteps sounded on the stair behind her. From her doorway she saw the baron climbing up towards his tower chambers, with his head bowed and a flask of wine in his hand. She closed her door and went to sit on her bed. After a time she rose to her feet again.

There would be guards at Aun's door, but they would not stop her. She wondered whether they would think it strange, provided she left the door ajar and did not stay long. With her heart beginning to beat at the impropriety of what she was doing, she stole along the corridor to the stair that would lead up to his room. It was as she hesitated with her foot on the first step that the door to the hall opened two flights below. The sound of voices carried clearly up to her.

'I think you may hope, sir,' said the chamberlain. 'I think you may. Neither Faul nor Develin will be content if His Highness weds the other's candidate. So we are at a mighty stand-off. His Highness uses this to order matters as it pleases him. And he is tired of the court ladies, and remembers her well. I may tell him that word has exaggerated neither her looks nor her bearing. Nothing is fixed, mind, but I should not be surprised if His Highness finds occasion to visit you himself before long – in passing, as it were.'

'His Highness does us much honour,' said Ambrose. 'And more than I or my cross-grained daughter deserve.'

'So far, I would say that a crossing grain has done neither you nor her harm where it most counts in this case. Quite the reverse. It is the stuff of ballads. And if Barius *were* set on remaining single, as he seems to be—'

'Let us not talk of that. When will he come?'

'I cannot say for sure. If I am right, there is to be a Royal Progress through these lands in the new year.'

'It is not widely known yet, but I had heard so.'

'Then expect His Highness to be one of the party. And do your best to ensure all are well entertained at Trant.'

'I am already giving it thought. One thing – will the King bring news for my guest, do you think?'

'Lackmere? Inchapter has the protection of his lands, and the profit from them. He is one of Develin's men. That party would not wish to see them surrendered, and His Majesty has little reason to anger them. Lackmere should not look for release before that changes.'

'It is not good. He frets like a badly-tamed hawk.'

'I am sorry for him, but he should have chosen better friends – or burned fewer villages.'

They were climbing the stair towards her. The chamberlain must be retiring early after his journey. And so Father was retiring, too. Phaedra fled.

Crouching behind the door in her room, she heard the footsteps fade. Doors closed. Other footsteps were on the stair – James the housemaster and his fellows, dousing the lights now that the Warden had gone to his bed. The lamp-glow from under her door disappeared. Only the cracks of moonlight from the window shutters lit the darkness of her room.

The door was shut. She was trapped.

She could not go to Aun's room now, with the house in darkness, and the baron probably drunk. And she would not know what to say to him. She did not know what to think. She wished she had not overheard. The chamberlain must have been drunk himself to talk so much. Or did the house of the prince spend all its days in gossip?

The prince!

She could not remember much of Septimus: a plain-faced, paunchy young man, unremarkable other than that he was a son of the King. To the rest of the world, no doubt, he was an even better match than Baldwin would have been. To Phaedra he was undoubtedly a worse one. And he lived at the King's court in Tuscolo, at the centre of its frivolities and intrigue and twisted justice. He had smiled at a strange face in the royal chapel, and there had been nothing strange to him about that because his home was forever full of strangers. He would never be master there, nor would his wife be mistress.

Trapped! She could do nothing but wait until they came to get her, however many months it might be before they made up their minds. She had learned enough since leaving Tuscolo to know that the world would never let her alone. There had to be an end. She had not expected it to be this. She was pacing the little room now, angrily, round and round. Now and again a word or a sound escaped her. She stamped her foot, hard. It hurt. She wanted to scream. Her bed stood against the wall, with its sheets rumpled where she had been sitting. Sleep? How could she sleep after hearing this? Somewhere in Tuscolo there would be another bed, bigger, richer, which Septimus would share with his bride. She had heard that on the wedding night of a prince men stood at the bedside with lit candles, for there must be those who could swear, if it came to it, that the heir of a prince was truly his.

Oaths and Angels!

She turned to the window of her room and eased the shutters open. It was a cool winter's night, although this side of the castle was sheltered from the wind that set the moon chasing among the cloud-thickets like a lord at hunt. She leaned on the sill, and the cold stone pressed back against her. Down below her the slope fell easily to the water's edge. She could see the clumps of trees within the dyke, the outline of the old buildings and the little grove that surrounded the ruined fountain court. She could see the moonlight on the lakewater, stretching a path from the far hills towards her across the lake: a moon-path away from this place where the walls pressed against her, but out of reach, out of all possibility.

There at the window, she must have slept at last. For it seemed to her as if the walls around her had faded. She was walking among brown rocks, and there seemed to be a low humming from somewhere that was almost too deep for the ear. She knew these things from before.

The moon appeared again. The brown rocks gave back, and beneath the thin soles of her shoes she felt grass. She seemed to be walking among trees. She was in the grove by the fountain again, with the damp air of night breathing on her shoulders. Oaks whispered as if they were alive. The colonnades were about her. The wavelets lapped and rippled a short distance away. Still that deep sound throbbed in her ear, and her feet turned upon brown stones among the roots of the trees.

Where are you?

She had met him here, when she had thought she must accept Baldwin. Now she needed him more than ever.

Where are you?

There was water in the fountain, reflecting the moon. The reflection wavered, and would not be still. The shadow of his head appeared beside hers on the water's surface.

Well met, he said.

Are you there? I can't see you clearly.

He kneeled before her and kissed her hand. Her fingers tingled at the touch of his lips.

You were calling me, he said. *I looked, and there you were. What is the matter?*

They will wed me to Prince Septimus, she said. *I must leave here, but I know no one and have nowhere to go.*

He was silent for a while, as if he were thinking.

How long do we have?

I don't know, she answered. *A few weeks. I must be gone before he sees me.*

Choose a number, then. Greater than five.

Eight had always been her favourite.

Good. On the eighth day of the new year wait for me in this place at the eighth hour after noon. Can you do that?

She thought so.

If I come in that hour, I shall give you what help I can. If I do not, I cannot help you at all.

Wait!

70

He paused.

Are you . . . (alive? real? She had known him for seven years. Now he seemed to be speaking as if he could step into the world outside her skin.)

He seemed to smile. For a moment she could see him clearly, standing before her with his hand on the fountain rim. She remembered how the fountain had become the cup in his hand. His fingers drifted over the water and seemed to pick something from the surface.

My name is Ulfin, he said, handing it to her. *These grow below my walls.*

Then the moonlight faded again, and the vision with it. She opened her eyes.

She was awake, standing at her window, shivering. The stone of the sill was hard and cold against her. The grove of the fountain court, which the moment before had so clearly been about her, lay hidden in darkness down the hill. Nothing seemed to move there. The light grew as the moon reared clear of the clouds. In her left hand, which he had kissed, lay a four-pointed white rose flower with one black petal. She looked at it closely. She had not seen its like before.

'So I am a witch now,' she muttered over it. 'Did you do that to me?'

Perhaps its silence was a reply. Perhaps it said that he too had changed. Somewhere, he walked in the light of day, under the same sun as Septimus and all the world that hammered at her door. He could help. And his lips had touched her hand.

Her heart was beating as if she had run all the way up the tower stairs.

IV

Steel and Darkness

he chamberlain left. January came with dark days and drizzle that whipped down the wind. Royal outriders appeared on the lake road and called for entry at the gates. There were four of them, sent weeks ahead of the great progress with instructions for each of the hosting houses along the way. The people of Trant watched them as they crossed the courtyards, and whispered to one another. Kitchen boys scurried down the passageways that they had sauntered along the day before. The stablemaster lost his temper over a detail and beat one of the grooms for it. Trant was roused, and nervous. The King was coming.

Phaedra noticed that the atmosphere in the castle had changed with the arrival of the newcomers, but she was preoccupied with her own thoughts. Time had gone swiftly. Father had said nothing of his conversation with the prince's chamberlain on the stair. It was as well, for she would not have known how to react. She found it hard to concentrate on the doings of the house, which were becoming more and more unreal to her as time passed. Sometimes, when people spoke to her, she took a moment to respond.

The flower had lain in a cup of water for a week until it had wasted away. The most real thing left in the castle was the small bundle – a purse and travelling clothes – that she had hidden under her bed some days before. Many times since then she had felt for it to make sure it was still there. It bulked in her mind like stone among shadows.

On the seventh night of the new year Phaedra retired to bed as she had a thousand times before. She did not sleep. When she closed her eyes and looked up into darkness, she wondered where she would lay her head tomorrow.

The next morning she attended the Warden's discussions with the King's men. Others from Trant were there too. The visitors spoke in turn. A marshal told them of the size of the King's escort and the accommodation they would need. A clerk wanted details of the complaints that would be brought before the King's justice while he was at Trant. A butler spoke of the personal wants and comforts of the King, and a huntsman about how he might spend his leisure.

Phaedra said nothing. As she listened, she realized why Trant was already beginning to hum around her. The demands on the household would be enormous. There would be fifty knights – fifty! – wanting board and sleeping room, as well as clerks, jesters, cup-holders and chamberlains – enough to eat three months' worth of Trant's provisions in the three weeks they would stay. Both royal princes would be in the party. It was not yet known which of the barons would join the progress, although it was a safe guess that if Develin came both Seguin and Faul would be along to keep an eye on him. Two princes, three great lords; and the King would not pay a silver piece for the board of his following or theirs for all the season that he was away from Tuscolo. Plainly, the crown had good reasons for such a progress, and reinforcing the King's authority in the lands he passed through would only be one of them.

There would be no women with the King's following. The queen was pregnant again (her seventh child, if it lived). She would not travel. The ladies of the court were to remain at Tuscolo out of respect for her.

'Well you may look pleased,' said the butler to Phaedra. There were chuckles in the room. Phaedra had to think for a moment before realizing that if ladies of the court had come her work as hostess would have doubled – more than doubled.

There would be over a hundred horses to be stabled and fed, with tack to be mended and all. Trant's stables would overflow. There would be banquets by night and hunts by day. Phaedra knew that without a miracle that night she would be filling every moment with matters of the King's visit for weeks. Still, she found her attention wandering: to the fountain; to the coming night; to the man in the dream. And the voices of the room would dim around her.

'What of the Baron Lackmere?' asked Father.

'A matter that touches the King's justice,' said the royal clerk. 'But His Majesty is in my opinion unlikely to make any further judgement concerning him in the course of this progress.'

'Therefore,' said the butler, 'it would be better if the

baron did not meet with the King at any time, nor did eat at the high table, nor at any table with the King's household. What you do beyond that I leave to you.'

So Aun's hope of early release was gone, as he had feared it would be. And there would be no other chance as good as this for a number of years. Father was making no protest. Nor did he when the clerk began to enquire about the ins and outs of the Bay knight's claim on Manor Sevel, feeling out how this dispute between the great houses might go when the King tried them. If Bay must have crumbs, then crumbs would be thrown to Bay. Trant was after a bigger prize. She shut her eyes briefly.

I must leave, she thought. I will save him from this.

Afterwards, when the midday meal was ended, she looked for Aun through the castle, and did not find him. At last she came upon his guards, lurking in the upper levels of the north-east tower to be out of the wind and the threat of coming rain. They pointed her to where the baron paced on the northern battlements above the great hall. She saw at once that he already knew what the King's men had said about him. When she approached he turned away, as though fearing she would try to comfort him.

'It is not a good day, I think,' she said.

He grunted, and peered over the battlements. She joined him, looking down the grey and white perspectives of the north wall. It was forty feet from the platform where they stood to the base, and another fifteen to the floor of the ditch. The ditch was supposed to be dry, but there was always a little water in it at this time of year.

'The wall bulges outward near the bottom,' she said.

'You don't see it, unless you are up here looking down.'

At another time he might have explained about building techniques – about the need for a broad base to the wall for stability, or some such reason. Today he scowled.

'I wonder at your workmanship here. The mortar is well enough at this level – no doubt because it is easy to come to. But are there not cracks between the stonework on the face of the wall?'

'You may be right, sir.'

'I should say so. Perhaps it will fall down one day, and then I shall be free.'

'You have better hopes of being freed, Aun.'

'Have I?' he said sharply. 'I suppose if you marry this prince of yours, you'll be a princess, and if you bear him the right number of sons, he'll listen to you. Then if His kind Majesty and Barius would only die without further issue, you'll be Queen Consort one day. *Then* you can persuade someone to let me out of here – if I haven't died or gone mad waiting.'

Phaedra paused, fighting the sudden anger in herself that would make her walk away. It was knowing he would not care that stopped her. And he had good reason to be distressed – as much as she did, she thought.

'I'm not supposed to know about that,' she said quietly.

'Neither am I. Neither is half the castle. Do you think anyone would tell me if it hadn't been rattling around the corridors since yesterday? These gabbling Tuscolo gaylords!'

'I do not wish to—'

'You're very young, my girl. May I give you some advice?'

'Do.'

'Don't think of making your father play your game. He can't, this time. And he won't try. What he has done for you has already been beyond all reason – another man would have birched the skin off his child for crossing him so. If the prince wants to marry you, he will – although if you ask me, he'll suffer for it in the Kingdom. But he can do it. Your father would not be warden for long if he interfered. I'm not telling you this because I like it. I'm telling you because that's the way things are.'

It might be a sort of comfort, to a man like him, to know that someone else was being constrained against their will. Rain began to fall in individual drops upon the stonework around them. After a while she spoke again.

'Sir, I would like to forget what you have said. For too many men are nothing but armoured bullies. And I think that when you have taken a man's arms and bullying away from him, and find there is nothing more, then he likewise is nothing more. And you and he and the Kingdom are the poorer for it.'

He glared at her, and she met his look, as she always did. Then she left him. When she looked back she saw him leaning over the battlements again, with the rain beating heavily around him.

So she spent the rest of the afternoon drifting round the castle, watching the men and women at their work and telling them absently what she thought would be needed when the King came. Then she went to the north-west tower to watch the evening. The rain had gone. So had Aun. The battlements below her were empty. The grey underbellies of clouds ranked one after the other, on and on towards the pale gleams of sunset. The weather was changing. The wind blew from the south. It was strangely warm. She looked down towards the olive trees that hid the fountain and thought: I must go. Even if he does not come tonight, I shall go. Perhaps I shall make the sail-folk take me down the lake to Jent, and ask the bishop to let me enter a convent there.

At the sixth hour that evening she sat through her last supper at Trant, with the oil lamps flaring above her. Looking down from her place at the high table, where she sat between the King's huntsman and his butler, she could see the household at the long tables below her. They had seated Aun on the one to her right, among the knights at the head of it. She could see him watching her, but could not read his face. When she looked again midway through the meal he was gone.

The tables clattered with fists and dishes, and Joliper the merryman came up with his lute and his banter to entertain the high table. The sights and the sounds touched her eyes and ears, but reached only to the edge of her mind. The King's butler was talking with Brother David, but she did not listen. The thought of the old court beneath the oak trees lay in her head like a dark, quiet pool. The supper went on in uproar along the banks, but the surface of the water was still.

'. . . So Wulfram came from the sea,' Joliper was saying in his sing-song story voice.

'. . . In Three Ships he brought Four Angels, and with them our people to a strange shore.

'There he bade his Seven Sons each take land for their own, and in their hands he placed One Thing.

'And the Thing was Iron.

'Iron in the hands of the Seven Sons won the Kingdom, and Iron in the hearts of their children shall see that it never is at peace.'

Joliper had ridden with Father in the long harrying of the Seabord when the last rebels had finally been put down. He would never stand up to Father, or indeed to any man that Phaedra could think of. But his hatred of what he had seen stirred in the lines of his ballads – even before the King's own men. (He also mentioned lice and dysentery whenever he thought Father would let him get away with it.)

Some time after the seventh hour, when they came to fill the cups for the second time, Phaedra rose to leave. She kissed Father goodnight, as she had done every night since she was small, and let her lips linger just a fraction longer than usual on his hairy cheek. If he noticed, he did not show it. But he smiled at her and there was warmth in his hug, which had not always been there in the last few months. Then he turned to the royal clerk beside him, and began to test the water about his long dispute with Falco of Bowerbridge, who claimed to be a free knight rather than to hold his manor from the Warden. Perhaps not one for the King himself, but for a panel of right men appointed to judge?

Father was not a bad man. He played the game as he must, like chess, and this was too good a chance for him to miss. A gift in the right place, even to this clerk, would bring a royal letter that would finish tiresome old Falco's claim to be a dog-knight as surely as if Father had burned him out of his home and killed anyone who tried to help him. It would be a manor to set against Sevel, if he lost that: a fair exchange for Trant, whatever came of the marriage. Phaedra walked from the hall without looking back.

The corridors were dark to her eyes after the lights of the hall. Purple splashes drifted in her sight as she walked. Her feet knew the way. Up the stair, turning after a dozen steps, and up again to the gallery from which she had heard Father and the prince's man talking weeks before. An emptiness was growing within her as she walked.

Now to the right. A torch hung above her door, shedding a pool of light in the passage. She went in and fumbled for the things she had placed below her bed: a light cloak, and the bundle small enough to hide under it. She was leaving almost everything behind. Even her cup-and-ball game lay in her chest alongside the dusty rag dolls that she had not played with for years. There would be nothing, as she hooked the cloak around her neck, to show that she was doing more than taking a short stroll within the castle before retiring.

She was ready. It must be almost the eighth hour.

She stood alone at the window a little while, looking westwards down to the lake. There was a moon out there, somewhere above thin clouds. The oaks about the fountain clustered in a mass of black below her, and the lake-face spread in deep blue-grey into the night beyond. She thought she could just – just? – make out a pale patch that might be the full-bellied curve of a sail, dipping silently above the water. She could not be sure.

There was one more thing to do. She left her room and felt her way along the corridor to the north-west tower, where she took the spiral steps down to the ground. The corridor here was unlit, but she walked forward confidently, running her fingers along the right-hand wall past one, two, three doorways. When her fingers touched wood for the fourth time, she stopped and groped for the door ring. The hinges opened with a moan.

The chapel was empty. The Flame of Heaven still fluttered on the altar, but the roof and the aisles were lost in darkness. She crossed slowly to the far aisle, bowing to the Flame as she had done every day for a dozen years, and walked down the chapel until she came to the stones in the wall.

She could hardly see them in this light, but she did not have to. She stood before them. After a moment she opened her mouth to say something, but stopped herself. Instead she reached out and touched each stone lightly, feeling for the names cut in the cold surfaces. Goodbye, Guy. Goodbye, Ellen, Anfred, Ina. Goodbye, Mother. I must go.

She thought, as she walked down the aisle to the main door, that families should weep at parting. But for seven years she had had only five stones and Father. Stones could not weep, and neither did she.

Set in Trant's west wall, under the lee of the north-west tower, was the small postern door. It was unguarded. Huge bolts held it on the inside, but her hands drew them back. The hinges groaned as it opened. She stepped through and closed it as softly as she could behind her.

Immediately she knew she was in the wrong place. She

had never been this side of the walls after dark before. She scrambled quickly down into the ditch (ankle-deep in cold water) and up the far side. No one called to her from above. Lights burned up there, but Trant's custom in time of peace was to man the gatehouse and let the walls look to themselves.

Down the hill, and the ground was soft beneath her feet. Her cloak was dark. She was beyond the reach of the torchlight now. There seemed to be no sound but the steady whisper of the wind and the slight scuff of her shoes on the grass. The first trunks of the grove loomed at her out of the night. She went more slowly, straining her eyes for the sign of anyone moving or standing beneath the trees.

'I should have brought a lantern,' she muttered to herself.

But what for? Carrying a light would only give her away to anyone watching from the castle. She knew the way. At least, she knew it in daylight. And it was not wholly dark, even here beneath the trees.

Her feet touched stone flags. Some of the trunks around her must be pillars. The old fountain stood before her. Her fingers reached to touch the dry rim. It was there. She felt her way down to crouch on its step, and slowly settled her back against the stone. She wondered how long she should wait. An hour, he had said. Could she judge the time?

The wind stirred in the branches. Between them, to her left, she could see the lights of the castle. Faint sounds clicked and muttered among the trees. Now and again she was sure she heard a footstep, but though she turned her head and strained her eyes she saw nothing, and then a gust would come and all the leaves would shiver, and as it died she would listen and listen and try, from all the meaningless patter of a wood at night, to pick a sound she knew.

It was cold. Her cloak was thin. Her feet and ankles were chilled. There were warmer things in her bundle, but she did not want to fumble and scatter her belongings in the darkness. She felt that if she did it would take her an age to be ready again.

Then she thought that she might as well be warmer and have something to do to pass the time. As she reached for the bundle she again thought she heard someone moving in the trees. More than one person, for the sounds behind her seemed very quickly to be followed by others to her left. She rose and looked around. Nothing moved. No one stepped forward to greet her.

So she waited. And the wind shivered and the grove clicked and rustled and dripped around her, and gradually the pounding in her heart eased, and she crouched and hugged her arms around her knees, and looked at the lights on the hill and wondered if she had strayed into a dream.

The cloud thinned. The light grew. A few feet behind her a voice spoke.

'Phaedra.'

Her heart jumped, and jumped again when she saw him. He was standing by the fountain, dressed in a heavy cloak, with the moonlight in his hair. Some restraint gave within her when she saw him, and she was smiling. So was he.

'You did come,' she said.

'I came. My ship is at the jetty on the lakeshore. Do you want to come with me?'

There were other men behind him, watching from the shadows of the columns and the trees. She rose.

'Yes,' she said. 'Ulfin.'

'No!'

A man stumbled forward from among the trees behind her. Metal scraped in a scabbard. A blade gleamed for a moment in the moonlight.

'She's not for you!' yelled Aun.

Phaedra cried out to him, but the knight was pushing her back from the fountain, drawing with his other hand. Aun checked his rush, hesitated. Steel flickered in shadow between the two men. Other hands took Phaedra and pulled as she looked back. The knight said something and then struck, and struck again as quick as a snake. Aun staggered away.

'Don't kill him!' she cried.

Distant voices called from the castle. The blades rang and the fighters stumbled. Aun beat desperately to keep the long blade away, and then swung at his enemy's head. The knight jumped back.

'Ha!'

'This is ridiculous,' the knight said. 'Get him off me.'

Men surged forward around Phaedra. She heard Aun shouting. There were lights and movement from the castle.

Her companion's hand fell on her shoulder.

'We must go now. Follow me.'

Blows and running feet sounded in the wood. From further off Aun was still shouting. 'Ho, Trant! Raiders! Raiders!'

A whistle blew by her right ear. The knight was leading her quickly downhill, out of the trees and along the lakeside. There were two others with him. More came running up.

'Is anyone hurt?' he asked the one nearest him.

'How do I know?' The man put a whistle to his lips and blew. Shapes moved on the slope – men running towards them.

'Come on!'

Before them Phaedra saw the long line of the jetty with the Trant boats rocking at tether. At the far end lay a long ship with her mast stepped and sail furled. There were men moving aboard. The knight led Phaedra out to it and jumped lightly down onto the deck. He held out his hand to help her after him. Behind her his followers gathered on the jetty. The man with the whistle was trying to count them.

'They've sortied,' said someone.

There were lights – torches – moving down the slope towards them from Trant. The men on the jetty scrambled aboard. The Trant boards pounded under the feet of the intruders.

'Push off.'

'Stand by me, Phaedra,' he said, from the stern of the vessel. She picked her way among the men and boards to join him. Oars swung and bit whitely on the dark water.

'Together!' urged someone near her. 'After me!'

There was a strip of water now between her and the jetty. She could still jump, and struggle back to her shore if she chose. She would have to jump now, if she was going to. The moment was slipping away.

He was standing beside her. They had touched, and she almost had not noticed. He was there, where she could touch him again. The deck lifted and made her decision for her. She reached to him to steady herself and hooked her hand into his belt. She allowed her fingers to stay where they could feel his warmth through the thin cloth.

Men were moving about them, and some looked their way. She wondered if they could tell what she was thinking, and whether it showed on her face, even in this light. She thought he must be able to feel her pulse through her fingertips and the fabric of his shirt, and if he could it would be wonderful, because he would already know what it was she did not think she could ever say. They stood together, and the taste of dark water was in her mouth.

On the hill above her was the mass of the castle, topped with torches, against the night sky. In that flat shadow lay Father, the knights, the dogs, and all the tattle-tale community of Trant. Collen, restless in his stable. The chapel, with the light on the altar. They looked down on her, and she departed.

Suddenly the night hissed at her savagely. She jumped.

'Keep low,' he said softly, and they kneeled together on the deck. There were torches and men moving on the jetty. Someone yelled at them from the shore.

The air hissed again, a hateful sound.

'Crossbow,' muttered a voice near her. 'More than one, maybe.'

'Hoist sail.'

There was a hiss and thump and a yelp from someone forward. The sail surged up the mast, flapping and rumpling in the night breeze. Men scrambled around it.

Then it shaped and filled, and the ship heeled under the palm of the wind. The oars rattled and came aboard. The thick ripple from the stem of the boat grew as their way increased. The jetty was well behind them now. Lights were moving there.

'Did you see to the boats?' he muttered to the helmsman.

'Threw the oars into the water and cut every rope we could find.'

'Thank you. In the bow, there! Anyone hurt?'

There was a pause. Then someone called back. 'Only splinters.'

'I think we've done it, then,' he said. Whether this was to himself or to her Phaedra was not quite sure. She was looking back at the torches on the jetty and in the castle, growing more distant with every minute, until the next headland hid the lower lights on the shoreline, and those in the castle fused into a single, high spark that seemed to follow them across the water. The shoreline dropped behind them and was hidden in the night, but she could see the castle light still.

Men were moving about the deck, loosening bundles, spreading blankets in the prow and stern of the ship. They gave one to Phaedra. It was stiff, and felt as though it had been soaked in oil. Someone pushed past her to take over from the man at the helm.

'Sleep now, rise early,' said the knight. 'We'll be warmer anyway.'

Phaedra realized she was shivering. The light she had been watching had gone. The moon was high – nearly full, but not quite. A fringe of shadow blotted one edge of the disc. Her knight and four others lay down in a row in the stern. She wrapped herself in her blanket and lay down with them, a woman not quite seventeen among these strange warriors. There was no privacy, but she was glad of the warmth. She did not feel at all sleepy. She looked up at the curve of the big sail above her, and at the moon, and tried to imagine what tomorrow would be like, but found that she did not know. She had walked off the jetty into the end of her world.

The water noise was different when she put her head to the deck. It was both deeper and shriller, and much nearer than it had been. Just the thickness of a few boards beneath her ear was Derewater – deep, and cold, and lightless. The men breathed and muttered beside her, and she felt warmer. The moon watched them gliding on the surface of the lake.

Ask nothing, ask nothing, sang the wake of the boat.

Someone stepped past her head. They were changing the man at the helm again. Somewhere forward she heard the low notes of a wind instrument – some kind of pipe, she thought. It had a breathy sound, less pure than she was used to, and the melody was strange. The moon had moved. She must have dozed. The ship washed purposefully forward in the unchanging dark.

Ask nothing.

Ask nothing of the night.

V

The Priest on the Knoll

 am the March-count of Tarceny.'

They were crouching at the rail of the boat, watching the sun rise over. The wind was strong enough to make the boat heel and to bring the big wavelets slapping against its side. Phaedra, huddled within a borrowed cloak, shivered constantly. Her body ached after a fitful night on the boards. There was, of course, still no hope of privacy. But the big sail was tinged with sunlight against the darkness of the lake surface, and a long black-and-white pennant cracked at the masthead. The sun flared on the distant water and licked the nearer waves with gold. For the moment she would not have been anywhere else in the world.

The western shore was much nearer now, and the steep wooded ridges were clear in the weak light. Ahead of them a large, flat-topped, dark-sided hill dominated the shore. The prow of the boat pointed straight for it. All that land must be Tarceny still. Astern, the lake stretched away, headland after headland blending in blue-grey shapes with the water until the shore faded from view. The east was a bank of mists. Trant, and all the country and lakeside she knew, was lost behind her. And north, under the bellying sail, the lake ran on without end. There were no other craft to be seen on the water.

'Our discomfort is almost past. That hill above the shore is Talifer's Knoll. Just this side of it is my harbour at Aclete, where we shall be able to show you a little more hospitality . . .'

He was the march-count. These men-at-arms were his; these crewmen were in his service. All those people busy on the hills, lands, woods, rents, dependencies – a thousand calls on his time. He was the peak of a human web that spread over the western shore of Derewater.

And of Tarceny! The Doubting Moon!

'Do – do not worry for me,' she said. 'Indeed, it is beautiful this morning.'

'You are good. I am not much of a sailor, myself. Boats have advantages, of course. It is most unlikely that we could be followed. Which is well, because I doubt either of us wishes harm to Trant. And even I can see that the view from the deck is sometimes a rare one.'

Phaedra stole another glance at him. He was still real; still there. Until now she had known his face as something in a dream – handsome, whole, but never an object for study. She had never seen details like the lines at the corners of his eyes and mouth, or the black stubble on his cheek and chin.

His face was long, and in repose it was solemn. Just now there was the faintest smile about him as he watched the sunrise, lost for a moment in thoughts of his own. He wore his black hair short. Three days ago he would have been clean-shaven. His eyes were a soft brown, his brows strong and yet not heavy. He must have been between twenty-five and thirty years of age. He wore black. Perhaps it had been chosen for the night's adventure, or perhaps because it was the colour of his house. She thought it suited him.

And she wondered at herself, for he was there – there beside her, as real as the day when before he had been shadow! It was almost as if it were she who was shadow now: she who was smoke without substance, beside him. She could not think what to say. His hand lay on the bulwark a few inches from her own. She wondered if she could take it in hers.

Suddenly he looked down at her. 'Am I right? Will they follow, do you think?'

Startled back into the complications of land and family, she sighed. 'They do not know who we were or where we have gone,' she answered. 'But if he believed me kidnapped, Father would hunt to the ends of the earth, with every knight and man-at-arms he could call on.'

And if he knew she had gone willingly?

Together they watched the sunlight on the waters.

'You left your home to escape a marriage that you would have refused,' he said. 'One that others would not have let you refuse. Had you stayed, there would have been great and lasting grief. You have spared your father that. It will have cost him a little of his pride. It has cost you your home.'

Men were stirring about them on the deck, moving to man sheets or to ready the mooring ropes. They were craning forward, watching the little group of huts with a jetty that clustered at the lakeside under the lee of a slight promontory. Beyond it rose the hill that he had pointed out earlier.

'I suppose you are right,' she said. 'I could not think what would happen if I stayed. I only knew that I had to get myself away.'

The boat drove on into the shallow bay. The point blocked the view northwards up the lake. The crewmen let the sail out, easing the pressure of the wind on the canvas, and their speed dropped.

'Do we need to move?' asked Phaedra.

'Better not now,' he said. 'They've room.'

The helmsman brought the boat upwind of the jetty. The men at the mast-ropes were looking back at him. A nod brought the sail roaring to the deck. The boat drifted the last few yards of its journey in towards the shore. Men were walking down the jetty towards them. Someone in the bow of the boat leaped clumsily up to the planks with a rope in his hand and took a turn round an upright post. Others were climbing up to join him. The boat nuzzled at the sturdy woodwork. Derewater was behind them.

'Good,' he said. He judged his moment as the boat rose, and stepped lightly up to the jetty. He turned and offered Phaedra his hand. She took it – with a tingling in her chest because she had suddenly been given what she dared not touch on the boat. There was strength in his fingers, and warmth, despite the night on the lake. She waited for the swell to lift the deck, and climbed up off the boat into a new world.

A small crowd was there to greet them on the foreshore. There was a score of men-at-arms, and others wearing black-and-white livery. There were people from the huts,

92

children scampering, men standing in the boats in the harbour to watch them come in: ordinary people, just as might have greeted her at any jetty of Trant's shore villages. There were smiles, laughter and chatter, as though some feat of arms or sportsmanship had just been performed. Men came to shake the boat party by the hand and slap them on the back. Everywhere there was the badge of Tarceny: a white moon on a black field, marked with a black device.

They were looking at her – glance after curious glance was thrown her way from the hurry of talk. When she caught someone's eye they would bow or curtsy, grinning, perhaps from embarrassment. Those nearer her mumbled a few words as they did so. She looked around. He was still on the jetty, with a handful of men about him. He seemed to be giving orders. He did not look her way. She stood among the crowd on the beach, wondering – what now? What did he intend? For she had not thought about what would happen after their escape.

A woman approached her and curtsied. Her name was Elanor Massey, she said. My lady must wish for a rest after her difficult journey. She would be pleased if my lady would allow her to offer her hospitality. It would be poor, but upon her word it would be the best that Aclete could offer.

She was middle-aged, a little below Phaedra's height, and smiling. She was dressed like a merchant's wife, although her head was bare. Perhaps she had put on her finest for the occasion.

'Why, thank you,' said Phaedra. 'You are very kind . . .' She glanced back. He still stood among his men; but now he was looking in her direction, nodding, although he could not possibly have heard what had been said. Then he was talking to his followers again, fist thumping urgently into his palm to emphasize what he was saying. He had known that she would be greeted like this, Phaedra thought. Perhaps he had given orders that it should be so. She had no idea why. She did not know when or even whether they would meet again. She did not want to leave his side. Yet the woman Massey was waiting, and there seemed to be nothing for it but to do as she proposed.

'Thank you,' she said again. 'It would be most welcome.'

'A night on a small-boat full of men is no fun for any woman. I've done too many of them myself. If you will please follow me, my lady. It is only a little way.'

The sun was well up now. She could feel the warmth of it already. It would be a fair day, for January. Beyond the crowd the foreshore was empty. Aclete was tiny – no more than two large houses, one of wood and the other of stone, on either side of the harbour, and a scattering of dusty huts and paths between them. Through the huts she caught glimpses of a stockade on the inland side of the hamlet.

Phaedra realized she should say something.

'They look very fine from the shore, these boats,' she said. 'But they are only a few feet of hard wood when you are in them.'

'That's the truth. I was raised in Velis, on the big sea. We had proper ships there, with decks and cabins and all. But you'll see none of them up here.'

'Because of the falls at Watermane.'

'That's it, my lady. Of course, you've lived on the lake all your life. Which is more than I have.'

'You are an experienced sailor, Mistress Massey?' Phaedra had never heard of a woman following such a calling.

'Not any more, if I can help it. I'm the harbour master here. That's a joke, isn't it? It was my poor Ralph, until he passed on ten years ago. Then we found there was nowhere to hold the meetings, except in my front room, nor anyone to read or keep the books and all. There was no one else to sort out the quarrels but me. Ralph left me every third hull in the bay, so they had to listen. Three years ago my lord wrote me a letter to say I was harbour master. Maybe he thought it was funny. But things have gone on these past three years the same as they did the seven before, so I must have been that all the time. Here we are, my lady.'

They stood before the big, wood-built house on the north side of the harbour. There were two maids at the door – girls Phaedra's own age, smiling and curtsying with the urgency of inner excitement. She stepped into the coolness of the hallway, smelling the strange smells of an unknown house. There was a big room to her left through an open door, with a dining table and fireplace; a small room to her right with something that looked like a chart on a desk; stairs leading upwards . . .

'Take my lady up, please,' Mistress Massey was saying. 'For I swear she's a right to be tired and would want a rest . . .'

Wooden steps were thumping under her feet. It was a steep climb. One of the girls was leading her up, the other

95

following. There was a big room overlooking the harbour. It was all made ready for her. It would be Mistress Massey's own, of course. A girl was asking her if she would like a drink of lemon juice. The other was pointing out clothes laid ready for her when she rose from her rest, gifts – *gifts* – from Mistress Massey. How would they fit? Perhaps he had been able to tell them roughly what height she was. Perhaps he had thought far enough ahead, before setting out, to realize what a woman arriving in a strange place after a night on a boat might need. He seemed to think of everything.

'Thank you,' she said.

She woke from a dream of running and running, and voices calling her name.

The room was quiet. The sun no longer fell on the unshuttered windows. The air had the cool flavour of a fine January afternoon, still warm enough to sit outside and yet far more pleasant than the dreary heats of summer. She was lying on a large, rich bed. She was in a village port in the March of Tarceny. The bed belonged to a woman who was harbour master. One of Mistress Massey's girls, who must have been set to wait on her, was sleeping in a chair. All Derewater lay between herself and home.

She must have slept for hours. She had had no idea that she was so tired. The night's adventure seemed long ago. She could remember running by the lakeshore, and torches, and the crossbow that had hissed like a sound of hate. But her mind, still half-waking, confused these images with others from the dream out of which she had just woken. She had been running not along the lakeshore, but in a dark place among brown stones. There had been a voice calling her; calling more desperately, fading . . . It might have been her father.

She sat up.

The room was still. There was no sound from beyond the window. Where was everyone? Where was – Ulfin?

He had been talking with his knights on the jetty – talking urgently. Had he swept on, about his other business, leaving her in the care of Aclete, deeming his own work done?

Softly, so as not to wake the sleeping girl, she stepped to the window and craned out. The harbour was a deep blue, wrinkling with light wavelets. Across the water was the stone house, which must be his lodge. Black-and-white pennants hung and flapped gently from spear-poles planted at the door. A dozen men were visible, sitting, walking listlessly. There were horse-lines by the stockade. His escort was still here, then. So he must still be in Aclete, too.

She turned from the window, with her heart knocking against her ribs, and drew a long breath.

The pile of new clothes was lying where they had left it, before a big glass. She tiptoed over to it. The dress she chose was simple and white, which she knew would go well with the colour of her skin. It had a high neck and buttoned down the front. She chose a golden girdle, but passed over the ornaments.

Her fingers were trembling.

She could not have said why she was dressing like this, unaided, when she had but to stir the sleeping maid to be dressed as she had been every day of her life. There had been no reason why he should have disappeared from her waking world as suddenly as he had stepped into it. Yet her fear that he would do so had been real. She was shaken; and knowing that he had not gone was important too. She wanted to think about it. She wanted to think about . . . *Ulfin.*

She had known him for years, and yet to name him made a stranger of him. It made him into that lord of Tarceny of whose house no man could say a good thing. He had sent heralds for her hand as if he had been any other noble in the Kingdom, and his men had been shown the gates within the hour. He had never mentioned it to her.

And after all these years, thought Phaedra, trying to steady herself, what did she know? His face was handsome, his hands long, his thoughts quick. He was the march-count. She knew his father had been a brigand and a pillager, who had chased the monks from his land and harried his own people outside his walls; but he had died by his own fire, she had heard, some years ago. She knew of no other family. What sort of a lord was Ulfin, then, to Tarceny, this place of terrible name where people smiled and curtsied and pressed their hospitality?

All the everyday things about him were strange or unknown. Only the memory of his voice recalled the familiar, shadowed dreams where they had walked together since she was a child. Her heart had leaped on seeing him, and had leaped again when her hand had touched him on the boat and assured her that he was there. And now he had not left her. He was waiting across the bay. She was here, close to him, and surely would see him again very soon. He knew her better than any man in the world.

It seemed impossible – a thing against all the laws of nature that she had learned or come to expect. In her mind it was like the moment when an eddy draws a leaf on the surface of some river pool upstream against the current. The eddy must break, the leaf must sink, and all be washed away; and yet, for a moment at least, some magical force sustains them where they cannot be. Like a leaf herself, she drifted without knowing it around the room. Her hands were locked together and her throat tickled with the memory of dark water. She was trying to imagine what he thought of her, but could not. The eddy drew her to the table before the glass. There was a hairbrush.

She picked it up and began brushing her long, black hair, turning her head to watch herself in the mirror. She rehearsed conversations with herself, mouthing her words softly. All the time she kept the brush moving as steadily as she could, seeking calm in the steady stroke, stroke, stroke, as she thought of the face and hands of Ulfin.

A sound behind her made her turn. The maid had stirred in her chair. She was barely awake, but she was staring at Phaedra with her mouth open.

'Why can't I look like you?' she said.

Suddenly Phaedra felt a power rising in herself, and she laughed. 'Umbriel writes what has been given, and why, and what else was given with it,' she said. 'But how do we read a book in which all things are written?' It was from one of Brother David's sermons. Just then, she felt sure he would have blessed her, if he had been with them. 'Let us go down now, if you are woken.'

* * *

'Who was that fellow who jumped out of the wood last night?' he asked.

They were sitting together at a table beneath a fruit tree outside the stone-built lodge. It was evening. The sun was low above the mountaintops to the west of them. Across the harbour Mistress Massey's house and the slope of the knoll beyond were all in shadow. The air was cool and moist.

He had sent to ask if she would take refreshment with him. When she had come, upon Mistress Massey's arm, the tables had been set beneath the trees with fruit and wine upon them, one small one for herself and Ulfin, and one long one at a little distance for a half-dozen of Ulfin's men and a crowd of folk from the town. The gathering was much what she would have expected at home – the same chatter, the same smiles; and yet it was not quite the same. Here and there among the faces were some who might have been part-blooded descendants of the hill folk. Earlier, a couple of musicians had played hill music on reed pipes and a drum. These things reminded her how near to the edge of the Kingdom she had come.

Phaedra was trying to guess why he had asked the question. It was not just curiosity, she thought. He would be testing the incident in his mind. Perhaps he was wondering if Phaedra had been followed to the fountain court, if she had known and, if so, what the significance of it was.

'He was Aun, Baron of Lackmere. A prisoner at Trant since the last rising.'

'Ah. I thought he seemed to know me. But it does not tell us what he was doing armed, and below Trant's walls.'

'He must have escaped. He had heard that his release

100

would not be granted soon. It made him angry. How he got out of the castle, I do not know, for there were always two men at his door after dark. Nor have I any idea how he came to be armed.'

'It was a short-sword. Not a knight's weapon. But his behaviour was strange for a prisoner, I think. First, he pauses in his escape to attack us. Next, although a fugitive, he shouts to raise the castle.'

'He was an impulsive man . . .' She felt Ulfin watching her, and hesitated. His questions had filled her mind with sudden doubts. For a moment she saw the world as he must see it, and found it complex, dangerous . . .

Could Aun secretly have been under orders to guard her? But that was madness. His imprisonment had been real. She knew that, even if Ulfin could not.

'Perhaps,' said Ulfin at last. 'He attacked a large body of men on his own. He was lucky to get away with it.'

'I'm glad you did not kill him.'

'In a way, so am I. But my thought is this. He knew me. Therefore, if he surrenders to Trant, or is recaptured, Trant and the crown will know where you are and whom to thank for your escape. That makes our position precarious, after all.'

'I see.'

She was not wholly certain what he meant. But her mind's eye showed her lines of soldiers, armour glittering in the sun, coming to force her home, and smoke drifting along the shore.

She looked around her, and felt her heart sinking. Talk rippled along the other table, unblemished by the fear of retribution. She heard Elanor Massey's laugh. People were smiling, looking her way, smiling again. The piper had begun to play, in long, low notes that hummed beneath the conversations like deep water.

'Why did we dream of one another?' she asked.

Ulfin was silent, looking out across the bay. When he spoke his voice was so low that she could barely make out his words.

'What do you remember of those dreams?'

When she could not answer, he spoke again. 'What was I carrying?'

'A cup.'

'It is a gift the Cup brings.'

'A gift?'

It seemed he was not going to say more.

'Was it not witchcraft?' she asked.

He sighed. She thought he was disappointed, as if she had failed some test of trust.

'I prefer to say *under-craft*, which is simply a March term for knowledge, or cunning,' he said softly. '"The Under-Craft Prevaileth" is a motto of my house. What it means is that you must use what you know, and if you know more than your enemy you will win. Phaedra, when Wulfram led his warriors over the sea to this land, the people who lived here at that time did not know how to work iron. When they found that we had weapons they could not break and armour they could not pierce, they were dismayed. They called our iron-working witchcraft because they did not understand it. And so we took the Kingdom.'

'It is not the same thing.'

'Not knowing, and fearing what you do not know, are

the same everywhere, I think. Knights and priests would call the Cup witchcraft, because with it I could defeat them, and they would not understand how. But there is no more evil in this than there was in Wulfram's iron. Less, I say, because I have not driven a people from their lands, destroyed villages, and left the survivors and their descendants to live in misery and barren poverty in the hills. The hillmen's grief with us is very great, Phaedra. What lies in the Cup is the tears of Beyah, who the hillmen say is Mother of the World. That is what you and I have tasted together. Now you share a knowledge I have shown none other since my brothers died. We have spoken enough of this. There is something else I want to say.

'Even when you were still a child, Phaedra, you were always clear to me. You are a rare thing. I do not just mean your looks or your birth, but in your spirit. You would not submit, though all the Kingdom leaned against you. If only for that, I am glad to have helped you as it was in my gift to do.

'You are now in the March of Tarceny. Here it is my law that no parent or guardian may order or prevent the marriage of one who is beyond sixteen years of age. You are free to remain as long as you wish as my guest, or, if you will, to go through all my lands. I shall be pleased to furnish you with any aid that you may ask.'

'You are – very kind.'

'That is freely given. But I have something else, and I hope you will hear me.

'My house is ill-reputed. Believe me when I say that is no fault of mine. It lies at my father's door, and should be forgotten. Still men are slow to understand us. We have little doing with Tuscolo, for we are stern, where they are gay; silent, where they gossip; true, where they are false. Yet my line is ancient and, except in latter days, it has been honourable. There is the true blood of Wulfram in my veins. Nor am I the least of my rank in the Kingdom.'

He was asking her to marry him!

'Most of all I am myself. I would not boast of my abilities, but I have made many studies and seen many places. On my honour I have neither broken a promise nor told a lie in all my living days. All that I am, and have, I would give to you, Phaedra. If you would but give yourself to me.'

A proposal of marriage should take months; there needed to be long negotiations over lands and dowries. And she was resisting all offers of marriage. All of them. Even . . .

Somewhere the voice of her dream was crying to her, but it was as if she was under water, and the sound could not carry. She looked into his face with her heart labouring beneath her ribs. He went on.

'Phaedra, the holiest man I know is within a mile of this place. I spoke with him while you slept. He is no vassal of mine, nor does he dwell on my lands or in any one other place in the Kingdom. But he has the right, and is willing, to wed us – if only you wish it.'

Over her head, the fronds of the fruit tree wavered in a light breeze. Already the branches were in bud. The sun dipped to touch the crests of the mountain, and the first full moon of the new year was heaving itself into view over Derewater. The world was turning about her, still slowly, but with the sudden firmness of the eddy that sucks the leaf to the centre of its whirl.

'Is he near?' she muttered.

'On the crest of this knoll you see. He will wait.'

At once she reached to grip his hand where it lay, palm down, on the table between them.

'Then let us go to him.'

'Are you sure?'

A last chance. If she passed this point . . .

'Say what you are thinking.'

Suddenly the words were running from her mouth like water.

'I remember – when all those knights' and barons' sons started to come to Trant for me – I knew that I had to marry one of them, and yet I knew it was impossible. I remember thinking that you should as well marry a clod of earth to a stream. I knew that because you were there before them. You were there all the time, and they were nothing like you. And now you have changed. I can see you, touch you, speak your name. Ulfin. And I have also changed. All the things that shaped my life have been washed away. Father, Trant, Fear – you have always told me not to be afraid. The only thing that has not changed is that I know you have been at the core of me all the time . . .' She looked at him, her eyes to his brown eyes and through them to his heart.

'Now, Ulfin. Let us do this. If we delay – they may come to take me from you.'

'Phaedra, I will often be away . . .'

'A day, two days in a year with you, better than none or better still than a whole year with any other man in the Kingdom. Ulfin, you've been – I don't think I can say all you've been to me.'

He got slowly to his feet, and stood over her. 'Then come here.'

She rose into his embrace. Then the world was blotted by his arms about her, his lips upon her face, and the thud, thud, thud of her own heart within her chest.

The tables were silent. She felt a host of eyes upon her as they stood, and she did not care. Above her Ulfin shouted, 'Hob!'

'My lord!'

'Send runners through the town. There will be a wedding this very evening, upon Talifer's Knoll – for those who are swift enough to catch us. There will be a feast at my door tonight. Send for food. Empty my cellar. Empty every keg and vat in the town, no matter how poor or good. And pay with gold! Send for torches. You there! Play a tune, and lead us on our way.'

There was a moment of stillness, and then the sudden clatter of people rising from the tables. Someone whooped. The player recovered, cried, 'Ho-ho-ho-ho!' and struck up a fast beat on his queer-shaped little lute. The man Hob bustled past, swearing to himself. Ulfin led Phaedra down to the track that ran from the harbour through the huts to the gate of the stockade. Others followed. The player was ahead. As they passed through the gates Phaedra could hear fists hammering on doors behind them in the town.

The road was rutted, and rough under foot. It looped to the west and north, around the base of the low hill. A hundred yards from the stockade a narrow goat-track curved steeply upwards, and then doubled back on itself, zigzagging up the south side of the knoll. They outstripped the player, who stopped on the slope to sing the others upwards. Behind them a score of followers straggled. Further back still, others were hurrying from the gates. From here they could look down into Aclete and see the people running between the huts.

She had not let go of Ulfin's hand. He paused beside her. They were both breathing heavily with the climb.

'It is a good place for this,' he said. 'You will see when we get to the top. Here the first prince of Tarceny waited for the lady of Velis, as she sailed up the lake to be his bride.'

'Look at the moon!'

'Yes. It is a good omen.'

He turned to the climb again, and she turned with him, thinking, Is this real? I am going to marry him! There's no one here from my house, no one to support me, no one but myself. I am going to marry him myself. All the lines of her past life seemed to rush together into this moment. There would be no stifled ceremonies, no buying and selling of rights or lands and the families that lived on them. Here, there would be nothing but the sky and an ancient place; and the two of them, running ahead, outstripping their followers in the joy of what they were doing.

The slope was easing. Aclete was hidden by the curve of the hillside, but all Derewater was in view, stretching into the north. The sun was down behind the mountains, which fumed with mist. The afterglow lit the sky, and across the water the moon was rising from its huge, yellow shape into the pureness of silver. The land about them was darkening. The rugged outlines of the hills

107

were dropping into shadow. The road below was a pale scar tracing north and west until it faded from view. From the very crest of the knoll Phaedra could see the beginnings of a wood that seemed to cover the northern slope. There was a lone, robed figure walking towards them from beneath its shade.

Ulfin turned, and spread his hands palm outwards, motioning those that followed to stop. Then he took Phaedra by the hand, and they went forward together. The priest approached them. He wore a long, belted robe, like a monk's, which was the colour of evening. His hood was up. Close to, Phaedra could see a thin and pale face within it. He seemed to be an old man, and yet he moved without difficulty.

'Who are you?' His voice was dry.

'Ulfin Ector, March-count of Tarceny.'

'Why have you come?'

'To be wed to this woman.'

The priest looked at Phaedra. Eyes gleamed within his hood. The outlines of his face were spare of flesh. His mouth was a little black hole that moved.

'Who are you?'

'Phaedra, of Trant. I would be wed to this man, sir.'

She realized that she should have said, *Phaedra, daughter of Ambrose, Warden of Trant*. But Ulfin had not used his father's name either.

'Your hands.'

Her hand was inside Ulfin's. They held them out together. The priest reached forward and laid his own hand on Ulfin's.

'Say the truth to one another. Let your lives be as a

mirror to one another. Keep the promises you have spoken. You are man and wife.'

Ulfin bowed. Phaedra took her cue and curtsied. When they rose the priest was already walking away from them, back towards the trees.

'That was short!' Phaedra gasped.

'We have been very honoured, Phaedra. To my knowledge, he has done this for no other in all his time.'

There was a note of awe in Ulfin's voice. The priest disappeared among the first trunks. From the sounds Phaedra thought that others, unseen, must have been waiting for him there.

'Does he live here?'

'Not he. He goes where he will.' He turned to her, and took her hands. For a moment they were both wordless. Phaedra found herself dropping her eyes.

'Now,' Ulfin said. 'We have guests to attend to.'

They turned and walked back towards the crowd, a couple of score of men-at-arms and townsfolk, that had spread in a wide quarter-circle at a distance from the marriage. Phaedra was thinking that the priest had told them to keep their promises, but they had made none. She wondered if that could be held against them, and whether Septimus could claim her back after all, if he knew. Perhaps she should find an ordinary priest, who could be trusted, and see if she could persuade Ulfin to let him say the words of the full marriage to them, to be sure.

Cheers and clapping spread as the watchers realized that the ceremony was already over. A torch flared brightly in the evening under the moon.

*   *   *

'What is that?'

The music had changed. The pipes were joining in a melody that rose over the clutter of noise below their window. It was a hill song, unlike any music of the Kingdom: a slow, measured sound, tinged with tears. Ulfin rose on one elbow from the pillow beside her and listened. The mingled moon- and torchlight fell on his right cheek and eye. The rest of his face was in shadow. But he seemed to smile, as if at some secret memory.

'That is the Great Lament. The World mourning for her child.'

She curled against him for comfort from the thoughts that rose in her mind.

His hand moved in the darkness. It touched her skin. Again she knew the extraordinary feeling of his fingers upon her, soothing now, and caressing until her body eased and she gasped softly in the sheets. She lay and looked up at him. His face was masked and beautiful as the half-moon on a brilliant night, and he was smiling again.

Outside, the lights burned on above the tables at Ulfin's door. The people talked and drank and laughed; the pipers played their breathy notes on and on as they had done for hours after their lord and his new countess had retired.

Here, in the closeness of his embrace, Phaedra had found pain, and indescribable sweetness. But most wonderful of all was this drift, drift drift on the edge of sleep in the arms of the man she loved.

VI

The Warden's Answer

merging from the high coolness of the hall, leaning on his arm, she heard the water playing a second before she understood where she was.

'Oh!' she said. 'It's like home. And like Tuscolo!'

She had been expecting the dusty inner courtyard where they had dismounted on their arrival. Instead she stood in a small paved court with two low fruit trees and a fountain. On all four sides were whitewashed colonnades, roofed with tiles, which gave shade from the sun. The air smelled sweet from the grey-green bushes – mint and rosemary – that stood in huge clay jars at the bases of the pillars.

'I thought you would like it,' said Ulfin. 'And it is in better repair than the one where we met in Trant, which must have been abandoned long ago. Can you name the seven houses of the Kingdom?'

'Tuscolo and Velis, Baldwin and Bay, Trant, Ferroux and Tarceny.'

'Exactly. Seven houses for seven princes, and you will find a court like this – or the remains of one – in each.

For that is the way we built when we first came over the sea.'

'Were there really seven princes? Are you descended from one?'

'No and yes. *The Tale of Kings* has been written and remembered many times, and in different ways. In each telling Wulfram rides up out of the sea in three ships, fleeing some war or disaster across the water that we do not recall. Straight away, he divides the land among his seven sons. Yet the seven are not always given the same names in the different tellings I have heard or read. I have counted eight names altogether. So I believe there were not seven princes, but eight. And some of them cannot have been born until well after Wulfram led our people over the sea. From his landing to the time my ancestor Talifer rode from Jent to conquer the March must have been twenty or thirty years.'

'Where is Ferroux? You do not hear of it now.'

'It is an unimportant manor house in Develin's country. There are those who claim descent from the line, of course, but the claim is false. The other houses also fell, one by one. The first house of Baldwin stands ruined since the end of the High Kings – although Faul and Seguin and all the royal house claim descent. And the traitorous stewards raised their tower on a nearby hill and call themselves Baldwin to this day. Trant is now in wardenship, as you know. Bay has a better story, but—'

'I liked Baldwin.'

'Not too much, I hope.'

'Don't be jealous. I did not marry him, did I?'

He laughed. He seemed surprised that anyone should speak to him that way.

'So you read histories, my lord?'

'There are some histories in the castle. And other works. Yes, I read. My intent is to understand how the Kingdom has come to the state it is in. Why is it that we, who are more numerous and better armed than all the wretched tribes around us, have warred for so long among ourselves and never sought to open up the lands that must exist beyond our borders? I wish the hillmen no ill. Yet it is a marvel to me that the strength of our people is turned so ruinously against ourselves. Surely our kings should rule us better.'

'I should like to see your books.'

'Everything I have is yours.'

Which was true, or seemed to be. A few hours ago she had been shown to a room and found a wealth of objects waiting for her – books, combs, mirrors, clothes, ornaments . . . A maid had been there – an elderly woman called Orani, who had a narrow face and that bird-like look that Phaedra was beginning to associate with the hill people. And already messages had been issued, to a dressmaker in Baer, the largest town in the March, and a jeweller in Watermane, to present themselves at the castle on the earliest date possible.

Best of all was the beautiful, beautiful writing desk, of wood so dark that it was almost black, with thin legs carved in the shapes of sinuous, scaled creatures. Running her fingers over its surface had made her want to fall in love with him all over again.

'You have been very kind. And I must ask for yet more.'

'Of course. What is it?'

'Pen, parchment and wax. I must write to my father

113

and bring him to accept what we have done. Also I have no signet ring as your wife.'

'Pen, parchment and wax you shall have at once. And I should write to your father too, for I have done him an injury and it must not become an insult. A signet ring will be more difficult. You could use mine—'

'For other letters, yes, but this . . .'

'Of course. And it will take any jeweller a week to prepare one . . . Wait.' He seemed to hesitate for a second, and then drew something from an inner pouch.

'There is this. It belonged to my younger brother. I had been wondering whether to give it to you, but – I think he would have liked you to have it.'

It was a signet ring, too large for her finger. On the boss was a single letter 'P' upon the moon of Tarceny. On either side of it letters – a 'c' and a 'u' – were carved into the outer surface of the ring. The ring itself was silver, shaped like the body of a tiny dragon that wove round and round on itself like rope, so that the boss of the ring was borne by its head, and its eyes peered out beneath the letter of her name.

'The dragon for eternity,' she murmured.

'Among our kind, of course that is true. But for the hill people his name is Capuu, the worm that lies along the rim of the world and binds it together; and he means faithfulness. You see him in jewellery and totems and even' – his finger touched the stonework – 'carved upon the rim of this fountain. There were three of us, my brothers and I, and each with a ring like this bearing the letters of each other's names alongside our own. Now they are fled, and dead, and I am the master of the house.'

She said, 'It is perfect, Ulfin. I will take care of it, I promise. What was his name?'

'Paigan.'

'A strange name.'

'An ancient one. And it should have lived on in him, but did not.'

'You must have loved him very much.'

He nodded. She waited, but he was looking firmly into the bowl of the fountain, and did not speak. So she stood in silence beside him, and looked at the steep roofs and towers of Tarceny around her.

The place was still bewildering. It seemed far larger than Trant, although not, of course, the size of the King's castle at Tuscolo. Its towers were taller, and thinner, and had looked almost graceful when her eye had first met them. She had ridden out of the forest and found herself on the lip of a broad, level valley in the hills, with the castle rearing from its steep and lonely spur opposite. The floor of the valley was covered in olive groves and had looked, from above, much like a huge garden. The afternoon light had played on the walls, and on the masses and masses of white flowers that grew in the tangled briars of the castle spur. As the cavalcade had poured down towards the trees the hills had rung with horn music.

Her hand traced the curves of the vast and sinewy beast that was carved around the rim of the fountain. She reached out to the jet of water that arched in uneven spurts from the centre. It was cool, but not cold. The droplets danced from her skin in the last of the sun. Somewhere, unseen, an ass or donkey must be turning the pump that made the water play, and a man must watch

115

her do it. Perhaps they were in the base of the little turret on the corner of the court, which jutted into the inner bailey. Surely they would not have been there all day. Ulfin would have commanded them there from other duties on his arrival, to add this little stroke of beauty to her welcome.

She turned, and with the base of her spine to the bowl, leaned back to look up at the sky. It was pure blue on this mid-January day, framed by the towers and battlements of Tarceny. Beside her, Ulfin stirred from his memories. She could feel his leg pressed against hers through the thickness of cloth. His hands were on her shoulders. Her skin rushed with blood, and he bent to kiss her neck as she had hoped he would.

Right revered and worshipful father [wrote Phaedra]. I commend myself humbly to you and desire earnestly to hear of your good spirit and well-being, as swiftly as your message may reach me. From the letter of my lord that accompanies this, and from the mouth of our messenger, you will learn that I have taken the hand and name of the lord of Tarceny. I write to tell you that I have done this of my own choosing and with great joy, for I never met a man more noble, wise, nor kind to me, save only, sir, your honoured self. Lest you think me of inconstant mind I tell you that this love has come upon me in no sudden wise, but has grown over time to a greatness that truly I cannot describe to you. Never did I feel more blessed than now, and it wants to me only your own blessing as father on this marriage to let me be the happiest woman that ever lived. This I pray earnestly that you send me as swiftly as you may give it. Right worshipful sir, you have cared for me and endured much for me. If I have ever caused you grief, lately or in my whole life, then I grieve in equal measure. I pray now that you will rejoice with me, for in this marriage you are rewarded with a great ally, who will be as strong and true to you as ever chance may need, and this because the love that my lord and I bear for one another shall mean that he will love you as I do, with all heart and duty that my self can afford.

Written this thirteenth day of January at Tarceny and signed with my hand.

She wrote it carefully, with many crossings out and insertions, and she was still not satisfied with it. It should have been longer, and yet she could not think of anything more to say that would not repeat what she had written already. She had great difficulty trying to explain when she had fallen in love. She did not want Father to think that in the end she had married on a whim. But she could not possibly tell him how, or for how long, she had known Ulfin before she had left Trant.

She had also wanted to copy the whole letter out neatly herself, so that all the page would be in her hand. But she took so long over drafting it that there was no time. Ulfin was waiting for her at the stables, to show her the new horse that he had acquired for her. So she gave the draft to one of Ulfin's clerks to copy onto a blank page that she had signed. Father, who could not write well, would in any case rely upon Joliper or someone to write his reply for him. And now that she had clerks in the house, she might as well use them like the great lady that she had become. The same thought led her to amend her opening greeting to a more neutral 'Right worshipful sir', and to delete the word 'humbly' from the first sentence. Then she hurried down to the stables.

Later, she regretted making those changes. And she thought, too, that she should have offered Father more apology than 'If I have ever caused you grief, lately or in my whole life'. (If!) But by then the letter had gone.

The towers looked out across wave upon wave of steep and wooded slopes, ridges sharp-backed and ragged with outcrops of rock, fading into the mists of the great mountains beyond. In the deep clefts streams rushed unseen, and roads the width of rabbit-tracks wound among the valleys, climbing and falling steeply. The villages were small, and far apart. In the day and a half of slow riding from Aclete they had passed no castles or manors. The first midday rest had been at a group of four huts by the roadside; the second, at a fork in the road.

It was an empty place, after the close, busy world of Trant: empty without and within. There was no priest – a thing which should have been shocking and which Phaedra knew she must change before Father and the others of her world learned about it. Apart from that, Ulfin's household was larger than the Warden's, but it was quieter and more ordered. The big rooms imposed something of their stillness upon the humans that moved between them. The hall rose three storeys to its high rafters, with the door to the upper bailey halfway down its length and a hearth spaced evenly either side of it. White steps ran up to the black-stained wood of the gallery, beyond which lay their sleeping quarters, and the floor alternated squares of black with white marble paving in a pattern that was almost regular – but not quite.

'Someone has been careless, sir,' she said one afternoon. 'For here there are three – no, five – black flagstones adjoining one another all higgledy-piggledy at this hearth. I am surprised you permit this disarrangement.'

He did not seem to be in a mood to be teased.

'The black stone comes from quarries beyond Baer. But the white is from Velis. At the time the stones were damaged, rebellion was beginning in the Seabord. Nothing passed south from the coast. We did what we could, and I have grown used to it.'

Phaedra had not seen a room designed around a single combination of colours before – not even at Tuscolo.

'Black and white are far more than the colours of my house,' said Ulfin. 'They are the colours of truth. They are clear, precise, and without decoration.'

'Like a chessboard?' (Aun had always referred to his board and pieces as 'black' and 'white', for all that they had been different shades of brown, and irregular at that.)

'You are still trying to tease me. But yes. Do you play chess?'

'I have begun to learn in the past year. My favourite piece is the queen. What is yours?'

'You should not have a favourite piece. You should use them all, as the game requires. When the time comes you must sacrifice them without mercy. Except the King, which you must guard with your life.'

So they began to play chess in the evenings. They played on a large, beautifully made board with pieces the colour of coal and pale ivory. Ulfin was skilful – far better, she judged, than Aun had been. He thought many turns in advance. His game was more subtle too. He loved to move a piece to a position of advantage, to let her worry about it until her hand was hovering over a knight or pawn for the counter-move. Then his head would shake just slightly, and she would look at the board again and see for the first time the bishop or castle his move had unmasked, its baleful threat lancing across to the heart of her defence.

She fought. She harnessed her own growing awareness of the game, of its complexities and tempo. She forced him into sudden exchanges in order to remove some piece that she thought his plans rested on. And so they played, sometimes game after game, in the early spring evenings in the hall at Tarceny, where the air moved through the long, slit windows and there was no sound but the clack of the pieces and the faint stirring of the hangings, rich with history, above them. And when her defences were swept away, and her king fell for the last time, she would grimace ruefully and take his outstretched hand, and together they would climb the marble stairs to the velvet dark of the sleeping quarters, where the moon gleamed on silk sheets and their hearts pounded within their cases of skin.

So Phaedra's idyll endured into the early days of February, when the first rain for weeks was spitting lightly into the dust, and the answer from Trant arrived to shatter the dream.

. . . Reckless, wilful and unnatural . . . Your father bids me write that he should give you the Angels' curse and his too, for you have shamed this house before the King and all the Kingdom . . . all the blood that he and his knights have spent

is set at naught . . . that he has sworn he shall bring you home,
and trussed if need be . . .

The War Room of Tarceny was lit with torches, and by the windows that looked out on the afterglow of sunset under a mass of cloud. The walls were whitewashed, the furniture was dark polished wood, which gleamed fitfully in the torchlight: a big table with benches on each side of it, and a huge chair, like a throne, carved with fighting scenes at its head. The only ornament on the walls was a portrait of a young man, with the long face of Ulfin's family and a sad look in his eyes.

Phaedra looked round at a dozen men, some unknown, others half-known, but to whom she could still not put a name. Hob, Ulfin's butler and close aide, was there. He occupied a low position at the table. The rest would be knights, each with several farms and manors and a dozen or more armoured men in the saddle. Some wore mail. In Tarceny men went geared for war even on their own lands, it seemed, and for the trodden road to their lord's gate. Most were older than Ulfin by a number of years. And these were none of the homely, if valiant, faces of Trant. They were the men who had followed the old count, hard and silent. They had done what he bid them do.

Now they waited for his son to speak.

'You know,' said Ulfin to them, 'that I have written to my lady's father, offering friendship, waiving dowry, and asking nothing but that he should be pleased to call me son. I have received no answer. My lady has also written, and has received some kind of answer, but little that gives us hope or encouragement. It is chiefly for that reason that

121

I have asked her to sit with us while we discuss these things.

'There is also the news that Abernay has brought me, which I shall ask him to tell us shortly. Lastly I have some news myself, which we should all consider and then decide what is best to do.

'First I shall say again, lest there be any doubt, that my lady consented to marry me of her own will, on March ground and under March law. There is no doubt of this case.'

His right hand, as he spoke, rested on Phaedra's arm. His left lay on a wooden chest, carved with intricate snakes and figures, which stood upon the table like a totem of authority. His language was formal, like a priest's. Phaedra could see the men round the table guessing what they were about to hear.

'My lady,' said Ulfin, turning in his chair.

'Sir,' said Phaedra, and her voice was a whisper. She tried to clear her throat, and spoke again. 'Sir, my father caused it to be written that he does not own us married, nor would he answer your letter in words.'

Someone grunted. It might have been a laugh, but the sound was too brief for Phaedra to tell if it were rueful or scornful.

'I do not think we need doubt his meaning,' said Ulfin.

'He cannot hope to win,' said Orcrim, the white-haired knight who was Ulfin's war master. 'We are five or more to his one.'

'If that were all, I would agree,' said Ulfin. 'However, let us think that, raging though he was, he seems to have delayed eight or ten days before replying to us. That is time to send other messages, and receive answers. We know the Warden is the King's man. And it seems to me not impossible that a certain royal prince may hold himself offended in this.'

There were one or two smiles around the table. Septimus did not command the respect of the March-knights, it seemed.

'Abernay, where is the King now, and who is with him?'

A knight – one of those in mail – leaned forward. He had a narrow face, with a pointed chin and black hair cut in a circular crop.

'I spoke with a merchant who had been sent across from Bay to make certain purchases for the King's coming. The King set out from Tuscolo on the last day of Christmas. He is now at Baldwin, but will be at Bay by the end of the month. Both princes are with him, as is the Lord Develin and others. They would be at Trant for a fortnight in mid-March, and would arrive at Jent for Easter.'

'That was his plan,' said Ulfin. 'Now I think it will have changed at least about where he spends Easter. My piece is this. That an order over the royal seal has gone down all the eastern shores of Derewater, for every ship and boat that may be commanded to be at Trant by the fifteenth day of March.'

There was silence in the room again. Phaedra could hear the flutter of the torches on the wall. At the end of the table, Hob was looking thoughtful. His eyes rested on the little chest beneath Ulfin's hand. Beyond the windows it was almost full night. Rain spat lightly on the sills.

She shuddered with sudden cold.

. . . that you have communed in secret with enemies of his house . . . that until he received your letter he knew not if you were alive or dead . . . daughter of a loved mother, who is dead, sister of loved brothers, who are dead, and should yourself be dead to him from this day on . . .

In the sleepless hours of misery and rage she had told herself that she could hardly be dead to him if he were about to set out across the lake to bring her back by force. He never meant the things he said in anger. If she were in Trant she could have faced him, and won. She could have told him that Tarceny was only an enemy if he chose to make it one. She might have made him see that this was the only way for her, and so have been forgiven. It was because she was here that she could do nothing.

But there was little comfort in such thinking. The truth was that she had fled because she was powerless, and that she had hardly asked herself what he would think or say. It had been a long time since Father had raged to her face. A part of her had forgotten what it was like. Written in reported speech, by a man trying hopelessly to soften what his lord had hurled at him to say, the words had hurt her in a way for which she had simply not been prepared.

And there had been Joliper's frantic, undictated post-script:

. . . Written this twenty-sixth day of January at Trant. Right worshipful and dear lady, I tell you he is grievous set with this, for he furies and weeps as I have not seen before. We must arm and practise every day and those who would not are beat until

124

they do. In very truth I wish you good fortune, lady, but there will be a river of blood before this is done.

They would take her from Ulfin!

His right hand still rested on her arm. She brought her own right hand across to grip it, hard. As if prompted by her touch he spoke again.

'You will know, friends, that since my father died we have given the King no cause to hate us. Yet I judge that he will think he has no cause to love us either, since we have not danced to the tune at his court, or made all his quarrels our own. At all events, I have no wish to wait until the King and my lords Baldwin, Bay and Develin are ready to meet me. If I do, I do not doubt that we should be hard put to it and that the terms of any parley would be harsh indeed. So – the key to their preparation is Trant. There they will gather their boats. There they will summon such of their knights as are not already with them. There the King will come, on the fifteenth day of March . . .'

The King, who was the Fount of the Law. He too was against her.

'. . . if we do not forestall him. So I mean to take Trant. With a royal castle in our hands, I guess we shall hear better terms.'

It was as if she was looking through a window into the room, seeing it from outside as he spoke. Her mind was in some other place, as his words fell calmly, naturally, into the talk of a world gone mad. She saw some of the knights nodding, as though defying the King to war was something that they had not thought of doing until now, but did not doubt that they could.

125

Others were frowning. Take Trant? Just like that?

'It must be the right stroke,' said Orcrim, from his seat at Ulfin's left. 'Better still if we wait until most of the boats are gathered there, so that we may seize them for our own use. Yet it must be done before the King arrives.'

'Indeed,' said Ulfin. 'I would not be known in the Kingdom as one who attacked his lord before any challenge was issued.'

'Ulfin!'

It was her own voice. She recovered herself.

'My lord. If you love me – no one at Trant is to be killed for my sake.'

'I know why you ask this,' said Ulfin. 'Although it is asking much. In war nothing can be certain. But,' he went on, looking around. 'But I too would not willingly shed any blood of the house of the man I would call Father. Therefore we must plan to come on them in such a way that no one in the house has a chance to draw sword.'

Now they were shocked.

'It's impossible!' someone protested.

'We'd have to have someone inside!'

'Not impossible,' said Ulfin. 'Difficult, yes. Difficult. But who tells me that what I would do is impossible?'

There was another silence, thicker this time. No one answered him.

'Good, then.' And he turned to Phaedra.

'Is there any way that we can come within the walls of Trant unseen? A tunnel, perhaps?'

Afterwards, when she looked back on that moment, Phaedra remembered his face looking down at her in the torchlight, her own heart beating within her, and the desperate need to help him persuade that room of war-scarred men of what must be done.

'There is no tunnel,' she said. 'Nor any stream or drain large enough for a man to crawl through.'

'How did you escape the castle, then?'

'By the postern door. It is in the lakeside wall, under the north-west tower. It opens into the ditch, and on the inside it leads into the courtyard. It is kept bolted from within. You will not force it without alerting the guard. But . . .' She hesitated.

'But?'

They were all looking at her. There was something in her that did not want to speak. She heard herself say: 'I was not the only one to escape the castle that night.'

'Lackmere?'

She nodded.

'He had chisels in his room, and a few blankets. When I saw him on the day before he was examining the north wall – how it bulged outwards at the base, how the masonry was cracked. I think he must have let himself out of his window, which was at the top of that tower, and worked his way down the wall, forcing his chisels between the stones for hand- and footholds.'

'Desperate.'

'He was in the mood to risk it. And there is no guard on the wall in peace. It may be a way for you.'

They did not like it.

'We'll have to get two-score men over the wall, in fighting gear!'

'Not two score,' said Ulfin. 'Only enough to reach the

127

postern from within. And it will be easier to climb than it was to descend.'

'That's true,' said someone. 'This Lackmere must have been mad.'

'Either he was mad, or we are. I never heard of a place like Trant being taken in such a way!'

'Enough,' said Ulfin. 'If a man can get out, a man can get in. One way or another, we must – and shall – reach that postern unseen. Now, my lady. The door is open. Where are the fighting men quartered?'

She leaned over the table, meeting no one's eye, and began to trace with her fingertips the outlines of her home on the dark wood. The air in the room around her was as thick as coming thunder.

An hour later, the gathering broke up. No one spoke. The knights filed from the room with set faces. Phaedra stood at Ulfin's hand, listening to the armoured heels crashing down the steps past the chapel door, where someone must have said something to rouse that bitter laugh from the others. The footsteps faded at last behind the futile *pit-pit-pit* from outside the window, of rain too thin to fill the tanks and cisterns or do any good but rouse the smell of dust from the land. Ulfin lounged in his chair, thinking. Slowly she curled up onto her stool and leaned across the armrest of the throne until her head was upon his shoulder. He put his arm round her.

'They are good fighters, but narrow,' he said. 'They only think in certain ways. Phaedra, I am sorry he has chosen this. It was not my intention. Yet with good luck we may yet laugh at it all from the other side.'

'They respect you,' she said.

Once he had spoken, they had not challenged him. They had not questioned the marriage rite, or the wisdom of plunging Tarceny into armed confrontation with the King. They had not even asked Ulfin where he had had his news about the King's order to the boats, or how reliable it was. Perhaps they thought they knew. Phaedra thought she could guess too.

Who tells me that what I would do is impossible?

'When were you planning to leave for Jent?'

She did not want to think of that.

'I wonder whether you should go at all,' he said. 'I cannot come with you now. There is too much to do.'

'There must be a priest in the castle, Ulfin. And this makes it the more urgent.'

'Why do you say that?'

His father had harried the priests and monks of the March until few were left but the craven who would oppose nothing he did. So Ulfin had never known what it was to live with the blessing of the Church. Perhaps that was why he did not seem to understand how he was seen in the Kingdom, for not having restored what his father had done. Yet he himself had shown her how the priests were actors in the play of justice.

What law could there be here, if his lands were unblessed? Nothing could be done in the March that could not be undone. Even a marriage rite – certainly such a hurried rite as they had had – might be declared void if bishop and King agreed that it should be so. They would take her away from him, and say that what the two of them had done was mere wickedness.

He would not be ready for that argument. Neither was

129

she. She thought that if they quarrelled now they would both be utterly alone.

'They will judge against us, in the Segne,' was all she said. 'Without even thinking—'

'There is so little time. If there is fighting, you cannot travel out of the March in safety. Jent will be busy too, full of pilgrims for Holy Week.'

'It must be a man we can trust, Ulfin; and that means we must choose him. Could – could we not send for the priest from the knoll? He would be—'

He had already said this was impossible. This time he did not even seem to hear.

'Perhaps it will help. They may try to pretend I carried you away by force, the easier to dissolve our marriage before wedding you to Septimus. It will be good, therefore, if you are seen to go beyond the March freely. And it may also conceal our intentions. However, you must not risk capture. Give them as little warning as you can that you are coming. And you must be back within the March by the twelfth day of next month. It will not be safe to stay longer.'

Still his arm was round her, and her head was against his chest. For a moment neither said anything more. She could hear and feel his heart, thudding against her ear.

That was her world, her whole world in there. She had thought, in the first days of her marriage, that she could not have been more in love. It had been astounding to her how her feelings, which had been growing deep within her through all the years that the two of them had met in their dreams, had come upon her so quickly and with such force. Through the Cup they had built a bond between them that she had thought was stronger than anything in the world. Now she knew that it was possible to love even more deeply. She loved him most of all when she thought that she might lose him.

Old soot, dislodged by the rain, hissed in the chimney. From the wall the picture of the young man regarded them with steady eyes. The border of the canvas was decorated with a great twisting snake, that reminded her of the dragon ring that now hung day and night upon a chain around her neck.

'Is that Paigan?'

'Yes.'

'How did he die, Ulfin?'

He stirred against her, and sighed. 'I am bound to tell you the truth, Phaedra. And so you may understand better why the priests do not love us, and why men take up arms when they hear the name of Tarceny.

'The truth is that my own father killed him, in this room. And that he did not lie long unavenged.'

VII

The Windows of Jent

n an opulent room of his palace, lit by high windows, the bishop sat like a worm at the heart of an apple. His walls were covered with pale-coloured drapes of soft pink and gold, but his gown was as plain as a novice's. On a small table at his hand were the remains of a meal of bread and water. He would have eaten before dawn, and would touch no more food before sundown. He could not have bathed for a week, nor did he wear oils or perfume. He smelled like a fieldsman from any peasant village.

These were the Lenten Days: the time before Easter when the Church demanded penitence. Even this bishop marked them in what he ate and wore; and devoted himself day after day to those who came to Jent at this time of year to beg his saint for forgiveness. And he was not pleased to be interrupted in his duties.

Red-faced and eyes popping, he leaned in his throne. 'I am told you were most pressing to speak with me.'

He gave her no title or greeting. There was no mistaking his anger.

From beyond the door at her back Phaedra could hear

132

the shuffle of the endless crowd of penitents, standing or sitting on the stairs and floorboards of the bishop's palace. The patient pilgrims had watched her force her way past them, using her rank to beat down the objections of the bishop's priests and door-keepers, as she had pushed and argued her way to His Grace's door. They might wait more than a day for their turn to enter his chamber and speak with him of what they had done. She felt as if something had rubbed off them onto her from their thousand pairs of eyes.

She opened her mouth to speak, conscious of the silks and jewellery that she had put on that morning without a second thought.

'Your Grace will have heard that since our last meeting I have taken the name of Tarceny,' she said.

'I had. I must tell you it is not one that I love. Did you wish me to bless your marriage, or to annul it for you?'

Annul it? No!

How could he say such a thing?

'If . . . If it please Your Grace to bless us,' she said carefully, 'we shall be thankful. I came because I find my house has no priest, and I wished to beg of you—'

'A priest? Indeed! It had been in my mind to ask what priest it was that had the gall to wed you.'

Surprised again, she did not answer. He must have seen by her look that she did not know the man's name.

'Of what church, what order?' he barked.

'He was a holy wanderer, known to my husband.'

'A mendicant!'

'Such was Tuchred Martyr, sir.'

'And such is every half-educated rogue who claims the

cloth to escape the noose if he is caught with another man's goods in his hands! And your father's blessing – you had that too, I suppose? Or did you send for it afterwards, to the man who raised you and guarded you all your little life, when you told him what you had done?'

Phaedra did not want to talk about Father. She was trying to remember whether the priest had worn a badge of one of the great orders – the Knotted Rope, the Lantern, the Staff . . . Surely he must have done, and yet she had not noticed. Her earrings jingled heavily as she shook her head, and her silks whispered to her. Damn them. And damn him too, in all his sackcloth and fuss!

The bishop raised his brows, waiting for her to answer, and she could not. She almost turned for the door then. But this was not Trant, and she was no longer a child.

'Your Grace – I came in good faith, and thinking you would be glad of my purpose. If you wish to speak of my marriage, I will listen. But—'

'*Listen* then. I do not love it that a child should wed without her father's let, or that a father should be so served after years of care. Nor do I love it that the royal house should be slighted. Nor do I love it that the Kingdom should be brought once again to the brink of war. I do not jest about marriage. Before long, some prince of the Church, and most likely myself, will be asked to judge on yours. When that time comes, it would be well for you to produce this mendicant, and for him to prove as you say. What you are able to tell of him now does not reassure.'

Silence seeped back into the room after his words. With it, once again, came the soft shuffles of the pilgrims beyond the door. The nearest of them must have heard everything he had said.

'Your Grace . . . I ask that you help me find a priest for my people at Tarceny, who have had none these twelve years.'

'Your people. And is it for your *people* that you ask this?'

She could only meet his look. 'Every soul in my house needs blessing, sir. I was not taught otherwise.'

He was trying to stare her down. She waited.

He rose, and began to pace to and fro before the throne. He was still angry – if anything he was angrier now than when she had first entered. She could see the dark wrinkle of the veins in his red cheeks.

'Blessing,' the bishop said. 'In the Lenten Days, my blessing is for those who come to me in penitence.'

'Indeed it gives me sorrow, sir, that I have had to interrupt your business today.' For that, at least, she could apologize (as if she could possibly have delayed here the length of Holy Week while he gave audience to a thousand pilgrims, one by one!).

But if he wanted to hear her regret her marriage, he would wait for ever.

'In truth,' she went on, 'I have had very little time, and must leave Jent again tomorrow. Yet it did seem to me' – she looked him in the eyes again – 'to *both* my lord and me, that our household should have one at least who would pray for it, and that this was the first and most urgent of all the matters that awaited us on our return there.'

He had turned away, and was looking out through one of the great, glassed windows that lit the room. It was a

135

huge thing, made of many diamond panes and worth, she supposed, as much as all the furniture and decorations of the room put together. She could not tell what he was looking at, but he must have a fine view over his city and the people who thronged to his shrines and palace. His hands were clasped behind his back. One fat thumb moved slowly round and round in the palm of the other hand. He was thinking. She could not see his face.

Surely, now he must see past his anger to where his own interests lay. Whatever the man thought of Tarceny, he would have a dozen reasons for wanting to rebuild the Church there. It would be discourteous, even dangerous, for him to turn down her proposal and to send the wife of his most powerful neighbour packing without ceremony. At seventeen years she thought she knew the realities of power.

'Well,' he said at last, 'it would be good if the eyes of the Angels were open in Tarceny again. I will think on it. But at present I have not the usual crowd of ordered idiots clamouring at me for a living.'

'Have you not, Your Grace? I . . . I am surprised that you should say so.' Bishops were forever having to manage the demands of their priests to find them places.

'Try me, and I may surprise you more. I have said that I shall think. Enough of this. There is a matter in which you may oblige me.'

'Your Grace?'

'This damned north wind,' said the bishop. 'It has blown for days, and few boat-captains will set out against it.'

'Indeed, Your Grace.' Did he want her to change the weather?

'There are many good folk who have come to this city

in faith and find it hard to return. One in particular concerns me.' He motioned her to stand by him at the window. 'Down there . . .'

The window looked out on the mighty spires of Jent. To her right was the old shrine of St Tuchred Martyr, with its white-finger tower and pointed roof. Beside it rose the new cathedral, a massive grey shape six times the size of the old shrine. It had been building for some twenty years now, and another lifetime would pass before it was completed. Huge crowds of Lenten pilgrims thronged and jostled at its doors. The square below the palace was seething with them, with their robes, their staffs, their asses and their voices.

The bishop was pointing to the north side of the square, where the ground dropped suddenly. There was a low stone balustrade with a clear view of the lake and the lower town. A single figure was standing there – a woman in a pale gown.

'Her turn came to speak with me three days ago. She has walked in the square each morning since, waiting for some way of returning to her home near Watermane. Since you say you must be on the road tomorrow—'

'You wish me to carry her north with me?'

She must have let her temper show in her voice, for the bishop frowned at her again.

'I had thought it was the custom for the great of strength to let others travel with them for safety on the road,' he said heavily. 'Indeed I remember that your father – and his daughter, for he had a daughter then – did join my company on the road from Tuscolo not two years ago. Do not mistrust me. I am not going to give you a leper or a brothel-keeper, although I have plenty whom it would do you good to meet. This is a knight's lady, but her party is too small to risk travelling by land on its own.'

Phaedra was about to ask why, in that case, the woman had not joined any of the caravans and bands of travellers that must leave Jent's gates every day. But he raised his finger to forestall her.

'Be kind to my penitents, child. You may be one yourself, yet.'

Penitence, marriage – there was nothing to be gained by repeating that part of their argument. She bowed her head slightly.

'Since you ask it, Your Grace. And I shall wait your answer to my request. I pray that it may be swift.'

The bishop grunted, and jerked his head. A side door to the room had opened. The bishop's secretary stood there. She was grateful that the bishop did not even give her his ringed finger to kiss as they parted.

'Follow me, my lady,' the secretary said, as the door to the bishop's room shut fast behind her.

They were in a dark, empty corridor that must serve as a back way into the chambers for the bishop's servants. The retinue with which she had arrived at the palace – Squire Vermian, Orani, the men-at-arms – was still camped somewhere among the crowd of pilgrims on the grand stairs on the far side of the bishop's chambers.

'His Grace wishes me to offer company to a knight's lady when I travel tomorrow.'

'Indeed, my lady. She is the Lady Evalia diManey, of Chatterfall. We must be swift, because she may not linger . . .'

She hurried after him, along the passage and down a set of back stairs.

He had been listening! The bishop must have posted him behind the door, so that he could hear every word of the interview. Suddenly she felt humiliated. She could feel her cheeks were flushing, and was thankful that it could not be seen in the dim passages. She followed the stalking secretary as quickly as she could without running, and with her head high. The man did not turn until they came by another side door to the main porch, crowded with pilgrims, where he stopped in the doorway. He was looking out across the square, trying to locate the woman whom the bishop had pointed to from the window.

'One thing,' she said to him, and raised a finger as if to prod him in the chest. 'I sent a message to warn that I would be coming. I asked for speech with the bishop this morning and then to meet with candidates after that. I know my message reached the palace the day before yesterday. Yet I think His Grace has not received it. He seemed surprised that I had come. And no preparations had been made for me.'

The secretary looked down at her. He was a young priest, with thinning sandy hair around his tonsure and the most prominent Adam's apple she had ever seen. He wore the Knotted Rope at his waist. She could see him thinking that she deserved no more and no less than the bishop had given her, for putting herself ahead of all the faithful folk.

'My lady, any message of import that reaches us is passed to His Grace. What he thought of your coming, other than what he has told you, I cannot discuss.'

'Well,' she said, 'I find it hard to believe that His Grace was well forewarned today. And I wish that you would not trouble yourself to accompany me now. You must be very busy. I do not think it would serve His Grace well if you lost any *more* messages while running after me. Would it?'

Then she stepped without cloak or escort out into the thick north wind.

It was a cheap victory, over a man who could not answer back. But she felt that *somebody* in the bishop's palace should know what she thought of the reception they had given her.

Phaedra crossed the cobbles, and she was alone. She was pushing like someone's messenger through a jabbering, droning, ill-smelling throng of pilgrims and townspeople in the great square between the palace and the shrines. No one seemed to know who she was. She had not seen her maid or men-at-arms since leaving them in the bishop's antechamber. There was no one to call for room, to shoulder the crowds aside, to help her past the puddles and potholes. She could feel the big windows of the palace staring at her back. Was His Grace still watching from behind his hangings, to see she approached this woman? Did he even care? She shied from the thought that this mission of charity might only have been a device to end the interview. He had been so angry! Why? Because of his old hatred of Tarceny? Because he had been forced by the incompetence of his secretaries to interrupt his hearing of the penitents? Or was it truly because of her marriage: because he feared that he would be caught up in the storm that followed it, and because at heart he sided with Father, not her?

She did not turn her head. If he was watching, she thought it better not to let him know that she was aware of it. If he was not, she did not want to know. She had travelled for a week to be here, and argued with priests for what seemed like hours. Her audience could not be over so soon, and with so little for it!

Phaedra skirted a group of singing pilgrims, and found the balustrade at the end of the square was empty.

Was all Jent conspiring against her today? The woman she had seen a moment ago from the bishop's window had vanished like a will-o'-the-wisp. Phaedra had turned off the bishop's man, and was separated from her retinue. There was no one to help her. And still she felt the palace windows at her back, watching what she did.

She stood, frustrated, looking north across the lower city.

The wind flew down the Derewater towards her, locking the boats in harbour, and washing over the white walls and red tiles, the tumble of roofs and the masts rocking at their moorings. The surface of the lake wrinkled darkly under the palm of the air. It was colder than at any time since the new year.

A little to her right was the head of a flight of steps, which must drop down into some street further down the slope. She crossed to them, and looked over. The flight zigzagged down the steep face of the hill. There was a woman in a pale gown, unattended, picking her way down the steps below her. Was this the one?

'Lady diManey?'

The woman walked on, but stopped when Phaedra called the second time.

'Yes – yes, that is my name.' She seemed to have been deep in thought.

'His Grace tells me that you are looking for a chance to travel north,' called Phaedra. 'I plan to take the road tomorrow, with a company. Will you come with me? It will be on your route.'

The woman stared at the air in front of her. She did not seem surprised to be accosted; but she shook her head without so much as raising her eyes. 'You are good, my lady,' she said. 'And His Grace is good if he sent you. But His Grace has forgotten that I am banned the King's roads, and must journey by water or not at all.'

Banned? Angels above, who was this?

And at the same time Phaedra saw why the bishop had asked her of all people to provide this woman with an escort. One reason why.

'Forgive me, my lady, for I have not made myself plain. I am the March-countess of Tarceny. I will be travelling to the west of the lake, through the March. The March has law of its own. And the roads there are not the King's, but my husband's.'

Now the woman looked up. Phaedra saw a pale, triangular face, with large eyes and a pronounced nose. There was something familiar about it, as though she had seen it from almost exactly this angle and distance before. A memory stirred in the darkness at the back of her mind.

Someone had been afraid.

'I had heard that he had married,' the woman said. 'So it was you.'

He and *you*. Who was this woman?

Lady diManey had put her head on one side and was looking up at Phaedra as if she too were trying to remember.

'And has His Grace told you why I am banned, my lady?'

'No.'

No. But now he did not need to.

'I – I saw your trial, at Tuscolo, two years ago. I was in the gallery, with some friends . . .'

Angels! The bishop had given her a witch!

'Is that where I saw you? Your face looking down – for some reason I remember it so clearly . . .'

Now she was climbing back up the steps towards Phaedra, watching her as she spoke. There was a wary look in her eyes, as if there might be reason to doubt Phaedra's good faith. Suddenly, wildly, Phaedra hoped that she would reject her offer, although it would be extraordinary if she did. A poor knight's woman looking to travel could be expected to snatch any chance to attach herself to the company of a great lady.

The woman reached the top of the steps and approached. She was tall, with big eyes and a softness to her skin. Phaedra, who a few minutes before had stood her ground in front of one of the most powerful men in the Kingdom, found herself almost trembling as this creature came on.

What did the bishop mean by doing this to her?

'My party is only three, including myself,' said Lady diManey. 'But we came by boat and have no mounts or harness—'

'I – I can provide that . . .'

The expense would not be nothing. But the time – there was so little time!

And the woman was a witch!

Lady diManey seemed to come to a decision. 'Then – I shall be deeply in your debt, my lady – if indeed you truly wish me to be of your company.'

She seemed to know that Phaedra was already regretting her offer. Phaedra hated that most of all.

'Of my company to Tarceny, my lady.' There was strength in the word 'Tarceny', and she clung to it. 'And thence an escort to bring you home. I promise it.'

In the smoke-filled, low-ceilinged rooms they had taken at the inn, Phaedra slumped into an ill-cut wooden chair by the fire.

'Vermian, attend me, please.'

Squire Vermian was one of the seasoned young fighters that Ulfin kept at Tarceny, waiting their chance to earn their knighthood from him, and a manor to support themselves and a family. He had a bluff, pleasing look with his hair cut close around his square head and his thin eyebrows almost invisible on his brown skin. Ulfin must have thought well of him, to have picked him to lead Phaedra's escort when none of the more experienced knights could be spared. But the city was not his element. He frowned helplessly.

'Mounts, my lady?'

'And harness, and a litter for my lady diManey. Four horses and a litter, by tonight.'

'Where—?'

'How am I to know? Ask the innkeeper.'

'I will ask, my lady, of course. But half the city is trying to travel. Mounts will be scarce.'

Of course they would. He was not just being stupid. But she was tired, shocked and disappointed. And he had no right to hand back problems she had given him to solve.

'Vermian, we will find it easier to bear each other if you—' Oh, for Umbriel's sake!

'Two, then, for her followers,' she growled. 'Four if you can, but two at a minimum, by tonight, at whatever price. The woman can have my own litter, if it comes to that. I will – I will ride Thunder,' she added, thinking of the big black gelding that Ulfin had given to her, who had spent most of the journey to Jent trailing riderless behind her litter.

'Yes, my lady.'

A great lady, ride her horse all the way for a week? He did not like it. But he knew better than to argue. He bowed and left, jingling in his harness of war.

Old Orani did not know better. She stood by the door, bird-faced and round-shouldered, gawping at her mistress.

'You going to ride all the way, lady?'

'We must leave tomorrow,' said Phaedra flatly. 'And we must take this woman with us.'

'Why's she coming with us, lady?'

Why? Great Umbriel!

'Because I have said she will. Now please help me. I want to get out of these filthy silks. I want something to eat. And then I want ink, and paper.'

'Yes, lady. Undress you, and then you eat.'

This, Phaedra was learning, was typical of the old woman. If she did not know how to fulfil an instruction, she pretended not to hear it.

145

'And ink, and paper, Orani. I wish to write to my lord.'

She had planned to spend the afternoon seeing candidates for the post she offered. That would not happen now. And after this morning she did not want to wander among the tremendous buildings of the bishop's city, as she might have done at another time. All the power of Tarceny seemed to be a stranger here. She would remain at the inn and compose her letter. One of her riders would have to be sent off with it before sundown. Ulfin would want to know how coolly Jent had received a request from his house. And writing to him would be a comfort, when no other comfort existed.

Still Orani looked at her, blank-faced.

'You ask the innkeeper, Orani.'

Heavens, why should *she* have to solve every problem there was?

Alone, waiting for her meal to arrive, she paced the room restlessly.

What did the bishop know of this woman? Did he even know she was a witch? Surely, yes. And he would know that courtesy demanded that Phaedra let the woman travel at her side, that she should talk with her, and look into her eyes the day long. What would the woman do? What could she *not* do? It was as if – yes, exactly as if – he had asked her to take into her party someone with a secret plague that the eye could not see.

Phaedra remembered the just-by-chance way that the bishop had looked out of the window. Nothing that happened in Jent around the Lady of Tarceny would be by chance at this time. Oh, he knew what the diManey was. He had known she would be out there. He might even have instructed that she should be. Throwing the two of them together was his purpose.

Why? To delay her? The bishop knew that war was coming. Was he giving her this woman in an attempt to keep the Lady of Tarceny in Jent for another day, so that he could more easily arrange her capture? But that was not going to work. One way or another she would leave tomorrow, with every one of her party well mounted, so that she could be beyond reach of pursuit when the fighting started. And there would have been other, better ways to hold her up – promising her a rich field of priests to choose from in a week's time, for one.

Was it to defame her, then – to show the world that Tarceny gave help to witches? But he had himself received this woman. He could not defame Tarceny without damaging himself. No, these were wild thoughts.

What was it she was really afraid of? Witchcraft? Her party would number twenty to Lady diManey's three. Even if diManey were a witch, she would depend too much upon Tarceny, for all things, to think of doing harm on their journey through the March. And the woman might well be innocent – altogether innocent. They had only said that she was a witch in order to kill her and take her lands. Phaedra had been sorry for her once. Why was she so afraid now? Fear was becoming a habit, in this new world she had entered.

The thought she clung to was that the bishop was testing her. He had wanted her to show a sign of humility. If she gave comfort to a friendless pilgrim he might after all give her what she had come for. That was why she was going to help the woman. That was why she did not recall Vermian, or send a brisk message around to Lady diManey's quarters, telling her to make other arrangements. There was still a chance of bringing home a priest, and so of making her marriage sure.

The bishop wanted Tarceny to have a priest. He had said so. He had said . . .

For a moment she stared unseeing at the warped timbers of the room around her.

If the eyes of the Angels were opened in Tarceny again.

Could the woman be a spy?

VIII

A Face on the Road

ow Michael guard us, my lady,' said the witch in the dawn.

The gate of Jent rang loudly with the hoofs of thirty horses, sidling and ordering in the narrow passage. The light was dim under the arch tunnel. The same battering wind that had blown for days shook the wooden doors on their hinges and flustered the black-and-white drapes of the litter of Tarceny, from which Lady diManey's face peered out at the throng around her.

'And Raphael guide our way,' Phaedra replied shortly. She did not complete the prayer. Nor did she acknowledge the diManey's look, or allow the conversation to continue. With a great groaning sound, light cracked from the top of the gates to the bottom ahead of her. Thunder, the big gelding Phaedra was riding, shouldered forward as the doors of the city opened to show him the road home.

Thunder was an idiot: Phaedra neither liked nor trusted him, for all that he was one of the first gifts that Ulfin had given her. The thought of a week on his back was bad for her temper. On the few long journeys she had made before, she had always been accompanied by a litter,

149

slung between two horses with a canopy under which she could rest when she tired of riding or the sun. Now she had had to solve the shortage of time and horses by sending her litter round to Lady diManey's lodgings. But at least she could still choose where in the cavalcade she should ride, and when or indeed whether she had to speak with her fellow traveller.

The night had been sleepless, with war and witchcraft and anger all circling in her head. No word had come from the bishop. No priest had presented himself suddenly, with a letter from His Grace in his hand. It was hardly likely now that some galloping chaplain would overtake them (and even if one did, she would have lost her chance of choosing the man). For the first time in her life she had failed absolutely to get what she wanted. She could not have believed that such a disaster could happen to one of her new rank: the wife of Jent's most powerful neighbour, and the child of an old friend, who had come so certain that His Grace would receive her well.

That a father should be so served . . . That the royal house should be slighted . . .

Father, and the bishop, and the King – it was so wrong that the pillars of the world should fall into outrage, so unthinkingly, against her! They thought that custom and a daughter's duty and respect for the royal house were nothing to her. They did not understand. She knew how far she had parted from the accepted way (at least, she did now). Yet if love was an offence against which bishops cursed and knights took up arms in outrage, then she must offend. Her past had nothing to offer. It was as empty as the obstinate road behind her. Their stupidity meant

150

danger, danger for the whole Kingdom. And if there was to be war between Trant and Tarceny, between Tarceny and the King, there was only one side that she could be on; and she must follow it. Love ran deeper than blood, and truer than the Fount of the Law.

They were the ones who could not see.

So she rode, and brooded to herself, and rode on in the cold northerly gusts for the first hour of her journey, until her conscience and the manners of her upbringing revolted at last against her own behaviour. Then she reined back to the litter, whose occupant might be entirely innocent, but would certainly have guessed by now that her patroness was sulking.

'These damned winds,' Phaedra said. 'It has blown this way for days, and may do so for many more. I dislike what it may portend.'

It was a day of superficial talk and long silences. DiManey was correct in her speech, and unforthcoming. Perhaps she was offended; or perhaps embarrassed. She showed no sign of wanting to ingratiate herself with the wife of a high noble, as a poor knight's woman might have done. Phaedra rode, and fretted about the daggers of politics around her. The memory of the bishop's red face returned and returned.

The first night of the return journey was spent at one of Ulfin's manor houses on the southern fringes of the March, where the knight who held it laughed loudly at the table and talked of fighting. Phaedra retired early, leaving him to bore the Lady diManey into the small hours. The man's lights were mere rushes, and the paper, like the pieces that the innkeeper had found for her the day before, was poor stuff, watermarked from a mill in Jent rather than the majestic, smooth pages from Velis that Phaedra was used to. Nevertheless, she needed to write her thoughts down. She wanted to make her case to the Kingdom. There was still one person living east of the lake who might understand.

Right Dear Madam and Good Friend, I recommend me to you and I pray that you will now rejoice with me, for you have bidden me marry for love, and I have obeyed.

She began by describing Ulfin's looks, his voice, the deep intelligence behind his eyes. She wrote of her wedding on Talifer's Knoll, so that she could state firmly (and at the same time remind herself) that it had been a true ceremony, however short. She turned over in her mind, word for word, the few things the priest had said to them. Speak the truth to one another. Their lives to be a mirror to one another. She decided that if she had had a hundred bishops preach sermons at her ceremonies, she could not have heard better. Between man and wife there must be truth, first and last, and true knowledge; like mirrors, they must show to each other the other's very self.

Keep your promises. There had been none, except in their hearts.

. . . a marriage both in law and in truth. Yet it is a marvel and a weary thing for me that many seem to hold themselves offended at it, and stir themselves to arms and terrible things, as if iron and custom should come before law and love. Indeed

152

this is a most heavy season for me, for those I love and honour above all in the world, save only my husband, are in this wise set against me . . .

She must be careful, now. A letter from Tarceny to the heart of the Kingdom could well be read by others, before or after it reached its destination. Even her own words could be twisted by hostile tongues.

Truly I honour His Majesty and His Highness Prince Septimus as I do the Sun, who rules the day and without whom nothing would live, but my heart must be with the bright Moon that rises above our nights. For we know that the Angels have given the day for duty, but they have given the night for love.

She re-read her letter, amended it and, working late by rush-light, wrote out the fair copy. Then she signed it, folded it and added the direction: 'To My Good Friend Maria, at the House of Sir Hector Delverdis, in Pemini'. Last of all she sealed it with the ring that Ulfin had given her. She looked down at the impression of the letters *cPu* superimposed upon the moon of Tarceny, in the stiffening wax.

The royal sun for duty, but the moon for love. It was already too long since she had lain in Ulfin's arms.

On the road the next morning she brought Thunder alongside the litter and made an honest effort at conversation with Lady diManey. She had decided that if her fellow traveller were a friend, she deserved more courtesy than Phaedra had shown her the day before, and that if she were indeed an agent of the bishop or the crown it would do no harm for her to learn how firmly set Phaedra was upon the path that she had chosen, and why.

The same thought led her to begin talking of Ulfin.

'So much changed for me after we returned from Tuscolo,' Phaedra said, as Thunder picked his way along the very verge of the narrow track beside the litter. 'All those wretches wanting me to marry! They made everything different, even Father, even my home. In the end I had to find a way to leave. And it was as if I found some strong under— I mean, undercurrent, bearing me out of there like a leaf on water. There was nothing left but my lord's voice telling me not to be afraid . . .'

There was a sudden alertness in Lady diManey's eyes – even surprise. Perhaps she had sensed that Phaedra had changed a crucial word, even as it had left her tongue. Perhaps she was just offended by the contrast that Phaedra had half-intended between their marriages. Phaedra met her look and waited, inwardly daring her fellow traveller to try to follow up what she had said, and at the same time resolving that she would be fifty times more careful over her words in future. Then Lady diManey dropped her gaze, and muttered an apology. They rode on in silence.

A little while later Phaedra caught the look again.

And yet with that moment they seemed to cross some threshold of intimacy in Evalia diManey's mind, for now she began to talk more; and of herself. She said that she made the journey to Jent every year, for penitence, and to seek solace from Heaven. She spoke a little of her new husband's manor house below the foot of the lake. She referred to him occasionally, mostly to say that he would be waiting her return; and once or twice she mentioned episodes from her childhood.

She was considerate too. The further they pushed into the steep hills of true Tarceny, the more trouble the doltish Thunder was having with the roads. Phaedra was tiring more quickly than she had expected. It was proving an effort to ride, to manage her idiot horse alongside the litter, and to keep a conversation going at the same time. Around noon of the third day Evalia diManey insisted, with some grace, that they should change places that afternoon. When they set out again, she somehow fell into conversation with the normally tongue-tied Squire Vermian, so that they naturally rode side by side, and the litter dropped behind. Phaedra found she could do what she really wanted, which, unusually for her, was to curl up among the cushions and have an afternoon's rest. The slow jog, jolt, jog of the litter was peaceful under the bright skies of Tarceny. Even the thought that she had given Vermian no warnings about their fellow traveller was little more than an ugly moment as she plunged beyond the borders of sleep and so out of the world.

It was the evening of the fifteenth of March: the night of the attack on Trant. Phaedra was sitting with Evalia diManey after supper in the long upper living chamber of Ulfin's lodge at Baer. Each had a bowl of wine to finish. The drink seemed to be on the diManey's tongue.

'. . . It was horrible. I was sick with it. I could think of nothing but the swords. When diManey appeared, I did not wonder who he was, or why he should risk his life. I don't think I could have done. Only I remember realizing that at least I would not be killed there and then, in front of everybody. Afterwards I even felt that it would be better to die indeed than to live those moments again.'

And a cup later, she said, 'You are very young. You have looks, yes. More, you are happy. You don't yet know that the only happiness worth having is the hope that it will continue. And how will you keep it? How?'

Phaedra looked into her bowl. She could feel sorry for her companion. She could even like her now. But she did not need lectures on being 'happy'. Happiness was a blossom that would come and go, but for someone else. For herself, she could see two lives opening before her – one maimed, one whole. She was not one person, she thought. She was a half of two, bound with a link as deep as dark lakewater, for ever. And now the small-boats of Tarceny would be stealing up to the jetty by the ruined court in the olive grove. She felt she could bear anything, any outcome at all, but that Ulfin should be killed.

She had lost her taste for wine. She turned and turned the remains of her cup around the bowl in a slow swill, praying to the Angels – keep him safe, keep him safe. Send that, for some reason, he does not try to lead his men over the wall. Send that the guard sleeps. Keep him safe, and let him come home.

When she raised her eyes again her companion was looking away, into the olivewood fire and some thought of her own. Her eyes were shining wetly, and blinking as they shone. So Phaedra watched the fire too, for a moment. And when they spoke again it was about other things.

She was woken that night by a queer sound, close to her bed. She lay and listened for it to come again. The night was still. The moon was up, behind a thin veil of cloud that dulled its light. Nothing moved in her room. But as she shifted in her blankets she heard it once more. It came from somewhere nearby, through the boards of a wall. A voice which moaned aloud, and then spoke. A woman's voice, which cried the name *Calyn*, and followed it with sounds of weeping. The weeping went on for some time. It pursued her into her dreams, where she climbed a slope of brown, jumbled stones towards a ridge from which the afterglow of the sun was fading. The landscape was scattered with huge boulders that looked like crooked people, all the same. She was losing her way.

She could not see the skyline now, or the two lights on the rim of the world that had been there so many times. Her feet were guided only by what seemed to be the angle of the slope on this rough ground. Still she stumbled upwards, skirting a double-peaked crag to emerge upon a lip of rock in the last sun. Beside her, Ulfin caught her arm and exclaimed, *We have done it, my love! Trant is ours, with not a life lost. And your father is our prisoner.*

Another day's rising, heavy with tiredness, facing another day on the road. But this was different. Today she would finally end days of travelling. They would be at Tarceny by sundown. She would soon say farewell to her fellow traveller, with perhaps a little regret as well as relief. She would be home.

A great door in the wall around her had opened. Ulfin was safe. Trant was theirs. So was Father, although he must be fit to be tied at this moment: less likely than ever to listen to his daughter's voice. Still, there must be a chance now to solve this quarrel. Somehow she must find a way.

She rode in silence for much of the morning, thinking round and round her problem. The tiredness of rising did not lift from her, and no answers presented themselves. In the afternoon, as she lay in the litter, a sudden and heavy shower of rain drenched the landscape. Sleepy as she was, Phaedra roused herself and had the whole cavalcade halt while she insisted that Evalia diManey join her in the cramped shelter of the litter. It was not made for two, and her companion's outer clothes were wet. But they laughed at their discomfort, and watched the good rain soak the land while their retinue trailed muddily behind them. By the time they passed the turn for Aclete, the clouds were breaking, and when at last they reached the edge above the olive groves of Tarceny, the skies were clear. A cool breeze was in their faces.

'This is the best place from which to see it,' Phaedra said. 'And the best time of day – look!'

'Wonderful,' said Evalia diManey.

They had come in the early sunset of Tarceny. The sun had touched the crest of the mountains. The air was moist. Below them, the olive woods were in shadow. But the castle opposite still stood in light, and its walls and towers glowed the colour of pale amber, floating above the clouds of moon roses upon the spur. There were flags flying from the turrets – long bannerets blown out by the March wind. The armour of the watchers flashed on the battlements with fragments of sun. Phaedra felt her heart lift as she looked out across the valley to her new home. And in that moment she had the answer to the problem that had been troubling her all the day long.

She would bring Father here. He would be made to give his word not to fight or run away, so that they might keep him in gentle captivity at Tarceny, as indeed he had done for Aun of Lackmere. He would be a difficult guest. She would be prepared for that. She could rule him, if she had to. And difficult or not, she knew she had been missing him. She could think of his big, turbulent presence with fondness. She would attend him, read to him, walk with him. She would show him the wide lands of Tarceny and the nobility of the house. She would teach him to see the tragedy of its past not with loathing, but with sadness. And she would let him understand how Ulfin and she loved one another and could only be together. She would win Father round, however long it took. She would beat a path to peace through his heart.

The litter swayed as the road dipped towards the olive groves. Squire Vermian had the horns blow, and at the same time voices from the bannermen at the head of the cavalcade cried for room on the road. Some fieldsmen from one of the villages had met them on the slope, toiling upwards with their donkeys laden with huge bales of firewood. It was a bad place for the horsemen, and tricky work edging the litter downhill in the narrow way, while the fieldsmen held the donkeys at the very lip of the track to give them room. There were three upturned faces marked with sweat and dust, and a fourth beneath a hood. Phaedra was lost in her mental campaign to win Father, and it was a moment before she stirred, and then started with the memory of what she had seen. She lurched to the side of the litter, craning back through the drapes to catch another sight of the party of fieldsmen as they

159

gained the ridge. She saw the last one turn in the track to look down: at the horsemen, at the litter, at her. In a gleam of sun he stood clear on the path, and his face was shadow beneath his hood. Then he disappeared after the others.

'Vermian! Vermian!' The litter swayed as she leaned out to shout ahead. The riders checked their horses. The squire lumbered back up the track towards them.

'My lady?'

'That party of men who passed us. The last man in it. Bid him come to me. I want to speak with him.'

The squire took a second to understand what he was being asked to do. Then he dug his heels into his horse, and the litter swayed again as he pounded past and up the hill, waving to the tail riders. Huge steeds jostled and whickered in the track. Iron clashed. The wet earth shuddered with hoofbeats, fading.

They waited. Phaedra glanced at Evalia diManey's face, and saw how her skin glowed softly in the light. She had paid no attention to what was going on. There was some thought, or memory, behind her eyes as she looked across the gulf to the castle. The dim echo of the gate-horn came to them. Phaedra remembered that Ulfin would not be at home. It would be the first time she had entered the place without him. She shifted in the litter.

'What is holding them?'

As she spoke the riders appeared again. One bore a man in front of him. They lumbered downhill towards the litter with their prize. Phaedra muttered an exclamation as they came near.

'Not this one! Not this one!' she said as they drew rein. 'I asked for the last man in the party. The *last* man.'

Vermian grunted something that must have been an oath. 'Your pardon, my lady, but there were three, and this was the third.'

The fieldsman seemed caught in a world beyond his understanding. She found his look almost painful, and wondered whether rabbits stared this way at an oncoming stoat.

'Put him down, you idiots. There were four. The last one in a robe and hood, and walking a little after the others.'

The riders exchanged glances.

'Call me a fool, my lady, but there were three when we came up with them.'

'Angels' Knees, Vermian!'

They were milling around her, these huge, clumsy simpletons. Big men on big horses, and the fieldsman still pinned to the saddle.

'My lady – what is it?' asked Evalia diManey.

'It's a circus – what does it look like? All right. Put him down, Vermian. And give him silver. You can do that, can you? Send some people back to have another look. I want that man. Promise him whatever you like, but for Michael and Umbriel get him to come to the castle. Now, let's be on our way.'

She turned abruptly in her place and faced forward, so that she need not see the looks she knew the horsemen were giving her and each other. They were idiots.

'He can't have walked fifty yards,' she muttered to Evalia diManey.

'Who, my lady?'

'If it was the man I think it was, he has caused me

much trouble,' said Phaedra grimly. 'Trouble and embarrassment – albeit unwittingly. It is the priest who wed me to my husband. I am going to find out for myself whether he will not accept a position when I offer it; if not, why not, and at the very least what his name and order is.'

The litter swayed into motion beneath them.

'What man?'

'The last one in that—' she broke off. 'You didn't see him either?'

Evalia diManey was looking at her as one might at a friend or guest who, halfway through an evening, has suddenly become drunk.

'I saw three fieldsmen and two donkeys.'

'You can't have been looking! He was there!'

'You saw a priest in that party?' There was something urgent in the diManey's tone.

'A man with a long pale robe and a hood. My lord chose him.'

Her companion looked back up the path in the growing dusk. 'I did not see him,' she said, almost to herself. 'I did not see him.'

To Phaedra that answer was the last insult. She was the lady of Tarceny, queen of the wide March. She had a score of men immediately at her command, each armoured and mounted at the cost of the harvest of several farms. She could not have the slightest task done for her, be it ever so important. A golden chance to set things right had just been let fade away into the evening. She clamped her jaw shut and watched the olive trees passing.

After a moment her companion spoke again.

'Phaedra – I am not sure who your priest is. But if you do see him again, I think you should be careful.'

Phaedra ignored her.

IX

Ill News by Water

he did not understand, then, why her mood swung so heavily against her companion that evening. The only thing she could blame Evalia diManey for was that she had used Phaedra's first name without being bidden. But Phaedra was not able to recover from the disappointment of missing the priest. The evening passed in long silences, while Phaedra brooded and Evalia diManey stared curiously around her at the high, black-and-white rooms of Tarceny. They both retired early.

Nor did Phaedra think it strange that she found it so difficult to rise the next morning. She dragged herself from her bed at last, in time to say a few meaningless goodbyes to the Lady diManey, who was about to set off with her party and a half-dozen of Vermian's riders on the final stages of her journey home to Chatterfall. Phaedra dismissed her companion's thanks with a smile and a wave of her hand. After that, there was another of those looks, but no more words. Evalia diManey left the gate in Phaedra's litter, and Phaedra turned to re-enter the maw of Tarceny.

She was busy with thoughts that would not wait to be

ordered. Ulfin had won a breathing space by the passage of arms. It would not last for ever, and there were things she could be doing to help put a settlement in place. She wrote to Ulfin, urging him to send Father across the lake, as soon as his word of honour could be secured. Then she penned a description of the priest of Talifer's Knoll, had it copied and instructed that it be sent to each of the seventy manors and settlements of the March, to be borne by special messengers from each to each so that news of the man's whereabouts might reach her without delay.

She found Vermian more difficult than she had expected about dispatching half his troop to ride over the March. Bullying him into compliance left her ill at ease and exhausted.

Her mind was restless, and would not concentrate. She decided to begin work on a great robe for Ulfin, such as Mother had used to make for Father. She told herself that this would make it harder for Father to pretend that she had been carried away against her will. She began to draw up lists of silks and materials to be ordered from Baer or Watermane. And, using the draft of her letter to Maria, she started composing an appeal to Septimus himself, to be delivered when Father's heart was won and her marriage proved. In it she would beg him to leave his quarrel and honour the new house of Tarceny, as it would him. It was to be a great piece – the decisive victory. In her mind's eye she saw herself once again before the thrones of Tuscolo, speaking this time not of Obedience but of Love. She tried to imagine the strum of the lyres that would carry her words in song down the years. But the words dried on the page. The image of the thrones shifted, too easily, too quickly; channelled by her memory into a scene of shadows and swords: the flickering torches, the murmuring crowd; and a woman on trial for witchcraft.

She waited, fretting, for news.

The house was full of echoes. Ulfin was away. (So also were his knights and most of his men-at-arms, but it was Ulfin's absence that she felt most.) Without him, the castle was strange. The household, a collection of ordinary people whom she hardly knew, moved about their hundred tasks behind closed doors, and left her. She lay in bed in the mornings, watching the light move and grow on the walls and ceiling. She took down books from the shelves, and read them. *The Death of Aurelian. Of Taliver and Velis. The Sacred Life of Tuchred among the Pagans.* Book after book, in scrolls or in great volumes that bound works such as *The Heraldry of the Seabord* with *A Discourse of Good and Evil* and *A Treatise of the Northern Seas* together under the same covers. *The Tale of Kings* appeared three times. She found that Ulfin had added short notes in the margins on many pages of the histories, and had written a number of scrolls of his own, so she hunted through his library to discover each jotting and trace the big curves of his letters with her finger. Then she might sit and hold the book against herself while she looked out of the window, missing him.

She looked for the small comfort of things that reminded her of him – clothes, brooches, his drinking cup: signs that in spite of his absence this was his home, and always had been. There were no portraits of him, nor of any of his family except the sad-faced Paigan in the War Room. She began to visit the War Room, in its emptiness, to look at the face framed by the twisting snake, and to imagine the subtlest broadening and strengthening of the artwork that would make it not Paigan's face, but his. Then she would sit on the stool to the right of the war throne, and lay her hand in her imagination upon her husband's arm. The little chest was gone from where it had stood under Ulfin's left hand.

'Why are there no toys?' she asked one morning, as one of Ulfin's body-servants moved around her in the outer chamber of the living quarters.

'Toys, my lady?'

Ulfin valued silence among his servants. They were not used to being spoken to. This one was an elderly man with a thin face and wisps of white hair, but he had the same black-and-white livery and, she thought, the same blank look that they all did. She was almost sure that he was called Patter, but she was still not confident that she knew everyone in the house by name.

'Of my lord and his brothers. From their childhood.'

It worried her that there was so little in the castle to recall Ulfin's boyhood here – no games, no school slates, no relics of adventures with his brothers. Good toys, like her dolls and cup-and-ball at Trant, were worth keeping. But there seemed to be no sign that three young boys had ever played and squabbled in these rooms and along these corridors. It was as if those years had been lost, or buried altogether. The living quarters – a sparsely furnished set of rooms with a few rugs, chests and low tables – bore no trace of them. This was another emptiness, and one that troubled her because without evidence of Ulfin's past in this place it was harder to imagine him living here all the long years of his future.

167

The man was putting a wooden chair back exactly where it had stood before she had moved it to the window to read.

'Don't know that they had many, my lady, or that he kept them, after.'

He moved on to the stone mantelpiece above the fire, replacing a candlestick, shifting a small box a few inches to the left.

Watching him as he moved softly around the room, Phaedra thought that the years when Ulfin had been growing here must have been difficult and unhappy ones. Neither Ulfin nor his servants liked to speak of the lives they had led under the old lord. Certainly Patter seemed very intent on what he was doing. He was probably avoiding her eye deliberately, and hoping that the conversation would stop there. It left a long and awkward silence between them. But he would be gone in a moment, surely. He had already done more than enough among the plain and spartan things with which Ulfin had furnished his chambers.

The silence lengthened. Still he moved patiently from item to item, dusting the chess set, adjusting the low table, replacing things exactly where they had been before she had disturbed them.

She watched him, fascinated, as every trace that she had been there disappeared beneath his hands: buried like the lost childhoods of Tarceny.

There was no priest like Brother David. There was no merryman like Joliper. Phaedra found no good companions among the household. As time went on she depended more and more upon Orani to carry her instructions to the others. But even Orani was not good company: elderly, bumbling and silent, with eyes that seemed deep but had nothing in them. She was competent at what she did, but when she spoke she rambled and changed subjects without pausing. She fussed among Phaedra's things.

So Phaedra drifted through the rooms of Tarceny. She looked at the faces in the fine cloth of the wall hangings. She even talked to them; she pitied them their wounds, or begged them to spare the beasts and men they pursued with iron. She scolded them in murmurs over the blood that ran down their hands, and wondered what it had been like for the young sons of Tarceny, growing from childhood under these eyes.

The evenings were colder than she expected, in this hill air. She shivered, and took to wearing a shawl.

She felt sick.

The litter returned after a week, and with it came a short note from Evalia diManey. It began respectfully enough, 'Right worshipful and especial good mistress', but went on, after expressions of gratitude, to conclude, 'I pray that the Angels attend you in all things in your new life, and also I pray that we may meet again, for friendship is a means of strength whatever the day may bring.' It was signed, very informally, with a large, curling E.

Phaedra's heart sank. In another time, perhaps, with other pasts, the two of them might have been friends. But there was a great gulf of politics and station between them. The woman had been quiet enough – even reticent – for much of their journey. Why was she now claiming a part of Phaedra's soul? Phaedra did not want to find out that the woman was a spy, after all; or that she was something worse. Five days in her company had given no clues to the questions that had arisen about their first meeting.

In the end, Phaedra's response did include a short invitation to come by Tarceny, when next Evalia diManey travelled to or from Jent. Phaedra calculated that the journey by land down the length of the lake, particularly across Tarceny's rough country, would normally take three or four times as long as it would by water. So the diManey would need some very strong reason to take advantage of such an offer. And if she ever appeared at Tarceny's gate again, Phaedra would be on her guard.

She was growing more tired in the afternoons. Her moods were still heavy, and she was sleeping less well. A new and awful suspicion had begun to steal upon her. She was missing Ulfin worse than ever. She wished she could speak with him, but he was not there.

She was in the War Room again, resting her arms upon the windowsill, looking north and west to the far mountains, when something changed. At first it might have been just the sun falling on a hillside, or the sudden memory of a lark that had been twittering a few moments before – but he suddenly felt *nearer*, as though some thought of him that she had already forgotten had parted the emptiness for a moment. It was as if she could feel his presence alongside her thought, growing more real and solid in the room behind her.

Ulfin! At last!

He was reaching to her, in the way that he had used to at Trant. He was using the Cup.

Phaedra.

I've been missing you, she said.

Is it not well, at Tarceny?

I can't imagine what it was like for you, growing up here.

She felt him sigh.

Only Calyn remembered our mother, he said. *It gave him strength that he could never share with Paigan or myself. All we had was each other, and hate.*

After a moment he spoke again.

Phaedra. Meet me at Aclete tomorrow evening. I must speak with you.

She could not stop herself from looking around, just as she had used to as a girl. Her hand reached for him, and into empty air. He was gone. She cursed herself and waited; but he did not come again.

It was evening once more, on the road to Aclete. The light was dull below the grey clouds. The journey was nearly over. The hulk of Talifer's Knoll was before them, blocking the lake and the town from view. It wore its cloak of woods draped on its northern shoulder, like some squat, bow-legged giant from the past. Phaedra started as her escort blew their horns.

'Vermian! Vermian – what are you blowing for?'

'My lord's standard is on the hill, my lady.'

Far off, horns were calling in answer. She could just make out the tiny figures on the skyline, stationed to see and be seen from the road. A long banner floated above them. Vermian – or one of his men – must have good eyesight if he could pick out the device on it at this distance. Perhaps it was the banner's shape, or some signal with horn and flag, that identified the party. Maybe

171

Vermian had made such rendezvous as this a score of times before.

'Is he there?'

'Most like, my lady.'

'Then let us go to him.'

I must speak with you. Why had he not simply done so? Or was it that what he had to say was so involved that it could not be contained, by night or day, in the fleeting visions of his cup? If so, then it must be Father, and her request to bring him to Tarceny. Ulfin wanted to talk it through with her, probably to argue with her.

But she had her own reasons for wanting to talk with Ulfin. She had been counting the hours until she could do so. And now she was at the foot of Talifer's Knoll.

Vermian checked the party with a call and a wave of his hand. He looked to her. He must have seen that she was not herself today. He said nothing, but his eyes asked, *Are you up to this?* It was no climb for the litter. It would be a bad one for any horse, for the slope was steep and thick with thorns and tussocks. Orani, looking thin-lipped and bright-eyed, rode on an ass. Thunder followed at the litter's tail. He was saddled and caparisoned for her, but the hands that had decked him in the dawn had worked in vain. She would not ride.

She was tired. Her stomach was uneasy and her throat tight. The motion of the litter made it worse. Her mind was sleazy with sickness, and with shock.

She sat on the rim of the litter and let them help her down to stand among them. The ground was hard and unmoving beneath her feet. The hillside swept above them. She was poorly shod for walking. It would, after all, be

172

more sensible to continue into town, and let Ulfin join them there. But he was waiting for her on the knoll.

'It is better when I stand,' she said. 'You may send the litter on, Vermian, and such others as you think right. Let the rest of us climb.'

Men were swinging themselves down from the saddle around her. Vermian was giving orders. The litter was moving. She set herself to face the hillside.

There was no path here. The tussocks were shin-high. There were thistles in the grass, which scratched her ankles and even her feet through the thinness of her shoes. She gathered her skirts and started upwards, frowning. At another time this slope, even pathless, would have given her little difficulty. She was not strong today. She felt herself beginning to breathe heavily. The men on the hillside above them were hidden by the curve of the slope. Her own party struggled behind and below her, the men slowed by their horses and their fighting gear.

On, on.

And the slope rose on and on above her. It grew steeper. She was going slowly, so slowly, picking her way around this anthill, past that thorn, another few feet upwards. When she stopped and looked around again she seemed to be only a third of the way up. The woods were to her left, watching her from under dark eaves. The going must be rough in there, rough for an old man's feet. Where are you now, priest, stumbling among the roots of my trees? Perhaps he knew secret paths. He had had companions, then: she had heard them moving in the wood. They would have helped him. There was no one to help her now. The crest was lost to view. She remembered this. She

173

had lost her way on the slope in her dream, and stumbled among the boulders. But Ulfin had been above her, and when she reached him he would give her good news in the sunset.

A man had halted by her, with the reins of his horse in one hand. He held his other out to her, with a questioning look on his face. How he intended both to help her and to lead his horse at the same time she could not imagine.

'My lady . . .'

That was Orani, sliding off the back of her donkey and offering to help her up. The patient beast stood by, tail flicking, blinking to keep the insects from her eyes. It seemed unconcerned by the climb. Phaedra shook her head. Orani's ass was Orani's. And she would not go to meet Ulfin clinging to its back like a sack of grain.

'On up,' she said. 'It will get easier.'

Her sickness had faded. It was only the weakness now, and she would not let the others see it. Push, push, push on upwards. And another thistle before her, with its bright purple blossom standing proudly among the grass stems at the level of her eyes. Step round it and climb on. Men were shouting, laughing. It was good that they were enjoying this. Someone blew a horn. There were figures above, coming down to meet them – men unencumbered by horses. The livery of Tarceny was all around her. Ulfin was not there, but a man – Squire Cradey – stumbled downwards to her and gave her his arm. To her right two men were embracing, while a horse, its reins released for a moment, ambled off along the hillside.

'Where is my lord?'

'Above, my lady,' said the squire.

'Is he well?'

'Well and unhurt, my lady.'

Thank Michael.

The slope was gentler now. The tussocks were more widely spread, and flatter. She could see the skyline above them, and the banner, and men clustered beneath it. Ulfin must be there. She smiled and felt stronger. It seemed so long since she had seen him.

He was not among them. When she came up to the banner, they pointed her to where he stood alone, a little way down the lakeside slope. He was not looking her way. He watched out across the grey face of Derewater, and the misty lands beyond it. There was something in his stance that spoke of apprehension.

I must speak with you. And yet now that she had come he would not face her. He seemed to be prolonging the moment before they met. He had something to say that he did not wish to.

I must speak with you. A silence had fallen upon the men under the banner. She sensed a sudden wariness among them, as they watched her look to her lord. They knew what he knew, and she did not. They knew what he had to say.

She walked down the gentle slope to where he stood.

'Ulfin, what is the matter?'

He looked up. His face was pale and he was ill-shaven. There was a darkness like bruising below his eyes.

'Phaedra – I . . . The truth is I do not know how to tell you . . .'

'Is it Father?'

175

He hesitated for a moment. Then he said, 'Yes.'

'Is he dead?'

'Yes.'

'You look terrible.'

She said it, and felt her face smile. The corners of her mouth twitched and the tiny muscles pulled at the edges of her eyes, even as his words as she had heard them crashed slowly though her guts.

'It has been a heavy season. The King and Prince Barius are also . . . So much has happened. Phaedra – the King is disappeared.'

She turned away and looked across the lake. She felt for the first time the keenness of the wind up here, which blew the folds of the banner out straight behind them. It flew into her eyes and teased them to tears. The land across the water was misty indeed. Father was gone. Dead, and the King with him?

Father!

She blinked. They would call her the worst traitor in the Kingdom.

'Why – why did it happen?'

'Because he was a good man! Because he didn't keep his dungeon in order!' The words exploded from Ulfin like protesting hounds. 'We were holding him and some others in a storeroom. It was not made for holding men. They broke out, and attacked my people. They were ill-armed, but they took us by surprise. My men defended themselves. By the time I got there he was dead, and two others with him.'

'Who?'

'I do not know the names, Phaedra. I can find out . . .'

She shook her head. At that moment, she did not want to know. 'I asked you to send him to me.'

He said, 'I did not have his word of conduct.'

Father would have been angry and ashamed. He might not even have listened. She had been asking too much, and dreaming that it would all be all right, because she had asked that it should. She could not blame Ulfin.

She took Ulfin's hand and held it.

'It is good to have you back again,' she said at last. 'I have missed you so much.'

'Phaedra – I cannot stay.'

She looked up. 'You must stay! You must! I can't . . .'

She broke away from him and ran a few steps, jamming her fist into her mouth. There was nowhere on all that wide, grey slope to go to. And she had no home any more – not Tarceny, without Ulfin. Not Trant, without Father, no! All those memories! Just a world of hillsides and grey skies and the wondering eyes of the soldiers above her.

I must not weep.

Ulfin caught her by the shoulders.

'Phaedra. It is grievous, yes. Now of all times I should be with you. But war may already be on us. I sent men under a flag of truce to the King's camp on the road to Bay, but the King and Barius were both vanished from it. Do you understand?'

She shook her head, choking with tears, and buried her face in his shoulder. Yet a part of her mind was watching from some unshaken platform in the middle of her brain. She felt it look askance, like an adult at the tantrum of some toddler. *Are you crying for Father*, it seemed to ask,

177

or because your husband has other things on his mind besides your-self?

'I cannot tell what will happen now. I have eighty men on the far side of Derewater, holding Trant for you. I must return at once, with eight hundred – a thousand. I cannot delay.'

It is both, she thought. Both. And if there is more fighting I may lose him too.

'One night,' she said hoarsely. 'One night. Ulfin, please. I – I have something to tell you as well.'

She felt him hesitate. She felt too the slightest shift in his embrace as he held her less tightly. The tension in his shoulders as he squared himself for what was coming.

'What is it?'

'I think I am with child.'

She had not believed it when Orani had told her for the first time, what her tiredness and sickness meant. She had not believed it because she could not allow it to be true. Even when her body, and the household's looks, had given her the lie, she had resisted the knowledge. It was only as she spoke the words that she surrendered to it at last.

Ulfin broke from her grip and walked a few steps away down the slope, looking out across the grey waters below. Then he turned to her again, and at last a slow smile crept across his face. And in her grief and her fear it did not seem strange that he too should think this was the most terrible news of all.

PART II

THE PALE PRIEST

X

Pain

A scroll in the library of Tarceny held a fragment of *The Tale of Kings* that she had not heard or read before. It told of a prince who led his followers into the pagan hills and there was surrounded by foes. Climbing to a high place, he raised his horn to summon his brothers to his aid. Many times he blew, but they were busy with hunts or wars, were at feasts, or yawned among their sheets of silk. They did not come to help him.

Once more the prince blew, calling across the leagues to the King, his father. *Come Wulfram, come, as in wrath you came from the sea!* The horn-note soured among the mountainsides. In his heart he felt his father's answer:

> *Wind whispers your words in dust*
> *On dying leaves. Thorns wave.*
> *Still are my steeds, my knights stir not.*
> *I lie among a hundred brave.*
> *Earth stops cold my mouth.*
> *My bones are litter in the grave.*

Ambushed, Phaedra wept.

She had not gone to his burial. She could not have stood by his coffin, with the eyes of the crowd upon her and Ulfin's swords guarding her from her own people. She had sent word that he was to be laid with Mother and the children, and a stone set by theirs in the chapel wall. One day she would visit, to see that it had been done.

His death was a presence, beyond the colourless doings of each day. It cast shadows in her mind. When they found the bodies of the King and Prince Barius in the thickets off the road from Tower Bay, covered with terrible wounds as if they had been mauled by beasts, no explanation had accompanied the news; but Phaedra could not feel surprised. It seemed to her that these deaths, though separated from it by days and distance, were swallowed into the one great Death that had happened at Trant. No further reason existed.

Grief made her eyes and shoulders ache. She suffered rashes, mouth-sores and a pain in the throat that lasted for days. There seemed to be a pit of emptiness in her stomach, which forced her to keep gulping. Her brain fogged when she tried to concentrate, and when she wanted to sleep it raced and would not rest. She wondered what kind of creature she was, to have allowed and even aided an attack on her own father's house. She was angry: in brief, spasmodic moments. Her nails dug into her palms, and she would stop to curse the world that had never warned her how frail her hopes would be. Sometimes she would be seized with anger even against Ulfin, who had sworn no harm would come, and yet had not been there to stop the swords as they cut into Father's flesh.

Most of all she raged against Father. *His* pride had brought the crisis. It was he who had called on the King, planned the invasion, and he who like a child had chosen to wreck everything when Tarceny had upset those plans without a life lost. Stupid, proud, blind, *selfish* man! What had he been thinking of, he and his unarmed handful, when they had prised the boards apart and rushed upon Tarceny's mailed fighters? All he had done was bring misery to those who loved him, and to his daughter most of all.

Life was so frail. It went cased in the thinnest of mail shirts among the swords of its enemies. The keystones of the Kingdom had fallen. The fighting might start any day. Malevolent chance had but to stretch its finger again, this time to touch Ulfin in the middle of some skirmish and steal him for ever. The thought came to her on the stair, on the edges of sleep, in dreams. Sometimes she found she expected to dream of him one last time, to say a final farewell and so close their brief lives together. At others she thought they would walk in without warning and tell her that he was dead. Then she feared that the servants were looking for her, and that when they had found her they would say that it had happened. So she avoided them, retreating to the passage above the hall gallery, listening for footsteps, and when she heard anyone pacing into the hall below, fleeing through the living quarters to the chapel, built into the north-west bastion below the War Room. There she would try to pray.

The chapel was a shell. Heaven did not rest there. She found a candlestick to stand for the Flame, but the light kept going out. She had no priest to perform the offices, or to promise her comfort or forgiveness. No word had arrived from Jent, and after these terrible events surely none would. In the stained and grimy windows the angels frowned: Michael the Warrior and Gabriel the Messenger, frozen in their postures above the altar. Raphael, Friend of the Hapless, stalked past without a sign. Umbriel, Judge of the World, wrote in his book as she kneeled before him. Her footprints showed in the layer of light dust upon the floor. She had never been so alone.

Yet even in her loneliness there was one that was with her, unwelcome, unspeaking, all the time.

It was nothing she could see or touch. It was weakness, sickness, a debilitating disease that stretched for months ahead of her. It softened her mind, so that she could no longer think clearly. It made her a slave to her own feelings. Soon it would begin to pull at her body, to swell it and distort it until she was hideous to look upon. She would waddle grotesquely down Ulfin's elegant corridors, resting at each corner as if she had travelled a mile. And then . . .

Mother had died in childbirth. Other women had done so too, in pain and blood. She could not imagine it. All she could think of was redness and screaming. It would come. She did not know how she would bear it. Sometimes she thought that perhaps she would survive it, but that the child would be born dead, or would die quickly afterwards, as her younger brother and sisters had all done. She tried to imagine herself and her son or daughter, playing together in a sunlit room as she remembered doing with Mother. She could not picture the child clearly. She did not believe such a future could be. There were moments when, exhausted by grief and from fear, she thought herself certain to miscarry. She would be free, and if all the world shamed her for it she felt she would not care. She would find ways never to be pregnant again. Still the child clung stubbornly within her, and she grew as the weeks passed.

There was a silent, grey-haired knight called Caw, who was left in charge of the castle while Ulfin was away. He had a lean face, white skin, and an inner hardness as though of flint. He did not seek her company; and she avoided his, except over supper, when custom demanded that they should sit together at the high table. They had little to say to one another. But one morning he came clanking in his mail and gear along the living-quarter passage and found her in Ulfin's library, trying to compose a letter to Ulfin at her great black writing desk. She looked up from the page at which she had been staring blankly for a quarter of an hour, and saw the knight frowning into the room. The sight of him there reminded her suddenly of the library at Trant, of another letter and another half-strange knight in the doorway. For a moment she wondered if Caw had come to ask her whether she played chess. Instead he showed her three folded papers that he held in his gauntleted hand.

'There are messages for you,' he said curtly.

'Come in, Sir Caw.' She supposed the letters must be the normal business of the March — suits, complaints or petitions — that would normally have gone to Ulfin, but in his absence were brought to her. She supposed that she was lucky there had not been more before this. At another time she might have been ready, even eager, to start learning the ins and outs of the day-to-day issues that must fill so much of Ulfin's time. But her mood was very low today.

Then she saw that the letters were addressed not to Ulfin, but to herself. She broke the seals and peered at the first one. It was badly written, in a hand she did not know, from a place called Hayley, which she thought must be somewhere in the north of the March.

Caw was standing by the doorway, watching her.

'It's a reply to my letter about the priest,' she said at last.

'Priest?'

'The man who wed my lord and me.'

'Hm.'

'The others . . . Yes, they are the same. I thought they must be petitions. Do people in the March not petition their lord?'

'They do,' he said. He sounded surprised at her question. Perhaps he had been thinking about priests.

'In my lord's absence . . .'

He shrugged. 'They come to me.'

'To you?' Why not to her?

'Yes.'

She looked at him. She, not Caw, was the wife of Ulfin and therefore the person of Ulfin in his absence. She should be doing more for Ulfin than she was. But Caw knew the March. He knew how to resolve the cases that could be resolved. He could advise her what to do; but a man like this would not willingly prop up a woman young enough to be his own child. So he was running all the March himself. He had said nothing of it to her. He probably saw nothing strange in what he was doing.

Her thoughts bickered wearily with one another, and she could not feel that it mattered.

He was waiting for her.

She turned back to the letters, and leafed listlessly through them. Two of them seemed to say that such a one as my lady had written of was seen near their village on such-and-such a day, but no one knew where he had gone. The third wove the most credulous tales around some mountain hermit, and gave him names such as John o' Locklegs, Grey Matt and Prince Under the Sky.

They were meaningless. And there would more of them, many more. And all meaningless.

Caw stirred, and cleared his throat. 'Must I hold the man who brought them?'

'No.' Even if replies were needed, she was not going to write them at once.

'It was important then,' she said. 'Now that all this has happened – I do not know.'

'All this?'

'Father, and the King.'

He said nothing. But she thought that he tensed at her words, as if he were afraid of what she would say next. He must think she was about to weep. A man like this must hate women who wept. Perhaps he just hated women.

Father, and the King. And still he was waiting for her. And suddenly she knew she could not keep her voice level.

'I don't see why!' she said hoarsely. 'I don't see what I have done!'

For a long moment it seemed that all of high, empty Tarceny was still around her.

'It is not your doing,' said Caw at last.

'No.' She put her hand on the letters and did not look up. At last she was able to say, 'Thank you, Sir Caw. If there are more, you may bring them to me.'

He left her.

A long time afterwards, she wondered if he had said: 'It is not *your* doing.'

She did not challenge Caw about the cases and complaints from the March, although she knew it was her task, not his, to hold court in Ulfin's name. She knew too that she, not Caw, should be touring the manors, shaking out the fighting men for her husband's war. But she rested at Tarceny, watching the March passing below her walls. And every day brought bands of men from the north or west of the land to sound their horns at the gates, to pause and water before hurrying on down to the lakeshore; for Ulfin was calling the March to arms beyond Derewater. There were knights from Hayley under banners, foot soldiers from valleys beyond Bellisfell under rough standards, settlers with hooks and hunting spears. The castle garrison was stripped to twenty men. Caw stalked and fretted, but did not speak. All he gave to her were matters that concerned her directly: the merchant who came to talk of the silk for Ulfin's robe, and the letters that came in answer to her notice about the priest.

There were many of these, ill-written, useless. She could see in their rude scribblings the reeves and elders huddled together over the page, thrilled to receive a writing from the Lady of the March, jumbling together all they could think of to please her, and – where the manor lord was absent – adding all the things he might want her to

188

know about the running of their lands (or, in a few cases, a number of things he clearly would not). Many seemed to assume that there would be a reward of money for finding the priest. Phaedra thought that before long she would have the courtyard seething with all the beggars and mendicants of the March, and every one claiming to be the man she sought.

None appeared. Whether they stayed away because of the fearsome reputation of Ulfin's house, or they did come, and Caw conscripted them for the war, she did not know.

One letter was unlike the others. Somehow, as spring grew towards summer, it had found a way across the lake to her. The script and spelling were clear, the hand familiar, if unusually hurried and disordered.

. . . He should have been a man of God, as he wanted. As prince he was too good for us. Now the Angels have him, and our hope with him, we are left in a dark place. The men are talking of omens. I do not know what will come. I fear the most terrible things. This cup had gall enough in it, but the more that we are now so set against ourselves and the men all arming for war. Some here who think themselves friends of Septimus will say you are bewitched. Others, though I would not listen to it, will say that even you yourself are a party to unholy things. Dearest madam, forgive me that I should write this, yet I believe it is truer friendship to say to you and not conceal from you that few will hear me when I speak for you, and that I am brought to write this to you in secret. Yet believe however I do in this, I know you still in my heart. And so I pray you forgive,

Your friend Maria Delverdis, who writes this to you on the
fourteenth day from the death of the King, and of his son Prince
Barius, of whom no equal has walked nor will again.

It had been written by candlelight, she decided –
perhaps after the house was asleep. And it had not come
direct from Pemini. Maria must have sent it to some friend
who was less likely to court danger or disapproval by sending messages direct to Tarceny. She had spared Phaedra
from telling her that. Re-reading the letter, Phaedra
suspected that Maria had spared her a lot. She could not
guess what 'unholy things' people were accusing her of,
but the idea that she might be bewitched must be the very
kindest of them. Eventually she settled herself to reply,
trying to write like the brave woman Maria seemed to
believe she was. She described the house and lands of
Tarceny, and wished that Maria might one day come to
see them. Then she put her letter aside, in the hope that
a day might come soon when it would be safe for Maria
to receive letters from Tarceny again.

Waiting, waiting. The weeks passed, and she could not
fill them all with misery. When the silks for Ulfin's robe
came, and with them the fine scissors and needles and
threads that Tarceny had not known in a generation, she
made herself begin on them. She told herself, with the first
crisp cuts, that fears might fail too. Just because she could
not believe in the future, it did not mean that good would
not come. All she could do was pray and pray in the empty
chapel for Ulfin to return.

And news came flying across the lake of victory.

* * *

She greeted his homecoming with garlands and a welcome-supper. He laughed as he held her, and he laughed again over his food in the hall of Tarceny. He was calling for his chess set even before the tables were cleared, and when it came he slapped a handful of pieces onto the boards in front of him.

'They came against us in three columns,' he said. 'From the north, under Baldwin; from the east and from the south-east.' He set chess pieces in an arc around a goblet that signified Trant. 'Say five or six thousand in all, to our fifteen hundred. We knew that the southern column was lagging, because Seguin had quarrelled with Develin and therefore was not pressing forward as hard as the others. So we were able to slip out to the south-east' – a black piece hooked outward from the castle – 'and come suddenly on Septimus and Develin from their southern flank. They collapsed at the first rush.'

His hand whipped a white knight from its place with a flourish. His tone was eager, almost boyish. His eyes were fixed on the pieces and his gestures were charged with the echoes of combat. Phaedra watched him with her eyes shining. It was so good to have him home – and safe, and in glory!

'Then we rode north and were on Baldwin before nightfall. There was a stiff fight for the road, because unlike Septimus they knew we were coming. But they had not been able to close up, and we got between Baldwin and Bay. Bay broke back the way they had come, and that was that. My riders chased Septimus to Tuscolo' – a white pawn skittered away across the tabletop – 'and Bay to the north. We took Baldwin, for the place was lightly held and the gate was open. We never even had to close with Seguin.'

'I am sorry for Baldwin,' Phaedra remembered to say. 'And for the men who died with him.'

'It is a pity. Still, Phaedra, such a death is a part of the life. Baldwin was ageing, and for him at least it came with honour. Develin was thrown from his horse and crushed in the press before any of mine even came near. If my hour must come, I would me a death as Baldwin died.'

'*No*, Ulfin! Don't speak of that. There must be no more of this! Let there be peace now. It has already gone beyond all reason.'

'It is not in my gift, Phaedra. There will be a pause, for the hot weather is on us and Septimus must re-gather. Whether he will now take charge, or Faul or Seguin, I do not know. But they have lost much honour. They will be at us again after the harvest.'

'Then I shall pray to Michael that you are wrong.'

Ulfin stayed for two weeks, in the hottest time of the summer, when men might die from heat in their armour and all campaigning ceased. They did little but sit together in the cool places, waiting for the sun to pass. He was silent much of the time, and seemed only to pay attention to the doings of the March when he saw a way to win more men or treasure for the campaign. She watched him looking out on the grand scape of the hills, with his mind turned inwards, unseeing. She saw Caw waiting to catch his master's attention, and being ignored. There was some coldness there. She thought Caw was hoping for release from his stewardship, but could not ask for it, and that

Ulfin was not prepared to let him go. When she tried to ask Ulfin about it he answered shortly and off the point.

He spoke with Phaedra on this and that, but even as he talked his mind was on other things. He seemed to think there was little use in trying to find the priest of the knoll. He was surprised that her pregnancy was making her sick (although she was able to assure him that it was better than it had been, and that indeed she was becoming stronger). And he would not talk about the coming child. She wondered whether he was superstitious, or embarrassed – or whether, like her, he was dreading what the birth would bring.

One morning he was gone; risen and out of the gate before she could drag herself from sleep. He left messages and keepsakes, but took most of the coin and all the men he could muster down the road to Aclete. She was hurt that he should let it seem to her – even if she did not believe it – that silver and mail meant so much more to him now than the woman who carried his child. She would have given years of her loneliness for a few more days of his company. She could not have them. All there was left that morning was the castle, the household, the child, and Caw.

Caw was, if anything, grimmer than before. It was clear he did not enjoy his post. He was hard to talk to. He seemed to think of little beyond war and the affairs of the month, and in his short way would speak of them if she wanted him to. She did not want to ask about those things, which were part of the present that imprisoned her. And Caw would not speak of the past at all. When she asked him about Ulfin's childhood his face hardened; he said only that his own father had broken his head and sold his marriage for a window of glass, but that he had never heard of any who had such a raising as old Tarceny had given his sons.

The afternoon she tried to talk to him about her father he got up and left the table with something that sounded like a curse.

The evenings after supper were empty places. She and Caw were the only two of rank at table. The household would clear the trestles and go about their duties, leaving them together, and they would look past one another until she could reasonably dismiss him. But Phaedra found that he did indeed play chess, and that this let them bear each other's company without the difficulties of conversation. By the middle of September they were playing every night. Caw always chose black. He was reluctant to make the first move, even in the opening dance of the chessboard. His positions were crabbed, tight and defensive. Phaedra had to do far more of the attacking than she was used to. Her mind was tired in the evenings, and although her sickness had eased, her thinking never quite had the focus that she expected of it. The games grew longer as the days shortened. The pieces moved *clip-clip* upon the board, separated by the long silences in which Caw thought and the air of the big hall hissed softly in Phaedra's ears. She would look up and see their reflections in a glass across the hall. The knight, in his dark tunic and his belted sword. The woman in the pale dress with the swelling belly. White flagstones and black, breaking into black irregularity at the hearth. Black pieces and white. Death and Life. And still Life lost.

194

Another evening, and the game was ended. It was late. Caw left her with a grunt that might have been a goodnight, and went to walk the walls. Phaedra rose too, frowning. She climbed the steps to the gallery and passed into the half-lit corridor that led to the empty living quarters. Her chamber was dusty and a little untidy. Patter was on other duties, now that Ulfin had carried away most of the younger servants to the war. However, Orani had left a bowl of fruit for her on the low table. She mumbled to herself, picked up an apple and bit it. It crashed into juiciness in her ears, and at that moment she thought she heard something else. She turned her head, wondering whether someone had stood for a moment in her bedroom doorway.

'Orani?'

There was no one there. Watching the door, she finished her mouthful, trying to chew without obliterating her hearing. Nothing moved. She picked up her light and walked softly to the doorway. There was no one in the corridor. From a little room a few paces away she heard the rumble of Orani's snore. The maid was supposed to remain awake to help her mistress retire, but she did not always manage it.

Phaedra closed the door as softly as she could. After a moment's thought she reached for and drew the old bolts, which were stiff with dust and disuse. They clacked home. Then she undressed and sat in her bed, finishing her supper and watching the door. She wondered whether it was something in the way she had bitten at the fruit that had sounded so like the scrape of a foot, and the sibilant rustle of a robe.

* * *

And now she was heavy with the child. It had woken in the late night, and its squirming had woken her too. She sat in Ulfin's library, wrapped in blankets in the October dawn, telling herself that there was nothing to be done about her discomfort. She could only distract herself until it eased. So she had come here to read by lamplight from Ulfin's books and Ulfin's manuscripts, while her stomach and bladder were crushed in turn by the shifting bulk of his child inside her.

The pages were uncut from their full size, so she had spread them over the writing desk that Ulfin had given her. They were the beautiful, smooth paper, watermarked with the sails of Velis, that she had sometimes seen at home. Across the cream-like surface Ulfin's hand, curving tightly to make the most use of space, had traced a family tree. At the top was a row of names famous in story: Wulfram the Seafarer, and the seven princes of the Kingdom. Below them Ulfin had listed for each the male line of descent, father to son. There were names she had known all her life – high kings and heroes. There were others she had never seen written or heard in *The Tale of Kings*. She could only wonder how Ulfin had known of them. One by one the lines came to an end. Only the seventh, headed TALIFER, went on and on, outlasting all the others until, at the foot of the third page, it ended in a row of names: CALYN, ULFIN, PAIGAN.

On her ring the letters *cPu* glittered, and the worm writhed in the weakening light of the flame.

Ulfin must have spent many hours on this, and she had many questions for him – or perhaps just one. But he was not home, and word came rarely from him across the lake. Sometimes when she slept, or even when she was awake, he would speak to her through the Cup. Such dreams were good but fleeting, and she could not tell when the next would be; nor could she will them to happen as she so often wished to. He was swept up in his war, crossing the Segne in relentless marches, seizing Tuscolo itself by a miraculous raid, and harrying Septimus and Seguin's forces when they turned to recapture it, until their soldiers melted away and Seguin was drowned in the bloody marshes on the road to Bay.

Now a group of barons had offered Ulfin the crown.

The news had come last night, and with it word that Ulfin had refused. Phaedra felt as if she had put a foot over a sudden precipice and had been snatched back before she was aware. Had he reached so far, it would have meant unceasing war. Even with his principal enemies fallen, too many people opposed him. If he lost, then all would be lost. If he won she would be dragged to Tuscolo, with all its whispers and intrigues, and the unceasing games of patronage that she knew she would loathe.

Turning in her sheets, fretting, trying to find a position in which she was comfortable, she had remembered these pages from other times in the library. Her sleeplessness had brought her to read them; to confirm that Ulfin was, or thought he was, the very last of the male line of the first kings. CALYN, ULFIN, PAIGAN. And his brothers were dead, and his child rested within her. He had never told her.

She lifted her eyes from the page. Outside a flight of doves – six or seven of them – whirred past the window. Voices called to one another from the towers and rooftops as the garrison looked out in the dawn. 'All clear, all clear. Stand down.' Men were walking along the battlements above her head, laughing and talking the short, idiot talk that soldiers always talk. The baby squirmed; she shifted. She could hear Orani moving about in the corridor, and someone, released from watch, settled to play his pipe in those long, breathy notes that would speak to her for ever of Tarceny and the hills.

Ulfin had refused. Whatever he thought the right of it was, he had known better than to advance his claim. Now, with these victories, there would surely be a chance of peace, and he would come home. She must start again on the robe, which had lain untouched for most of the summer.

She began to scroll the sheets up again, noticing as she did so that the number of princes at the head of the first page was not seven, but eight. On the right-hand end of the row was a name: PAIGAN. It was the same name as Ulfin's brother. There was no line of descent at all.

'Orani! Orani!'

She blundered in the darkness. Heaven knew what time it was. It might be midnight, or an hour before the late December dawn. Her foot struck something and she staggered against the side of the bed.

'Orani!'

There were sounds in the corridor. Hands tried the door to the outer chamber. It shook. Orani's voice came, muffled by wood.

'It's bolted!'

Of course it was. Phaedra fastened it every night now,

198

after a dream of a shape in the corridor a week ago. She felt her way across the huge space to the door and struggled with the bolts. As she was drawing the second one, the pain came again. She sank to the floor, bending double. The door jerked inwards and struck her thigh. Orani stood over her in the darkness.

'Lady?'

It was a moment before Phaedra could speak.

'What's happening? Orani – what's happening to me?'

She knew of course. It was the child. She had been waiting, day in, day out under the grey skies of November and December for something to begin. Now it had – but what? Was it birth? Was it miscarriage? Were these pains just something that would happen, and go away, and come again? No one had told her. She had not dared to ask.

Was it the beginning of death?

'Ulfin!'

Orani's hands were under her armpits. Together they staggered back into the bedchamber. Phaedra kneeled on the rug, with her face buried in her arms, while Orani muttered and felt among the bedclothes.

'Your waters gone, lady?'

'I— What?'

'You don't know, do you? Not to mind – you would if they had done. Don't seem to, at least not on the sheets here. Need light.'

'It hurts!'

'Is it hurting now?'

'Yes – no. It will in a minute. What is it?'

For answer the older woman ran her wrinkled hand up Phaedra's thigh to her swollen belly. Phaedra opened her mouth at the indignity, but said nothing. She knew she needed help. They sat together in the darkness, waiting. Then Phaedra gasped. The pain grew. It went on. She shuddered, and heard herself whimper.

'Little thing's in a hurry to get out, though,' Orani was saying as she withdrew her hand. 'That's what it is. Thought it might come tonight, for Puri's hens all laid together yesterday, even the old one. An' your feet are small, lady, so it'll hurt before it's better.' She rose to her feet. 'Need a light.'

'Send for my lord!'

Ulfin was two hundred miles away, on his way to or from a parley in the Seabord.

'Need a light, and some help. You bide there, lady. It won't come before I'm back.'

Phaedra heard her leave the room. She stifled another sob. She knew she should be brave. Whatever happened now would happen as the Angels willed it. But there was nothing in her to be brave with. She knew nothing about birth. No one had told her about it, and she had never wanted to ask. She had not expected these terrible spasms. She thought that Orani was right, and that the end would not come for some hours. Yet she had no faith in the maid's rambling birthlore.

She might go down into red darkness before Ulfin heard of it, before the messenger even left the castle. She, the start of all the Kingdom's troubles, would disappear in a meaningless end; and the Kingdom would war on, oblivious.

Then the pain began again.

Orani returned, her face lit from beneath by a lamp,

so that her nose and chin cast demonic shadows up her eyes and cheeks. There were other faces with her. Other people, people of the castle, were being brought into their lady's bedchamber to see her shudder and shriek in grossness upon her pillows. Phaedra cared, but did not care enough to try to send them away. She bit her wrist when the pain returned, and it helped. She did it again and again, until they noticed and bound it and gave her a leather strap to bite, which was not half as good. There was warmth and wetness over her legs and belly, and warm, wet cloths mopping at her face. She began to scream.

Sometime when the grey light was seeping in through the window, she knew she was about to die. She tried to say prayers between her spasms, but the pain came relentlessly and stopped all the words, so that she had to begin again. She opened her eyes and looked up at Orani.

'Fetch the priest!' she gasped.

'Still a while. You're doing not bad, lady. Puri's said she's seen better an' I say I've seen worse . . .'

Either she had not heard or she had not understood.

'The grey priest! The one who married us!' *Ulfin, where are you?*

'Him! You don't want *him*. You'll be fine with us. And we'll need a wet nurse, though maybe you don't want to think of that now.'

'The priest!'

Whatever else Orani said vanished in Phaedra's rush of agony. She could not think. She could only wait for the next. And the next.

And so on, for hours.

There was a strange time, when the pain ended and the weight left her. It was daylight. The sheets were bloody, and her legs were bloody, and women gathered and showed her a bundle of white cloth, in the middle of which was a small face of red and purple with its eyes shut and its mouth open in a thin, wheezing bawl that went on and on.

'Boy!' cried the women excitedly. 'Boy!' And someone ran out and down the corridor, calling.

Phaedra dragged herself to a sitting position on the bed and peered at the bundle. The eyes remained fast shut. There was a thick, black thatch of hair upon its head. She took it gingerly.

'So light!' she gasped. 'Is this all there is?'

Someone laughed. They were all laughing. And outside, voices were calling. A bell was ringing. Horns and trumpets sounded from the walls as Tarceny declared its heir to the world. The purple mouth opened and wheezed. The limbs, like rolled cloths, moved feebly.

'Hush, baby,' said Phaedra, rocking it. 'Hush, little thing. You can rest now.'

XI

Angels and Shadows

he woke suddenly in the chair in her living chamber. It was deep night. The lamp at her hand had sunk to the merest green spark. The air was close. Some sound had roused her from her dreams.

She stirred. She was still fully dressed. In her hands she held the great belt she was making to go with the robe. She had been trying to decide whether it should be re-made with eight precious stones, one for each of the first princes. She must have fallen asleep over it. She remembered dreaming that it had become a great chain of shimmering water, which bound Ulfin and her together as they lay among the brown rocks. Ulfin had wept and pulled at it, but he had remained bound as the shadows of his enemies crawled from the boulders to reach him. Then the dream had changed, or she had moved into another dream; because Ulfin had gone, and the shadows had gathered around the cradle that held her son. She remembered long, clawed fingers which had reached in over the cradle's rim as the baby had squirmed in his swaddles and tried to cry.

Her heart was lurching, and she felt sick. She listened.

There had been a sound. It had entered her dream. It had been – it might have been – footsteps in the corridor.

She got to her feet, and picked up the lamp. The oil was nearly gone.

People in the corridor, at this hour? Orani, still awake and wondering if her mistress was ever coming to bed? Unlikely.

Then, unmistakably, she heard the sound of a door-latch lifting. It came from the corridor. It must have been the latch of the library.

The library was where the baby now slept, with Orani and his new wet nurse. She fumbled her way to the door of her room, drew the bolts and stepped out into the corridor. There was almost no light. She lifted her lamp, but it told her nothing.

'Who's there?'

There was a movement, she thought, in the darkness by the library door. For a moment she had the impression that the shadows had shapes.

'Who's there?' she said, advancing with her feeble spark in her hand.

She reached the library door. There was no one there.

She thought there might have been a footstep – but only one. Even then, her hearing had been confused by her own movements.

The library door was slightly ajar.

She leaned on the door-frame, and peered in. She heard the rumbles and sighs of Orani, sleeping on the floor. There was no sound at all from her niece Eridi, the wet nurse, or from the cot that held the child. There was no one else there.

Holding her breath, trying to still the rustle of her clothes, she crept forward to the cot. The baby was there – quite still. She bent closer. There was still no sound. She put out her hand, and drew it back. She did not dare to touch him. So she hovered and waited through the long, impossible moments for the breaths that did not come.

Then, with her head only a few inches above the swaddles, she heard it at last: the faintest sigh. And again. And again. The child lived softly in the little locked world of his sleep.

Phaedra straightened in the dark room, and lifted her lamp. One of the sleepers had raised her head from her pillow and was looking at her. It was Eridi – the new girl, whom the Orani had brought to the castle when the baby was born.

'Did anyone come in here?' Phaedra whispered.

Eridi took a moment to reply. Phaedra crouched at her bedside, holding the lamp so that they could see each other's faces.

'Who came in?' she asked again.

'You did, lady.'

In Eridi the mixing of hill-blood and Kingdom had produced a big face, with a straight strong nose like a mare's. Her eyes were dark. Now they seemed like black marble as they stared at Phaedra.

'Before that.'

'No, lady.'

'You heard the door open?'

'I heard you call, lady.'

The girl was afraid, Phaedra thought. She had seen

something, or heard something. Now she did not know what to say. This house must be very strange to her. Even Phaedra herself must be frightening to a hill girl who had only ever lived in a hut.

'It was some watchman, wandering where he should not,' Phaedra said, as she rose to leave. It was not reassuring, but it was the best she could think of. 'Maybe he was drunk. Keep your door bolted, anyway. I'll have the man found and whipped in the morning.'

She went out again, and waited by the door while Eridi rose and slid the old bolt home on the inside. Then she moved carefully up and down the corridor, looking in doorways and the curling stairwell by the chapel entrance. Her light showed her nothing.

There had been more than one of them; and she did not think they were guards. One might have been a man. The other, she thought, had been shorter. She had heard one set of footsteps. She wished she had heard two.

There was a dank feel to the air, as though she were walking by the edge of a stagnant pool.

She was tired – aching with it. And there was no one here now.

At last she returned to her chamber and slid the bolts home on her own door. She set her useless lamp on the table. There seemed to be nothing she could do. She must speak to Ulfin. It was a comfort to know that he must already be close: camped somewhere on the road up from Aclete. He would be home tomorrow. All she had to do was wait until he came. From the windows drifted the scent of the moon roses, opening in their masses on the slopes below. It must be nearly dawn. She was exhausted. She needed to sleep, if she could.

And still she had not finished the robe. She had meant to complete it tonight, working as late as necessary, so that it would be ready for him in the morning. But the later she worked, the less satisfied she had become with what she had done. The belt, the bad hem, the lack of colour in the trimmings: it would not be ready in time for his arrival in the evening. She must hide it, and finish it at leisure for the time when he came home for good. He would guess what she was up to, if he looked at the accounts; but to her tired brain it did not matter. Tomorrow her gift for him must be their son.

Ulfin strode up the steps from the courtyard. His knights followed in a clatter of armed heels. From the shade of the hall door, Phaedra saw, with a suddenness as if she had forgotten, how tall among the men he stood. Her limbs were hollow with tiredness, but she could feel herself smiling and her heart lifting suddenly at the sight of him. He was home.

'My lord.' She curtsied.

'My lady.'

He seemed leaner than she remembered. There was a hardness about his eyes. She wondered if he was as tired as she was.

'My lord, your son also waits to greet you home.'

'Where is he?'

She turned to the nurse, who handed her the bundle. The baby was awake and quiet.

'I'm sorry, Phaedra,' said Ulfin. 'Give him to me.'

She felt no fear as he shut his eyes and took the baby. He turned in the hall doorway. She thought he would lift the child high to be cheered by his knights on the lower steps. Instead he paused a further moment, and began to descend. The armed men hesitated. Was he coming down to them, or passing through them? He was passing through. They were letting him through. Where was he taking the child? In the courtyard his horse stood, saddled.

White-haired Orcrim, Ulfin's war captain, stepped up to meet him, in mail from foot to chin.

'Hail to the heir of Tarceny,' he said, in a voice pitched to carry to the whole crowd. 'And he has your brother's look, my lord.'

Ulfin glanced again at the child. He might have stepped around Orcrim, but now the knights were crowding up to him and he could not move. From the higher steps Phaedra could just see the face of her son, cradled amid the forest of armed men, turning from head to grinning head around him. The strange men with their big voices held no alarm for him, and he blessed them all with his smile.

'Sir,' she called. 'I would name him Ambrose Umbriel.'

Again she sensed his hesitation. Yet there was so little she could do for Father now.

'He has your young brother's look, my lord,' said Caw clearly, at his elbow.

Why were these fighters suddenly so insistent about a baby's looks? And it was nonsense. He was round-headed and red-faced, happy for the moment; but in a second he would start to cry.

'Yes,' said Ulfin at last. There was a queer note in his voice. 'Yes, maybe he has.'

208

Abruptly he passed the babe into the mailed arms around him, and was pushing through his knights and down the steps. Beyond the crowd she heard his voice calling for his horse to be unsaddled.

The baby began to cry. She prised him from the embrace of an embarrassed knight, rocked and tried to hush him, and felt embarrassed herself with Orcrim and Hob and all the other knights watching her do it. Eridi was at her shoulder, reaching for the child, and Phaedra let him go. As his wails receded she faced the knot of armed men and found words to welcome them back to the home that had been hers for barely a year and that they had known for a lifetime. She led them up the steps and into the hall, where stable-cups were brought to the hearth. In the absence of both father and son they drank to the health of the line. No one seemed to know what to say, so the same things were said again and again. Orcrim was silent: his mouth a short, straight line, his foot prodding absently at the irregular black stones around the hearth. Something was bothering him. Caw was by the door. She saw a look pass between them, as if they were men who had conspired in something and did not know whether it would work. Caw peered out of the door again, pulled a face and gave a half-shrug. Ulfin was not coming in. At least not yet.

Twenty minutes later, when the last of the knights had bowed and clashed off to their quarters, she went herself to the door. The sun was down. Caw was crouching on the top of the steps. He grunted, and pointed with his chin. A figure was pacing the west wall, high above their heads. It did not look their way.

Phaedra crossed the courtyard to the wall steps and climbed to the parapet. The sky was clear, a deep blue overhead, brightening to green as it reached down to touch the jagged black line of the distant mountains. The air was thick with the flavour of moon roses. He was standing on the north-west fighting platform, facing out towards the hills and the last light of the evening. She heard him laugh: a sharp, barking sound, as if some restraint had given suddenly before a torrent within him. His hands were flung high above his head. For a moment he stood there. Then he turned to retrace his steps, and she ran to him along the wall.

'I had to think,' said Ulfin.

'Will you not tell me?'

They were walking in the fountain court under the moon. The water was still, but lights had been set at intervals along the paths to glow and flicker in the night air. From the hall came the sounds of the supper they had left, with the knights at the long tables bragging to Caw of their exploits and saying how good it was to be home.

'Why the name you chose for the child? Ambrose for your father, but—'

'Umbriel?'

Gabriel stood for Glory, Raphael for Compassion. Michael, a favourite of knightly families, meant Courage. Phaedra had chosen Truth for her son. Ulfin would know that. He was asking something else.

'I wanted – well, a protector for him.'

'A protector.'

A deep breath. Even as she began to speak, she did not know quite what she would say.

210

'I – am frightened, Ulfin. I have a feeling – I think I see things. At first it was not much – loneliness and night-fears. But now I have Ambrose, and I am frightened for him.'

'Fear may show you enemies where none exist.'

'Ulfin, do not play with me! How many times a day do you think I tell myself that? But I *am* frightened. I thought I would die with Ambrose. I thought you would die in the fighting. I do not see enough of you. If you cannot be at home, even a dream would help. We used to talk long, and drink water together—'

'Hush!'

'Now it is a few words, snatched here and there, and months between!'

She stared at him, and saw how he looked at her.

'There will be no more dreams.'

'Why not?'

'Because – because we have been in dangerous places, Phaedra.'

'I do not know if I have or have not.'

'You bear the mark. What is it you fear? What have you seen?'

'I do not know! I do not know if they are men, or if there are more than two. I have seen two. But I don't know if they are there at all! They are robed. Like—'

'Was there any smell?'

She shook her head slowly. His eyes held hers. After a moment he spoke again, so softly she could hardly hear.

'We have been in dangerous places, Phaedra. If we had not, we should never have come together across the water. Now, for our own sakes, we must no longer. And as

211

we cease to – to do what we have been doing, then these things, if they are indeed there, may cease too.'

'I want you home.'

'Phaedra, I cannot. I have started something across the water that I must finish, or there will be no peace until they finish with me. I have some bitter enemies now. Develin's widow, for one; some of Seguin's party; Baldwin's sons. And there are others, in the Seabord and elsewhere, who have never loved an overlord and will do their best to see that none arises. It will be a hard time, and it will mean danger for you too. And for Ambrose. Especially for Ambrose. You must guard him well. Are you listening, Phaedra?'

'Yes,' she said miserably.

'They suspect me, in the Kingdom. They suspect what I – and you – have been doing. But they do not know. They must not. So long as it is just suspicion, then men who wish to ally themselves with me can ignore the talk of witchcraft. Powers like Jent may stay neutral, rather than league themselves against me. If Jent came in against us now it would be deadly. They must not know . . .

'So. I shall lay – certain things – in the chest in the War Room. Locked, and I will keep the key. I will tell this to no one but you. Not to Caw, not to Orcrim – they guess, but they too do not truly know. It is better if they do not. Therefore do not suffer any to enter the room or to know what lies there. And be careful. Be careful.'

She nodded. He was talking about the Cup. He was not going to use it any more, because it was too dangerous. And there would be no more dreams.

He watched her for a moment more, then patted her on the shoulder.

'And the name. There is no wrong in it – not in either of them. But the combination has a significance that you do not seem to have realized. Think of the initials, A and U.'

'It means nothing to me.'

'It will to others, I think. You know that after the Sea Kings – Wulfram and his sons – their descendants became the High Kings. Their rule ran all across the land and under them there was peace. Now we have the War Kings. Their dynasties are short, their strength is diminished, and their rule is marked by rebellion and failure. So. Do you remember the name of the last High King?'

'Aurelian.'

'His seals bore the first two letters of his name embossed upon them. A and U. In the ancient tongue they are the first two letters of the word for gold. The time of the High Kings was a golden age, and after Aurelian was betrayed to his death the crown passed out of direct descent, and that age came to an end.'

'Ambrose is not going to be King,' she said quietly. 'You have already refused the crown, Ulfin.'

'I have. I have also made it plain that the Kingdom must strive to return itself to how things were under the High Kings. So many people still think that the crown is precisely what I want. And' – he chuckled – 'and the more aware of them will see proof in the name you have chosen. They'll think you did it on purpose. But then they think— Well, let us not trouble what they think, so long as they cannot show proof. Meanwhile, I have a gift for my son. It may make things easier. Come.'

He led her back into the hall. The tables were empty

now, except for the kitchen boys clearing the dishes. A few knights lounged before the hearth and looked up as they came in. Ulfin crossed to the foot of the gallery stairs, where various bundles had been laid. He took from one a small wooden box, which rattled in his hand, and opened the lid. Inside was a pile of circular white stones, milled smooth, bulging in the centre and thin at the edges, so that they might fit well into a child's grip.

'These will make good playthings, I think. Try not to let him lose any, for I am fond of them. There are thirty-one.'

'I have been wondering what happened to your toys.'

'They were not meant for toys. They were cut by Calyn, my elder brother. We were estranged for years before he died, but when he lay in his last sickness in the Seabord, he had them sent to me. I've carried these with me ever since.'

'They look like chequer pieces.'

'They are not chequer pieces either. But that reminds me. Do you still play chess?'

At last she smiled slowly, and felt her skin blush. 'I have been practising. But Ulfin, it is late.'

'One quick game.'

She smiled again. 'It may not be as quick as you think.'

She woke on a grey and dreary February morning, and the pillow beside her was empty. He had warned her that he found it easiest to part while she was still sleeping. Now he was gone, risen before the light came, and vanished into rumours of war.

It was harder this time, far harder than it had been before.

He had said that Caw was to keep an armed man posted over Ambrose at all times. Then the damp weather brought chills, and struck four of the garrison down with fever. There were no longer enough men to mount a full war-watch on the walls. Caw lengthened the duties, but the guards became tired and slept at their posts. If Ulfin had been there Caw might have driven his guards to the limit and never breathed a word. But he told Phaedra outright that he saw no reason why his men should rock cradles. In the end she moved Ambrose's day room to the big chamber below the fighting platform in the north-east tower. This meant the servants had to carry enough firewood up the stairs every day to keep the room warm, but also that the soldiers on the roof, which was the castle's main watch-point, were close enough to be deemed to be guarding Ambrose as well, thus releasing an extra man for other duties. (It also meant, from Phaedra's point of view, that Caw would not be tempted to put a half-sick man in the post, to sit and sweat his fevers over her precious son.) She found a gong in the living quarters, so that Eridi or whoever was with Ambrose might summon the guards in an emergency.

Eridi was dubious. She had enjoyed having the company of a man all day.

'What am I to do if an assassin comes, lady?'

'Bang the gong and sell your life dearly,' said Phaedra. 'Just remember to bang the gong first.'

Phaedra kept the iron key to the locked War Room in her jewel box, nestling among the gaudy brooches and rings. Every few days, at times when others were busy, she took it and climbed the stairs past the chapel to see if all was still well. The carved chest rested on the War-Room table with its lid closed. Even without moving it or trying to lift it, she thought she could sense things weighing within. Her fingertips stroked the dark carvings and prised idly at the locked lid. It was shut fast. The nights and days passed silently, and the wood was cold.

She shivered.

The touchstone of Ulfin's presence was gone. All the questions she had not needed to ask while he was with her were crowding in again. Doubts wormed in her mind: about the war, and the chances for peace; about her thought that she was spied upon; about the 'dangerous places' where they had drunk the water and walked among the rocks for so many years. Over the early Easter, she fasted and kneeled in the chapel. She listed her fears before the silent Angels, murmuring in the quiet room above the sounds of the armed watch around her, the calls and the clink of mail, and the hollow whispers within.

A man from Mistress Massey at Aclete waited for her in the hall, with a letter that bore the seal of the Dancing Hound. Evalia diManey was on her way to Jent on pilgrimage. She would land at Aclete on her way home, and come up the road to Tarceny to her Dear Friend, whom she had not seen for a full year.

There was no enquiry whether it was convenient, and little by way of respectful greeting from the woman of a dog-knight to the lady of one of the highest lords in the land. The boldness of it was striking. Of course, hospitality could not be refused to a gentlewoman on pilgrimage. Phaedra thought of writing that there was contagious sickness at the castle, but she had never told such an outright lie in her life. So she pursed her lips and begged Caw to dispatch the minimum escort to Aclete. And a week later she stood at the top of the hall steps, with the shadow of the doorway across her back; and Evalia diManey rode into the inner bailey, waving from the saddle.

'Well,' said Evalia, as they greeted one another on the steps. 'They tell me that you have had a child, though I could not believe it to look at you.'

'You are kind,' said Phaedra, 'if, I think, less than truthful today. And you have not changed by a hair. It is good of you to come so far out of your way to comfort a lonely woman in her home.'

'Not so lonely now. Where is he?'

'Asleep.' Why was she so eager to lay eyes on Ambrose? 'We shall not see him again until tomorrow.'

'Then I must contain myself for a few hours longer. In the meantime' – Evalia glanced over her shoulder, to where her tiny retinue were dismounting, unloading and leading their beasts away – 'in the meantime I have brought you a present.'

The man climbing the steps towards them was the secretary of the Bishop of Jent.

'You were rather cold to him,' said Evalia, as they walked together on the west wall the next morning, while the priest was at prayer.

It was a bright day, and there was birdsong, and a light breeze flapped the standards against the flagpoles above their heads. Below them was the silent hillside of lank grass and massed flowers, and away to the west the low cloud-shapes that were the mountains.

'Cold? Was I?'

'You hardly spoke to him at all. Poor Martin. He was telling me he had pressed His Grace most particularly for this post.'

'It surprises me. I think we displeased each other in Jent.'

'Perhaps he does not remember that the same way. However, if you are wondering why he left such an excellent position to come here, so did I.'

It was precisely what Phaedra had been wondering. Chaplain to a noble house was a good place, but to be secretary to a bishop must be even better.

'I will tell you. He wants to go among the hill people. The heathen.'

'Heathen? The March was converted long ago!'

'No, the real heathen, beyond the March. My dear, I have brought you a young Tuchred.'

'He wants to go into the mountains?'

'He is hoping you will release him at times. I hope you will too. He is very earnest.'

It fitted with what she remembered of him, and this far it was plausible.

'So long as he does not require much escort,' she murmured.

Jent, an influential player, had taken neither side in the troubles of the Kingdom. So this Martin might indeed be all he appeared to be. He might even be a sign that His Grace wished to please the more successful party in the struggles. To refuse the bishop's own secretary would be a public insult to a powerful man, and Ulfin's enemies would be quick to ask why. Yet she remembered the bishop's hostility towards Ulfin, shown even before the raid on Trant. She remembered his implausible plea that he had no one around him at that time. She could see now that he must have understood at once how she planned to use any priest he gave her to strengthen her case against her father and the King. A year later he had chosen to send her his own secretary – his creature, not hers. To accept this man into the household would be a leap in a dark place.

Her eyes lingered on a shadow, impenetrable, in the window of the western tower. Nothing moved there.

Ulfin had warned her to be careful. She would have to watch closely what this man did at Tarceny. If he wanted to be away from the household for long periods, well, it would not be difficult to grant him leave – so long as he truly went into the wild mountains and was not spying around the March. She would need to make sure. If either bishop or secretary showed a false sign, then insult there would be.

She felt so much older than the girl who, a year ago, had gone in her silks to beg His Grace for a priest.

'Well,' she said at last. 'May the Angels be pleased to help us, so long as he chooses to be among us.' And if that sounded trite, their help was no more than she truly wished for.

Evalia did not reply at once. She was looking ahead of her into the great spaces of Tarceny, with the little frown of thought upon her smooth face.

'The help of Angels is a rare thing,' she said. 'Of course you hear often of new appearances or wonders, seen by someone you have never heard of. No doubt they are grown many times in the telling. I have seen nothing with my own eyes, and nor, I suppose, have you. But diManey thinks he has seen an Angel. And the strangeness is that you were there.'

'Your husband?'

'Yes . . . yes, my husband . . . Do you know – I began by hating him? When I came out of my fright and was able to think for myself, I mean, which was not for days after the trial. I thought he had fallen in love with me as I walked past. A bumpkin panting so hard for a pretty woman that he would risk death for it! Oh . . .'

'It is what some of us thought, in the gallery.'

'When I knew him better I saw there was more to it. Of course he was outraged by the way they had arranged the ordeal to kill me, but if it had been just that he'd still have been wondering what to do when they cut my head off. He is a *good* man. Once you see beyond his looks there is no fault you can lay at his door. If there is a fault it is in me. If I cannot be at peace in diManey's house at Chatterfall, then where in all the world? But he is not . . .'

Not? Not who?

'It took me months to prise it out of him. He says there was one, dressed roughly, who appeared beside him in the throng while the accusations were being read out. You know that Raphael is portrayed on altars in a peasant's or a pilgrim's garb. Adam does not remember what the pilgrim said. He says he only remembers that when the man had spoken he felt he knew exactly what to do.'

Phaedra nodded. She was worrying at that other, elusive thought which teased in the back of her mind; a name unspoken, bitten off a second before it was uttered. Ulfin? That was the contrast; but Evalia had never met Ulfin (nor did Phaedra want her to). No, it would have been the man that Evalia herself had loved, and his name had been stifled because it was too painful – because she had remembered that it would not mean anything to Phaedra. Or perhaps because it would . . .

'Adam says he seemed to be an old man, a priest in a long, pale robe and hood.'

Evalia looked sideways at her. She knew what she had said.

Her words were like doors that opened on dark corridors that led in bewildering directions. She seemed to be so much older than Phaedra, and cleverer. Phaedra did not know which way to turn.

Be careful. *Be careful.*

'So he stepped out in front of all those people and went up to the swords. I do not know what he thought would happen – whether God would give him the victory, or the King quail before the revealed Truth, or whether he would die then and there because he had been told to. The one thing he had forgotten was that his house was under the King's protection.'

'It became clear that there was something like that to it,' said Phaedra.

'His father had been crippled in the King's service. When you think about it, the King must have scores of obligations like that – to look after so-and-so's children here, and somebody's widow there, as if he did not have enough to do looking after the Kingdom as a whole. A king must need a memory deep as a well to keep them all.'

Deep within Phaedra's memory a name stirred. Calyn.

Calyn? She had heard Evalia cry it aloud in the night, in the lodge at Baer. And had not Lackmere said it too, all those years ago at the round table in the inn? Or was she overlaying on both memories a name she already knew?

Evalia was waiting for her to speak. Phaedra knew she was expected to follow up the story, and that the best thing would be to do so with a witless stream of questions, as if she were a devout woman who had entirely missed the meaning Evalia had intended. She could not put the thoughts together. She stood in that air of sunlight, birdsong and moon roses, staring firmly into the distance, saying nothing because she could not think what to say.

Her companion turned away with a movement of her shoulder which said, *Well, if you won't . . .*

'I have been waiting to ask if you know what is the meaning of the shape on the Moon,' said Evalia at length. 'It has such a sinister look.'

Phaedra looked up at the limp banners, and felt her face draw into a smile. 'Sometimes it is one thing, and sometimes it is another,' she heard herself answer. 'Different hands have their own interpretations. I believe some have held it to be a moon rose, which has one black petal and the rest white. My lord's father ordered that it should be a bat wing.'

'What a thing to wear on your badge!'

'Such was the man . . .'

Words were coming at last to give her the space she needed, with the force of the anger she nursed at that evil lord.

'Such was the man,' she said. 'He lived in armour and thought of nothing beyond his stomach and his sword. There was once a settlement below these walls, but there is none now. Who would rest so close to a lord that might burn the roof-trees of his own people for a whim? And he tried to raise his sons in his image. I have long wondered why there were no playthings in the house from the boyhood of my lord and his brothers. But my lord has told me that they were allowed no toys but wooden swords . . .'

Now it was her turn to watch sidelong, for a change in Evalia's face.

My first toy was the head of a man, Ulfin had said at last, when she had pressed him on this the night before his departure. *All dried with the eyes gone. Some enemy or unfortunate that we rolled around between us. I remember it. I wish I did not.*

She saw Evalia's eyes flicker. The woman knew what she had left out: that grisly plaything the lord had given to please his sons. Calyn had remembered it too, and how could he not? Calyn of the Moon Rose, Ulfin's elder brother. Perhaps the same sighs had escaped him when his lover had led him to speak of his ruined childhood.

'Now the old lord is gone,' Phaedra went on, as levelly as she could. 'Dead at his hearth after a life of wrong-doing. The Moon is free of his stain. As for my lord, he says he has no fixed idea what the shape should signify. Sometimes he thinks it is a mouth – that the Moon is pulling a face at what it sees here in the world.'

'I like that no better.'

'I think *he* likes that it may be one thing or it may be another. The Moon sees everything, and yet what it sees

leaves it uncertain. That is why it is the Doubting Moon
– the secret of truth.'

'Meaning the more you know, the more you know you
don't know.'

'Indeed.'

Indeed. A few moments ago this woman's poise had
wavered – unbalanced by the sudden weight that had stirred
at Phaedra's word 'husband'. For a moment she had become
again the inward, unhappy woman from their journey the
year before. Now she was as smooth as the surface of a lake;
as bold and well-spoken as when she had ridden in through
the gates, and yet almost certainly lying, or at least hiding
things that it would have been honest to tell. What of it?
That she was hiding her past with Calyn proved nothing.
But it was an important truth, and she was concealing it,
even as she made her gambit about the pale priest.

For that matter, her whole story about diManey might
be a concoction. Phaedra had herself given her all the
material she would have needed, when they passed the
priest in the litter. So! She would take more care in what
she said. And when the woman was gone, she might think
again about this Martin who had been served up to her
so suddenly—

A movement at the turret door caught her eye.

'. . . A man whose mind leans to uncommon places,'
Evalia was saying. 'He must be a strange one to live with.
You must love him very much, for all that I think he may
have done a foul thing to you. What is the matter?'

Phaedra turned back from the turret to meet her look
carefully, keeping her face blank. Distracted once again,
she had barely heard what Evalia had just said.

'It is nothing,' she replied. 'I think – shall . . . shall we see if Ambrose is awake? I would like to see how he is.'

'Is anything the matter? Can I help?'

Phaedra made herself smile as she shook her head. 'It is nothing,' she said.

XII

On the Stair

t was nothing. It was always nothing; when she looked round, or raised her light, or turned the corner of the corridor. The nooks and passageways were empty. They were frames of wood and stone and plaster that held no image and perhaps only the faintest smell – so thin that she could not have described it. She would wait and listen, staring at the blank walls for some sign.

Nothing.

The incidents were fleeting, gone almost before she was aware of them. Her mind was playing tricks. And she remembered herself as a nine-year-old girl (half her life ago now), starting and turning when a man's voice spoke at her side; and when she turned, he would be gone. But he had been real. He had been Ulfin. And this . . . Ulfin had not seemed able to say.

As a girl, she had learned not to look. She had found that if she kept her eyes on some point ahead of her, he would remain, and could be spoken to. She had believed he was her brother Guy at first, who had not after all allowed death to make him abandon her. And by the time she had understood that he was not, she had already begun to trust him. This was different. She could not be still when she felt the presence of the watchers. To sit, watching her fingertips, thinking that one of *them* might be behind her – she neither dared nor wished to dare. It was better to look, knowing as she did so that the shadows would be empty. Let them trick her. Let them mock her, so long as the looking drove them away.

There was no one to talk to. She did not want to frighten Orani or Eridi: she could not afford to lose either of them. She dared not trust Brother Martin. As for Caw, if he had seen anything he gave no sign of it, although she watched him closely at chess and at other times. Perhaps the things were as invisible to him as the pale priest had been to Vermian on the road from Baer. Or perhaps he had indeed seen something, but was pretending he had not. Why? What did he guess? To speak to him would be to ask for help – even to be believed. She was not sure he would grant her either. He was more sullen than ever now that Ulfin had come and gone again, and left him once more in the post he hated.

So she spoke to no one of her trouble. She was Trant's daughter and Ulfin's wife – the Lady of Tarceny, who should not be afraid. If the shapes she saw meant harm, then maybe they could be harmed, and she had armed men within call who could do harm if it came to that. For now, what she was seeing (if she was seeing it) had as much substance as the flick of a bat's wings. They troubled her pulse-rate; nothing more. She could school that. She could treat them as if they were the insects that swarmed from the hillsides. Madness came from the

227

blood, she had heard. There was none, surely, in *her* family.

They came and went at the edge of the light. Very well; there would be more light. She complained of eye-ache in the lengthening dusks of summer, and had lamps placed in every corridor and around every room in use in the living quarters. Forty rushes burned every evening in the great hall, and the night bugs from the dewy hillsides wove and died among them in hundreds. She watched the servants from the corner of her eye for signs that they thought her wasteful, or deranged, or heedless of the risks of fire. And perhaps she saw it. But she thought that they too were glad of the light. Rushes were replaced as they burned low. Doors on dark, unused rooms were shut, and kept locked.

Ulfin did not come home that summer. Instead, he wrote more frequently than he had done (perhaps because he was writing at the same time to Caw, for money and more soldiers). The malady of the Kingdom persisted. He held the Segne, the heart of the land. She heard that nobles had rallied to him. But to north and east and south other powers watched. Some were openly hostile – especially in the south, where the Develin was strong. Elsewhere, the barons used the weakness of the Kingdom to do as they would; and who was to stop them? The Fount of the Law was dry.

Raid was followed by counter-raid. The strength of some lord was tested, and his villages withered in fire. Orcrim hammered interminably at the gates of Bay, but the household that had been shamed at Trant crouched behind its walls and would not yield. In June Pemini fell, bloodily, to some of Ulfin's allies, and the town was sacked. Phaedra sent anxiously for news of Maria when she heard, but no answer came.

One September morning, more news arrived.

Phaedra was on the north-west fighting platform, looking out over the hills and groves of Tarceny. She was remembering the view from the walls of Trant, which would have been all busy with people harvesting in the fields at this time of the year, when she heard a footstep behind her, and a man spoke.

'My lady?'

It was Martin, the priest, standing alone on the fighting platform.

'Good morning to you, Martin.'

She thought, once again, that she should find time to ask him how he liked his post, and to talk about what more he might do here. She felt guilty that she had so little for him to be busy with, other than leading in prayer the house-servants and kitchen staff and those others of the household whom she could compel to attend chapel. At the same time she still wanted to watch how he did, and in particular how often he wrote letters to Jent and other places. He was correct and polite, but she could neither bring herself to trust him, nor decide that she definitely did not trust him. It had crossed her mind more than once that she should have his letters intercepted, but she had done nothing. He remained a stranger.

'I heard the men-at-arms talking in the courtyard, my lady. Word from the Segne has come to Caw. I thought perhaps it would concern you.'

Dear Angels, what had happened now?

'I think you were acquainted with Elward of Baldwin, my lady?'

'Yes.' Elward. Young, handsome, high-born . . . She remembered him clearly, standing before Father's chair. 'I almost agreed to marry him.'

'Then I – I grieve to tell you, my lady, that he is dead.'

Dead.

Down below the walls, the olive groves whispered in the light breeze. Once, she might have thought that a man like that could not possibly die. She knew better now.

'Did we do it?'

'My lady?'

She sighed. Of course *we* had. *We* seemed to do everything.

'How did it happen, Martin?'

'He must have been with Septimus in Develin. Early this month he rode north with a small troop. He slipped past my lord's force at Tuscolo and arrived unexpectedly at Baldwin. The gates were open – there were harvest trains coming and going – and they got in. But they were too few, and the garrison was alert. They were cut down in the courtyard – Elward and all his followers.'

Cut down in the courtyard: in the courtyard where he must have played as a child. He deserved to have loved someone else.

'He was an honourable man, Martin. I knew no wrong of him.'

And yet another love would not have saved him, because he had also loved the house where he would have brought her to live. He must have hated the thought that the flag of Tarceny had been placed so easily on his walls.

He would have brooded on it, during all the dreary months of campaigning, until he could no longer bear to wait for the chances of war to return him home. Then he had taken such as would follow him, to his end and theirs.

'We should say a rite for him, Martin.'

'At noon? Will you summon the house?'

'No, now. Just you and I.'

He led the way down to the chapel (so much cleaner, lighter and better ordered than it had been before he had come). There they kneeled side by side for a long hour before the Flame. She followed him through the prayers and responses, and listened to his address to Umbriel, in which he prayed the Watcher of Heaven to count twice every good deed the dead man had done. He said the ancient words as though they were new, and marked each appeal with a silence, in which she could almost feel the air drawn past her cheek to the stillness of his prayer.

Afterwards they walked the fountain court together, among the scents of mint and thyme.

'My thoughts are with his mother,' Phaedra said. 'To have lost both her husband and now her son . . . As a wife and mother myself it seems to me a grief beyond bearing. I cannot think that the Angels intend such things.'

'I doubt that they do, my lady.'

'Then why do they permit them to happen – and to the best among us?'

'The Angels do not permit, nor do they prevent. That is not their charge. Nor do they busy themselves only for those who are counted good. "If the miser gives gold to a poor man," Holy Tuchred tells us, "we have seen Raphael move his heart. When the coward knight turns upon his pursuers, there Michael rides upon his helm. And if a lying man speaks prophesy, you may look for Umbriel behind his eyes." Their paths are within us, in the most secret places of our thoughts. In as little as a gesture or a word, we may glimpse their light among the evil we have made.'

'But evil walks. It may touch us in so many ways!' cried Phaedra in frustration. She was thinking of the evil that might walk in shadows, rather than on sword-edges or sickness; but she dared not be more specific. 'What hope have we if the Angels do not themselves take body to intervene?'

He frowned. 'The body is only the battleground. The true fight – where we need all the help the Angels give – is for the mind and soul.'

Dogma, dogma, thought Phaedra.

'Do you know my lady diManey's story – how she was delivered from an ordeal that was meant to kill her?' she asked.

'I know what Adam diManey thinks he saw. And I know that His Grace and the lady spoke of it behind a closed door before you came to take her home, but neither have said what they think is the truth. Yet I know His Grace will have told her, as he has said to me, that if the Angels came to rescue each victim and right every wrong, they would long ago have led us back to Paradise, and left none of us the wiser.'

Phaedra was silent. She needed comfort, and it was not being given. If the Angels did not protect, or cure, or avert evil – what good could they bring in this world where disaster followed disaster in terrible succession?

Looking back, she could remember the days at Trant when she had almost agreed to marry Elward. Then she had met one more time with Ulfin, had drunk once more from the Cup, and had found the strength to resist, one more time. What if she had not? There would have been no war. Father would have been alive. Baldwin, in its sunbeaten pastures, might yet have been as good a home as Tarceny with its loneliness and shadows. Ulfin; her son Ambrose; everything bad and good in her life seemed to have flowed from that moment when she had lifted the Cup to her lips and seen the tiny oak leaf circling on the face of the water.

'Is it well with you, my lady?' asked Martin suddenly.

He was looking at her closely. And he was either a very good actor, or the concern in his eyes was real. She was sure she did not deserve it. She could imagine how she had seemed to him since he had arrived at Tarceny – cold, distracted, distrustful. She must be a poor mistress. And even an honest man would ask himself what it was she so feared.

'I was wondering – how much longer will you be with us before you go into the mountains?'

He frowned slightly. 'We agreed I should leave after All Hallows, my lady. But that I would return before the Lenten Days.'

'I shall be sorry to lose you.'

She had not answered his question, but they both knew that that in itself was an answer. He could not press her again. After a moment she thanked him and dismissed him, thinking that even if he was indeed the bishop's man, Tarceny would be lonelier yet when he was gone.

And the past was a closed door. Elward was dead, and it was idle to dream of having married him, for she never would have done. Even then, Ulfin in his absence had been more real to her than any man she had met in the light of day. Now – how many times more so! She could close her eyes and remember the depth of his look, and the *thud*, *thud* of her heart as he held her in his arms. He might be hundreds of miles away, and yet she could still feel the witchcraft of his touch upon her skin.

And there was Ambrose. Squalling, petulant child: his uncle's long face was indeed showing now, where Orcrim had claimed so implausibly to see it; but the boy's clear eyes and (she believed) his mulish spirit were all his own. She would not have changed one moment of her past if it meant that he would never be.

Then she laughed, and she flung her arms to the sky as she had seen Ulfin do when he first met her son.

Martin left in the late autumn. He went on foot, with a donkey, some rude gear, and no protection but a staff and the appearance of little to steal. He seemed determined to find some hill settlement where he could spend midwinter, but promised to return in the spring. Phaedra watched him dawdle at the slow pace of his beast in and out of the olive groves below the castle, until he was finally hidden from sight. Now the chapel was empty again, and there was just Caw at her table. in the evenings.

The Lady of Tarceny, she had never felt so alone.

Her troubles were beginning to grow. That night, as Orani was brushing the tangles from her hair, Phaedra started and exclaimed aloud. After a few seconds she rose and hurried down the corridor to the room which was now the nursery. Ambrose was awake, but quiet, mouthing at one of Ulfin's stones while Eridi sang him one of the droning lullabies of the hills. Stones and other toys were scattered on the floor of the room. Lamps flickered quietly in their places. The two were alone. So she returned to her chambers, ignoring Orani's stare, and settled herself before the mirror again. She watched the glass intently, looking past the brush and hands of her maid to a certain corner of the wall beyond where, a few moments before, she had locked eyes with something inhuman.

A face. Not a man's face, or at least she thought not. What she had glimpsed had seemed more like . . . like a demented cockerel under a cloth hood, staring and gibbering in her glass from the shadows of the far side of the room.

There was nothing there now. The robe, still unfinished, stood like a headless shadow and did not move. The hanging behind it had pictures of fight scenes from the ancient stories of the Kingdom, but surely not the patterns that could conjure such a thing for a sleepy eye. And Orani, standing beside her, did not appear to have seen or felt anything.

Phaedra sniffed. Was there a smell?

'We must have more lights,' she said.

She wrote guardedly to Ulfin. When his answer came it brought little comfort. She must watch and trust no one.

Especially she must watch over Ambrose. Ulfin could not say when he would be able to return.

> Things cannot go on as they are, here. And yet I cannot tell what will change it. No one wants Septimus for King. Yet it suits many to support him, that there should be no King at all. I wish that I might resign the game and withdraw west of the lake. But it would not end there. For the sake of Ambrose and those who follow us, I must finish what we have started.

He also said, curiously, that he hoped she would retain Orani and Eridi in service, for he thought they were good at what they did. It was the first time that she could remember him noticing anything to do with her domestic arrangements since those few weeks after their marriage, eighteen months ago. She wrote back that the weather was bad, and that Ambrose was crawling.

Her letter crossed with the news that, a year after they had first offered it to him, he had again refused the crown.

The weather was indeed bad. The light was dim. She had rushes burning in the corridors in the middle of the day, despite the constant risk of fire. They gave off a heavy, sour smell and some fumed so badly that if she had indeed been suffering from eye-ache it would have made things worse rather than better. The air was damp, and chilly in the wind. A round of colds began among the household. Phaedra worried about keeping the tower room warm for Ambrose, keeping the fire going, keeping a flow of dry wood coming up hourly from the woodstore in the arms of kitchen boys.

She was crossing the upper bailey after a short meet-ing with Caw and the guard captain about duties. Her head was full of the numbers – a guard and three servants sick, a sergeant and four gone to recruit men for the war. Another guard asking leave to marry. There were too few horses. She knew that Caw would soon ask her to release her horse Thunder to the garrison, which would spark their first argument in months (she did not have much use for the animal, who was a lump – but there were limits!). And with these preoccupations she looked up in the dank day at the north-east tower for the reassuring plume of smoke that wavered thinly up the inner side. It was not there.

She stopped and waited, but it did not appear. Had the fire gone out? Or was the wood in the hearth so dry that the smoke was simply invisible in this light? Caw's voice sounded behind her, ending a conversation with the guard captain in the doorway to the inner gatehouse.

She hurried across the courtyard. If the fire had gone out, it would either be because Eridi had allowed it to – in which case she was in for a tongue-lashing if the room was a jot less than *very* warm – or because the next lot of wood hadn't appeared, in which case some kitchen boy was going to spend a day or two doing something *very* unpleasant. She entered the hall and climbed the gallery stairs, passed into the living-quarter passage and turned to her right. A flight of wooden steps took her up to the next level, where the house-servants were quartered, and to the door to the tower room. It was shut. She lifted the latch, which clacked in her hand, and entered.

It was nowhere near warm enough. The floor was

littered, as it always was, with Ambrose's stones and other toys. The room was empty. The fire was out. There was no one there.

The smell. Not the woody scent of dead embers, but something thick and damp, like old stone at the edge of pools. She knew it at once.

Then she saw Ambrose.

He was a half-dozen steps up the stair that curled up the side of the chamber to disappear into the tower wall. He was struggling, on hands and knees, to make the next step.

There was someone on the stair above him . . .

Dear Angels!

A figure – it was smaller than a man – crouched in a heavy, hooded cloak, with its head bowed. The boy was climbing towards it.

It leaned forward.

'Stop!' Nothing changed at the sound of her voice.

There were soldiers on the roof above. Somewhere in the room was a gong to call them, but she could not think where. She could not take her eyes off her son. His tongue was clenched between his lips as he reached for the next flight of stone. His head rocked. He uttered a little grunt as she watched.

The crouching thing lifted its head. Beneath the hood it seemed eyeless, toad-headed. Something crunched. Flecks of stone trickled down the stair.

Long fingers that were not a man's stretched towards the child.

'Amba!' she said, louder this time. The boy looked round and saw her.

I'm busy, his look said.

If she stepped forward he would turn to climb again. Two steps above him the fingers hovered like the roots of black trees. Water glistened on them. She must not look. She must look at Ambrose. At Ambrose.

'Come down, darling. Please – come down.'

Slowly the boy turned.

He frowned in concentration. He hesitated. Then he tried a step downwards.

He fell.

Phaedra cried out, and lunged up the stair to catch him as he rolled over and over down the stone steps. Above her the stair was crowded – the hooded crouching thing, stinking, a few feet away, and beyond it, another figure – a man in a robe and hood, looking down, coming down the stairs towards her . . .

It was him! It was *him*!

'Help! Help!' Down the stairs, and she nearly fell. Somewhere beyond a door feet pounded on wooden steps. People were coming. She turned, snarling, with her child in her arms, to face the enemy.

The stair was empty.

Ambrose bawled and bawled. The tower door rattled and Caw flung into the room, with Orani behind him.

'There's someone up there!'

Caw leaped to the stair foot. Phaedra saw him check as he registered that there was no one on the lower steps. He drew his sword, listened, and crept to the point where the stair disappeared into the thickness of the wall. There he paused.

'Where's Eridi?' asked Orani.

'Quiet, damn it!' Caw trying to listen, as the tower rang with Ambrose's cries. After a few seconds he called loudly upwards.

'Ho there! Tower guard!'

There was a pause.

'Sir?' came a voice, echoing down.

'Is the stair clear?'

'Clear, sir, as far as I can see.'

'Come on down then, and take care.'

After a moment there came the sound of armoured heels upon the steps. Watching Caw, Phaedra could see the moment when the guard lurched into his view. The stair was clear.

'Have you seen anything? Inside or out?'

'No, sir.'

'There was!' cried Phaedra. 'On the stair, two of them!'

'All right!' Caw swore under his breath. 'All right, let's do this properly. Up the stairs, you, and sound the alarm.'

'Sir?'

'Sound the alarm! Something's been here. Either that or you and your fellow have been pissing down the steps, to make it stink like this. Get the inner gatehouse to drop the portcullis and keep it down until I say otherwise. Then the two of you clear the roof of the living quarters. It's the only place for them to have gone. Hurry.'

'Sir!' Feet clattered on the stairs, fading.

'Now, dear, don't cry,' Orani was saying, as she prised Ambrose from his mother's grip. 'There, there. *Next* time you turn round an' come down *backwards*, that's the way. Nasty fall, was it? There, there . . .'

Ambrose wailed on, but less loudly. Phaedra looked at her hands, and found she was shaking. She wanted to cry too.

And no one else had seen anything.

'Take that child down to the gatehouse, quick,' said Caw. 'It'll be safe enough there until we have sorted this out.'

'And *you* get out too!' he barked.

Eridi had appeared in the door with an armful of wood, and was gawping at them. Orani hustled her out, babe in one arm. Ambrose's keening receded. The door closed. Above, a trumpet began to sound the harsh notes of the alarm.

Phaedra was left in the room with Caw, still perched on the stairs.

'I suppose you think I'm mad,' she whispered.

He looked at her, as though he was about to agree. Then he said: 'You'd better see this.'

Phaedra climbed up the steps towards him – nine, ten, eleven: he was standing precisely where the crouching thing had been. He moved his foot as she approached. Sunk into the lip of the step was the mark.

It was if the stone had been worn, or crushed by some impossible weight. She touched the stone. It was damp. The place stank.

It was smaller than a man's print. Smaller even than her own. And rounder. On one side of it was another mark that might have been a little claw. Other pits and blemishes in the surface of the step showed where the creature had rested. The stairs above and below were clean.

Phaedra stared at it. The mutilated step. The fresh

241

sweep of the step below, with one of the Ambrose's white play-stones resting on it. It had been that close. And the face of the man she had seen on the stair, intent upon the capture.

Footsteps above them roused her. Caw replaced his foot on the marks as the soldiers came into view and hurried out onto the parapet above the living quarters. Then he removed it and bent over the step.

'I think I can get this slab up,' he said in a low voice. 'We'd better give out it was worn, so the child slipped.'

'What are you going to do?'

'Hide it. Bury it, when I can.'

'Why?'

'Why do you think?' He looked up angrily. 'It needs just one loose mouth about this, and we're all done. My lord too. And that's another thing. Don't go writing any of this to him.'

'What!' Ulfin was the only one who could possibly help.

'Not in writing. I'll send him messages to get him back here. You can do the same. If you like, we'll craft it so that if he reads both together he'll get the idea. But they go separately. There's to be nothing anyone can read about this. Damn! I need a chisel.' He stood up, breathing heavily.

'You stay here,' he said. 'Make sure no one sees it. Act mad, or whatever. In fact, that would be a good idea, for they'll find nothing on the roof and will wonder what it was all about. I'll be back as soon as I can.'

Without waiting for an answer, he turned and hurried down the steps and out of the room. Phaedra sat heavily

242

on the step below the marks – she could not bring herself to sit *on* them – and tried to think about what he had said.

Tell no one. And what if they came again? Tell no one. Not the guards, not Orani, not Eridi. Try to get Ulfin back here without telling him why.

Dear Angels!

She played absently with the white pebble, thinking: Tell no one, not even Caw. Not about the face on the stair, beyond the crouching thing. Tell no one that it was the pale priest of the knoll.

They found nothing. Phaedra's anger ran like a wave through the household. A kitchen boy was put in the stocks for failing to deliver the wood. Eridi was beaten by Orani for leaving her post to get it. Men scurried when the lady expressed a wish, and watched her sideways, wondering.

The messages left for Ulfin within a day of each other, bearing as much as Caw would allow them to say. Letters from him arrived almost at once, so for a moment Phaedra believed that he already knew what had happened, and was giving them the answer. But when the seals were broken her hope faded. War was deepening in the Kingdom. He was leading a column to harry the Seabord, drawing soldiers from Trant and Tuscolo. Caw must send replacements to the weakened garrisons, in case Septimus raided from Develin. He must also send money. The letters bore no thought of troubles west of the lake.

Caw swore, and rode the next morning for Baer and the south of the March, where he reckoned there were manors that had yet to give as much as Ulfin's other lands

243

to their lord's cause. He took only three riders with him, and yet with sickness, and messengers abroad, his departure left the garrison with just nine fighting men until the recruiting party should return. Caw's last words to her were: 'Remember – tell no one. We all depend on it.'

Phaedra nodded dumbly, and watched him ride out of the gate. She liked him so little. Yet to lose him now was almost more than she could bear.

For the first time she was truly mistress in her own house. And yet she had never been so ill-prepared for it. Indecision took her, even as she gave instructions for the simplest tasks. For at the same time as ordering the day-to-day functions of the garrison, she must also try to guard against the enemy they had never seen and could not be allowed to know existed, but might appear at any moment among them. How far would Patter be at that time? Would Arianda be within call? Was it safe to let Barnay gather wood on his own? Her mind grappled with the movements, and the recurring need to find reasons for tasks to be done in unusual ways. If her brain was too slow, as it often seemed to be, she would take refuge in irrationality and order them to do it anyway. And when they had bowed and left (shaking their heads, no doubt, as soon as they were out of sight) she would lose faith in her own decision, and call them back, or struggle to stop herself calling, and yet wish that she had done. She would watch them secretly, and yet suspect that they knew she was watching; but she could not rid her mind of the images of clawed shadows rising from the well or the woodpile around the servant who, in the last few seconds, would become her son. Then she would turn abruptly to walk the walls or corridors, waiting for another half-hour to pass so that she might reasonably visit Ambrose again, wondering when she might hear from Ulfin, and what she would do that evening when the light faded. And at dusk she took her blankets and lay beside Eridi on the floor of Ambrose's room, rising every hour to tend the lights around him before they failed.

Ulfin did not answer. Night came, and came again, and still he did not answer.

Sometime on a dark evening she went with a single candle to her writing desk. There, heavy with exhaustion, she broke the word that she had indeed never truly given to Caw. She wrote a short side of parchment to Evalia diManey. Trust her or not, she did not know. But if Ulfin would not or could not answer, she would treat with the one person who might know what was to be done.

... I have seen again that person I sought on the road from Baer. It is in my mind that you bade me then to have care. It would confirm me greatly if I knew your reason ...

She knew, as she wrote, that it must look and read like the scrawlings of a madwoman. But she did not have the strength to write it out again, or the will to wait until strength might return.

The message went, and the garrison reduced to eight men. The house watched her from under lowered eyes and ignored her bidding when they thought she would not notice. She could not trust them. Yet she could not watch for ever. Her blood sank, and her head lurched with the heaviness of sleeping and the horror of being asleep. She dreamed that she moved among shadows, in strange halls and corridors where people passed and spoke to her, and then passed without speaking, and at last ceased to appear at all. She was climbing the long stairs in the bishop's palace, leading up and up to the chamber where he waited to tell the penitent that their shadows were their own and would hunt them no more. The place was empty of people. The stairs were not wood but stone, and after a long time they were narrow and began to curl to the right. Something scuffled above her, and turning a corner she saw the small round clawed prints in the stone, with a film of water in the bottom that smelled of the edge of pools. They led up towards the room where Ambrose lay in his cot, playing silently with a bishop's robes. And she followed with her heart and feet stumbling together, knowing that the door to his room was already opening, and still the tracks led on and on and on up the empty stair.

From Tarceny to diManey's house at Chatterfall it was three days, in anything but an easterly wind. Phaedra expected no answer for a week. When she looked up on the evening of the fifth day and saw her messenger standing in the hallway door, her heart dropped to her shoes. The winds had been wrong. He had failed to get a boat. He had given her precious message to someone to take when they could. He had shrugged his shoulders and come back to tell her that he would not do as she had bid. She felt her face harden. Bitter words rose within her. The man stepped forward and offered her a paper that was not her own. It bore the Sign of the Hound.

'She said I was to have five in silver if you got this 'fore sundown today.'

Phaedra blinked, and broke the seal at once. On the paper was a single line of writing.

'Yes. Yes, thank you,' she heard herself say.

Evalia had committed no secrets to the page. The line read:

Come to Chatterfall. Bring your son and whoever you need, but come at once.

E.

XIII

Chatterfall

t the head of the Derewater stood a knot of flat-topped, tumble-sided hills, thickly fleeced with low thorns. Here the lake, flooding north, divided and embraced the massif in two great arms. The main body of water washed the western and then the northern slopes as it bent to crash at last over the great falls. But the lesser arm turned east at once, wandering in a narrowing creek through the steep hillsides.

Up this sleeve of water crept a boat under oars. The thorn slopes towered ahead and on both sides. Their reflections darkened the surface of the lake. The sun was falling to the west. It was a still evening, with very little wind. Beyond the constant *splash, splash* of the oars the rough banks slipped backwards and gave no sound.

Phaedra, crouching in the bows, saw the faces of her party all bathed in that soft light. The fishermen, father and son, who worked the oars: the old man's brown skin was lined as deep as yew wood. Orani, Eridi, Ambrose; and the two guards huddled uncomfortably in the stern. One of the men was a recruit called Massey. He was a poor cousin-by-marriage to Elanor Massey of Aclete, with a burly, red-bearded look that lent confidence. Phaedra had chosen him because she found it easier to trust a new man than any of the guards at Tarceny, who had either seen nothing all year long and thought her mad, or had seen or guessed too much, and had done not a thing to help her.

The other man was a fellow with a lean, dark-dog face and a tendency to chat regardless of whether he was receiving a response. His name, of all things, was Orchard, and Phaedra would most certainly not have chosen him if chance had not picked him to carry her earlier messages and proved that he could find his way to Chatterfall with speed. It had been his infernal optimism that had led them on into the wilderness the night before, until it had become plain even to Phaedra that it was too dark to carry on to the lakeshore in safety; but it was also he who had led them on down to Neff's Jetty in the morning, and had found a crew of father and son from east of the lake who were willing to take a gentle lady and her retainers back with them that day.

Just two men. She had not dared to reduce the household further. Until the recruiting parties returned, the garrison was already so weak that any passing band of brigands might take the castle if they had enough rope. Moreover, she wished to travel in secret. Without a full troop of soldiers her best protection from ordinary enemies was anonymity. Her party carried no banners and showed no devices.

She had travelled in fear. The memory of the night still pressed upon her – her very first in open camp, tossing in the dark of the wasteland above the lake, with its whispering scrub and hard little rocks edging up from every foot of flat ground. The dawn had been terrible: she had cursed and tried not to weep as her guard challenged again and again something that blundered and stirred among the thorns. Friend, foe or wild animal? Nothing had come forward. The wind had hammered them on the march, flapping cloaks, tossing the thorn-scrub and flinging sudden spits of rain at cheek and eye; she had turned constantly in her saddle to look back at the overcast hillsides and at the man riding last behind her, to see that he was still there, and still a friend. She had waited restlessly among the huts and rocks around the jetty while the guards haggled with the fishermen for passage; fighting the urge to barge past her men and push coins into the fishermen's hands, knowing that she could not. For who could such a woman be, travelling almost unescorted with her son and paying for haste in gold?

They had boarded at last, and the water had widened between her and the shore. The wind had steadied out of the north, bellying the sail and drawing the boat swiftly along in a broad reach across the head of the lake. The hills of Tarceny had receded slowly behind her, and the menace that she felt among them had receded too. She had lived all her life above the Derewater, and although these parts were strange to her she still felt it was a friend. Somehow she did not believe that the sorcery could chase her easily across the deep water. She had slept for a while, pillowed on Orani's knee. By the time she had woken again the wind had dropped, blocked by the close hills. The crew had lowered the sail and were shipping oars for the last stretch to the landing.

For a while the hills ranked close on both sides, falling

steeply to the water. But around sundown the slopes to the south eased. The hills retreated a few hundred yards. There were trees, a track, the occasional building. The reeds grew. A forest of pale yellow stalks reached six feet above the level of the water. Wild fowl landed in flights of grey wings, shrieking as dusk fell. *Splash, splash* went the oars, casting ripples in widening rings on the dark surface, stirring the pale-yellow stalks that glowed in the last of the sun.

There was a channel cut to the shore, a makeshift jetty and a group of huts nearby. There they landed and stretched their limbs. There was an inn of sorts, smelling of wood smoke. The party was able to rest and drink clean water while someone was sent at the run down the track to warn the house at Chatterfall of the arrival of a gentle-woman, with her child and retainers. The inn folk loaned them lanterns, so that they could walk the last hour to Chatterfall in the dusk. There were no horses, but it was possible to hire the single donkey, which Eridi rode with Ambrose, wrapped and asleep before her. The track topped a rise and fell steeply through an oak wood that rang to the sound of water falling. Down and down it went, in long looping curves, for the northern slopes of these hills dropped several hundred feet further than the southern, towards the Seabord plain. They saw lights moving through the trees ahead of them. There were men's voices, shapes moving on the track in the twilight that resolved into a figure on a large horse, and others on foot bearing lanterns, calling as they approached.

'Adam diManey, my lady,' said a pudgy voice. 'Come to welcome you in my own lady's name.' He was addressing the shape of Eridi, who was the only one in the party on any sort of mount.

'Sir, you are good,' said Phaedra from the darkness by his stirrup. 'And I thank you for your welcome and your protection.'

'. . . Come to welcome you,' said the knight, recovering. 'And to let you ride my horse, if you can manage a knight's seat. Alas, my lady's saddle is still a-mending.'

'But I shall be happy to walk, if it is not far.'

'Then I shall walk with you,' he said, and he swung himself heavily down. 'It is not far – a furlong or two. You can hear the falls clearly. These are my acres, and I am glad to welcome you to them. I have heard much about you.'

'Sir, if I were frank with you, that is little comfort.'

'I meant that I have heard much of you from my lady. And you need have no fear of what she has said.'

'She has been kind indeed.'

Firelight, and the second evening since her arrival. She was not so tired now, after a day of doing little by the small wooden manor house, among its stockaded outbuildings and in the olive groves under the waterfall nearby. She could look around at the room, flickering dimly with the light of the small flames from the stone hearth. If her eyes lingered on a patch of shadow, it was more from habit than anxiety. The shapes that had haunted Tarceny had no place among the undecorated timbers of diManey's house. She was confident of that, at least for now. There would be time to rest here.

There would be time to watch Evalia with her lord. Phaedra saw the formality between them, which was proper, and guessed that it persisted in private. An hour ago, when the tables had been cleared and Ambrose put to bed, Evalia had produced her husband's flute and whee-dled him into playing before their guest. He had played a number of airs, not badly, and had talked with Phaedra about the pipes of the hill people, and why the sound they made was so different, from their size and from the very reed of which they were made. He played them the Great Lament of the hill folk: a solemn, simple air that Phaedra remembered at once, and that yet sounded purer and more controlled from diManey's pipe and under his roof-tree. And then he had switched once again, and played 'South Wind' – the song of the lake-sailor, homeward bound, which each of them had known from their childhoods. Phaedra caught Evalia's half-smile and knew that her friend had led diManey to talk of things he felt confident of and play as he would have wanted to play for his high-ranking guest. She watched Evalia watching her husband fall gently asleep in his chair, and saw two people who had been thrown together on a long journey. She wondered what they thought of when they lay side by side in the darkness.

Now Adam slumbered by the fire. The chess pieces, with which she had forced an honourable draw against him earlier in the evening, stood frozen in their places at his right hand. Most of the servants were abed. It was time to speak.

'What made you warn me to be careful?' she murmured.

'I was worried about you,' said Evalia. 'I still am. I saw you go up alone into that evil place—'

'Tarceny?'

Evalia hesitated.

'The old lord is dead, remember,' said Phaedra.

'Phaedra, there is not one of the seven great houses – not one – without its own long tale of ruin and misdoing. You might think that some devil has played his game with each of them; and indeed I think one has. Yet Tarceny's story is the longest and perhaps the foulest of them all, over many generations. And there you were. You seemed to be so happy then. And beautiful, and young—'

'I am losing my looks.' Somehow it did not seem difficult to voice such a private grief here.

Evalia shook her head. 'You are tired. You have been for a long time. And you have lost faith in yourself. Looks fade quickly when that happens – I should know. But you will win them back again, perhaps more quickly than you would think possible.'

Phaedra watched the flames. She remembered how everything was more difficult than it had been before. She seemed to have been afraid for so long, first with the birth and then these other things. Ever since Father had died. Or even before that, with the raid coming, the Kingdom arming, the priest on the hillside who had disappeared.

'I do not know what to do,' she said.

For answer Evalia touched diManey's hand. The knight snorted and opened his eyes. Phaedra watched him realize that he had been asleep, attempt to look as though he had been awake all the time, and then understand that both the women knew he had been napping and thought it funny that he should pretend otherwise. Evalia inclined her head towards the bedroom.

'Hum?' said diManey. 'You ladies want to talk secrets? Very well.' He heaved himself from his chair and allowed Evalia to help him across the rush-strewn earth floor to the doorway. Then he rumbled again and felt his way unsteadily into the darkness beyond. Evalia returned to the fireplace with a slight smile on her lips.

'What did he mean?' asked Phaedra.

'Not what you are thinking. We might be talking about the secret of good looks for all he knows. He has guessed that you are in some sort of trouble. He supposes it is because the wars are putting you in danger, either from your husband or from his enemies.'

'The latter is likely enough.'

'Indeed. Now we are alone and may talk of what brings you here. However, we must be careful. I trust all who live in this house; but it is better for them as well as for us that they should not hear what we say.'

Phaedra nodded. After a moment she drew the chess set on its small table over to where they sat and began to arrange the pieces. 'Let us look as though we are playing. Or if you don't know how, let us look as though I am teaching you.'

Evalia smiled and waited until Phaedra had finished. Then she reached out and moved a white pawn forward in a classic opening.

'Tell me,' she said softly.

Phaedra put her chin on her hands and studied the board. There seemed to be so little to tell.

Dreams. The whisper of robes. Shadows shifting in the corner of her eye. The thing she had seen in her mirror. The thing on the stair and the mark it had left.

The face of the priest. The words were difficult, and her voice hesitated. She wanted to lift her head and look suddenly into the shadows; to listen for movements beyond the door. Her fingers were digging into her palm as she talked, so she used them to move another piece.

No, she did not know how many there were – several, she thought. No, she had not spoken to any of them. Or at least none had answered her. (Evalia seemed to think that important.) No, she could not name the priest. Yes, she was sure it was the same as had wed her. Could she be sure he had sent the thing on the stair? Yes, he had been with it, like a man controlling his dog. And she had glimpsed them together before – a hooded man, and something smaller, at the library door. What else did she know about him? Only what Ulfin had said. That she was privileged to have been wed by him. That he was 'holy'.

'Does your lord practise witchcraft, Phaedra?'

Phaedra blinked. Evalia had just executed a move that was both unexpected and devastating. She had no more idea how to respond to the white piece now sitting inside her defences than she had to the question she should have foreseen days ago. She looked up under lowered eyelids to read Evalia's face. It was a mask of concentration, frowning on the developing complexity of the board before them.

Be careful, said Ulfin's voice in the fountain court, under the moon of Tarceny.

'I think he understands more than I do. But all his attention is on the war, as if it would tear him to pieces if he turned aside.'

'But does he practise witchcraft?'

256

Phaedra opened her mouth to answer. The words stuck. She could not say them. She could not betray Ulfin with her tongue, whatever Evalia might guess from her lengthening silence.

'I can send no letters to him,' was all she could manage. 'Caw is against it. And I truly believe he would prevent them from going if he suspected they said too much.'

'This Caw is not a fool,' said Evalia dryly. 'The powers of the land have no mercy for those who do these things, and little justice for those suspected of them – as even my case should tell you.'

'Were you not innocent of those charges?' Phaedra moved a piece in a wild counter-attack.

Now it was Evalia's turn to pause.

'Perhaps you would trust me if it were your own secret, and not his,' she said solemnly. 'If you do not want to tell me what you know, perhaps that is an answer in itself . . .'

She was waiting for Phaedra to interrupt her. She had offered Phaedra help and comfort: a shelter for herself and her son, when no one else would. In doing so she must be putting herself at risk from the enemies of Tarceny. She had a right to expect the truth. And Phaedra knew that she had already said enough to let Evalia spin any story of witchcraft she wished to against Ulfin and his house. Even if she made a firm denial now, Evalia must guess that it was false. Such a lie was more than Phaedra could utter. But she could not, *could not*, say the words that would expose Ulfin further.

'I have told you what I have seen, Evalia.'

A truth that concealed was a lie also. She frowned unhappily at the board, and pushed forward a pawn to strengthen her defence.

'Well,' said Evalia at last, 'I cannot blame you. If you could have said more, I might have been able to help you more. As it is, I will tell you what I can. I know no more of these things that have troubled you than you do yourself. Although . . . I might guess that that which moves like thinnest smoke and that which weighs so much as to leave its mark in stone may both be creatures of deep places, where the rocks press fast together and the ways through are open to no body on the surface of the earth . . .

'But this is guesswork. And I too am evading a question under the guise of an answer. I was not innocent of those charges, Phaedra.'

Phaedra's heart sank. In that one short sentence, freely spoken, Evalia had willingly placed her life in Phaedra's hands.

'I do not regret what I tried to do,' Evalia went on. 'Although I should have tried a knife, or poison, rather than this. I did not have that sort of courage. I was a young bride to Luguan's house. Like you, I suppose, I had grown up with stories of princely marriages and the happy-ever-after. I found how different it could be. The man was a beast. After eighteen months I was truly in despair. Then the rising came our way. The Seabord barons came fighting with a luck or skill that seemed far beyond their numbers. They killed Luguan – for their own reasons. One of their allies was the Knight of the Moon Rose—'

'Calyn, my lord's brother?'

For a long moment Evalia was silent again. Then she

rose and went to a low chest to one side of the hearth. The lid was unlocked. She took something from among many other things within it, with a sureness that showed she had known exactly where it lay before she opened the lid. She brought it to Phaedra in the palm of her hand.

'I do not carry it any more. It is not fair to Adam. Nor do I keep it in the bedroom. But I could not send it back, with those other things. It was his. He was truly the best man I have ever known, Phaedra. What is more, he loved me, and I him. I shall never have those days again.'

It was a ring, made to look like the body of a dragon twisting three times upon itself. The head bore a great boss on which was set the letter C upon the moon of Tarceny. Phaedra turned it in the firelight to find the letters on either side of the boss.

'U, C, P,' she murmured. Her own ring nestled heavily against her skin.

'"The Under-Craft Prevaileth" – it was his saying, and he would study those letters as you are doing, and whisper the words to himself. I remember how he would smile, then – as if it had cost him a great price. He once spoke of a ring that he and his brothers had broken in the mountains. It meant something terrible, I think. Because of that he was aware of powers that most did not dream of, and could work with things that most would call forbidden. He could see far, and speak far, and pass where no man should have been able to pass – many things. He used it very little: so far as I know only to help his friends among the Seabord barons in their fight against Tuscolo. He was a sick man when the tide turned against the rebels, and he died without even being aware that he and I had passed into

Seguin's captivity. That was eleven months after he had first ridden through Luguan's door.

'Seguin wanted Luguan's lands, which were now mine after Luguan's death. He could not make up his mind whether to wed me himself, or make me marry his thirteen-year-old bastard or one of his toadies. For my part I had lost my lover, I was childless and I saw myself returning to another heartless marriage. I had no thought for my safety, for I believed all the good in my life had ended with Calyn's.' She smiled bitterly. 'Although it was not long before I was trying to pray for my life, whether it would be good or no. But at that time I saw no reason not to use the knowledge Calyn had left me.

'What I learned, and what you must look for, is this. There are powers. They do not seek much from the world or the people in it, if indeed they are aware of us at all. They were here before the Angels came. Some among them may tend to good, and some to ill. I suppose like all powers, some can be used for either or neither.

'Then there is one – perhaps more than one, but only one that I have seen – who is an intermediary: who has learned the secrets of those powers and can use them. He seems to be an old man in a long, pale robe, like a priest's. I have heard him called the Prince Under the Sky. What his true name is I do not know.

'Finally there are the suitors – people such as I, or as Calyn sometimes was, who meet and deal with this intermediary for a specific end. What I sought was Seguin's death. I obtained the means to achieve it. If I had been prepared to pay a fuller price, I should have achieved it indeed.'

'Price?'

'I think there is always a price. This intermediary – he is a man, I think, or was once. But he is not moved by the things that move men. He has access to power that makes all offers of wealth meaningless, and yet he demands acknowledgement. He demands some sacrifice on the suitor's part to recognize what he gives them. I do not know why. Perhaps there was a time when he made his own bargain, with some power or some other intermediary, so that even he has a price to pay. And that price is measured in the misery of our world, and his hatred of those who come to him.

'So there is a price. It is never, I think, mere gold. But – to give that which should not be yours to give. That is his currency. If not – your blood, your strength, your warmth. Calyn had given enough of himself for a plain fever to carry him off as if he were a child . . .

'Even to bargain, that is a price. Yes. Once you begin – it may not seem it – everything you say may seem fair, every exchange just common sense. But you cannot unsay what you have said. You cannot take back what you have given. You cannot give back what you have been given . . . Oh, Phaedra, what may seem a good enough bargain at the time, you may well regret later. When he moved Adam to spare me at my trial, I thought he had saved me because he wanted me as an ally. Later I supposed it was because he still needed me as a pawn, for his own ends. Now I am sure that the reason, the one reason he chose to help me, was that the price I paid him would be meaningless if I did not live to endure it. What it was I will not say. I will only say – take care. If you see him again, take care.'

The firelight shone wetly in Evalia's eyes. Phaedra

frowned upon the board in front of her, trying to puzzle a way forward through the interwoven threats and protections. At length she moved a piece on the board before her. Evalia looked at it, shrugged and moved a castle in a wholly irrelevant manner.

A power, a suitor and the intermediary. Which was the enemy?

'It is three moves from checkmate,' Phaedra said, raising her voice for the first time. 'And I thank you.'

Evalia shrugged again. Phaedra was leaning forward to demonstrate when she heard Ambrose call from the guest room.

'A mother's duty is never done,' said Evalia, almost wistfully.

Later Phaedra woke in her bed. She had neither dreamed nor felt anything to alarm her. Her mind was turning on and on over the things it had spun in its sleep. It was almost completely dark. Only the faintest square patch showed where the window was open to the night, and the shape of one of Ambrose's white stones (which seemed to get *everywhere*) on the sill. Evalia's fingers must have packed those stones, when Calyn her lover was cold and dead; packed them and sent them to his brother.

Evalia had demanded that Phaedra trust her. Phaedra had already trusted her, with herself and her son. But she had not been willing to talk of Ulfin. And although Evalia had talked willingly of Calyn, the comparison was not a fair one. Calyn was dead, and could not be harmed by the powers of this world. Ulfin went in peril of his enemies every day. Even Evalia's confession might have been less than it seemed to be. Surely she would already have said the same in penitence to the Bishop of Jent, and have his protection for it?

Phaedra turned in her blankets, restless at her own thoughts. The bishop was many days away. He could not protect Evalia from terrible rumours spread at this end of the lake. His part in this had ended when from his high window he had pointed the two of them together. (Had he foreseen this discussion, even then?) Evalia had trusted her. She had given nothing in return. She had not been able to, any more than she had been able to accept any of the men who had come to Trant for her in the days when she had not known if Ulfin was anything more than a dream. She could only accept Evalia's trust, and take what she had been given.

A power? She knew none. Except that Ulfin had once said that the Cup held the tears of someone who, to the hillmen, was Mother of the World. The hillmen lived in the mountains. The brothers had 'broken a ring' in the mountains. Deep places, where the rocks pressed fast together: perhaps there was some unholy power in the hills – a relic of the time before the Angels? Orani might know something, if Phaedra could find a way of asking. And yet the priest was no hillman. Evalia was saying he was the intermediary. She had called him the Prince Under the Sky. There had been a letter that called him that, written from somewhere in the March.

She must speak with Ulfin. Only Ulfin could give her the help she needed. She remembered his evident faith in the priest, and at the same time her own utter dread at the sight of the priest's face on the stair.

Ulfin, help me!

Ulfin. If one thing was clear, it was that Ulfin had himself been a 'suitor'. Then, at the time he had come to see Ambrose, he had told her that he would use his under-craft no more. Why? Had he changed his mind about the priest? Had the price become too high?

Ulfin – what price have you paid? Are you now inwardly so weak that the smallest wound or fever will take you from me?

The campaigns marched on, one after another, carrying him away. When would he return – weeks, months? She might never see him again. She lay in the darkness, trying to build a picture of his face in her mind. The clouds were thickening, hiding him, as they hid the moon. The light was fading. The ghostly underbellies massed across the sky like the plumes of armies: like a frozen fall of water a thousand miles high.

She slept, and the waters roared in her dreams.

XIV

The Man in the Reeds

t was a boy in the distance, plodding along the road by the lakeshore. He was alone in the sun. Beyond him the reed beds wavered and the blue lakewater wrinkled in the breeze. Across the strip of water a herd of goats was loose on the lower slopes. The clonking of their neck-bells carried clearly across the water.

'. . . In a month or so it will be summer, and truly hot,' Evalia was saying dreamily. 'Then the surface of the lake falls and the stream sinks to a trickle. Last year it dried completely for three weeks, and the falls stopped altogether. I thought the grasshoppers would drive me mad.'

It was a warm day. Sitting in the shade of a little grove on a low rise, with Evalia lying beside her, the servants at a distance with the horses, Phaedra felt as if it might already be summer. The boy trudged on up the road towards them, as if on some errand. Beyond him a man was cutting reeds.

'Watermane, of course, never dries. That's where the lake truly empties. Our falls are just a thing it does for fun.'

Phaedra said something to show that she was listening.

265

Not that Evalia really meant her to pay attention. Her talk was idle stuff, light and unending, to let two gentle ladies while away an afternoon in each other's company. And even Evalia was silent for a moment, lying full length on the thin grass and looking up at the sun as it glanced between the leaves.

Phaedra could not relax. She was muddling with a sense of depression that would not go away. She had realized, as the weeks passed, that Adam diManey was reluctant to discuss the politics of the Kingdom with her. That morning, when the subject had come up briefly, he had hesitated and picked his words so painfully that it was obvious he was trying not to give offence. As a free knight, and one under a ban at that, he was able to take sides in the Kingdom's troubles or remain neutral if he chose (which he did). Clearly, he was at best reserved about Ulfin's cause. As one who had stood up against the practices of the old court at Tuscolo, and had suffered for it, she thought he should have been a sympathizer. Either diManey, a genuinely good man, was blind to the real needs of the Kingdom, or he saw some reason why Ulfin's entire effort, and her own sacrifices with it, was at fault or would fail uselessly. Perhaps he hated the chaos that war brought more even than the bad justice of the order that had preceded it.

The boy had left the road. He was making straight for their trees, wading through knee-high grasses and past the low thorns that lurked among them. It was unlikely that he had left property among the trees on the hillock. Village boys did not walk up to a group like this casually, if they could instead wait at a distance until the party had gone. Whatever his business, it concerned Evalia's party. Phaedra watched him come. He could not have been more than eleven years old.

It was only when he was a few yards off, when he looked around the people under the trees and came hesitantly forward, that she realized he was looking for her.

'Man told me to give you this,' he said, holding out his hand.

It held a chess piece.

Beside her, Evalia rose to look. Phaedra reached out and took it.

'He said he'd like it if you came alone,' said the boy.

'Did he?' she said, almost to herself. 'And where is he?'

'That's him.' He was pointing to the reed cutter, a furlong up the track by the shore.

Evalia was at her shoulder. Phaedra heard her gasp as she saw the chess piece. She knew at once that Evalia's mind had flown back to the night, shortly after her arrival, when they had murmured together over the chessboard.

'It's all right,' she said. 'This is no eavesdropper.' Or at least that was not what the piece was supposed to say. 'He's just telling me who he is.'

It was the figure of a knight, roughly cut and stained brown. The face had a crazed, lopsided look.

'He must have carried them with him down the wall,' she muttered. 'Dear Angels!'

He was bareheaded, and so roughly dressed that he might have been a peasant himself. It was only when they came close, along the spit of land where he was working, that they could see the leather of his boots, the unconvincing way in which he thrashed among the stalks with his sickle, and that

267

his chosen spot was a poor one for good reeds but was well placed to hide him from anyone passing on the track close by. He had no punt, but a rowboat nosed among the stems. The sickle he must have taken from the boy. He straightened as they approached. Phaedra, helping Evalia pick her way along the narrow strip of land, felt the tension in her companion's grip as they neared him.

'Well met,' he said. 'I see you are in good health.'

'Indeed I am, sir. As, I hope, are you and your family.'

He nodded. 'And I wish health to your son.'

Phaedra smiled. He might know, or guess, that Ambrose was at Chatterfall, but she was not going to tell him.

'Sir, my companion is the Lady diManey, whom you may have once known as Luguan. My lady, this is the Baron Lackmere, who was a guest in my father's house.' She allowed herself to linger just a fraction on the word 'guest', to convey the double meaning and to rob the man of any respectability that her recognition implied. For until she discovered what he wanted, she would not concede him anything.

Indeed he was a rascally sight. His skin was lined and tanned from long exposure to the weather. His hair was tangled and there was thick stubble on his chin. His boots were spattered with mud. The tunic was faded and torn. From a bundle of reeds on the dry land peeped the hilt of a sword. Phaedra's eyes caught the chipped green mark of the oak leaf on its pommel, and looked away. If he had his chess pieces with him then presumably all his other worldly goods were also stowed nearby, perhaps aboard the small rowboat. He stood straight enough, with the old, angry look in his eye that she remembered.

268

'Let us sit,' he said.

They found themselves places on piles of cut stems. The reeds rose around them and hid all the lakeshore from view.

'I was sorry to hear of your father's death.'

'You are good, sir – to have sought me out to tell me so?'

'I found you were here quite by chance.'

He was looking at her, as if to assess what sort of woman she had become in the time since their last argument on the walls of Trant.

'Do I need to guess what chance brings a former baron to these reeds?'

'Ah. You think I am an outlaw? Of course. I am sorry that my appearance is something rough these days. But it is hard campaigning, and not a life without the law, that makes me look so. My lady, I should tell you that I am restored to my lands and forgiven my deeds. I appear before you Baron of Lackmere in truth as well as in name.'

'I am pleased for you, sir. If I may enquire who has done this?'

'The only one who could. Septimus, prince of the house that decreed my ban. When I heard that that old woman Inchapter was dead with Seguin, I sought the prince out straight away. I offered him my sword – at a time, I may say, when others of whom he had thought better were sheathing theirs. The widow of Develin herself stood by him at that moment, and although she knew me to have been an enemy of her house, she counselled the prince to accept and restore me, for at that time he needed men sorely. Things go better with him now.'

'And worse for the Kingdom, for now there are two

equal powers striving for mastery, where before one was in defeat.'

'Equal?' He grinned sourly. 'I tell you, the balance is tipping faster than you think. The chief town of Tarceny is Baer, is it not? I know within a day who has come and gone from its gates. You have a lodge there. If you were to hang a green or a blue cloth from a window, and then travel south, or west, before you had gone two days you would have heard from me.'

Green or blue: Trant's colours, and Lackmere's. And Septimus had followers in Tarceny.

'Did it ever occur to you that my lord might have helped you regain your lands whether or not Inchapter was dead?'

'It did.' For a moment Aun frowned, as though he found it hard to say what repelled him from Ulfin's cause. 'I had unpleasant dealings with him once. And we have crossed swords, as you know.'

Dealings? They must have been before he came to Trant. She remembered that he had known Ulfin even as he leaped at him out of the night. *She's not for you!*

'I know. Yet I trust that my lord has the judgement to overlook such a scuffle if it meant righting an injustice in the Kingdom.' (She was not convinced that there had been any injustice in Lackmere's fall; but Ulfin needed followers too.) 'Further, if he understood that your hostility had been from some old misunderstanding, and not any fault of his' – she let the thought dangle for a second, and saw Aun frown again, as if he did not agree – 'I believe he would have done at least as much for the service of your sword. He might not even mind that it was a sword purloined from my father's castle, and one that you had tried to take his head off with.'

She finished with more force than she had intended. The baron only laughed.

'If you knew how much effort it took to remove it from where it had been set without my guards noticing, to hide it in a bundle of wood, carry it up to my rooms, carry up every other stick of wood I needed in the next fortnight, so that no one should think that there was anything strange in my carrying the first bundle, keep it there for six weeks undiscovered, *and* get it down that damned wall, you will know why I do not exchange it for a nobler weapon. It was my one achievement in eighteen long months at Trant. And I am not ashamed of the reasons for which I first drew it. Next time he and I meet, I shall wear mail, and we will see what advantage his long blade and pretty swordsmanship bring him.'

There was a light in his eye as if he were anticipating the coming fight. She looked away across the leaves. At length he spoke again.

'I do not often go among gossiping company,' he said. 'Even so, you might be surprised how often I hear others talk of you, and what they say.'

'I do not listen to gossip at all, sir.'

'You are not concerned, then, at what is said of your part in the fall of your father's house?'

'And what is it that you think should concern me?' She could guess at some of it. But she would dare him to repeat it to her.

Aun pulled a face. Then he shrugged. 'I had supposed you had heard before this. Traitress, is one thing.'

271

'False, but it does not surprise me.'

'Witch, also. And – well, witch will do.'

'Witch and . . . ?'

He shook his head.

'*And*, sir?'

'Whore, then!'

She stared at him levelly. 'Well,' she said softly. 'It seems that beaten men may spin much out of very little things. What I did, sir, was to say to my lord that you had found it possible to escape by climbing down the wall of Trant, and therefore that it might also be possible for the wall to be scaled. What was done then was done with skill and courage by the men of Tarceny, such that no life was lost at all in the taking of the castle. Which I count the greatest feat of arms in all this sorry war. My father's death – you may not have heard – occurred some days later, when he broke out of his confinement. He attacked his guards and was killed.'

'By Caw of Enderby, I have heard.'

Caw!

'Now,' he said. 'If you mean that *my* departure from Trant showed Tarceny the way in, I must say that I doubt it. I came down that wall from a window I had prepared. Perhaps I could get back up it again, if I had need. But forty strangers in war gear, and without alerting a guard? If that is true, then I shall bow my head to your father when we meet beneath Michael's wings. But I do not think it. My own guess is that Tarceny has other means, and uses them.'

The reeds stirred in the wind and sighed. Caw. Father. Caw.

'I did not like the way the King died so suddenly on the road to Trant,' Aun said, half to himself. 'Just as his force was gathering, like that. It has opened the way for—'

She was angry now. Angry on Ulfin's behalf. 'Sir, it seems we are in different camps, you and I. Nevertheless, I can say this to you. Neither my lord nor I wish you any harm, and I hope that when reason prevails in the Kingdom you will be able to live peacefully in your home at last. But my lord is guiltless of the things you accuse him of. And he does not desire the crown. He has refused it twice—'

'And will he refuse it a third time? I wonder.'

'He has refused it. And he did not desire my father's death, nor did I, nor that of anyone at Trant. You have my oath on that!'

It was Aun's turn to pause, looking away across the reeds to some vision of war beyond them.

'Well,' he said at last. 'I suppose I came to find if you were a willing accomplice in Tarceny's doings, or a victim of abduction in hiding from your so-called husband. I had hoped it was the second, and what gave me hope was to find you this side of the water when I know Tarceny is hurrying back to the other.

'It seems you are more the first, although you may not realize, for example, that a fighting man cannot set out to take another's house without wishing him other than the most grievous harm. Or that in politics it is often necessary to refuse more than once what you would most have others give you. Perhaps you have been bewitched. At all events you are yet young, my lady. I do not forget that.

And one day you may need my help. Well, if you do, I have told you how you may come by it. Maybe it is better for both of us if we say no more now.'

'You were very calm,' said Evalia, as they picked their way back along the lakeshore in the sun.

'Was I? I did not feel it.'

'I'm no good at times like that. I cannot move or speak. I feel like a mouse.'

'He would not have hurt us,' said Phaedra, thinking that if Evalia had believed there would be serious danger, she deserved more credit than she was giving herself for following Phaedra into the reeds. 'He loathes my lord – I guess because my lord would not side against the King in the Seabord rising. But that is a different matter. I do not think he will tell others that I am here. He was a captive at Trant. For eighteen months I was almost his only company. You would not think it to hear him speak perhaps; but I am afraid . . .'

Pace, pace, along the dusty track where yellow grass tufted among the hard ruts, and a skylark singing somewhere in the blue overhead.

'I am afraid he is in love with me.'

How time shifted the perspective of things! She had barely thought of Lackmere in the past two years. Now she could see that his bitterness and despair at Trant had not only been caused by his imprisonment. At the time she had been receiving suitor after suitor, and he was already married to a woman with whom he barely corresponded. And then he had risked his neck to escape, and yet had turned aside while still in earshot of the walls – had roused the castle, indeed – in an attempt to prevent Ulfin from carrying her away. Madness. Now he had sought her out again.

'Of course, he may be changing his mind even as I speak. It was a most depressing talk in a number of ways.'

Evalia was waiting to ask her a different question.

'I see the servants did not stay for us,' Phaedra continued sourly, looking up at the wooded hillock where they had rested earlier. 'I suppose we will have to walk home.'

'I sent them back to the house,' said Evalia.

'Did you? Why?'

'Because— Ah!'

A rider had appeared on the track ahead of them. Dust rose in a low plume from the hooves of his mount. He was moving heavily, and yet seemed to be hurrying. Sunlight gleamed dully on mail and helm. Now she could hear the double thud of the hooves: a lumbering trot that rose to a canter as the rider saw them. Evalia waved her arm. They could see the lance-pennant, flickering darkly about the tiny point of iron. Now they could feel the ground shake beneath their ankles with the vast weight of the approach. He was almost on them – a mountain of flesh and jingling harness, mail and weapons. The rider's visor was up. It was Adam diManey, puffing and pulling and bringing his huge beast to a stop on the track where they stood. Phaedra blinked in the dust.

'He's gone,' Evalia was saying. 'He had a rowboat and went off across the lake. No harm has been done.'

DiManey looked about him, searching the reed beds and the surface of the lake. He was gasping for breath.

'Came as – quick as I could. Who was it?'

'One of Septimus's followers. He wanted to parley only.'

'I don't think he'll come back,' said Phaedra.

DiManey was without leg-armour, shield or surplice. He had not stopped to put on his padded undercoat, but had thrown his mail on over his shirt when the servants reached him. He was still panting. His horse had been ridden hard. Phaedra saw him exchange glances with Evalia. They had been afraid.

'The others are following with horses for you,' Adam said. 'I suggest we find some shade until they arrive.' He swung himself ponderously down from his perch, and began to lead his mount up the slope.

Phaedra followed, thinking that if Aun had found her, then others might do so, even without his help. They would find that Ambrose was there too. DiManey might be able to keep his lands free of petty outlaws, but he could not stand against a baron's raiding party. If they came here she would have to surrender at once, or it would mean a bloody death for diManey and possibly a traitor's death for Evalia too. But Ulfin was across the lake now . . .

'Is it not Caw of Enderby whom your lord has set to hold Tarceny?' Evalia murmured in her ear.

'It is.' It was the question she had known Evalia would ask.

She could sense Evalia expecting outrage. And, in part, she was right. Phaedra had never even asked herself whose hands had swung the blade that had cut into her father's flesh: who had stood over him as he had choked and bubbled in his own blood until at last he was still for ever. She had barely wondered what embarrassment it was

Caw had caused to Ulfin that he should be consigned to his appointment, eating at her table a thousand times, slow to meet her eye, rude when she spoke of home, and anxious that his lord should release him from his duty! And yet she knew that Ulfin must have known, and moreover, that he had chosen Caw for that very reason.

She had no sense of betrayal. She thought she could see the matter as Ulfin had done, looking Caw scornfully in the eye. You killed this man. You guard his child, and grandchild, and eat in silence the guilt of what you have done. He had not explained to her, but she saw now that he had not needed to. What he had chosen to do was wisdom: dark and cool as water in a cup of ancient stone.

'I must go back,' she said.

'Back!'

'To Tarceny. My lord is there now.'

Once again, that long stare. She met it. It was Evalia who dropped her gaze.

'Say what you are thinking.'

'Is it . . .' Evalia shook her head, as though suppressing her thought. Then she seemed to change her mind again. 'Is it – what that man said? Are you sure you are not bewitched?'

The air was thick with heat. In the puddles of the stream Phaedra could see the pale shapes of the oak-leaves of last summer, lying drowned and still.

Suddenly she laughed. Because Ulfin was across the lake, and treading the soil of Tarceny.

'Bewitched? My dear friend, I am: utterly.'

XV

The House in the Hills

mbrose had grown in the weeks at Chatterfall. He had taken his first steps on Phaedra's nineteenth birthday, with Evalia releasing his hands in the olive groves and Eridi beckoning him across the grassy floor. He showed far more interest in their homeward journey than Phaedra remembered him doing on their flight from Tarceny. In the boat, he wanted to sit by the rail and reach out to the brown wavetops, running just beyond his fingers' reach below the taffrail. When one splashed up at him, he sat back, startled but not unhappy.

'Ooh! We'h!'

'Yes, darling,' said Phaedra. '*Very* wet. Please be careful.'

So he spent half the remaining trip at the rail of the boat, with Orani, Eridi and Phaedra all taking turns to keep an arm around him while he leaned over the side in his efforts to catch another wave, or watched the wrinkling lake-surface with solemn eyes that gave no sign of what he was thinking. His child's face hinted more strongly now of the long and delicate features of his father's house, but the way his black hair was beginning to curl at his ears and collar reminded Phaedra suddenly of her own mother. She thought that if Father could see him, perhaps he would not be altogether ashamed of her now.

Orchard had crossed the lake the day before, to retrieve their horses from the manor to which they had been entrusted. He was waiting with them at Neff's Jetty when the boat landed. He had news too. Ulfin had indeed crossed the lake. But he was not at Tarceny. He had set out a day or two before, for Hayley in the northern part of the March. No one had been able to say why.

'Very well,' Phaedra said. 'We will go to Hayley.'

The narrow tracks took them through a part of the March that she did not know, where the hills rose more steeply to rugged, bare crests, so that once or twice a day when the path lifted above the tree line she could turn in the saddle and look back to astounding views east and south over the March. She found that Thunder was more easy to manage than she remembered, and realized that this was not because he had changed, but because she had. She no longer expected him to behave like old Collen, but knew him as a horse in his own right, with ways and reactions that she was coming to understand rather than fight. She began to pay attention to her own riding, and to feel an improvement as she did so.

The true mountains crept nearer, showing white flecks and patches on their high peaks, where the snow lay packed in shady gullies and still had not melted.

Hayley was a single, square keep within a curtain wall. Pennants flew from its battlements, but Ulfin's standard was not there. Phaedra almost cried aloud with disappointment, and hurried down to the gate to demand admittance and news. The castle warden, astounded by the appearance within a few days first of his lord, whom he had supposed to be fighting deep in the Segne of the Kingdom, and then of his lady, who had disappeared without trace for a full season, could give only the barest of information. Ulfin had been at Hayley. Indeed, most of his escort was still there. My lord himself had gone on into the hills, accompanied only by two herders and a small flock of goats. The warden did not know why. It was a thing my lord had done before, although not recently. He would return in a week, maybe a few weeks. The warden would do everything to see that my lady was comfortable until then . . .

'I am going to follow him,' she said.

The mountains rose in line after line of disappearing blue. They were vast enough to hold a dozen armies unseen from one another. They were silent: bare slopes and deep valleys; lonely huts; the crowns of cloud that gathered above each peak, so that a clear sky at dawn changed slowly to a huge mass that billowed along the mountaintops by evening. North and west of Hayley a valley ran between two great forested spurs. The path Ulfin had taken went in that direction. Phaedra demanded trackers from the warden, and four more escorts, whom she had Massey pick from the garrison as though he were a sergeant. She took donkeys and provisions, dogs for hunting and to keep guard. She had them ready at dawn, every strap and bundle as her father would have done; cried the Traveller's Prayer aloud in the courtyard; and led her small cavalcade from Hayley's gate as the tips of the mountains turned gold.

They passed the March-stone before evening that day.

'For what it is worth,' Massey said. The Kingdom had no real border here. Some years all the villages for a week's journey beyond the stone might pay tribute. And now? Massey shrugged. With the garrison at Hayley stripped for the war, it was doubtful that my lord's law ran any further than the warden could spit from its walls.

Where are you, Ulfin? What madness has lured you from the battle for a kingdom, from the hunt for your wife and child, and brought you alone to these places? Are you seeking something, or fleeing it? I am groping among your footsteps, looking for signs in this empty land. I have only my feet, my eyes and my will. By day I look for goat droppings and the far sun-flash of metal, by night the spark of a distant fire. Let the Angels lead me to you, if only they fly in this land.

The going was slow. The paths were not paths but bare places where men and beasts might go with care. A day's journey would take them into, along and across a single valley. They saw no one, nor any beast but the big-winged carrion birds that turned lazily above the hillsides. The mountains were vast.

They were vast, but the ways among them were few. And slow though horses and donkeys might be, a goat flock travelled more slowly still. They did come across droppings, signs of grazing and, once, an old campfire. Even so, Phaedra was not prepared for the moment when, following a tiny path, they crossed over a shoulder between two peaks and came upon a score of goats stripping bark off young trees, watched by a pair of boys just sprouting their first beards, and beyond them a man in mail, sitting on a rock. He looked up as she approached.

'Ah,' he said. 'I was wondering if it was you.'

'You knew we were following?'

'Since yesterday. This morning we saw you carried the pennants of Hayley, so I waited for you to come up.'

'What are you doing out here?'

'I am on a journey which, I hope, will put both your troubles and mine behind us. Do you want to come along?'

She slid from her saddle and flung her arms around his waist.

'Yes,' she said.

And now this sloping, stony ground under her back that pressed her spine and discouraged sleep. The dark awning rippling over her in the breeze that had followed them up the valley all day; from the open end, above her feet, in meaningless distance the black mass of the mountain opposite and a few low stars above; Ulfin stirring and muttering at her side. She could feel his warmth through the folds of blankets between them. Beyond the awning, the sounds of Eridi hushing Ambrose's sleepy protests from their shelter nearby. The donkeys stirred at their tethers below the little camp. The goats were silent. The watchmen had let the fire die to embers.

'Did Caw show you what he found on the step?'

'No. He described it to me, but he had buried it. He did the right thing. So did you, I think. At least it will have confused them. It confused me, certainly, and others. It was a risk, nonetheless. If one of Septimus's followers—'

'I know. Friends hid me—'

'Don't tell me where.'

'I was so afraid, for Ambrose above all.'

'Those things could not come at him. All the same, it is right to be watchful.'

They lay in silence together. His hand began to stroke softly down her ribs and thigh.

'Who is the priest, Ulfin?'

The hand stopped. 'What? The fellow you hired into my house?'

'No, not him. And I did not hire him, Ulfin. We agreed he should come.'

'Jent is not a friend, remember.'

She remembered that Martin must be somewhere in these hills too. She wondered how he was faring. He might be as close as the next valley, and yet as good as a thousand miles away, for they would pass by him and never know that he was there. Their party seemed utterly alone in these vast places.

'Who is? I believe that not all of the March is safe, either.'

'You'll have to tell me about that.'

Aun's scornful face rose before her eyes. She wondered if there was anything she could say that would bring the two men out of danger from each other.

'Tomorrow, Ulfin.' He had not answered her question about the priest, either. With Ulfin beside her, that too could wait until tomorrow. But if his presence made some fears remote, it brought others closer.

'I've heard the war is tipping against us now.'

He sighed. 'It always has been. At the beginning, I had the – the tools you know of – to bring success despite that. If I deny myself those, then yes, it is hard to see how . . . This hot weather should bring a respite for a few weeks at

283

least. I have ordered another muster at Tarceny for my return. We must raise money. I fear we must begin to sell things we would rather not part with, such as jewels, and even your writing desk.'

'I had thought of it already.'

After a moment his hand began to move against her skin once more.

Beyond the awning Eridi was singing softly, lulling Ambrose to sleep with the tones of the Great Lament. The notes spoke of loneliness and loss, and the endless emptiness of the hills. Each one sounded as if it had been born for the first time in this great and dark corner of the world. Phaedra turned her head to listen.

'What is it saying?'

Ulfin's hand moved upon the flesh of her thigh beneath her nightdress. He said: 'It talks of the time when the world shrugged, and turned to stone, and the giants came. Beyah, the Mother of the World, turned her back on her people to weep for her lost child, and only the world-worm Capuu dared approach her. It may include memories of when we invaded and drove them into the hills; but there are other things, myths or happenings from an older time. Or nonsense.' He paused. His fingers pushed slowly across the slackness of her belly to her ribs, and crept on towards her breast.

There was a cry – a man's voice. It came from somewhere above them, as they picked their way along a scrubby slope that fell to the valley floor a thousand feet below. Phaedra checked Thunder and looked about her. There was nothing to be seen among the green thorns. Her view forward was obscured by Eridi, riding on her ass with Ambrose. She could not see Ulfin or the soldiers at the head of the party. She could not see whether they were getting ready to fight or not. The world had shrunk to the few square yards of hillside immediately above her and the vast view out across the valley to her right. Listening, trying to still Thunder (who was less use than a donkey on this ground), she felt a sort of humming in the air, as if of music played somewhere just beyond the reach of hearing.

Then the cry came again.

It was uphill, and somewhere ahead of her. It was too far away, she thought, to have been directed at them or uttered by anyone aware of their presence. There were men up there, and what they might do when they saw the party she did not know.

Eridi was moving on. Beyond, Phaedra could now see Ulfin waving them forward impatiently. She kicked Thunder into motion, on up, making him pick his way among the scattered boulders and thorns while the flies of the hillside wove around his ears.

They came suddenly up to a spur of rock that rose above the main hillside and jutted out and down towards the edge of the valley. Along its back a broad path ran, six feet wide or more, downhill across their route. She could hear the music now. There were hill pipes and drums and voices intoning low notes somewhere just beyond sight. Ulfin was shooing the soldiers to keep to the track-side as the leading hillmen came into view.

Her first impression was how small they were. None of them seemed to be more than two-thirds the height of Ulfin, standing tall at her stirrup. Even Orani and Eridi, whom she thought of as having hill-blood, were half a head above any of them. There were twenty, thirty, in a crowd, pacing down the track towards her. They bore no weapons, and seemed to be dressed in rags. Phaedra wondered for a moment whether they had seen Ulfin's party from far off and had come to meet them. Ulfin did not seem to expect them to stop. He stood to one side of their path as they came on to the steady beat of their drums.

Then the cry came again, a long and trailing sound from the lips of the leader, with his eyes half closed and his head flung back towards the sky. The pipes flowed in behind, filling the space with a simple, steady melody that Phaedra had never heard before. The procession was passing Ulfin and his soldiers with barely a second look. She watched them stalk by. They wore brown blankets and went barefoot. She saw the weathered, bird-like faces, the dark and greying hair, the skin deeply lined. They walked on down the hillside from, she guessed, some settlement above to some shrine below. Some were carrying figures on poles – gods or spirits, she supposed.

The pipes and the voices had stopped. The hillmen passed to the steady beat of the drums, sad faces, solemn faces, some that looked curiously up at her and others that stared fixedly ahead as they marched. Further uphill, a hillman in what must have been a chief's dress had stopped to speak with Ulfin. Beside her one of the herders was explaining something to Eridi and Orani, pointing out across the valley to where the hillside opposite ended in a huge shoulder of rock and a new valley opened. Far beyond, a huge peak rose, white-capped and purple-sided with the shadows of the clouds.

'That's her,' the boy was saying. His hill accent was so thick that Phaedra had to strain for the meaning. 'Beyah. She don't answer, of course.'

'Beyaah!' cried the voice at the head of the column. And the pipes began again. The hillmen were passing, droning in their low voices below the breath of the pipes. The leading gods of the procession were followed by bizarre and colourful figures of other gods and spirits, including a long, red worm with a crest and great eyes which needed three poles to support the length of its body. 'Capuu, world-worm,' the herder was saying. 'Catches her teardrop in his teeth for the people. An' tho' she bash him one in the mouth, so he spits teeth when he come to the ground, still he don't drop the tear but lays it in front of the people an' tells them what it is. Mica-mica, uh . . . star-spider spin-the-night; Apta and Axapta, the twins; and Prince-Under-Sky.'

A doll-sized figure of a man, hooded and in pale robes.

Prince Under Sky. Evalia, and a memory of one of that mass of futile letters from the manors of the March, when she had been searching for the priest. It might have come from somewhere near Hayley.

'Ulfin . . .'

He was still talking to the hill chief, and had not looked her way.

They spent the night in the huts of the hillmen. Ulfin spoke with the chiefs and translated, commenting on the hill sayings and customs, and giving advice on how to eat the food. Phaedra said little. And later, when he slept peacefully beside her, she lay awake for a long while and stared at the open door and the pale night beyond. *Be careful*, said a voice in her mind. *Be careful.* And it was not the voice of Ulfin, but of Evalia diManey.

Opposite the village, perched on a shoulder of the far hill-side where the two valleys joined, was a long, low shape of stone. It was more regular than any rock outcrop, and broke the skyline in silhouettes that spoke of roofs and even, possibly, of chimneys. Ulfin pointed it out in the morning as the sun fingered along the rim of the valley and picked it from the shade below. It was a house, and the end of their journey.

It took them most of that day to clamber down into the valley and up the far side. They finished with a long, nervous stretch on a path as wide as a rabbit track that ran for a mile along a steep hillside among the thorns and scrub. The sun was westering, but lingered on the path and warmed the air, drawing sweat and the hum of insects in little clouds about the eyes and ears. Then the path rose, the crest of the hill dropped to meet it, and they were on a finger of rock above the world.

The mountains, wrapped in their evening cloud, reared in a wide circle around her. They rose beyond the green hillside where they had spent the night in the village, and ranged before them in blues and sunset-pink snow-fields around and up to the great massif of Beyah far to her right. Immediately ahead the path dropped along the spur to a small gatehouse, with slit windows and battle-ments like any wealthy house of the Kingdom. Nothing moved upon its walls. Beyond it were glimpses of other buildings, marching off in a row to the end of the spur. Phaedra laughed when she saw it. To find something so familiar in all that strange landscape was the strangest thing of all.

'Does anyone live here?' she called to Ulfin.

'I do,' he said. 'When I am here.' He walked forward to the gate. There was no moat or drawbridge. The path ended in the wood of the door, with the squat turrets lurking on either hand. Something flew from the gatehouse roof in a flutter of wings as he dragged the door open. There was a short, dark tunnel. Phaedra kicked Thunder forward. The gateway smelled of stone and emptiness. The hooves clattered loudly in her ears. Ulfin was waiting beyond, in a small courtyard with buildings on three sides and a low wall open to the great view of the mountains on her left hand.

'Welcome to my house.'

'Has it a name?'

'I think so. But I have not found it yet.'

'More importantly, has it water?'

'Come and see.'

He helped her down. Taking her hand, he led her through a low colonnade opposite the gate and into another courtyard beyond.

'Oh!' she said.

It was a small fountain court, like Tuscolo, like Trant, like Tarceny. The same colonnades, with low buildings behind them. The same fountain dribbling in the centre of it. Phaedra walked forward. She saw the same wide basin and the faded beast-carvings. Here, as in Tarceny, the body of a great snake or dragon coiled around the rim of the bowl. The water did not come in spurts, as in those other places. No pump was worked in all this deserted place to lift the water in its steady trickle, barely clearing the lips of the rearing beast before running down its front to the wet circle of the stone.

'Where does it come from?'

'It is cunning. A concealed pipe runs down the hill from a cleft far up the mountainside. It rises here, not just for show but so that those in the house may know whether their water line is still intact or not. From the bowl it runs to a cistern below our feet: a good, deep reservoir so that even if foes find and cut the water the house may still stand a siege.'

Phaedra looked around. It was not, in fact, wholly like the other courts she had known. For one thing, the colonnades ran along only three sides. The fourth was open, like the forecourt. Nothing but a chest-high wall stood between the floor of the court and a sheer drop down to the hillside below. For the second, it was irregular. The open side was the longest, admitting a wide view of the mountains around to Beyah herself. The far colonnade slanted back from a round platform at the end of the court to join the rear cloisters at a broad angle. And a great stone chair rose like a throne beside the fountain. There were steps up to it, and more carvings on it. Ulfin climbed up and seated himself.

'This place was built by people of the Kingdom,' he said. 'In the last wave of conquest after Talifer took Tarceny, they came here. They slaughtered the leaders of the hillmen and made the villages pay tribute. But they were too few. They needed help from the Kingdom, and the princes were busy with what they already held. Their leader sat here, waiting for months, years, but no help came. Now they are gone. And to my knowledge no man of the Kingdom has trodden here since, until Calyn and I found this place, a dozen years ago.'

He was silent for a moment, looking out at the great panorama of mountains.

'I shall come here when all is lost,' he said.

XVI

The Place of White Stones

ere, on this knuckle of the world, they idled through the days. Great birds drifted in their lazy circles, brown-backed when they flew below the level of the walls, and black against the sky above them. Ulfin had given over most of the goats at the village as a peace-offering, but they had kept a half-dozen for milk. There were small fruits from the bushes to eat, and game upon the hillside. The water from the spring was cold as melted snow.

They put the guards to repairing the roofs that had decayed since Ulfin's last visit, to clearing nests from the gatehouse and stopping the holes of the tenacious mountain-rats where they had burrowed among the walls. Ambrose played with his pebbles in the courtyard, yelling at the silent mountains and covering himself with dust. Phaedra and Ulfin walked along the hillsides in the sun. It was cool up here, in this high air. She imagined that even in the summer it would be possible to walk out at midday. Nevertheless, they did not go far. In that tilted world no path ran level. It was an effort just to scramble a few hundred feet back up to the house of an evening, as the sun dipped towards the peaks and all the mountains fumed.

On the third afternoon Ulfin led her from the gates and turned half-left, climbing the hillside in a direction they had not taken before. The way was steep and pathless, but clear of thorns. The house dropped away beneath them.

At the crest Ulfin paused. Phaedra climbed up towards him, breathing heavily in the mountain air. He pointed silently to the range of peaks before them, sweeping up to the great shape of Beyah away to their right.

'You can see why the hillmen say the world is a bowl, or cup,' he said.

'How did the mountain lose her child?'

'In the village across the valley, it is part of their story about the beginning of the world. In others, they will say it was when the giants came.'

'Giants?'

'Us.'

'I can see why you come here, Ulfin.'

'What has the Kingdom to this? Especially in summer, when the mountain air is cool. My brothers and I came here every year for five years, making friends with the hillmen and bringing them gifts as I have done this time. We climbed to this point often. We found what I will show you now.'

He turned away from the view and faced the hillside. A wall of low scrub rose before them, from which a boulder of white rock stood tilted like a sentry asleep at his post. Taking her hand, Ulfin stepped into the bushes.

'Be careful,' he said. 'It quickly becomes steep.'

293

For a moment she did not understand him. Then she saw him step downwards, felt his hand pulling, and realized that the scrub concealed not a rising hillside but a sudden drop. A space was opening before her as she followed him down among the thorn-roots. She was at the rim of a natural amphitheatre, some fifty yards across, facing up the valley towards the mass of Beyah, wreathed in cloud. The slopes were bare, and fell steeply from grey-coloured rock to brown. Ulfin had released her hand and was making his way carefully downwards. A perfectly circular pool of water lapped the cliff edges sixty feet below.

'Place your feet with care,' Ulfin said.

Phaedra looked around her. You could see nothing beyond the rim of the bowl except the sky above and, opposite, where the cliff above the pool was much lower, the peak of Beyah. The rim was crowned with white and grey-white boulders, like the one they had passed – some straight, some shapeless, some leaning drunkenly. Chance had not brought them there, scattering them at such even intervals along the bowl. Some vast workforce had laboured to bring them across these impossible hillsides – or down, perhaps, from the peak above – to stand like watchers around the rim.

Even as she completed her careful descent she could feel the spell of it. There was barely a ripple on the face of the water, blue-grey under the sky. The brown cliffs climbed above her to their crown of white rocks. Something moved in her – as if long ago, in a dream of another life she had been in this place before. It fitted. Ulfin was crouching on a narrow shelf by the water, looking up at her. Perhaps he was expecting her to say something. Right at his knee there was a notch in the rock, a foot or more across. He saw her eyes fall on it, and smiled.

'It is where the Cup was carved from,' he said.

'When?'

'At least three hundred years ago. But it may be older still.'

She did not feel surprised. The surface of the pool was smooth as a mirror in which the blue sky swam deep below. 'Can you bathe?' she asked.

He shrugged, as though she had still not asked the right question, but might yet do so. 'Of course – with care. There are a few yards of shallows, and then the bottom drops into nothing. I do not know how deep it is. It goes right to the heart of the mountain.'

Phaedra looked at the opaque surface. Her skin crept a little at the thought of those sudden depths a few feet from her, unseen. It was warm by the edge of the pool, and her dress (rough, short-sleeved for the summer and short-skirted for the hills) was prickling with sweat. So she removed her sandals and felt her way outwards with her toes. The water was cold – even here in the shallows with the sun warming the rocks around it. It had a thick, filmy quality, and as she looked down at her feet she saw them as through a veil: blanched shapes upon the dark stone beneath her soles.

She could feel Ulfin watching her.

Abruptly she stooped and, gathering a double hand-ful of water, flung it to her face. It splashed and cascaded and trickled down the inside of her dress in a shock of cold. She did it again, more gently. And again. After a while she felt her way outwards further, until the rock dipped beneath her feet and she could no longer see the bottom. She splashed herself again, and looked at the depths, and thought of flinging herself outwards and the deep cold enveloping her body. Her dress was soaked, and clung to her skin. There were bright droplets on her arm, winking in the sun. She looked round at Ulfin, and saw that he was watching her. He was half sitting, half kneeling by the edge of the pool, in his black doublet and hose, resting on one arm in a way that made her think of the lean muscles tensed beneath the cloth. He smiled, and she felt her blood move. She knew what he must be thinking.

Slowly she turned, and began to pick her way back through the shallows. She drew herself from the edge of the pool, with the water clinging heavily to her lower dress and pouring from its hem to the rocks. She retrieved her sandals, but did not put them on. Ulfin was waiting for her, not looking her way, stirring the surface of the pool with his hand. She began to step carefully around towards him.

He had brought her to this place. It was a sanctuary for him; and therefore for her. Her skin had begun to tingle with the thought of his embrace. She looked down on him and smiled.

He was not looking at her. He was watching the water, as if things were moving in it that she could not see. And when she thought he had finished, he stirred it again with his hand and muttered.

'Ulfin,' she said.

He did not seem to hear.

'Ulfin.'

Again she thought he had not heard. Then he picked himself to his feet, straightened his doublet, looked at her and looked away again across the water.

'Back to the house, I think,' he said.

She dropped her gaze. 'I'm sorry,' she said.

She was surprised and hurt. And Ulfin was already moving, not back up the way they had come but on around the pool, clinging to the steep slope and clambering along the rocks. She sat and put on her sandals, watching him go. As ever, his progress was easy and precise, and yet, knowing him as she did, she sensed some unease or uncertainty about him, as if half his mind was on what he was doing and the other on some thought that was troubling him. After a moment she began to follow.

The way around the pool was awkward, but no worse. Time had stripped rocks from the sheer cliffs, so that a thin apron of brown rubble lay at their feet and at the edge of the water. The far side was much lower than the cliff down which they had come, and sloped more easily. No doubt it was the way that Ulfin would normally have approached the pool, had he not wanted to show her the place from its most startling aspect. He was waiting at the top, either for her to catch up, or because he was turning some thought in his mind. He was standing by, and kicking lightly with his boot, a great grey-white monolith four or five times the size of the others, which had clearly fallen outward from its place and lay full length down the outer slope.

'A good stroke,' he said.

'What?'

He looked up. 'I am in the wrong place. There is nothing I can do about it.'

'What do you mean?'

He sighed. Then he shrugged. 'It does not matter. Let us go and see if they are ready to start supper.'

He turned left along the slope without waiting for an answer, although he must have known that it was an hour too early. Orani would only just have lit the fires.

There was a path here of sorts, looping around the outer face of the rock shoulder on which the house stood. Like almost all the paths in these hills it was barely wide enough for a single foot, let alone for two people to walk abreast. It faded away in places, demanding all the walker's attention to keep from an ugly fall down the hillside, and ended in a rough scramble up a steep slope that brought them to a point below the back of the house, from which they could climb to the gate. When they reached the outer court Ulfin walked on, saying nothing, and disappeared on into the colonnades around the fountain court. Phaedra looked around for Ambrose, whom she had left playing in the dust, but he was not there. So she took herself over to the wall to sulk at the great view. She could hear voices in the house around her – calling this, saying that, laughing. She wanted to shut them out. She wanted to rail at the mountains that were failing her.

After a while she stirred, and looked around. The first thing she saw was one of Ambrose's pebbles, wedged at the foot of the wall. There was another not far away. He must have lost or forgotten them. She began to pick them up absently.

'Umbriel writes what has been given,' she was saying

to herself. 'And why, and what else was given with it—'

'Nooaw!'

Ambrose had emerged from the shadow of the inner arch. He was standing unsteadily on his feet in the middle of the courtyard, watching her. She stopped, wondering what the matter was. He started to cry. Something was wrong.

'Hush, my darling, I'm coming . . .'

His wails became worse as she walked over to him – much worse. For a nightmarish moment it was as if her very approach was making him afraid, and yet she had no choice but to continue to walk over to him, to find out what the matter was. He held up his arm, not to be picked up, but for something else.

'It's all right, my darling. I'm here. Have you lost Eridi? What is it, my darling . . . ? No, I'm just picking them up so you don't lose them. Amba! Don't snatch! *No*, I'm picking them up, I said. Dear Angels, what *is* the matter?'

He was prising at her fingers, crying '*No! No! No!*' at her. She had never seen him like this before. For a moment the world flipped over in her mind, like a coin spinning, so that suddenly she was the child looking at a world that was a red face and shouting, and something that was forbidden.

He knew something. He understood something. What was it?

'Amba! Let go! I said, let go!'

Still he clung, and pulled, and cried to her. Now he had hooked his fingers into her palm to touch the white stone that she gripped there.

'All right, my darling. Please don't cry like that. Is this what you want? There . . .'

He took both of them, prising at her fingers to get the second one. Then he set out on his hands and knees for the wall. Phaedra watched him replace both stones more or less exactly where she had picked them up. Then he squatted down and began to play with the dirt by the wall as if nothing had happened. She realized her heart was working just a little harder than it had a right to. He had reacted so strongly, and yet with so little cause . . .

Something had been wrong, and he had had to replace the stones to make it right. What child's game had he been playing, that had been so real to him? He had not been just angry, or upset that his pattern had been spoilt. He had been afraid.

She turned slowly, looking about her as if seeing the place where she was for the first time. She saw other white stones by the wall. There were more by the buildings, and in both gateways. They were all around the courtyard, in a ring.

A ring. A ring that, a moment ago, she had broken.

Now she was afraid too.

She dreamed that she stood by a white stone, one of Ambrose's stones grown to the height of a sleeping sentry. She moved around it, and found that the rocky ground dipped into a pool in a bowl among the rugged hillsides. Opposite her a woman the size of a mountain sat and wept for a son lost at the beginning of the world. Phaedra began to climb down. Around her the shapes of stones rose like teeth against the sky, and one shaped like the white king of the chessboard lay fallen on the outer slope. She was close to the waterside, pausing over the surface and the impossible depth beneath it. Shadows moved on the far side of the pool. There was a smell that she knew, but had not noticed here before.

'Why have you brought me here?' she said to Ulfin. There was no answer.

She was awake, and the bed beside her was empty.

Her heart laboured. It was still night. She had no idea what time it was. She hauled herself to the rough stool by the side of the bed and sat there, waiting for the dull-brown fogs of sleep to clear from her mind. Ulfin was not in the room. He had gone out somewhere, at this time.

Ulfin was gone. He had slept fitfully much of the night, muttering and turning, sitting up and staring at the darkness. When, sleepily, she had asked him what the matter was, he had muttered again and lain back down. Now he had disappeared. Something in the air of the dark room told her that the door was ajar.

She crossed to it, and emerged barefoot in the colonnades of the fountain court. Orani lay, snorting lightly, on her pallet by the door. In the dimness Phaedra could see the black hulk of the throne rising with its back to her.

For Ulfin it would have been a natural thing, if he had been bothered and could not sleep, to go out and brood there while the stars turned. Perhaps he had done so for a while. But she knew, as she picked her way round to the front of it, that the chair would be as empty as it had been for centuries before he came.

There was no moon. A quality in the night, perhaps the very blackness of the mountain shapes against the pale sky, told her dawn must be near.

And now she was truly afraid. For if Ulfin could have

gone nowhere far in the mountains at night, the presence of dawn opened numberless possibilities. *I am in the wrong place.* Where did he think the right place might be? Was he trying, even now, to get there? Twice before in their marriage he had risen like this and gone away to the war. Never before had he left without warning. And why so suddenly, if not to ensure that he could not be followed?

For a moment she stood there, with her knees quivering in the air of the night and the stones of the court gritty beneath her bare feet. She thought of leaving Ulfin to disappear, to come back (if he would) that evening, or the next day, or – when? They had food, guards – surely he had not taken the guards. They could keep themselves here. And if need be they could return to Hayley, unless for some reason the mountain folk were suddenly grown hostile.

No. He was slipping beyond her reach. She did not know when he would return, and whenever it was might be too late. She must be quick.

She hurried back to her door, pausing to give Orani a shake as she passed. In the room she found her clothes and shoes by feel, and threw them on. Orani was sitting bolt upright among her blankets when she emerged again.

'Lady?'

'Orani, my lord has gone out. I do not know where or for how long. It may be nothing. But I am going to follow him.'

'Now, lady?'

'It's nearly dawn. You are to stay here. If we return today, well and good. If not . . .' She paused, thinking. 'If not, you must go, at dawn tomorrow. This place is

302

dangerous in ways I do not understand. You must make the men take you back to Hayley. Massey will do it, if you tell him I asked it.'

Orani was staring at her. Phaedra wondered how much she had understood. She did not have time to repeat herself. She spoke again more slowly.

'Whatever happens, you and Eridi must see that Ambrose is safe. If all else fails, remember that he has friends at Chatterfall. Go there quickly and in secret. The knight and his lady there will help you. Or you may make your way down the lake and seek sanctuary with the bishop at Jent. Orani . . .'

'Lady?'

'You know my son's enemies are not all of the day.'

'Yes, lady.'

'Those stones – the charms my lord gave. What did he say should be done with them?'

'He told Eridi, lady, when he first gave them. To keep them round the little one always.'

Those things could not come at him. All the same, it is right to be watchful.

'See that you do.'

She turned, and hurried along the dark colonnades to the forecourt. The gateway was black as pitch. She did not see the man in it until she stumbled into him.

'Who . . . ?'

'Who's there?'

It was the sentry, of course.

'Who is it? Grayme?'

'Buckliss. My lady,' he added, as he recognized her.

'Have you seen my lord?'

'Five, ten minutes ago, my lady. I was watching him go off along the slope. Then I thought he must ha' left the gate open, which he did. So I come down off the roof to close it.'

'Did he look as if he was going far?'

'He'd a loaf with him, my lady.' The man's voice was taking on a wary note, as he registered that the lord was off and the lady seemingly did not know where or why he was gone. Phaedra did not care what the man thought. A loaf would see Ulfin through a day. It would not get him to Hayley, but he might find other provisions before the day was ended. She must catch him quickly. But she must be prepared in case she did not.

'Do you have any food or drink with you?'

'Only water, my lady.'

'Give it to me, please.'

He looked at her for a moment. Then stepped out of the gateway and fumbled at his belt. The leather bottle he gave her was almost empty. She did not dare stop for more.

'Which way did he go?'

'Left, my lady, and down a bit.'

He was not going to Hayley then. He was going back to the pool.

'Let me out, please.'

The man fumbled with the bolts in the darkness. Grey light cracked from top to bottom of the arch as he pulled one great wooden door open. Outside it was nearly dawn. Phaedra hurried out into the cold mountain wind.

He had gone to the pool. In that dim light she was unsure of striking the path by which they had returned the previous day. She was unsure too of the loose-pebbled descent under the walls of the house. Instead she took the way she remembered – up the slope, tending to the left, climbing to the viewpoint by the thorns and the white stone. Somewhere the sun must have been rising; but there was little sign of it in the sky except, away to her left, where the mountain ridge above the village stood sharp and black against a pale grey with the slightest flush of rose.

She paused to listen for some sound beyond the hiss of the low wind in the thorns. There was nothing. Her feet crashed and scraped loudly as she pushed among the undergrowth, looking for the way down. She found it. Before beginning her descent she paused, and faced the white stone. Running her hand over the surface she found an area at the tip which was less smooth than the rest of it. There were indentations, as if of an iron chisel. She could not tell how old they were. There, a piece perhaps the size of a fist had been cut from the rock. Enough, she thought, to mill down to the sort of smooth pebble a child might play with. When she had descended through the scrub far enough to gain a view of the pool and the clifftops she paused to count the other stones.

There were thirty-one.

Voices sounded across the space before her. On the far side of the pool, on the very crest, stood the priest in his pale robes. He had his back to Phaedra. Below him, by the fallen monolith, was Ulfin. Only his head and shoulders were visible from where Phaedra crouched below the thorns. The words were indistinct, but the two were arguing.

If either looked her way, she would be in plain view. But the light was dim and her clothes were dull. If she did not move she might go unseen. She strained to catch the voices. Ulfin was the louder – urgent, angry. She could almost hear his words. The priest's voice was softer and more level. And yet she thought that he too was angry. What was happening? At one moment Ulfin seemed to be urging, almost begging, for something the priest would not consider. The next he was waving the words of the priest away with a furious gesture, and placing his hand upon the fallen monolith in a manner that appeared intended as a threat. Now the priest was answering again. At length Ulfin nodded, as if he were still not satisfied with the bargain, but knew that he was going to accept. Together they walked down to the water's edge. Phaedra watched as Ulfin kneeled before her enemy, and drank water that the priest had lifted from the pool with his hands.

Suddenly Ulfin had risen and was striding quickly up the slope towards the fallen stone. The priest was looking up towards where Phaedra crouched on the cliffside. She could not tell, at that distance, whether he had seen her. Her mind's eye saw again the cold smile she had seen on the stair of Tarceny. Then he too turned away, and the hillside was empty of him.

Perhaps he had gone behind some rock that she could not see. Perhaps he would emerge in a moment, following Ulfin or walking by the edge of the pool. Phaedra crouched, counting. He would come in sight in a few seconds. In ten. In twenty.

He did not. And neither her memory nor the growing light suggested that there was any boulder on the far rim of the bowl behind which a man might have disappeared so. He was gone into the rock, and she was alone above the pool.

Ulfin had passed the ridge. She must not be left behind again. She must not be deceived by light or lover; led to think this had been a chance meeting, any more than Ulfin had meant the white pebbles to be a child's toy. Somewhere down there the truth had glimmered for a moment, like a fish below water. She must catch it. As quickly as she dared, she committed herself to the descent.

Ulfin had met the priest. He had known – he must have known – that he would find the priest here.

Quickly, quickly. Don't fall.

He had brought her here, knowing the priest to be in this place.

He had let Eridi and Orani into his secrets. Why? Because they would not ask questions of him. They would take his pebbles, those little childish pebbles that had seemed to get everywhere, and make sure that Ambrose was surrounded with them, because he had told them to. As he must have told them not to tell her. And she, mother of the child, wife of the lord, had been left unaware, just as she had never been told that Caw was her father's killer.

'Ulfin!' she groaned, as she landed by the pool.

He hadn't told her because she would ask questions he did not want to answer. Yet he had always had answers for the questions she did ask – *Tell the truth*, he had sworn. And surely they had been true, as true as they had been deft and slanted to leave her as accepting and ignorant as before. They had left her trusting in the bond between them; the bond that now drew her on.

Quickly, quickly.

She was slow. The rocks were uneven, the water, where she splashed briefly into it to ankle-depth, shockingly cold.

. And now she was nearing the point where the priest had stood. She did not know if he had been aware of her before he had disappeared. She did not know where he had gone. She had a horror of meeting him and, worse still, the things that might be with him. She was going more cautiously, pausing to look around her. A man who disappeared so easily might reappear again without warning.

Angels! He had been *here*!

Her caution gave other parts of her mind time to think. Ulfin had gone back down the slope, the way he had come. He might have been going back to the house. He might be halfway there by now. She did not think so. He had taken provisions. Whatever his business with the priest, he was starting on a journey. She had nothing but thin shoes, thin clothes and a water-bottle that was almost empty.

The latter at least could be cured. She paused for a moment at the water's edge and looked around. Nothing moved. Uncorking the bottle, she thrust it into the water and watched the silver air bubbles gollop out until it was full. Another look around. Still nothing. She corked the bottle and hurried up the low slope to the point where the priest had stood.

She looked into a different world.

She should have been halfway down a steep mountainside, with the dawn growing in the pink sky and the green of the thorns and scrub-grass beginning to start from the grey, and the distant ridges black against the sky. Now the colours had changed. The land seemed darker, as if thick clouds had dimmed the rising sun. The shape of the hillsides had altered, although they retained in their low rises and ridges a suggestion of the mountains they had been. The sky was heavy, as if with thunder, and yet there was no breath of wind in the air.

Ulfin was in view, not far off, but walking away from her down a slope.

'Ulfin!' she shrieked.

He seemed not to hear her, and she sprang forward. Almost at once she lost her footing, for in the light and the slope there was something deceptive, and her feet did not strike rock where they expected it. She stumbled and slid, rolling and banging and bruising herself down the slope. When she checked herself, Ulfin was looking back at her from twenty yards off.

'Wait!' she said. Her voice sounded flat in her ears.

'What are you doing?'

'Following you.'

'Why the devil . . . ?'

There was something wrong about his voice too. Just as there was about the light, and the dark brown-rubbled landscape around her.

She knew this place. She had stood among rocks like these in a hundred dreams. Around her was the same barren landscape and the impossible curve of the distant ground, upward and upward until it seemed to be all cliffs of a gigantic scale that rose to a skyline far above her head. Away to her left two great lights glowed above the world's rim. The air throbbed with a sound so deep that it was almost beyond hearing. And everything was brown.

'You cannot stay here,' Ulfin said. 'You must go back.'

She looked back the way she thought she had come.

309

A few paces away, up a shallow slope, was the edge of a dark pool that lay among a jumble of boulders. Around it, standing stones rose like the teeth of some vast beast. She had dreamed of it last night. And she could remember now, years ago, how a nine-year-old girl had crept among its rocks in the dreams after her mother's death, peering into the black depths until the man had spoken in the shadow beside her.

'No,' she said.

XVII

The Deep of the Cup

e seemed to realize that even if she had wanted to find her way back to the daylight, she could not.

'He's let you through,' he said. 'To make a fool of me, I suppose.' He hesitated. He was wondering whether to lead her back up the slope, and presumably whether he could find the way back out of the brown rocks that she could not.

'I am in a hurry, Phaedra.'

'I am coming with you,' she said.

'You cannot. The others—'

'They have their orders. They will be as safe, I suppose, as at any time since I wed you.'

'I must go far and fast. To linger is to die, in this place. You cannot come with me.'

'I shall come with you, my lord—'

'If you come it is your choice and I am not responsible—'

'Indeed. And you shall tell me what it is—'

'Shall I?'

'You are sworn to, if you remember, by the one you left on the hillside above us.'

311

Ulfin muttered an exclamation, turned and began walking at a brisk pace across the brown land. Phaedra followed.

For a while she judged it better not to speak. In a little while he would have controlled his anger and surprise. When he had come to accept her company, they might talk. For now she must concentrate on keeping up – if she could. It was not so easy in this strange place.

Strange? She had been here before. She had walked among rocks like these a hundred times, in the dreams when Ulfin had met her with the Cup in his hand. She remembered them. She had never seen them with her waking eyes. She had never felt how dry the land was, or the emptiness of the humming air upon her cheek. She had never seen so clearly how the distant scapes of the world reared up all around her, as if she were walking within a vast bowl.

The light was dim. The ground was rough. There was a curious, oppressive quality to the place that teased her senses. Sounds were flattened and distorted. And sight – there was something wrong, or odd, about the distances. Perhaps she was confused by the way the world curved. The outlines of rocks were clear and sharp, but the way they shifted in her sight as she passed them did not match where her mind placed them. She could not tell without reaching out to touch them quite how close they were.

She stumbled, but did not fall. He was waiting for her. She had fallen behind again.

'Where are we going?' she asked as she came up.

He turned away. 'Tarceny,' he said. 'I must lay my hands on every man and beast and get them across the lake in a week. Less.'

It was the war then. Strange, that the explanation should be so understandable.

'Why? I thought campaigning was done for the summer.'

'They have been cunning. The widow's soldiers threaten Tuscolo, so Orcrim has drawn men from the garrison at Trant to aid the capital. But the real target is Trant. Trant is the key. If I had ever had the time to attend properly to Bay, it would be different. Now they have seen that without Trant I cannot reinforce across the lake. Septimus is leading a column against it now. Orcrim is unaware. I must head Septimus off.'

'How do you know this?'

'I saw it in the pool yesterday.'

She found she was not surprised by his answer. It chimed with so many things: the way he had watched and stirred the water; his behaviour then and on the way back; the cleft from which the Cup had been carved, in the rock beside the pool.

The pool that held the tears of Beyah.

Stride, stride, stride, swiftly across the shifting landscape of brown stones. He was ahead again slightly, although not so far that he could pretend not to hear her.

'Why did you not send Orcrim a dream – since you seem to be using your under-craft again?'

He neither stopped nor turned round; but she could tell that the question had made him angry again.

'I cannot reach anyone with thought from here. The pool is not the Cup. I do not own it. I would need power over it that I do not have.'

'Who does then?'

He did not answer.

'Ulfin, who is the Prince Under the Sky?'

'If you know enough to ask, you must already know the answer. Or do you mean, why is he called that? If you want to know, it was because he had no land. His brothers took everything there was. So he came here.'

'He is no priest, Ulfin.' In her hurry to keep pace she almost jostled against him. He turned, and his face was angry.

'I never told you he was. No, if you think, Phaedra, I did not. And before you speak, you would do well to ask yourself why I should have troubled myself to say more, when you plainly could not believe what already I had told you. Do you imagine that I did not know why you sought, at such risk, to bring an outsider, a priest, into our household? Did you think to persuade me to go through an empty ceremony that would make meaningless our hour upon the knoll? My lady, you are wed to me, and with the force of all the laws of our people, for there is no one living with more right to bind us than he who has his royalty straight from the loins of Wulfram.'

'You yourself have proved that you and your brothers were the last living of Wulfram's line. I have seen the scroll.'

'And you have misread it, for the last born we were, but the last living we were not. My lady, you and I were wed by the last of Wulfram's sons, Paigan, who has no issue, nor any need of issue, for he walks in his own flesh to this day.'

She stared at him. For a moment her mind was accepting what he was saying, incorporating it, linking it with other knowledge – Paigan, the prince. The eighth son at

314

the head of Ulfin's scroll. Landless. Came here after the conquest of the March. His settlement failed. The stone throne looking over the valley . . .

'Ulfin, do not spin me stories. Do not try to scare me—'

'Think what you like.' He was hurrying forward again.

'He would have to be *hundreds* of years old.'

'He is.'

'Ulfin – you don't mean it! Dear God! He *married* us. What price did he—?'

'Enough of this, Phaedra!'

Ulfin leaped a dry stream bed and started up the far side without waiting. He was trying to put more distance between them.

'He is the intermediary, isn't he?'

'What?' The question had stopped him.

'The intermediary. The one who has given you your power. And there's something in that pool that is the source of it.'

The tears of Beyah. The pool held the tears of Beyah, which the world-worm had brought to the earth in his teeth.

'How do you know these things? Who have you spoken to?'

'You are not the only one who has treated with him, Ulfin. You know Calyn did before you, and used his power to aid his rebel friends. No doubt your brother Paigan did too—'

'My brother Calyn feared too much, and failed. My brother Paigan did no more or less than you, my lady. Do not judge—'

'And what price did you pay?'

He turned his back and began to climb out of the gully they were in. She looked at the stream bed and judged it too far to leap. So she scrambled down into it and then out the far side. Ulfin was near the top of the slope, black against the brown sky.

'What price did you pay, Ulfin?'

As he crossed the skyline, he broke into a run.

'Ulfin!'

The slope was steep. She forced herself up it, panting. Pebbles gave way beneath her toe and she slid, grazing her hands. Then she recovered. Hurry!

She gained the ridge. The landscape before her tilted gently down to her right before rising again. It was thick with boulders, and the light was dim. Ulfin was nowhere to be seen.

'Ulfin! Ulfin, I can't see you. Wait!'

There was no reply.

She was growing weaker. She had drunk some water, but it had not helped. Something else was missing; some unknown element that nurtured life was absent from this place. Her feet were dragging, and she had begun to stumble when she should not have done.

At first she had hurried forward, expecting to catch sight of Ulfin almost at once as he emerged from behind some boulder or climbed from some dip in the ground. He had not appeared. Then, when her confidence had failed, she had dithered for a long time on a low ridge and subsequently tried to retrace her footsteps to the point where she had lost sight of him, in the hope that he would return for her. She did not understand how distances worked in this place. When she had gone as far back as she thought she had come forward since losing him, and still had not reached anywhere she recognized, her confidence failed again and she halted.

She had called, and waited, and called again. There had been no answer. Nothing had moved on that awful scape, where rocks and ridges merged brownly into the upward sweep of the bowl of the world that surrounded her. She was utterly alone.

At last she had begun to walk again, trying to keep to the direction in which she thought Ulfin had been travelling; hoping to find some sign that would guide her onwards. And her line grew more wayward, as she chose that side of a ridge rather than this, left around a boulder and right along the lip of a gully, until it no longer mattered which way she was headed, for all ways were equal and ran to an end among brown rocks.

Still that thing within her that more and more she named 'the bond' held her up and led her forward. She had followed Ulfin into the mountains, and had found him. She had followed him through the pre-dawn on the high ridges, and had come upon him. In this place too she would find him and pass with him back into the day. She must not think of any other possibility.

She stumbled again. Breathing was hard, and growing harder.

She came to a halt for a third time in half an hour, swaying, looking around her and the changing, changeless stones.

Angels, help me.

She was on her knees; but she had not kneeled to pray. She had fallen painfully, and did not remember falling. She wanted to rise, but did not. All directions were the same.

It was a place no different from any other in this land. She could see, with eyes accustomed to the gloom, the powdery-dry surface of the rock shaped like a severed pig's head by her right hand. She could see the ill-defined patch of shadow beneath it, in which clustered pebbles and grains that were each as brown and dry and powdery as any of the great boulders around her. She could feel the hard surface, the grit beneath her chin, as she rested against the rock. She could hear, in the ear pressed to the rock, the scrape and sound of the footsteps approaching her.

Ulfin, help me.

There was a movement beyond the boulder to her right, and stones slipping beneath a leather-shod foot. A voice calling.

'Are you there?'

'Yes,' she said.

She felt, in the silence, that the speaker was surprised. That he had expected someone else to answer, or to use different words.

'Who's there?' he said.

Who was there? What did a name mean in this place?

'I am,' she said. Still she rested against the boulder. She was weak, shaking. The man came into view, moving cautiously. He wore a brown robe, roped monk-style at his middle, and his head was bare.

'My – lady?'

'Martin? What – what in heaven's name are you doing here?'

318

'I followed . . . He woke me by my campfire. Did you see . . . ?'

'Ulfin? My lord?'

'No! Did you not see . . . ?'

They stared at one another. Then Martin walked to the edge of the slope, looking left and right down it as though sweeping it for some sight of another traveller.

'Well,' she said, when at last she found her voice. 'I am glad that whoever it was led you here, Martin. Although you may well not be.'

He looked around, at the sky and the rocks. 'What is this place?'

'A place between places. I have been here in my dreams.'

'Are those stars?' He was pointing at the two lights, low upon the skyline above them. 'They do not look like—'

'I do not think so.'

Capuu lies along the rim of the world, and binds it together. If she could somehow climb all the way up there, what would she see?

'The air is trembling.'

'Yes,' she said. Distant understandings were beginning to stir in her mind. 'We are within the Cup.'

'I don't understand.'

'There is a cup, or bowl that . . .' She stopped, her mind grappling for words that could make plain the mysteries that she was beginning to unravel. 'The surface of the Cup encompasses the whole world. Each point upon it compares with a place in the world. Those who are able to, may travel from one place across the bowl to another,

319

arriving there many hours or days before they might have done if they had taken the ordinary road.'

Martin looked around him. 'Have you water?'

She gave him her bottle. He shook it, then seemed to change his mind.

'Better that we save it,' he said, as he handed it back to her. 'How do we get out?'

'I do not know.'

He seemed to think about what she had said.

'We are not meant to fail, my lady. We can be sure of that.'

'Where were you camped?'

'In a valley in the foothills on the edge of the March. A day west and south of Hayley.'

So she was south and east of where she had started her journey. And she had come a distance that would have taken her at least four days of ordinary travel, if the way had been passable at all.

She closed her eyes and rested against the stone for a moment, drawing strength – strength from this knowledge; from Martin's presence in the desolate place.

When she opened her eyes again she looked around. Away to her left and right the light-brown dusk melded with the rising background in the same monotonal hue that it had done ever since she had entered the place. But before her, she now saw, it drew together darkly and seemed more close. Something lay there, half-concealed in the distance. Or maybe it was nothing. A place where the brown earth dropped away into nothing. A vast cleft running from half to her left away to her right almost as far as she could see. A cleft. A place that lay deep in the mind of the world.

'It's Derewater,' she said.

'Where?'

'There before us. There! He must be somewhere this side of it. He is going to Tarceny, to rally men and take them across in ships. If we are quick we may catch him.'

She struggled to her feet and set off again across the dry land. Martin followed.

'My lady – who did you say was ahead of us?'

She had forgotten that he could have no idea how she had come here. 'My lord himself. Ulfin, March-count of Tarceny. He was in a hurry, Martin,' she went on. 'So he came this way. I followed him, for I did not know what he was about. We must catch him, and speak with him quickly.'

With the loom of Derewater to guide them, Phaedra had some confidence in her direction; but she was still weak. She stumbled often, and once or twice she fell. And although she would pick herself doggedly up, mouthing Ulfin's names to herself like a litany, and set herself to walk on, she knew her mind was tiring and her legs were growing less steady. Martin was stronger, for he had been less long in this place. At first he simply put out a hand to steady her if she tripped. Later he was walking alongside her, with her arm in his as if she were some ageing relative whose limbs had grown frail with years.

Once he said a prayer to Raphael, aloud. A little later she made him repeat it. Then she tried to get him to teach it to her, for it was not one that she knew. The words slipped quickly from her brain, and she was left each time only with fragments.

They bore on together across that dark land.

It was their third or fourth rest in what might have been an hour. She was leaning against a rock, for she did not dare to sit or lie down now. And she was bracing to push herself upright again when she paused, and looked at the place around her. The ground sloped gently up to her right, as she faced back the way they had come. The rocks were like any of a thousand other rocks in view. And yet a sense of recognition itched somewhere in her mind, where her memory could not reach it.

The more she looked, the more certain she became. In some dream or memory, she had met with Ulfin here. Perhaps they had drunk the water from the bowl beneath the big finger of stone on the ridge above her, once, or many times, when he had wooed her from afar as a child.

'This way,' she muttered, lurching from the stone.

Martin followed.

She turned to her right, and pressed on uphill. She knew the slope of brown, jumbled stones that climbed towards the ridge, which was suddenly glowing as if with the last light of a sunset in all that sunless land. The landscape was scattered with huge boulders that looked like crooked people, all the same. Her feet were guided only by what seemed to be the angle of the slope on this rough ground. Still she stumbled upwards, skirting a double-peaked crag to emerge upon a lip of rock in the last sun.

Suddenly there was a change. The air was moving with the wind of the day. The terrible, brown world was gone. There were colours around her. It was sunset – a living sunset. The horizon was level with her eyes again. The green and gold of the land was fading into evening. And the stone was even beneath her feet. It was level, because it was paved. And before her a low wall rose battlemented, and she stumbled to it and clutched the edge of it.

She stood on the north-west fighting platform of Tarceny, and the banner of the Doubting Moon cracked overhead in the wind of the living world.

She rose and turned. Martin was sitting slumped by the parapet, but he picked himself up as she approached. There were no guards in sight. Voices were calling distantly from the outer court.

'Let us be inside,' she said. 'There may still be time.'

He followed her down the steep and narrow steps that descended from the platform, past the War-Room door, to the passage below. Here Martin grunted and, turning to his right, entered the chapel. Looking back, Phaedra saw him drop to his knees before a stained-glass window and bow his head. Above him the figure of Raphael, Friend of the Hapless, trudged on across a weary landscape with his staff in hand. She left him.

She made her way from the chapel to the living quarters, from the living quarters down through the hall to the upper bailey. Voices were calling. She passed servants, who stopped from their hurrying to stare at her as she walked by. The guard at the gate was watching the outer court-yard, and did not see her approach. When he found her at his elbow he jumped visibly. Phaedra ignored him.

The outer court was a turmoil of horses and wagons. There were forty or fifty men in the saddle, and others hurrying to marshal on foot. There were banners, knights riding to and fro, their voices hoarse as they bellowed for the fiftieth time for speed. Ulfin was among them, scowling at the mess. He must mean to set out now, with every man and more that he had brought with him to Tarceny three weeks ago. And it would be dark in two hours. Perhaps he was planning to march through the night.

Trumpets were sounding, and the gates were open. At the far end of the bailey the troops were beginning to file out into the evening. Ulfin had seen her. He sat still for a moment, and met her eyes. Then he was urging his horse over towards her, gesturing for the guard at the gate to fall back.

He bent in the saddle to talk down to her. 'I have one thing to say to you, my lady,' he said. 'If you love your son, let him not near me again.'

'Ulfin . . .'

And she saw in his eyes that he loathed her.

He did not wait for her to answer, but turned his beast in a great clatter and dust to join the companies that were filing through the outer gate. Pikemen, horsemen, banners and bowmen, merging into one black mass of helmets and weaponry as they passed out beneath the reddening sky.

She stood for a long, long time at the inner gate. Night fell, and the distant sounds of the march faded to nothing. When the torches winked upon the walls, she turned and went indoors.

In the living quarters, the writing desk and a number of other items had already gone. There was no paper, so she went to the library and cut a strip from the bottom of one of Ulfin's scrolls. On this she penned a few lines: a bald appeal to him to return and speak with her. As she finished, a kitchen boy came hurrying in to ask if she had everything she needed. The household must have gone into convulsions at their lord's sudden arrival and departure, and the realization that their lady was among them, without so much as a maid attending her.

'A special messenger for this, to follow my lord as swiftly as may be. I will go to my chambers now.'

'Food and drink, my lady?'

'Water, to my chambers, but no food. No food.'

Why? Why did he not love her? What had she done — what had she *not* done? Loved him, waited for him, upheld his war, borne him his son. He had no reason to hate her. He had loved her. He *should* love her! He had said that he did.

Then why did he not come?

'Dear Angels!' Her voice broke as she uttered her cry.

How many days had it been now? Eight? They passed one after another in endless, endless pains and dreams, in sips of lukewarm water and rising with the dawn to pen, each time more laboriously, another appeal to him to return. And every day some stupid maid or servant would try to bring her bread or broth, and she would curse them brokenly until they took it away.

Father was watching, from under Michael's wings.

Somewhere beyond one of these nightfalls he must be waiting. She tried to rehearse the words with which she would justify her life. I did not betray you. If you had only understood, not tried to force me, it would have been well!

He had not tried to force her in anything. His eyes would look on her, daughter-traitor, witless and deceived. Impossible to get forty men in war gear over the wall. There would have to be a man inside. In the Cup he can pass where men cannot pass – from the wilderness to the north-west bastion of Tarceny; from the lakeside to the postern passage within the walls of Trant. Who tells me that what I would do is impossible?

'No!'

Father was dead. That could not be undone. Ulfin was gone. He might yet return. And somewhere beyond this grey world was a place where Ambrose played in the sun. And she would plod, plod, plod until she came there.

The image of him (sitting on the dust, looking round for her) reappeared through the clouds of exhaustion. It troubled her that if Ulfin did not come, then Ambrose might not see her again. She would never see how he grew.

'Amba,' she whispered, over and over. 'You are all that is left of the world.'

She dreamed that he nodded and ran ahead, dodging among the brown rocks. Careful, my darling. It is easy to get lost here. He ran on in his clumsy child fashion, knowing the way. She followed. Her legs ached and her feet tripped. She lost sight of him. The ground dipped, and she followed it, treading around the stones that looked like people, until she saw the child, looking down into the great, rock bowl and the shadowed pool that she remembered.

Amba, come back.

Shapes flitted and stirred among the stones. Rock broke with a small, crunching sound under immense weight. There were tracks – clawed prints in the ground. They smelled of the edge of dank pools. Ambrose was gone.

She was peering over the edge in his place. Somewhere

326

a mountain wept for the child that was lost. The pool below her was lightless, deep and black, like the pit of the world. She looked into it, and there was nothing: deep nothing that weighed around her neck and dragged her down towards it. She had been here before, one half of her life ago. In the shadow beside her a man moved and spoke.

Will you drink?

I thought you would never come, she said. *Why have you been so long?*

He smiled, and held out the great Cup. The water was dark within it. She lifted it to her lips.

It was different. It crashed sharply upon her tongue, like the sudden shock of salt. She looked up, surprised and hurt, into the eyes of the man beside her. He was smiling at her still, terribly, as a snake might smile at a young bird. His eyes were deep pits. Something like a chain shattered in her mind, and she thought that she screamed.

For a father, the life of a son, said the pale priest. *For a king, the life of a king*.

She sat bolt upright in her bed. Martin stood beside her, with a bowl in his hands that smelled of some gamey gruel.

'He won't come,' he said. 'For Raphael's sake, you must eat.'

The gruel too tasted salty; like tears.

PART III

THE TRAITRESS

XVIII

Cold Morning

he War Room was lit with the first grey light of the world. The face of dead Paigan was a shadow in the corner. The benches and the chair were empty. The table was bare, its writhing carvings lost in the dimness. On it, bolted to the woodwork, stood the low chest. Phaedra ran her fingers along it, and they tingled at the touch. She reached out her hand and tried to lift the lid. It stuck for a moment, and then opened with a grunt of metal as the hasp freed.

There was nothing in it.

The inside was lined with dark cloth. Objects had rested there, and the fabric was crushed. She probed with her fingertips, trying to make sense of the marks. At one end had sat something heavy, with most of its weight pressing in two places. Its rounded surfaces had scored two ruts into the lining of the chest. She thought instantly of the Cup. She had never seen it with her waking mind, but the size and the weight and the shape that she remembered were right for it to have rested on its side and stem there.

At the other end of the chest was a fainter mark: a

331

small rectangle, as of a box containing something heavy. She could not tell how old it was, but it might from the size of it have been the little box of white stones that Ulfin had given to Ambrose, without telling her why, over a year ago. She thought that the cloth might retain an impression for that length of time. Between them had been something else, large and rectangular. It had lain there more recently than the box, although its edges were not as sharp. She looked and prodded for a long time before deciding that it might have been a book.

The things were gone. Ambrose – Angels send – played among the white stones in the mountains, and Ulfin had taken the other two to war, as he had done before. As his brother Calyn had done, with these things or others in the Seabord rising: Calyn who had 'feared too much' and yet had paid such a price that it had cost him his life.

Great Umbriel – what price had Ulfin paid?

And Paigan, his younger brother, who must have been named after that eighth son of Wulfram who still haunted the world? Ulfin said he had done 'no more nor less than you'. So he had drunk the water with Ulfin, who had loved him; and then spoken such words of it, perhaps, that his father had flown into a rage and slain him in this room. What price? None perhaps for Paigan, and yet Paigan too was dead. Round the rim of his portrait the great world-worm twisted in oils, and the letters at its head spelled CaPuU; *cPu* nitched the tiny dark letters of the snake ring on the chain around her neck: the ring that had been his. Each brother had had a ring, with the letter of his own name set between the other two. Calyn's, Evalia had said, had recalled the motto of his house: 'The Under-Craft

Prevaileth'. The ring of Ulfin must spell *cUp*. She had never noticed, or understood.

She left the room, empty. The stair wound downwards towards the chapel, from which Martin's voice rose in the morning office.

Her legs carried her down, but were not strong enough to hold her standing in the little aisle while the morning songs endured. So she sank into the wall-bench and waited, eyes closed, for the notes to die away. At length Martin dropped his hands from prayer and turned.

'I am glad to see you up, my lady.'

'They tell me it was only six days.'

'Only?'

'When I was a child I went without food for a fortnight, and would have gone to the end if my father had not himself surrendered. I had not thought I had become so weak-willed. Martin, I want to talk with you.'

'Now?'

'If you please.'

He looked hard at her. 'Is this penitence?'

'I think it is – at last.'

'Do you wish to kneel? We can perform the office from your seat, if you would find it easier.'

She thought about it and nodded. He took his place beside her and began to murmur the opening prayer, while Phaedra looked up into the four faces of Heaven.

'I have three things to tell you,' she said.

'The first is what I said a moment ago. When I was nine years old I set out to starve myself to death because my mother had died and I thought my father would remarry. After two weeks he promised me he would not.'

'Wherein lay the fault?'

'It – was blackmail, and an act of lovelessness. He doted on me, for I was the last of his family. And when I had shown him that I might starve myself at will, if I chose, he could not rule me any more. After that he was bound to do as I wished, and so was everyone in Trant; even, when it came to my marriage, to offend great lords of the land, for fear that I would begin to refuse food again. I was—'

'It is also taught that the intent of self-destruction should be cause of penitence.'

'I know.' She thought to herself that Martin's former master would have had his own views on that point; but she had not come to argue.

'Umbriel, write what has been said,' whispered Martin at length. 'And Michael, lend us courage to face the enemy within.'

'The second is that shortly after that time, I began to meet a man in the places that you and I travelled when we returned to Tarceny a week ago. Together we drank a – a . . . love philtre.' The words 'love philtre' sounded wrong. They could not describe the meaning of the Cup, year after year of it, but she could not think of anything better. 'The bond persisted between us. We loved each other, and I became his wife, in a ceremony that – was a true marriage, but took place without my father's blessing.'

'Wherein lay the fault?'

'Witchcraft,' she whispered, because she knew that she must. And she did not say: *I was a child, I trusted him, I knew no better.* Penitence could not come to Umbriel dressed in excuses; only the thin cloak of filth that she had borne ever since she had begun to taste the water and that she now felt at last, clinging to her skin as she spoke. 'And betrayal. I had forced my father to give me love, and I—'

'Umbriel, write what has been admitted,' said Martin softly. 'And Gabriel, bathe the heart of the penitent in Glory.'

Phaedra hesitated, partly because he had cut her off from saying that which (at that moment) she felt most keenly, and partly because he had changed the order of the office as she understood it. Gabriel, Messenger of God, should have been accorded the last and greatest place among the brothers of Umbriel.

'The third,' she said at last. 'When my father called the King to help him bring me home, I told my husband how I thought my home might be taken in an armed raid.'

'Wherein lay the fault?'

'Betrayal.'

She had seen in her mind's eye a means of attack on her home. She had spoken of it to those men – hardened, armed killers from the former days of Tarceny. She had hoped, stupidly, that no harm would come of it. And yet she had preferred that lives at Trant should be at risk rather than that she should end the quarrel by returning there. She had not even considered the possibility.

It had been betrayal, although Ulfin had had no need to follow her wild plan, and must never have intended to. There would be no need to climb a wall with forty men in war gear if you could walk among the brown rocks and appear suddenly within your enemy's castle, perhaps with one or two most trusted men, and so open the postern door to your storming party before the guard was aware.

Despite the bond between them – perhaps even because of it – he had allowed her to believe that it was she who had shown his men the way into Trant, and to the ending of her father's life.

Ulfin!

Slowly, from the fog of her desolation, the outlines of his mind were emerging at last. The past was becoming more than just event after event. He had planned each move, like a chess player, long in advance, seeing clearly where others had gone in blindness. Trant had been the key. Holding Trant he had the road to the heart of the Kingdom. When had he first known that? Long before ever he had lifted the bolts of its postern door and let his swordsmen in. No, even before he had raised the water to her lips one part of his mind had known what the end should be – not just Trant, but Tuscolo, the empty throne, and the changes he would bring around it. He could see far, and speak far. She had been a fool to suppose that, given such power, he would use it only to woo a young girl in a lakeside castle. How had he gained such victories? Why had the gates of Baldwin and Tuscolo opened so suddenly?

How had the King died?

A chess player. And yet he was not in his element. The world was less precise, more perverse, than he allowed for it to be. Fathers denied him the hand of their daughters for the sake of an ill reputation earned a generation before. Doors that should have held gave before imprisoned men, so that their blood would be spilled to his shame. The stubborn barons would not yield to his harrying, and the

336

widow of Develin so hated him that she armed the enemies of her house against him. Even his 'under-craft' twisted from his purpose, so that the bonds of love that he should throw about his beautiful bride should be bonds for him too – in some unfathomable way a weakness or impediment that he had not intended, and from which he could only break free at the cost of allowing the woman who had been blinded with love to understand at last the secrets that he kept from her: the name of her father's killer; the name of the one who had married them; the charms he had placed around her son, set by two serving women who, because of their ignorance or credulity, he trusted more than he did his wife.

How he must have longed to be free of the love-bond that he had wished upon them both!

The last she had seen of him was the loathing in his eyes. Hatred, because she had become to him a burden and a threat. She had pursued him with her questions among the brown rocks, imagining that he must answer her with the truth. But he had already escaped her. The priest at the pool had given him the water that released him. And so he had left her in that terrible place.

Ulfin!

There had been a time when he had talked about leaving the night and entering the day. There would be no more magic. He would do things in the plain, ordinary way that others did them, and let the secrets of twilight sleep. On the battlements above her head she had seen him laugh and fling his arms to the sky, as if he had been pushing something away, or crying '*Stop!*': towards the peak of Beyah, the ruined house on its great spur; towards the pool that held the dark tears of the Mother of the World. It had been a gesture of defiance, and refusal.

What had changed his mind? The sight of his enemies, pressing in upon him, with no power but their numbers and iron. Without the magic he would fail. So he had gone back. He had become a suitor again; a suitor to the undying priest, Paigan Wulframson, Prince Under the Sky, who must have found the pool and its power, even as his own brothers abandoned him to his stillborn kingdom in the mountains three hundred years ago.

Where had Ulfin been, when Father was slain? She could remember his words on the knoll as clearly as if he had spoken yesterday. *By the time I got there, he was dead.* Where had he been? She had supposed him to have been within Trant, almost, but tragically not quite, within call. What if he had not been there? If he had been within the Cup again, travelling north to some point where no one could expect him to be?

How had the King died?

And what price had Ulfin paid?

'My lady?'

Martin was waiting for her to go on. She shook her head.

'My lady, before I close, I must ask whether this witchcraft persists between yourself and your husband.'

'It did until a week ago. His bond was broken then. Mine – a day or two since, as I fasted and waited for him. I do not love him any more.'

'So – you are now free.'

'Free. Although . . .'

The priest, grinning at her as the water had crashed

through her mind. He had spared Evalia to suffer. Was that what he had now done for her? Her hands were shaking. Famine, anger or dread? She felt them all.

'. . . It is the manner in which I have been freed gives me the greatest cause for fear.'

Ulfin! You did . . . Oaths and Angels!

Martin must have been waiting for her. At length he said: 'If there is more that you would say of this, I beg that you do so under Penitence and not—'

'There is not, Martin. And I came to you because I have begun to understand things that had touched upon me; not because you have already walked with me in places that could only have been reached by witchcraft – although I am glad that our shared journey must at least have made it easier for you to believe what I have been saying.'

'Indeed.'

'Close the office, please, Martin.'

'Umbriel, write that which has been owned, and that which has not been owned. Seal it in our minds and hearts until the Day of the Call of the Dead. And Raphael, Compassion of God who walks in the dark places; Friend of the Hapless; Light on our Path; Wise, Tender, Commanding . . .'

'Thank you,' she said when he had finished and was helping her to her feet. 'I had never heard that prayer before. Still, it does not seem wrong to have him take precedence over his brothers at Penitence.'

'My lady, I think that he may have taken an interest in this matter already. And that most directly in a manner I would never have believed.'

'You are saying . . . ?'

'That I was woken in my camp by a man. He was plainly dressed – as if he were a peasant or a pilgrim. Yet his voice was not like that. He led me to find you among those rocks. There was no escape from them, and yet we escaped. I remember telling you then that I did not think we were meant to fail.'

A pilgrim?

'What did he look like, Martin?'

'I can hardly say, my lady. It was dark, and by the time I was fully awake, he was already walking away from me. Yet – yet I can think of no other explanation than that it was Raphael himself.'

Phaedra felt no movement in her empty soul. Great and compassionate as Heaven might be, she could not imagine that it would have stooped to help her. And there was another ugly, horrible possibility that the word 'pilgrim' roused in her mind.

'Can you be certain? I remember you saying that the Angels moved only within us, and did not appear in body as we suppose they do. And I cannot think that he should have chosen to intervene for me at all, no matter through what agency.'

'They who think themselves furthest fallen are often the most near to help. And I know what Tuchred teaches, and what I have said. Yet there was one who woke me in the night from my camp and bade me follow. I rose, and pursuing him I found you, in need, in that place – I do not know what to believe. I wish I could send a letter to His Grace, but—'

'I may have a message for him too. Can you send it for me?'

She saw a sudden wariness come over him.

'It would be better if I were not seen to be writing myself,' she said.

'You know Caw opens my letters, my lady.'

'What! No, I did not.'

'Not long after I came here I saw that a message that came for me had been opened, and then re-sealed with some care. So when I wrote the reply and handed it to the messenger I watched what he did. Before leaving he took it to Caw. He has done so with every message I have sent outside the castle since then. Not that I have had occasion to do so often.'

'You should have told me.'

'For a while – forgive me – I assumed it was at your orders.'

Phaedra remembered a time when her first thought about Martin had been that he was the bishop's spy.

It was that little extra lurch of anger and of guilt that made her decision for her. There, in a corridor outside the chapel, with one hand on his shoulder and the cold draught flowing down the stair, she knew what she was going to do.

'Caw is still in the house, is he?'

'My lord has left him in charge, with some strength, for they believe Septimus has raiders in Tarceny. Whether that will remain so after my lord's latest victory at Trant I cannot say.'

'I will not stay under the same roof as Caw.'

Again, Martin was waiting for her to go on. People were always waiting for her.

'Martin, I need you to do me another service.'

'My lady.'

'Go to Hayley. If Orani and my son are not there, have the garrison send into the hills to bring them down. I will need to tell you how you may find them. Once they are at Hayley you should set out as if to bring them back here. Then you must turn secretly aside, and take them to the manor of diManey beyond the lake. Its name is Chatterfall, and they will be safe there for a short time . . .'

He was listening, thinking. He did not seem in the least surprised that he was to set out again, so soon after his sudden and extraordinary journey home.

'Will the soldiers co-operate?'

'You will need to choose the right ones. There is one called Massey, another called Orchard – they have been there before. Do not use any others unless you must. Martin, there is one further thing. I do not know who it was who roused you from your camp. Maybe it was a power of Heaven, maybe not. There is one who walks in the robe of a pilgrim or priest who is no friend. If ever you see him again – I beg you to be careful.'

Martin looked at her for a long moment. She saw him understand that, even under Penitence, she had not said all that she should have done. Then he nodded.

'And what will you do?' he asked.

'I will go . . . I will go to Jent.'

Another lie. She would go towards Jent. But not even Martin should know what it was she was planning to do.

XIX

Ordeal

er new maid was called Hera. She had been sent, generously, by Elanor Massey in response to a letter Phaedra had written the day she had ceased her fast. Hera was the same girl who had fallen asleep in the chair while waiting on Phaedra two years before. She smiled openly, and had come with a warm recommendation. All the same, Phaedra thought her both very young and not altogether sensible. So she was less surprised than perhaps she should have been when, an hour after their arrival in Baer, Hera came flying into the upper room where Phaedra was resting, threw herself down and, seizing Phaedra's hand, kissed it. Somewhere nearby a church bell had begun to ring.

'Your Majesty!' Hera said.

'What?'

'I'm sorry, mam. I just wanted to be the first to call you that. They're saying in the streets that he's been crowned! I'm going to serve you really well, Your Majesty. I'd never have believed—'

'Dear Angels, girl' – although Hera was almost exactly

her own age – 'I am not crowned yet. I may never be. Whatever they are saying in the streets, it may not be true. He has refused the crown twice—'

'He's taken it, mam. He truly has! So perhaps the war will be over,' Hera said. For she had quickly decided that her mistress must be unhappy at her lord's absence.

'He has won battles before, and not brought it to an end,' said Phaedra dryly. 'Now get to your feet and be useful, will you? Look,' she said, lifting the green cloth she had been fingering in her lap. 'You have made me spill my drinking water on this sleeve. Hang it out of the window to dry, please. And you can tell me whether the people are planning to storm the lodge at the same time.'

A few scattered cheers broke out when Hera appeared at the window.

'They think I'm you, Your Majesty,' she said, and waved at the crowd below. 'I think they'd like to see you, if you are willing.'

'If that is what they want. But I shall not be called "Your Majesty", Hera – by you or them.'

'No, mam.'

'That's to be quite clear. Let the word be sent from the door. I shall want to go out in the town soon, for I have Sarcen silks to order for my lord's robes. I do not want to find myself part of a procession.'

'No, mam.' Hera was still smiling, waving from the window. 'What colours, please, mam?'

'What?'

'What colour silks, mam?'

'Oh. Black, I suppose. And gold,' she added sourly.

Gold for a king. And green – the green cloth of Trant,

hanging from the window of the lodge: a signal for the man from the reeds of Derewater.

Lying awake in the night, remembering. *And will he refuse it a third time? I wonder.* She could picture the scorn in Lackmere's eyes as he had spoken to her of her own naivety. *In politics it is often necessary to refuse more than once what you would most have others give you.* So now Ulfin had what he had sought from the beginning.

Again and again she remembered his face as they had talked in the fountain court about Ambrose's name. Without saying a word that was untrue, he had led her to believe the opposite of what was true. He had duped her so many times, and most of all about his will to be King – the Fount of the Law, which in him would be founded on lies.

She could not sleep for anger.

Once she cried his name aloud. 'Ulfin!'

She remembered how, in that very room, she had heard a woman's voice crying the name of Ulfin's brother in the night. Even Evalia's loss, she thought, was less terrible than her own. At least for Evalia the memory of Calyn was whole.

The small hours of the night seeped past. She turned in her sheets, dozing, dreaming among images of Ulfin smiling, Ulfin speaking, Ulfin frowning in thought as he offered her the white stones for Ambrose. The white stones now lay scattered in a room where Ambrose slept. Such little things they were, hidden in the darkness. The shadows moved. Something cracked beneath a clawed foot close by. She saw Ambrose wake and begin to cry. She saw

Eridi lift her head from the pillow to listen. Across the chessboard Phaedra met the eyes of the priest.

When the time comes you must sacrifice without mercy, he said. *Except the King, which you must guard with your life.*

She looked down and did not answer. There were very few pieces on the board, and most were black. She prodded another white stone into place around her son, and prayed that the ring might hold.

A day and a half of dull riding south of Baer, as they were plodding slowly through low-limbed woods, a horseman surged onto the path ahead of them. He was helmed and armoured. Another followed at his tail, and others with him – five, eight, more.

'Put up your arms,' one shouted.

A crashing among the bushes behind her told that others were emerging from the woods to cut off their retreat back down the road. The sergeant who led her escort reined around, looking for a line of escape as his half-dozen men fumbled for their weapons. The ground among the trees was rocky and treacherous.

The horsemen were beginning to close from the front. In a few seconds they would charge.

'You had better do as he says,' said Phaedra.

The sergeant was neither young nor noble-born, and had the sense the moment needed. He grunted an order to his men, who dropped their weapons to the ground. The ambush party approached from front and rear. Orders were being given – to her own men – Move over there, put your arms up, hands together, *do* it, damn you. She looked around, but could not see any face that she recognized.

The leader towered over her on his charger. He took the reins of her horse. He did not say anything. His helm hid most of his face, although a mane of black hair peeped from under it, and there was something distantly familiar about his eyes. A rider nearby spat at her. She watched dumbly the little fleck rolling down the pommel of her side-saddle.

'*Vixen!*' one screamed at her.

Then they put a sack over her head.

Patience, patience. She had gone in the dark before. The hood rasped at her cheek and chin, and her breath huffed in the cloth before her lips. There were chinks of daylight rising from where it opened around her neck. And she did not have to see. All she had to do was ride, and wait, for however many hours it would be until they lifted the hood from her head again.

She told herself that it was important that they should treat her as a prisoner. It must not seem to her soldiers that she was being handled any differently by their enemies. She wondered why Lackmere had chosen so open a way of contacting her. (If he had chosen it, for she had not seen him yet.) She had been expecting him to fall in with her company disguised as a priest or a merchant, so that they could speak privately on the road. She had taken a small escort because it increased the chances of finding a moment to talk unheard – not because it would make falling into an ambush easier. There would be a lot of explaining to do at Tarceny, if she returned there after this.

If she returned. She had no idea what would happen now. She could hear, not far away, the sound of Hera whimpering as they rode. Presumably she too was blind-folded. Phaedra could feel the sound sawing at her own nerves. She wanted to utter some rebuke, sharply, at this silly girl whom she barely knew. She did not. Hera had much less idea than she why they had suddenly been pounced upon. Earlier that afternoon she had been still blissful in her sudden proximity to the new queen, full of dreams and thoughts about the future. Now she was being herded along by rough, armed men. Angels knew what fears were in her mind.

And no doubt Hera had a sweetheart somewhere who still loved her – who had not abandoned her and to whom she had expected to return. Perhaps she had not betrayed her own father to death. Perhaps she still thought the world was a place in which good things would happen and go on happening, in which a soul might be free of its own guilt and seek for something more than just the undoing of what could not be undone.

'Hera,' she called, trying to keep her voice soft so that no one would be tempted to shut her up. 'Hera.'

There was no answer, but the whimpering stopped.

'It won't last, this. It won't last for ever.'

Still there was no answer. Whatever Hera was think-ing, she was silent in her hood. Phaedra rode on, and did not know whether she pitied her maid or envied her.

It did not last. An hour later, after a steep climb and then a long descent by running water, her horse was pulled sharply to her left. She could hear others of the party ahead of her. They had slowed. Her mount plodded forward under somebody's guidance, and began to climb a slope. Instead of the *scrape-clip-scrape* of hooves on rocky paths there were dry leaves and twigs under its feet. The sounds had changed. They were not in the open. The noise of wind in branches was overhead as well as around them. They had turned off the path and plunged into trees. Instinctively she crouched in the saddle, hunching her shoulders against the imagined sweep of low branches. She wondered if her captors would care if she caught a knock or a twig in the eye.

'Take our masks off,' she said.

No one answered.

'Take them off,' she said. 'We can't remember the way now. And it won't help you if we crack our skulls or fall in the bushes.'

There was a halt, and low words spoken among their captors. A horse rode up close to her left. A hand hauled the hood roughly from her head. Light exploded in her eyes.

They were, as she had thought, in a wood. It might have been any wood anywhere in Tarceny, for it had the same steep slope and green leaves and the sound of rushing water somewhere below. Down there a rearguard of their captors had assembled, sweeping leaves across their tracks. Others were taking the hoods off her followers. Her men, she saw, were bound. Hera's face looked drawn and miserable. Phaedra tried to give her a smile.

Lackmere was still nowhere to be seen.

'Forward,' said the leader.

He had removed his helm, and his thick curling hair fell in a mane to his neck. Watching his back, as he rode a slanting path ahead of her up the slope, she saw the faded design on his surplice. There, faint on the brown and weather-stained cloth, an eagle spread its wings above a battlemented tower: Baldwin. He was one of Elward's brothers – probably Tancrem, the middle one, as the youngest could barely be carrying arms yet. That was why she had thought she recognized him. And Phaedra felt a slight chill in her stomach. For while it was something to know her captor's name, she could not think that any in the House of Baldwin would be well-disposed towards her.

They breasted the slope, and suddenly there was a camp before them. It occupied most of the flat top of the hill, under three huge oaks with awnings spread from their branches. There were a score of men and a few women there, watching them as they rode up. There were horses in lines, and a cooking fire with the thinnest wisp of smoke above it. It was a strong place, defensible, in that the hill was steep sided; well concealed, for until you climbed to this level you did not know it was there; and yet it lay within ten minutes of at least one path, and offered its inhabitants the whole cloak of the forest to hide in if some force were to come against them.

Faces were turned towards her. She was scanning them for signs of Lackmere when Tancrem, dismounted, appeared at her knee.

'Down,' he said, and held out his hand.

'Thank you,' she said as she alighted. 'It is good to see, and to walk, after so long.'

'Stand there.' He was pointing to a spot in the middle of the camp. She turned and walked silently to where she was told. Her other followers were being hustled off somewhere. People were gathering around her, in a half-ring.

She looked round at them, and found that it was impossible to look a crowd in the eye.

Men came forward with drawn swords. They laid them down in a row on the leafy forest floor.

There were six. Three pointed towards her, and three away. A young man, bareheaded, stepped forward and began reading from a scroll.

It was a charge of witchcraft.

All the voices that had spoken to her, murmuring in her ears now. In the rustle of the leaves she could hear Father talking, but she could not catch the words. Evalia – how hard it was to think at a moment like this! Little Ambrose cried 'Mama', and looked around for her. And still she stared across at the young man reading, on and on, and could not speak.

It was the accusations themselves that steadied her. The reedy voice bore in upon her confusion. It stated this, described that, all things that she was supposed to have done; things that even her bewildered mind could reject at once. This was not, as she had for some terrible moments supposed, her confession to Martin returned to bring her to her ruin. This was a credulous, ludicrous concoction; a miscellany of all the frightened whispers that man could pass to man in a defeated army. Martin had not betrayed her. He must still be striding north to Hayley, as she had bidden him, to meet her son and take him to safety. And knowing that, she could think again.

They were going to kill her. They were going to blow a horn three times and then take her somewhere and cut her head off. Now the thing that she felt most clearly was

351

anger. Anger not because she had come in good faith to talk with them – they were armed men and enemies and might kill her if they chose – but that they should go through this mummery first, to give themselves the excuse, which would stand in no one's eyes except their own, that what they would do was both holy and right.

She looked around at the faces in the ring. A score, two score of them, crowded several deep on her left, strung thinly around behind her and to her right. On that side there was a young fighter with bowl-cut blond hair, and a tall woman, whose face recalled a shadow of a memory. The woman was frowning at what she saw before her. They were a beaten, sullen band. They would barely enjoy this little revenge.

The young man had finished speaking. Lackmere was not to be seen.

The horn blew. Tancrem and two others stepped up to the swords. The others were young, like him, and like the one who had read the charge. They were Tancrem's clique – a little sub-group in this desperate band. So Tancrem was the one behind this. He stood there, with his dark eyes burning with the memory of his brother, waiting to hack the head from the woman his brother had loved.

'Should I not answer first?' she asked, pitching her voice to carry clearly across to the ring.

She saw Tancrem frown.

'Be quick,' he said.

She paused, and looked around her. She must speak calmly, and keep speaking. The charges – she had barely been listening to them, except to register that her dark arts were supposed to be behind their defeats, that she was the mastermind, urging her husband on to bring misery on the world. She could not let those idiocies go unchallenged. But even admitting that she had charges to answer seemed to play the game for her killers.

Another voice was in her mind: far back, in the sun by a well in Tuscolo.

'She has nothing to say,' said Tancrem.

'I was just thinking. I've seen something like this once before. After it was over, one of my friends said – what was it? That because some dog-knight from the back of nowhere was ready to fight, the woman who was on trial might be innocent. But if no one had wanted a fight with the cut-throats who had been put up against her, we'd have known she was guilty and had her killed.

'What she meant was that any man who steps forward to fight, on either side, must think he can change the past, as well as the future. Which is more even than the Angels may do. And as she said – what do knights do *but* fight?'

She looked around at the ring, to make them understand that it was them she was talking to. The young fighter with the bowl-cut hair was bending to catch something that his hooded neighbour was saying. The woman beside him was turning away from the crowd. Perhaps she was disgusted with the scene. Others were listening. Phaedra knew she must keep talking – talking like the elder sister that she had never been. Now, as if to the young man who had read the charges: 'I did not catch all you said. I don't think I needed to. Where did you get all that from? I have never conjured anyone – unless you count praying that my husband would come home. I have never enslaved anyone, by any means. I have never killed or tried to kill anyone' – she thought for an instant – 'except myself. And for that I have been penitent before the Angels and a sanctified priest—'

'That's enough,' broke in Tancrem. 'She has denied the charges. Blow the horn.'

As if she had not heard him, and still to the man who had read the charges, she continued. '. . . A sanctified priest. *You're* not a priest, are you? For a moment I thought you must be. You do know that justice must be blessed? Anything else would be a terrible risk. But I think it would be hard to find any priest within a hundred leagues of Jent who would do this without the bishop's permission. He is very firm against ordeals – he's told me so himself.'

'That's enough. You've had your time and wasted it.'

'Do you doubt me? You could ask the Baron of Lackmere. He was present at the time. So if you really want to press these complaints I suggest we had all better go—'

'*No!* Blow again!'

Tancrem was in a hurry. He had not denied knowledge of Aun. So this was Aun's party. She should insist that she had come to see him. But Tancrem would know that. He was trying to get his bit of murder done while his leader's back was turned.

Think of something – anything!

'A moment!' she cried. The man who had read the charges hesitated, with the horn part-way to his lips.

'I see you have not untied my men—'

'They are dishonoured. Tarred with your brush.'

'They are low-born, Tancrem,' said someone else.

'Low-born!' he repeated.

'In the eyes of Heaven, does that matter?' She must be careful about this. No farmer put in a mail shirt would stand a chance against a war-trained knight. 'If they were to choose my side, and my side was right, then—'

'Enough! Blow.'

The horn rang through the forest. Its harsh tone blotted her train of thought. It was one more step closer to death. She could feel her control slipping. She wanted to grab one of the swords and fight. But they would love that, these sweaty bullocks. It would give them everything they wanted. They would chop her up like butcher's meat.

Someone had walked up to stand at her left. It was another youngster – the boy with the bowl-cut hair. He stood at the hilt of a sword that pointed from her.

'Chawlin!' Tancrem's voice mixed scorn and exasperation. 'Get back.'

'No.'

'Chawlin!' the others cried. 'You idiot!'

He shook his head stubbornly. He must be a misfit here, part suffered, part mocked by the main band, with little to commend him but a mind of his own. Still, his appearance at her side made no sense. And now one – two of her men were on their feet beyond the ring, calling hoarsely for their bonds to be untied so that they might stand for the swords too.

'Chawlin, for Michael's sake, this is *serious*.'

'*I'm* serious.'

The moment of farce was a gift. She exclaimed loudly and marched towards the gap he had left in the ring. Tancrem yelled, but she kept walking. They were not stopping her. The show was falling apart. There was no one in front of her but the old man in the hood, who lifted his eyes as she approached.

Cold eyes, and a cold smile that she had seen before.

She must have halted. Someone's hand had closed on her wrist. Somebody gripped her shoulders. Behind her the men were scuffling. She saw the priest turn and vanish, and no one else had seen him. They were herding her back towards the middle of the ring, where the boy Chawlin was on his hands and knees, trying to rise as others pinned him. A voice called. The fuss stilled. Three newcomers had appeared from the forest, pushing their way into the throng. One was the tall woman whom she had seen earlier. Beside her was Aun of Lackmere. And the third was a plump young man whom she also knew.

'The Prince.'

People around her were kneeling.

'What's this, lads?' His voice was round and jovial, as if he were scolding a pack of truants. 'Holding a court? From whom did you have your licence, in this our realm?'

No one replied. The crowd remained kneeling, heads bowed.

'Law is a thing for debating,' Aun was saying. His voice sounded harsh after that of Septimus. 'But I would speak with the one who let off a horn in this camp for all the world to hear.'

The woman was at Phaedra's elbow, pulling gently at her arm. Phaedra found her feet were unsteady. She had to lean on her companion's shoulder. They made their way towards one of the awnings, where a few big logs were set on end for stools.

'Thank you. I can manage,' she was saying, even as her knees trembled and made her lean more heavily.

The priest! What part had he played in all this?

'Are you all right?'

'I'm not hurt. Just shaken. Dear Angels!'

'Can I bring you some water?'

'In – in a moment. That would be kind. One thing . . .'

'What is it?'

'I thought I saw – is there an old man among you? He's someone I have met before.'

'Jan Brig? He's not very old—'

'No.'

'With a scar on his face? That's Jan Brig.'

'No scar, and much older. I thought he wore a pilgrim's or a priest's dress.'

The woman was puzzled. She looked around. 'I can't think who you mean. I'd know if anyone new had come to us—'

'No matter. I – I must have been mistaken.' Phaedra eased herself down onto the log and buried her head in her hands.

The priest. He had been talking to the boy who had taken her side. Then the boy had come forward to fight for her, as Adam had done. What did it mean? The birdsong of the forest mingled with her bewilderment. The wind stirred the branches but there were no answers in the blowing of the leaves.

What did it mean?

She had been expecting the woman to go and fetch water. She had not moved. After a moment Phaedra looked up at her, wondering what was wrong. The woman was watching her, with her head cocked and her brow furrowed.

'Do you know I've been hating you?'

Phaedra stared at her.

'You don't remember me, do you?' the other said. 'Amanthys diGuerring – although that was not my name then. We sneaked up and watched a witch trial from the King's balcony in Tuscolo, and it all went wrong, like this one did. And afterwards you and I fell out over something silly that one of us said.'

'I – remember.'

'I've often thought about you since. And just now I heard you quoting poor Maria at them – as if I were seeing the past played out for me again, and all my sins with it. I knew the baron and the prince were walking by the stream, and I had to find them. You were lucky. I might have been looking yet. Water, was it? Nothing stronger?'

'I'm all right. I just need time. In fact, I need talk. Can you stay a little? Tell me what you're doing here.'

'Very well.' She settled on a log beside Phaedra. 'It isn't happy, but I'll tell you if you like. I am the camp master, I suppose. I don't fight. I just see that there is food for the men, hay for the horses, water, that the camp is clear of filth, that the fires don't give us away, that we pack and go in the right order – oh, all the things that they don't have the sense to do for themselves. In a moment I should go over and see that your men are comfortable. We can't untie them, I'm afraid . . .

'Why am I doing this? That's the unhappy bit. I got angry. About eighteen months ago, I think.'

She stopped, and looked at Phaedra. 'You have a child, don't you. Alive?'

'Please Heaven.'

'I lost mine. I was pregnant when my new husband joined the host that was coming to clear yours out of Tuscolo. I rode in a litter most of the way to see the fun. Well, you know what happened. My horses were taken by all those brave squires and soldiers in their hurry to get away. I was staggering in the mud with all the others. By nightfall I had lost it – and my husband too, although I did not know about that until later. He was not a bad man. I remember lying all bloody in the back of someone's wagon with six wounded men and thinking what a horrible, horrible incompetent mess it had all been . . .

'That's why I hated you, for a time. We all did. And the men go on hating. It's what keeps them going after all the defeats. It's been bad since they heard about this last one, and those knights your husband had beheaded because he claimed that they had changed sides. Sometimes they do stupid things, or try to – like Tancrem just now. We make all the mistakes in this war. Your side doesn't. But they won't give up.'

The fair-haired boy walked past. He barely noticed them. He had a bruise on his soft, round face and a faraway look in his eyes, as if he had been talking with Angels.

After a little Phaedra said: 'It is not my side any more, Amanthys. That is why I came to speak with Aun. I will talk to Septimus too, if he will hear me.'

It was Amanthys's turn to digest what had been said. 'I'm sure he will. He probably intends to come over anyway, when he has finished cracking heads. I'll see if I can fetch him.'

The crowd was still on its knees, heads down while the prince scolded them. He had authority, that man, after all his disasters.

'What is he doing here?'

'He's trying to get back to his friends. Your husband's soldiers cut him off from Develin. So he crossed the lake to give them the slip. Lackmere went to meet him, which is why he wasn't here when we got news of you coming south. If Tancrem had realized they were back he might have thought twice before launching his bloody little play.'

'One more thing,' said Phaedra, as her companion rose.

'Yes?'

'You said "poor Maria". What happened?'

A shadow crossed Amanthys's face. 'She was in Pemini when it fell. You know that your people sacked it. That was six months ago, and I have heard nothing since then.'

The priest had sent that boy to stand for her; as he had sent Adam diManey to stand for Evalia before the steps of the King. If he had sent Chawlin, then it was he who had roused Martin from his camp and led him among the dark rocks to find her. Did he think she was his pawn, or did he merely want her to live to see her son taken at last by the dark things that surrounded him? She could not guess what twisted reasons had moved him. But she had trusted Ambrose to two men who thought this deadly enemy was a sending from Heaven, and to one flawed woman who had once been in his power. Now there was nothing she could do.

Amanthys had gone. On the flat hilltop people were moving around the camp. Phaedra sat and stared unseeing across the trampled grass, like a player at a board who has seen that all her pieces are in check.

Phaedra's Price

letter came a few days after her return
to Tarceny. In the bare writing cham-
ber Phaedra looked closely at the seal.
The brown wax, set with the Dancing
Hound, had not been tampered with.
And when she broke it she found that
Evalia had been careful.

The page began with a gushing passage on the news
of Ulfin's coronation. A casual reader, even a spy, might
have looked no further for its purpose, nor seen anything
in it more than the witterings of a woman with too much
time and too little brain. Phaedra had spent weeks in
Evalia's close company. She could almost see Evalia, as
she scratched through phrase after silly phrase in the
yellow lamplight with her small, cynical smile on her lips
and the muffled pouring of the falls in her ears. Martin
must have told her that letters might be opened in
Tarceny. Even if he had not done so, she would have
guessed.

Towards the bottom of the page Evalia had under-
scored the last phrase of a paragraph. While the line
appeared to give emphasis to the empty-headed words

above them, it also marked them off from the two short paragraphs that followed.

Adam is well, although in truth I must say that I suppose him to be well, for he is so taken with his diggings and his plantings that I have hardly had the luck to speak with him in these past few days. First in his heart is a little oak seedling that came with a knotted rope around it one day. It seems to thrive where we have set it, for all that the ground is stony here. We watch it closely.

Dearest Phaedra, I remember my first sight of you. I cannot say why your face stood out among those around you, but I did wonder even then who you were and what it was you thought of what was before you. I do not know what you are going to do now. I do know you must be busy. But wherever you go, remember that there are many who wish you happiness, and among them remember first your

E.

The knotted rope – the badge of his monkly order – was for Martin. The seedling was Ambrose. He was safe, and guarded, at the time the letter was written. The garrison at Hayley now supposed Ambrose and his followers to be at Tarceny, just as Tarceny supposed him to be at Hayley or in the hills.

She penned a short acknowledgement to Evalia's letter, as a grand lady might in response to a request for patronage that she did not wish to grant, but that had come from someone she did not wish to offend. The only expansion she allowed herself was to recall the story of diManey's vision, and to add that she had now heard that the monks of the Knot knew of similar things. Indeed she knew one who had had a vision that was very like. She would write more on this, but the matter was too great for such a letter.

She sealed it, thinking of her son. Did he miss her – did he remember her, and look around, and ask a one-word question of Eridi: 'Mama?' There was no way of knowing.

And one part of her did not wish to know the answers. This was less, she thought, from fear of what they might be, than because she did not deserve it. She must stifle her questions and wait. Even the few sentences in Evalia's letter were too much kindness, too much danger. After reading it for the fourth time, by candlelight, alone in her room, she lit it at one corner and dropped it in the grate. She watched the yellow flames creeping around the parchment, blackening, destroying, concealing. *When the time comes you must sacrifice without mercy. Except the King.*

I have castled, she thought. I have placed my king where he may be guarded – by thirty-one white stones, and by the wits of a woman I once despised. I have warned her as best I can. Now I must play.

And she knew that Evalia's final words had not been a veiled plea for patronage, but the sentences of a friend who did not know whether to write farewell.

Long after night had fallen and the parchment had turned to wispy black fragments she sat by the grate, turning over thoughts in her mind. Ulfin, as he ran from her in the dark country. Amanthys and her story. The suffering the war had caused to her, and others. Father. Elward. Maria, lost in Pemini. Ulfin.

Opposite her, under the window, lay huge bales of black and golden silks that had come up the road from Baer that

364

afternoon. Heaven knew where they had found them, for Baer itself did not make cloth of this quality, and yet it had been but a fortnight since she had gone down to the warehouse and spoken with the merchants there. Some hero must have abandoned all other things (wife? family?) and gone hotfoot to Watermane, haggling and bargaining and doing whatever was humanly possible to please the whim of the new queen in the time she had set for it. And he had done well. He had found precisely the blacks and golds in good silks that had flitted idly into her mind that afternoon in Baer. She should remember to send a reward, if there were enough coin in the castle for that.

The more so because his efforts had been vain. She would have accepted any cloth of any colour that arrived at the gate. The same sweating scullions would have hauled it all the way up the same stairs to her room. The price, any price, would have been paid by any means possible. For the cloth did not matter. What mattered was that when the door was shut and the scullions and Hera were gone, her fingers, questing deep within the roll, should find there what they sought. Others had been busy while the unknown merchant was abroad. And in this they had made no mistakes.

The room was cold. She could hear the low wind droning in the chimney and soughing beyond the thick stones of her wall. She must make her move.

Rising from her place, she took an earthenware bowl in which lay a mass of the little four-pointed moon roses that thronged below the walls in spring. These had been cut a week before. They were limp and lifeless, and going brown at the tips. She tossed them and the water in which they lay out of the window. Next she took from the foot of her bed the bottle she had brought with her on her dark journey from the hills. She shook it. It still held the water she had drawn from the pool. She pulled the cork.

Slowly she poured the water into the bowl. It splashed and swirled, scattering the candlelight in fragments across its surface. She peered at it, touched it with her fingers. It was just water, smelling sourly of the inside of a leather bottle. The clearest thing was her own reflection, like a hooded shadow on the face of the water. She hesitated.

She was about to do something she had never done before, and that she did not know would work, or why. Ulfin had not answered the letter she had sent urgently to him on her return to Tarceny. She had known he might not. So she must try this way. It was a way that she could never, never, discuss with those who might count her a friend. She was in a dark room, feeling for the door.

This was not *the* bowl: not the Cup, which she had seen only in her dreams, like a vast goblet in Ulfin's hand. This was ordinary clay. But the water – the water came from the well under the sky, where the great shape of Beyah plunged reflected into its depths and the priest crept around its rim upon heels three hundred years old. These were the tears that had fallen in love, and rage and darkness, from the eyes of a being of the beginning of the world. She had felt – had drunk from – the love that was in them. Perhaps no one in the world knew the strength of it better than she. She had seen their darkness flitting in nightmare shapes around her son. It had left its mark upon her stair. It was the rage of a goddess who had lost her own son when Wulfram's people came.

This was the power that the cheated prince had turned against the line of his father. 'We live by truth,' the bishop had said, and what was the Law but the exercise of truth? Now the priest would place Ulfin, his lie, at the very heart of the Law. Such a rage and darkness – surely Ulfin and his brothers would never have dared to meddle with it, if they had truly understood it! Perhaps only a mother could.

And now she must meddle too.

The tears were born of the eyes of the goddess. What Phaedra needed now was their sight. If there was a way, it was here. Here, within this film of water, within the rough clay surface beneath, which shifted as the water moved, grown like rocks on a barren landscape. The light was dim. There was something wrong, or odd, about the distances. The water knew her. She could see the outlines of rocks in the bowl.

The world was a bowl. Every place in the world had its point on the bowl's surface. She need only look. So – how to find it?

Ulfin had done this. Or at least, his presence had come to her, waking or sleeping, as she went about the ways of Trant and Tuscolo long ago. She was not now walking from one place across the dark land to emerge in another. She was sending thought, a dream, as Ulfin had done. And thoughts should fly.

She bent over the bowl again, more confidently now. She remembered the way into the place of brown rocks. She remembered Ulfin. She felt for him, away to the east, camped with an army of iron around him, resting or sleeping. Yes, and the water knew him too. A mind as beautiful and cold as a mountain valley, where the clefts flow darkling with corrupted streams. She stood, it seemed, on a flat-topped rock like a million others in that place, looking down into the space before her. There was a room, lit by torches. It was the upper floor of some lodge, on a road from Tuscolo to the south. Distant campfires glittered at the windows. A mailed foot shifted beyond the door. The room was scattered with papers, clothes, armour. A dirty plate and an empty goblet stood upon a low table by the bed, and on the bed itself he lay face down and stirred as she watched him.

Ulfin.

He muttered and shook his head. His sleep was heavy. She did not have much time.

Ulfin, come.

'Phaedra?' He moaned. He was seeing her.

Ulfin, come quickly.

Her vision was fading. The water in the bowl intruded. Candlelight danced on its surface and marked the shadow of her reflection. She could see both that and at the same time the room beyond, where Ulfin was starting from his sleep.

'Phaedra! What are you doing?' His voice was faint. Her reflection on the water blocked her view into the room, like a hooded shape. A hooded shape. It was not her reflection. The picture of a face floated there. Pale eyes glittered. Its lips moved, and spoke.

'What price will you pay?'

She looked down into the face of the priest, on the surface of the water. She had almost expected it.

'What price will you pay me, woman, for my power?'

Phaedra! No! A voice that drifted from a hundred miles away.

'I? Pay you?' She gathered herself. 'Nothing!'

Her fist banged upon the table. The water slopped. Even as it settled, she saw the face reforming on its surface. Like a paper mask, it had no depth to it. It reflected nothing – she was well back from the bowl now, trembling a few feet from the table. Yet it floated there, as if it meant to stay. After a moment she took a scarf and draped it over the bowl, so that she would not have to look at what lay inside.

She was shivering.

Pay? There was nothing to pay. This was not knowledge she had had from him. This was not the Cup he had carved. These were the tears of Beyah, which she herself had gathered and he had never owned; never, for all the terrible strength in his eyes. It was well that she had not spoken longer with him.

Phaedra, said Ulfin behind her.

'No!' She jerked round.

He was gone.

Of course, he would try to reach her at once. She had not thought of that. He would be desperate to know how she had done what she had done, what bargain she had struck; whether his powers were now under threat. That was right. But he must not get the answer through the Cup. He must come himself. And it was beginning to dawn on her how difficult it might be to make him.

The room was cold and empty. The hour was late. She should build up the fire.

On the table her bowl sat, covered by the green scarf. Outwardly it was plain. There was no sign of what had been floating on its surface when she had last seen it. Had it gone? If it had gone, perhaps she might be able to use the water again. She could keep calling Ulfin until he came. She reached for the corner of the cloth. Before she lifted it her fingers checked.

It had gone. Surely it had gone now.

There was no sign, no sound within the bowl. The cloth was chilly to her touch, the colour faded and yellow in the lamplight. She knew what must lie beneath it, floating like a mask on the surface of the water. She dropped the cloth and let it lie.

Phaedra! What have you done?

'What price have I paid, Ulfin?' she asked, with her eyes on the bowl.

The low wind droned and stirred the ash-motes in the grate.

'Would you tell *me*?' she shouted, and spun to where he must be standing. A shadow flitted, and the vision was broken. There was nothing there.

After thirty heartbeats, waiting for him to come again, she kneeled and began to make up the fire.

What was her price, to bargain or to sell? In a leafy clearing in the woods, three days to the south, with the wind thrashing in the treetops and the grey skies flowing by above them, she had set it, watching the tubby young man with the brown stubble whom half the Kingdom held to be the Fount of their Law. He had not returned her look, but stared at a point before him on the gold-brown mush of the forest floor, and listened as she spoke.

'I have a son . . . less than two years old. When I last saw him he was just beginning to walk.' (Little Ambrose, rising to his feet in a world of three mortal dangers. The first, the nightmares in the twilight beyond the ring of little white stones. The second, the chills and the fever that daily robbed mothers of their sons all through the Kingdom. The third . . .)

'. . . Of all men living I suppose he must be counted among your greatest enemies. Your soldiers would think they did you a service if they killed him, for some see him as the heir to your throne.'

The prince, nodding as though she had made a reasonable point in some scholarly argument. Aun, sitting on the far side of him frowning. Perhaps he did not like to be reminded of her son and, by him, of her marriage.

'I do not ask the throne for him,' she had heard her own voice say. 'Nor riches, nor titles.'

She remembered the face of the prince, as he thought. The man whom she would have been made to marry. So ordinary: so desperate after his latest disaster that he had fled deep into his enemy's heartland to escape pursuit. Perhaps he knew – surely he must know – how much less of a figure he was than his brother, or even his father. By his own admission it had been one of his frequent headcolds that had kept him from joining them on their last, fatal hunt. Did he grudge them their lost glory? Or was it for their sake, and the sake of those around him who had lost their true kings upon that terrible day, that he had carried on?

For what kept a man like this going through defeat after defeat and humiliation?

'He will have my protection,' the prince had said at last – in a voice that had more firmness that Phaedra expected. 'My soldiers shall not harm him, so long as he does not offend my law or commit treason towards my person. Even if, as a grown man, he does, and is brought to me for it, I shall pardon him. Once. After that I may not help him.'

She remembered her hesitation.

'He cannot do more,' Aun had said.

In the iron world of politics no man, not even Ambrose, could be immune for ever. The King would lose face and following if he pardoned a man twice. Once would be bad enough. Phaedra remembered the bustle and excitement at the royal court when the King had thrown the favour of a baron to the winds to preserve a country knight who had stepped forward for an accused witch. There had been some good in old Tuscolo.

And if Ambrose grew into a man with a heart like Adam diManey, she could not be sorry.

'It is enough,' she had said.

The bowl lay on the table behind her. She had not spoken to the prince of this, nor asked any protection for herself. It occurred to her that his men might take her and burn her and put Ambrose somewhere safe, and think they had fulfilled his vow. She barely cared. She thought too of Ulfin, bending every power at his disposal to find some clue of what was happening in Tarceny. She could fend him off while she was awake. It was only necessary to be aware of him. But in her dreams they would meet halfway, in the land of brown stones. That must not happen. So she must not sleep. Or at least she must sleep when he was not expecting it, which could not be now. She must find snatches of daylight hours in which to rest, until he came.

The fire was laid. Taking some light tinder, she opened the lamp and held it to the wick until it glowed and the tiny flames began to lick at the tip. Then she lit the fire. She watched it flutter and grow, before turning back to the table.

With a flick of her fingers she cast the cloth aside and looked down into the bowl. The face floated in the water before her. The eyes opened and looked into hers. The mouth opened to speak.

With an oath she picked the bowl up and, stepping to the window, flung its contents through into the night outside. A low laugh sounded on the wind.

XXI

The Powers of Iron

t was the old moon, sinking towards the horizon, and perhaps a third past the full. It was still bright enough to silver a great quadrant of the sky. There was no star that could stand near it. From the north-west bastion Phaedra could see the marks upon its cheeks. She could trace the pure arc of its rim and the uneven ripple where the disc dropped into shadow.

The moon was falling. In the past half-hour that she had paced up here, wrapped in furs against the night winds, it had dropped perhaps a half of the remaining distance to the horizon. Soon the lower edge would break upon the jagged mountaintops, lining the ridges with silver until the light diminished and the dark hours before dawn began. And she had nothing better to do than to pace, pace, pace up here, watching it go.

It was the eighth night since she had called to Ulfin through the bowl.

There had been a dog barking somewhere among the olive groves, more than a mile away. The deep, round-throated row had carried clearly. What had startled him? A fox? A line of silent horsemen, passing? A bad dream?

He was quiet now. She could hear the sighing of the winds. The olive branches shivered. Some twenty yards away the mail of a watchman jingled against stone, and muttered words were borne to her by the moving air. Below, men slept. And out there, men slept, in their little huts with the low roofs and families of six or more huddled all into their one room where they might snore and keep warm together. It was such a seething world, even now; and the same, still moon so far beyond, shining down on all of it; looking a thousand night-watchers like herself at once in the eye, even as it sank towards darkness.

Umbriel, send that my son sleeps well.

Something clinked among the olive trees. She looked where she thought the sound had come from, among the shadows a hundred yards down the slope, opposite the postern gate. There was nothing to be seen. No clear shapes of boughs or men stood out down there. The hillside was a patchwork of shadows and silver grasses, shifting as the wind stirred the boughs – too much for tired eyes. In the moments that followed she wondered if she had heard the hiss of a whisper. Were there men down there? If there were, they must surely have seen her, standing at the parapet under the moon. And within the castle there were other noises, hurried steps of men crossing the outer courtyard. A hinge somewhere cracked. A man was talking somewhere, voice low in the night, but she could hear the sudden surprise in his tone. A horse whickered. And suddenly a dog barked in the outer court, again and again, until a man's voice yelled at it for quiet. More steps – mailed feet climbing stone stairs, moving quickly and yet with as little sound as armed men could hope for.

Ulfin was home.

She sighed, and drummed her fingers lightly on the battlements of Tarceny. She had already decided that she would not go to lie down. He would know that she had not been sleeping these many nights past. He had come in force, and by night, as if to surprise his own castle. There had been no challenge at the gate. Most likely Caw or the gate-captain had simply woken to find his lord standing by his bed, bidding to open without a sound or a moment's delay. Perhaps he was already in her room, searching it lamp in hand for any sign of water, bowl, book or other artefact that might confirm she had dealt with things beyond the world. It was better to wait. The castle watchmen would tell him where to find her.

The moon had dropped to the rim of the world. The sharp, flat shadow of a mountain peak pressed upwards upon its disc. Its shape was changing to a monstrous skull.

'I am here, Phaedra.'

'You have taken your time,' she said, without turning.

'I want to know what you have been doing.'

'Waiting for you.'

She heard him step up behind her, and turned to face him. He looked down on her, and in the fading moonlight his face was iron.

'You have done things that are forbidden. I want to know why, and by what means. And why you then would not hear me. Tell me now.'

'Why? Because I wanted you to come. Why would I not hear you? Because if I had you would not have come. The means I used you know as well as I.'

'Do not play with me, Phaedra.'

'I am not playing! I starved myself and you would not come! I wrote to you that I had been taken – Ulfin, I was nearly killed! And you did not come. They took me from a road in the heart of your lands and tried me for my life! Did you even read my letter?'

'You were in not a farthing of the danger you stood in when you spoke with me. Why did you do that? What did you give?'

'Nothing. Ulfin, they—'

'I do not believe you.'

'Dear Angels!' She turned away and strode across the platform, wrestling with her own anger. 'I gave nothing, Ulfin. What I used was the remains of the water I took that morning from the pool. I made no bargain. I spoke to you before he could prevent me. I would not have done it if you had answered my letter. I have done nothing since but throw the water away.'

'You threw it away? When?'

'That night. Ask him, if you do not believe me.'

Ulfin paused. He seemed in doubt. 'Where is Ambrose?'

'Safe.' It was a weakness in her defences. She leaned on the parapet and looked outwards, to prevent him from reading her face.

He was waiting for her to go on.

'Are those your men in the grove, Ulfin? Did you think I would run when you came? Why don't you call them in and let them—'

'I asked you where is Ambrose. Do not evade me. I am your king, as well as your husband!'

'Are you now? Yes, I had heard. Well, Your Majesty,

your son is safe. Which is more than could have been said for his mother a fortnight ago. But you do not care about that, do you?'

'You were not in danger. Where is he?'

'I was in danger, Ulfin. In your very lands—'

'All the Kingdom is my land—'

'And for all your kingliness your queen's throat would have been cut if Septimus had not been there too.'

'Septimus?'

'Three days from where we stand. Does that interest you at last?'

Ulfin paused again. He was tired, as she was. And perhaps he was beginning to believe her. He had not for one second showed concern at her story.

'So that was where he went. He will be long gone by now – back across to Bay, or to the Seabord. And you have not answered me. Where is Ambrose?'

Ambrose, Ambrose, Ambrose. What price did you pay, Phaedra?

What price did you pay, Ulfin?

'Have you looked in Hayley?'

'He is not there, Phaedra. I know he came there and left. Where is he now?'

'When you still loved me, you told me not to tell you. But do not worry. I would not put my son at hazard, even if you offered me a crown.'

And it was so easy to walk away.

She lay exhausted on her bed in her inner room, and could not sleep. Her head seethed. A false step, a word spoken in the wrong tone, a sentence that he might have known from his spyings was not true, and she would have been lost. But she had held fear back with the palm of her mind. And he had not prevented her from leaving when she chose.

Speak the truth to one another. She had spoken the truth and lied with every word – as he had done since the day they were wed.

The tired dawn crept through the windows. The doors of her wardrobe stood open. Around her bed lay the piles of silk cuttings in some disorder. Ulfin had pulled them aside, presumably to look under her bed. Witchcraft was what he had been looking for. He had not disturbed the gown, still hanging on its frame like a black ghost with no head. That was what mattered.

She heard the door to her antechamber open, and the soft steps of a man in the next room. They paused, as if he were listening. She wondered whether to call that she was awake, and so perhaps make him go away again. But perhaps he would then come in, and question her further. Undecided, she lay quiet. Presently she heard him moving again, to and fro across the antechamber, moving things, looking behind curtains, casting about by daylight for some sign that was not there.

She wondered if he would try to speak with the grey priest, and if so, what the monster would say.

It was a long time before she heard the door close again.

Later Hera came, bringing a lunch of fruits and bread. Phaedra ate lightly, telling Hera between mouthfuls what instructions must be passed to the household now that my lord was home. As she spoke she looked closely at her maid, who sat with eyes downcast and answered in monosyllables. She was miserable and awkward. Phaedra was on the point of asking her what was wrong when she realized what it must be.

Hera had been questioned, and not kindly. It would have been about Ambrose and signs of witchcraft, of course. And possibly about their captivity in the woods beyond Baer. She would have been told that her mistress had done something terribly wrong. Perhaps she had been threatened, to prevent her telling Phaedra what questions had been asked, and was terrified that Phaedra might try to worm them out of her.

Phaedra said nothing. As soon as she could she dismissed Hera to go about her business. It would be far better to let the girl find something to do than have her sit trembling on a stool in the antechamber all afternoon. She thanked the Angels that Martin had still not returned.

So the long afternoon wore on, and on. She spent hours sitting at her window, looking northward to the wooded ridges that ran like huge rollers across the land. They were thickly covered. Nothing could be seen moving there. And so she stayed until the light went grey again, and the colours faded. The detail was lost upon the ridges and the hillsides flattened into shadow with the coming night. When Hera came to light the lamps Phaedra smiled at her and asked for two, and then sent her down to the chapel, to prepare, she said, for a vigil that she would keep that night for her father's soul.

As Hera's footsteps diminished along the corridor Phaedra took the two lamps and set them, side by side, on the sill of one window. She waited, counting. After one hundred she took them down and counted again. Then she placed them in the window for a second time, and a third. At last she stopped, and waited.

Minutes seeped by.

She sighed, and set her teeth, and stared at the black ridges. Why . . .

A light showed among the trees. It was so much nearer than she had been expecting that at first she discounted it. It faded, and reappeared again, and then again. Each time it had moved a little, as if some traveller had been walking among the trees with a lamp, moving parallel to the castle wall and a little uphill. Not, by itself, something to alarm a watchman on the walls, but enough to keep him staring outward at that one ridge, wondering when the light would appear again.

Phaedra felt along the collar of the robe. Two years in the making, never finished: the silk was cold as metal beneath her fingertips. She found the seam, took the collar on both sides of it, and ripped the robe from collar to waist. There, hanging coil upon coil on the frame, was the forty feet of rope that had come concealed in the silks from Baer. She climbed on a stool and wound one end round a roofbeam, knotting it as best she could. Then she fed the rest of it yard by yard through the window, where it hung close in by the small bastion that housed the living-quarter stairs, and so was hidden for most of its length from any watchers on the north-east tower.

It was a dark night. The moon would not rise for some hours. Phaedra settled herself to wait again. What was a little more waiting, after so long? She should try to enjoy the dark and quiet for a little while. Things would be

381

moving soon enough, and faster than she would wish. She seemed to herself to be approaching a corner in the passage of her life, not knowing what she would find when she turned it. Some destiny hung only a few moments away. She did not know what. In one future, rippling in the pool of her mind's eye, she saw Ambrose grow to manhood at Chatterfall, and Evalia telling him what sort of a woman his mother had been. It would not be all bad. Evalia had always been generous.

No, Phaedra! There were a thousand chances yet. One way or another this intolerable life would end soon. She thought of the words that had passed on the fighting platform, and sighed.

A door opened in the antechamber.

There were footsteps in the next room. Ulfin's voice called.

Retrieve the rope? There was not time. Close the door and bolt it? The fastenings were old. He would be instantly suspicious.

She took a lamp, and stepped out to meet him. 'Sir,' she said.

He was standing in his evening gown, with his fine black silk doublet, traced with gold, and the long sword at his hip.

'I had expected you at supper, my lady.'

'I was tired.'

'A pity, since you had gone to such lengths to bring me home. For I have decided to return in the morning.'

She sat slowly on a stool and looked at him. 'Will you do nothing about the raiders, my lord?'

'They are not more than Caw can handle. Spies more

than raiders, I guess. And I do not think they were the reason for what you have done.'

She looked at her feet. 'No one enjoys a sword at their throat, sir. Nor does any wife expect to be ignored when she sends to her husband for protection.'

He settled in a chair, looking at her. 'Where is Ambrose?' he asked.

Behind her in the bedroom, something creaked. She did not dare turn round. She could not remember if she had even shut the door.

He was watching her, waiting for an answer.

Abruptly she leaned forward, took the chess case from its low shelf, and opened it on the table between them. The dust was silver on the black and white squares.

'Will you play, my lord? If you win, I may tell you what you wish to know.'

His head tilted slightly to one side, as if he were trying to read her thoughts. 'I will win,' he said.

'You will find my game has changed, sir. Let me play white.'

'White? If you wish. It will make no difference.'

They set the pieces on the board before them. Phaedra clapped the white figures into their places, making as much noise with them as she dared without being so loud that he would begin to wonder why. The black pieces went deftly into their rows, with the sound of a cat's footfall. She left one pawn out in the middle of the board. Ulfin had made his move before she had finished setting the rest of her pieces. It was the knight to the queen-bishop third, which she had not been expecting. She had to stop and think.

In the silence, the rope creaked again. Phaedra wondered if somewhere she could hear the ghost of a leather sole on stone. Ulfin looked up. She clicked her knight forward, and his eye fell on the board again.

He played quickly, and so did she. She would have liked longer to think, but she must keep his mind on the play. And already she was in trouble. Somehow, in an equal number of moves, he had far more force on the board than she. Now she must bring her queen forward – Aun had always told her not to do that.

Clip, clip, went the pieces. (*Grunt*, went the rope in the room beyond.)

Surely he must hear it now. And she must move again quickly. Her queen was under attack.

'You will lose her,' he said.

'But you have not seen what I am doing.' Her hand hovered. His eyes followed it. And ignoring the danger, she pushed a knight forward into his defence.

It was a wild move. A farce. She saw the disgust on his face. And then his expression changed. His eyes flew to the door of her room. Within, the sound of cloth and boot wrestling on the stone sill. A heavy body landing upon the floor. A man grunting. A step. The door handle turning.

Aun stood in the doorway, breathing hard.

Ulfin leaped back from his seat with a shout. The table rocked and crashed to the floor. Phaedra was on her hands and knees, scrambling among the chess pieces. She reached the outer door and slid the bolts home. Then she turned.

The men faced each other over the tumbled furniture. The swords were out, and held low. Ulfin's eyes flicked towards her. She was in easy reach of the iron in his hand.

Aun was a long second away across the room. She crammed herself backwards against the door, snarling. But Ulfin looked back at Aun.

'All right,' he said, settling into a crouch. 'Come on.'

In the bedroom, the rope creaked again.

Aun came with a rush, beating at Ulfin's blade. The long sword evaded him and slammed into his ribs. Aun staggered and struck. Iron rang in the room, again and again. Aun jumped back, panting.

'Mail,' he said, patting the baggy doublet he wore. He grinned.

'Ho, there!' cried Ulfin. 'Ho, there! Help!'

Then Aun was coming forward again, feinting, hacking. Ulfin blocked. They did not have room to circle. Aun was trying to get between Ulfin and the door, but again he was beaten back. Ulfin looked to the door too, but the bolts were thrown and he would have to open them while keeping Aun at bay with the other hand. And he would have to cut her down first of all. Phaedra cast about for a chair, a stool, to put between herself and the sword.

'Help, guards, help!' cried Ulfin.

The rope creaked. A second man was climbing through the window.

Ulfin attacked, cutting for Aun's head and immediately his thigh, but Aun went down on one knee into the blow, grunting as the blade struck his elbow and back. Phaedra winced, and winced again and yelped as the short Trant sword caught Ulfin full in the face. He fell without a cry.

Aun stood over him for a moment, and then fumbled for a knife from his belt.

'Don't kill him!' Phaedra said.

He looked at her.

Another man was standing in the doorway to the bedroom. Beyond him, the rope was creaking again.

'Are you hurt?' said the newcomer.

'No and yes,' said Aun. 'But I'll heal. Did they hear?'

Phaedra put her ear to the door. There were distant sounds beyond.

'I don't know.'

'How many on the postern door?'

'Two, I think. You go right and down the steps, then right through the storeroom passage. They'll be in the little room at the end, to the left of the door itself. I don't want you to kill them.'

A third man was scrambling through the window.

'We'll go then. Wave the others round. We can't wait.'

'Chawlin's on the rope.'

'Then wave the others off. Chawlin can guard him,' he said, pointing to where Ulfin lay motionless on the floor. 'Let's go.'

They stepped to the door, weapons out. Phaedra saw the long streak of her husband's blood on Aun's blade. She opened her mouth to say something about not killing, and closed it again, knowing the thought was futile.

The bolts clacked back. The door opened into the dimness of the corridor. No one challenged. One after another the men stepped out silently.

She was alone.

She took Ulfin's sword and placed it out of his reach. It was heavy, and cold. She supposed that if the soldiers came up from the hall now she might threaten them with it, but she would do far better to bolt the door again. In fact, she should do so now. But . . .

Ulfin lay sprawled on the floor of the room. He was face down, but he was trying to lift his head. It was bloody. She heard him gasp.

Slowly she stood and went into the dark bedroom, where the rope jerked and creaked to itself. There she tore a long strip from the bale of precious, useless black silk by the bed. As she did so a pair of hands appeared on the rope outside the window, and a head. It was the young man from the forest glade. He was having trouble.

'Here,' she said, and helped him to scramble over the windowsill. He collapsed in a heap, apparently exhausted by his climb.

'Where are they?'

'They've gone on down. You're to stay here. Come and help me.'

She took the silk into the outer room, and kneeling beside Ulfin, lifted his head. His face was coated in blood, and there was a widening pool of it on the floor. It seemed to be flowing thickly from his cheek and forehead. She pressed at it with the cloth in her hands, and tried to wipe it away. It was useless. The boy came and supported Ulfin's head, while she wound the silk clumsily round and round and tied it in place. Then they lifted Ulfin's shoulders and dragged him into the inner room and laid him on the bed. They looked at one another. They were both bloody, and there was a long trail of it on the floor.

'We need more bandages,' he said. 'And water.'

'Take what you need,' said Phaedra, pointing to the ruined silks. 'I'll find a jug. I'm – glad it's you, Chawlin.'

It was as near as she would ever come to thanking him for stepping forward in the camp.

Hera had left a jug of drinking water on one of the tables in the antechamber. But the table had fallen in the fight. The jug was smashed and its contents had soaked into the rug. Phaedra hesitated, looking around her. She could hear shouts not far away. Someone was blowing a horn – an alarm, she guessed. She could not remember when it had started. Feet sounded in the corridor, coming towards her at a run.

The door was still open! She had not had time to shut it!

A figure skidded in the doorway – armed, looking inwards. It was Tancrem. His face hardened when he saw her, but he did not enter.

'How do we come at the hall?'

He must have come up from the level of the storerooms. There seemed to be others with him.

'Go on along the corridor. Before you reach the tower door there are steps going down to the right. They take you to the gallery. What's happening?'

'The inner gatehouse is ours. But they are holding the hall, and there are more in the outer bailey. Stay here.'

He turned and clattered back down the corridor with others at his heels. Somewhere someone was screaming, on and on, the sound blotted by the blasting of the horn, and emerging again. Who was in the hall? Men like Caw, like Abernay, fighting unarmoured and part-armed for a lord they did not know had fallen? And she needed water. She looked out into the corridor, and it was empty.

It seemed the shouting increased as she crept along in

Tancrem's wake. She could hear metal clashing now, and someone cry out in pain. At the tower door she listened, and could hear nothing beyond it. Either the guards above had abandoned their posts, or they were keeping very still.

From the hall rose a riot of combat. Men were calling for surrender, others yelling defiance. She stumbled down the wooden steps. The gallery was empty.

The hall below was chaos. Tables were overthrown, and food spilt across the floor. Here and there men were lying sprawled like drunkards in a scene of orgy. Tancrem and his men were clustered at the door, through which others were flowing in – also Septimus's supporters. They were clearing a table from the doorway, which must have been used as a barricade by the defenders until Tancrem's party had rushed them from the gallery steps. At the far end of the hall a half-dozen Tarceny men had upended two tables and barricaded themselves into a corner. They were hopelessly outnumbered. They had seen her.

The horn had stopped. For a moment she could think. She saw Caw's grey head among the defenders.

'Put down your weapons!' she called. 'Put them down!'

For a heartbeat's space they stared at her. Then they were yelling at her, curses, defiance, threats. She saw an arm raised, flung forward. Something flew through the air towards her. A knife! It tumbled as it flew, and clattered uselessly against the wall a yard to her left. The men at the door bellowed and swarmed forward – twenty or more of them, hurling themselves at the tables. Iron danced in blood, and from the gallery a woman of nineteen stared bright-eyed at the murder she had unleashed in her home.

XXII

The Powers of Shadow

 man lay huddled among the potted mints of the fountain court. It was Vermian, and he was dead. His head and forearms were a ruin of sword-cuts, as if his last act had been to throw up both arms to cover his face. He lay with his mouth open. In the light of Phaedra's lamp his half-closed eye glittered with a sickly fire.

It was over. The leaderless men in the outer bailey had surrendered. Before the gatehouse Prince Septimus had kneeled and, in his gladness and gratitude, kissed the hem of her bloody robe. She had seen the wounded – Caw among them – carried to a makeshift hospital in one of the dormitories. She had watched the captives being herded into a stout storehouse where they could be guarded. She had seen them look across at her. A man had been kicked and cuffed by the guards for shouting something that she had not heard.

And now they were gathering the dead.

Someone was crossing the court towards her. She rose, and lifted up her lamp. Martin emerged out of the darkness and looked down at the man at her feet.

'He was planning to marry,' she said.

'It takes blood to stop a war, my lady. And if it is not stopped, then it will have blood anyway. With good luck, this one may now be caged.'

Phaedra turned her head. She wanted to shut away the terrible images that danced in her mind. She wanted to cry, and being unable to, she felt sick; and tired.

'When did you arrive?'

'A half-hour ago. The postern gate was open, and no one was guarding it.'

She looked around. 'Have you seen Hera?'

'She is in the chapel, and the door is locked. I should go back and tell her it is safe to come out. But I wanted to find you. Are you hurt?'

She shook her head. 'It is not my blood,' she said dully. 'It is Ulfin's.'

'They say he is asking for you.'

'I do not want to see him.' She knew she would go. '. . . Ambrose?'

'Well, when I left him. When he understood I was coming here, he gave me something for you.' He fished something from his pouch and handed it to her, seeming to smile for a moment. '"Give Mama," he said.'

It was one of the white stones, lying warm in her palm. Her fingers closed on it.

Martin stooped over Vermian's body. 'I will bring this one in.'

'Will you need the lamp?'

'No.'

'Don't forget Hera.'

He grunted, and she could tell by the sound that he

had indeed forgotten, despite reminding himself of her only a moment before. And she remembered that she had been looking for water to wash the blood from Ulfin's face. That had been hours ago. Thought had shattered under the impact of the things they had both witnessed. The mind saw image after image, forgot them and moved on. And she must move on too.

The courtyard was dark and quiet. The stone bowl of the fountain glowed in the lamplight as she passed it: that place where Ulfin and she had kissed in the sunlight on her first day in Tarceny. The bowl was empty. Its waters were silent now.

Chawlin rose to his feet as she entered the antechamber. The door to the bedroom was open. She could see the light beyond it, and the shape of the man upon the bed.

'How is he?'

'Conscious. He's in pain, of course. I think the bleeding has stopped.'

'Sit down, please.'

Someone – Chawlin, presumably – had righted the tables that had been upset in the fight. The mess had been cleared. The blood had been mopped away – no, surely not. But he had dragged that rug across to cover whatever marks remained. The room had a subdued and peaceful look. Apart from Chawlin himself, a mild-looking boy with a naked sword across his knees, there was no sign that anything had happened here.

Phaedra hesitated. Through the window she could see, dimly, the shapes of the wooded ridges rolling away to the north of the castle. The night was lighter than it had been.

Somewhere beyond the towers and clouds the moon had risen again, paling the overcast sky to a dull, colourless glow. She felt a sudden wish to be out there, moving across the vast floor of the night, and away from this torchlit stone where swords cut flesh and all her deeds were remembered.

Out there, in the soft darkness. But the night had never been her friend. There was stone under her feet and a lamp in her hand, and beyond the door lay the man she had betrayed.

She stepped through and set her lamp on a low table. Chawlin – or someone – had been busy in here too. The blood-soaked rugs and sheets were piled into a corner. The silks were pushed beneath the bed. The rope was gone. Ulfin lay with his head heavily wrapped so that only one eye was visible.

He was looking at her.

'I'm here,' she said.

'What – happened?' Speaking seemed to hurt him.

'The castle is taken. Septimus is here. You are his prisoner.'

'Why?'

'Why did I . . . ? Do you not know?'

'No.'

His one eye was watching her. It did not look angry, or accusing, but bewildered. That was worse. For a moment she could not look at him. Don't kill him! She might as well have let his throat be cut then and there. For they must kill him. They could not allow him to live. Not after all he had done. In some market square, before a thousand people . . .

'Why – why do I have to justify myself to you, Ulfin? You would have left me to die in the rocks. You—'

'But you were not – danger.' Still he was looking at her.

'Was I not? Was I not? Do you misremember, now? Or are you hiding it even from yourself?' She rose.

'Phaedra!'

'Do not be afraid. I am not leaving.' She walked to the antechamber door. Chawlin looked up. No doubt he could hear every word.

'Please pass the word for Brother Martin,' she said. When he hesitated, she added: 'He is the castle chaplain. You will find him in the chapel below, I think.'

She closed the door. Chawlin shouted down the corridor beyond.

'Martin found me,' she said. 'You did not know that he had been in that place, did you? He will tell you how it was with me after you left. And then I think he should hear what you have to say.'

'You want a penitence? I do not. Not to a priest.'

'To me, then.'

After a long moment he said, 'If you like.'

The eye had turned to the ceiling. What she could see of his face was more relaxed now. Perhaps his pain was receding. Or perhaps – more probably – he was learning to bear it.

They waited.

After a while his head turned. 'My men?'

She cleared her throat. 'I know nine are dead. There may be more. Abernay was one of them. Caw and Hob are wounded. They are in the hospital with some others.

The rest are held.' She left out the thought that some might be – probably still were – hiding from Aun's hunters in corners of the castle.

'You tell Septimus – kill them.'

'What?'

'I wish them no ill. But if any live, they will hunt you. And Orcrim. You must catch him. And—'

'I want no more bloodshed, Ulfin.'

He seemed to smile. After a little he said: 'There will be. These men – follow Septimus. But they will fight. When I am finished, they will fight among themselves.'

So he knew there was no hope. Of course he did.

'Septimus will hold them.'

'Septimus will be fighting. Foremost. And Lackmere. Over you.'

No!

No. They would not. Enough was enough. When this was over . . .

Septimus had sought her hand. Would he not do so again? What would Aun do? And there was the March. Tarceny would be hers if Ulfin were gone. And the Trant manors. Tarceny and Trant: keys to the Kingdom. Someone would want to get them, through her. She saw the long, weary game opening up ahead of her. Something in her heart went cold.

'I had thought to ask clemency for you,' she said, and wondered why she had even bothered to hold out a hope he must know was useless.

'They will not see me hanged.'

There was such a flat finality in his voice that for a moment she thought she had misheard.

'I was King,' he murmured. 'And a fly in a web. Both at once. Now it is over. It is not Septimus—'

'What are you saying?'

'Does Ambrose still have the stones?'

Her fingers clenched around the pebble in her palm. She said: 'Yes.'

'I have doomed myself. But I am glad, Phaedra. It is better. And I may look my brothers with a straight eye when I see them.'

Another silence. Beyond the window the sudden swell of rain. It was deep dark out there now.

'Calyn knew,' he said. 'We felled the stone together, but even then he saw further than I. He tried to warn me. And his last act was to send me the white stones that he had carved from the teeth of Capuu by the pool. Not even the love and the rage of the Mother of the World can pass them. Perhaps if Calyn had not . . . But I had already begun by then. We had spoken. I had been given the bowl. And I had seen you at the poolside. Yes, I had made my bargain.'

'Bargain? What bargain?'

Behind her the door opened.

'The chaplain, my lady,' said Chawlin.

Martin had changed into a dull robe, and wore his hood thrown forward about his face. He stepped up silently to settle beside Phaedra.

'What bargain, Ulfin?'

He was looking up at the ceiling. 'One I have failed to keep.'

'And the terms?'

'Go – with me.' His mouth clamped shut.

'Perhaps I can help you,' she heard herself say, in a calm, dry voice that might almost have belonged to another.

'You wanted power, of course. The Cup gave that to you – the power to see far off, to walk in dreams and to cross the world by moving in the dark places. Many tricks like that. I think you have written them in a book, which may not be far away. It gave you the power to love and be loved by one with whom you chose to drink from it. You bewitched me, Ulfin. Did you think I would never learn what you had stolen from me?'

Her voice was shaking. Ulfin lay, and Martin sat, like statues as she spoke. Neither made a sign. She drew breath. The price . . .

'But first of all it was for the life of your father, to avenge the brother to whom you had bound yourself through the water.

'Do you know that in two years in this house I never wondered how you had brought an end to your father? Yet it was there for me to see. Caw dealt quickly with the marks we found on the stair. So quickly I think – perhaps – that such things have been found in this house before. By the hearth in the hall where you broke the floor patterns with black marble, because you could not get the white.'

Still he did not answer; and the rain beat heavily at the night outside.

'How else, you may say, could a friendless young man come at so armed and cruel a lord? Yet you went further. When Trant had fallen – by your under-craft, although you allowed the world and me to think it was my own faithlessness – you sought the life of the King. And the King died—'

'You lied!'

She looked at him.

'You said – you had not spoken with him.'

'If I have lied to you, Ulfin, I was not the first to deceive. And I did not lie. I did not speak to him. He spoke to me, by the pool, as he handed me the water that broke at last the bond that you had laid on me. That is the truth. And it is the sort of truth you have been telling me for two years. And what of me? Why did you enspell me – enspell us both – for all those years? Was it for Trant: your foothold in the heart of the Kingdom? Or was it because – because only through me could you pay your price?

'How *could* you live with me, Ulfin? How could you have wed me, and looked me in the eye, knowing that the price you would pay would be *the life of our son*?'

'No!'

'*For a father, the life of a son*, he said. *For a king, the life of a king* – Ambrose Umbriel, the King who would be. That was what you would rather have left me to die than say. And that is why I have done what I have done!'

'I – did not know him! Phaedra!' He jerked up onto one elbow. His face writhed with pain. She saw the open neck of his shirt, and a little black key on a chain against his pale skin. She saw him gather himself.

'What you say is true—'

'True!' She laughed shrilly. 'I never thought to hear you say that. "Speak the truth to one another." What a curse that was! "Keep your promises" – including the

398

promise you had made to him. What was the other? "Let your lives be a mirror to one another." We have both led our fathers to their deaths. You made a bargain to be King, and offered your child. I made a bargain with the King, to save your child. And my price was you. Dear Angels!'

'Phaedra – think what you will. But do not think that I gave a child I knew for power, or wed you for any other cause than yourself. When I first made my bargain – I did not know what the price would be. He only said he would tell me when the time was right. I was young, grieving, hating everything. I would have given anything I had or thought I ever would have to be avenged on my father. After that – I used – what he had given me. There was never a word of price. If I thought at all it was only to assume he was showing me favour as the last of his own father's line. And he showed me you, by the poolside. Do you remember? You were close to willing yourself to death when I spoke with you.

'Yet had I known then what the price would be I would never have asked to wed you. Believe this. It was only when I spoke with him after the taking of Trant that I understood what he intended. And by then I was committed to war with the King – a war I could not win without his help.

'So I returned, when I could, to you. I was going to take Ambrose then. Yet when I saw him – when I heard the name you gave him – when I knew how I loved you – I could not give him up . . .'

It was Orcrim and Caw who had forestalled him, pointing to an imaginary likeness with the brother whom he had loved. They had guessed, these men he would now have her kill. They had saved her son while she was blind to the danger. She drew breath to speak. But it was pointless now.

'So I refused the Prince Under the Sky. I gave Ambrose the stones I had kept for my own protection. I surrounded myself with armed men – he and his can take hurt from iron, Phaedra. I would not use the power he offered, although my men paid dearly for it. And I went into the mountains, where you found me, to tell him he could not have what he wanted, and to make another bargain.'

'You found you needed him more than he did you.'

'If I was to prevent – this – yes.'

'You trusted a maid and a wet nurse with secrets you would not trust to me.'

'They understood what you would not.'

'You mean they did not ask the questions I would have done! And you left us there. You went to use the power you knew could only be paid for in one way. You had him free you from the love you had cast on both of us, so that you could bring yourself to pay it. This was Ambrose's *life*!'

'There is another interpretation.'

She stopped. He had crowned himself on his return from the mountains. Why then? For a king, the life of a king. He had made himself a king indeed, whereas Ambrose . . .

'You mean you would have offered yourself . . . ?'

'Not if I could – help it. I hoped time would find me a third chance. But if nothing else . . .'

He had demanded Ambrose of her. Yet he had also warned her to keep Ambrose from him. If he had truly been caught in this web as a youth . . . If he had twice put himself at risk for his child's sake . . . For the first time since she had stepped through the door, Phaedra felt her conviction waver. The bitter clarity that had driven her speech was blurring. And as the wrong she perceived in him diminished, the things she had done seemed darker.

He must have seen her uncertainty, and known that his words had counted. He looked at the priest, as if to see whether Martin had understood too.

He froze.

Then, like a snake, his hand shot out and clutched the corner of the priest's hood. The sudden movement made him cry with pain. The hood fell.

It was not Martin's face beneath.

A small head, almost hairless, which wore a thin circlet of gold. Yellow-grey skin that stretched tightly over the skull. Eyes were set in deep sockets like pools in dark rock. The grey priest looked impassively down at the man before him.

'Once again you twist the truth, son of Talifer,' he said. 'You shrank from giving me the boy. Yet you supposed that if, despite you, I should come past your pebbles and take him, you should be both debtless and blameless, and that fault should lie with the three witless women you left to guard him.

'I will have my price. There is no third chance. There is no second chance. If a man would cheat me I take my price twice over. Your life is forfeit to me, son of your father and self-made King. Yet you shall not so save your son. The boy cannot stay within the ring for ever. One day I shall have him too, and then our bargain will be fulfilled.

'Except for this,' he went on, turning to Phaedra. 'I make one offer only to you. Twenty years of life, for either your husband or your son. The other to be mine at once, or as soon as a message may reach across the lake. Choose quickly.'

Phaedra could not answer. How had he come here? Where was Martin? But Martin's voice was sounding beyond the door, talking with Chawlin; puzzled, but unworried: ten feet from where she stood eye to eye with the grey priest.

'You think against me, daughter of farmers? You cannot. Your life is mine three times. I sent the priest-fool to find you among the rocks. I sent the boy-fool to stand for you at the swords. And most of all because I woke the girl-fool who lay starving her body for a love that had already betrayed her. You are mine. You cannot deny it.

'Choose. Twenty years is a good life. Many a child born tomorrow will die sooner. Or fifty years for the man, and maybe you will get more children yet.'

Could he deliver Ulfin from execution? Would he? But she could not offer her child's life. He must know that. He must know, and Ulfin must know, what choice she would make. If he had spared her, it was to be his tool. They were waiting for her to speak. The world was his eyes, like black pits, willing her towards the edge.

And a little white stone that she clutched in her hand.

He had spared her to bring Ulfin defeat. He had spared her for this moment. He wanted Ulfin to hear her condemn him. And still she would have bargained with the grey priest.

'I refuse.'

'You may not refuse. I will have one or other, or both. Choose.'

Nothing was real but the little stone that had been sent to her by her son.

'No.'

'Twenty-five years!'

Suddenly she laughed. She could not guess what purpose moved the priest. But he had shown weakness, and although she was still afraid she knew that she both must and could resist. And Ulfin was struggling to raise himself, his eye fixed on the apparition, the lamp shadows sweeping across his face; rising behind him like a black, twisted angel on the wall.

'Old man! Creeping, scheming dotard! What do your bargains and promises mean but the corruption of those that treat with you? Have you done nothing in three hundred years but bring ruin on each of your brothers' houses? Because they left you no land but that you could not hold. Envious, joyless, cheated! Hear me. I will pay your price – *our* price – with my body. But then be you gone, for my house is debtless to you.'

'You are mine, and your house will be mine, and only then will I be done with you.'

But Ulfin answered, Ulfin and more than Ulfin, for there was a light behind his eye and a power within his words that came from far beyond the man.

'Hear these words, Paigan Wulframson. Listen well. Least of your father's sons. By the last of your father's sons—'

'Enough!' The priest spread his arms. The room was filling with shapes and shadows. There was a sudden, strong smell as if of dank stone. Strange mutters and cries swelled around them. Ulfin's voice rose above them, pained and cracking, yet suddenly with the weight of trembling stars.

'By the last of your father's sons shall you be brought down!'

And then they were on him.

Shapes with low, hooded faces rose around the bed. Floorboards broke. She saw Ulfin's head forced back, his leg kicking. Something with eyes and a beak billowed in front of her, buffeting her sideways like a blast of wind. She fell. She heard Ulfin scream.

'Chawlin!' she cried. 'Chawlin!'

The room was crowded. The door erupted inwards. Chawlin was there, sword in hand. Martin was at his shoulder. She saw Chawlin seize a shadowy limb, saw the creature turn and *crow* in the face of its challenger. Chawlin recoiled with a cry.

Martin was yelling the names of the Angels. Phaedra scrambled on her hands and knees, and struck with her fist that held the pebble against a leg of stone. It jerked away, dragging her with it over the broken floor. The sword whipped and sang above her head. There was a clatter and a shriek. Feet were running in the corridor. Men were in the antechamber. Everyone was shouting or shrieking.

They had the sword. Two, three clawlike hands clutched the blade, black against the bright metal. Chawlin was pulling at the hilt. Past the gibbering, crowding things Phaedra saw across the room the face of the grey priest watching her. Then he turned into the wall and was gone.

The room was empty.

'Dear Michael!' said Chawlin, and leaned against the wall.

The chamber stank. The floorboards were scarred and splintered. The bed was broken. Ulfin lay huddled in a mess of blood beside it. Phaedra crawled over to him, and stopped when she saw the wounds. The chest, the arms, the legs, the face were all gouged with bloody tracks. Martin was at his shoulders, turning him. She bent over the wreck of the man.

Even now he was not quite dead. His good eye flickered at her. The mouth moved.

'Raise – the King's stone. Hillmen – help. Raise . . .' He tried to cough, and could not.

'Ulfin?' she whispered. There was no answer.

Someone was kneeling at her side. It was Septimus. She looked at him, and realized that the room around her was crowded with his followers.

'These are the same wounds my father bore,' he said. 'And my brother.'

'And, I guess, the old lord of Tarceny,' someone added. 'Justice has a hard face. Is he dead?'

'Yes,' said Septimus.

After a while the prince rose to his feet. 'Madam,' he said. 'There is much here that may be guessed at. And much, no doubt, that will never be known. But if you know any of the causes of what has passed here, you have a duty to reveal them to me.'

'I do,' she said. Gingerly she eased the cord that held the little black key from around Ulfin's bloody neck, and rose to her feet. She was thinking how his heart had beaten against the key to his secrets, as hers had beaten against

405

the ring he had given her. His heart was still now. Hers too.

She looked around her. Aun was there, and Tancrem, Chawlin, Septimus and a half-dozen others, watching her as if she were about to grow horns and a tail.

'If you will follow me.'

She led them to the War Room. The black chest was on the table, locked. The wood gleamed in the lamplight, writhing with shadows and the carved creatures upon it. She saw Chawlin peer closely at them and look away. She tried the key, and it clicked in the lock.

The chest was no longer empty. Within lay a stone bowl, with a stem and a base like a large cup. Beside it on the cloth lay a book. Septimus lifted the bowl out and looked at it curiously. There was something like a snake carved around the rim.

'Rude workmanship,' said someone.

'It was cut by the hand of a prince,' she said.

'Did he show you the purpose of these things?'

'No. The Cup I have seen only in my dreams. He would gather water in it, in which to see far off, and so defeat his enemies.' Aun was nodding. 'He could cross great distances swiftly, and pass doors that were locked. It helped him in this. And – there were other uses.' She remembered the taste of the water in her dreams, warm, and sweet as the faintest honey. 'The book I have never seen before, although I guessed it must exist. I do not know if there is now any witchcraft in them. I believe it came through them, from beyond.' She used the word *witchcraft* for the sake of her listeners. It had a strange feel on her tongue.

406

Septimus lifted the book and turned a few pages. She could tell at once that neither he nor any of those craning over his shoulder could read well.

'It would be best to destroy them,' someone said.

'Not yet,' said Septimus. 'There may be something that can be learned from them about this evil that has threatened us. But we shall not treat them lightly. The Cup shall remain here, secret and guarded. And Lord Lackmere, you shall take the book into the south. Keep it in your home, and let none approach it without my permission.'

Aun hesitated for a second, as the book was put into his hands. He looked at Phaedra and then at Septimus, who was already returning his attention to the Cup. Phaedra could see, written on his face, his dislike of the mission he had been given. It was not just the book. He did not want to go into the south, to return to his family and live at home. And from Septimus's bearing she guessed that the prince knew it, and was nevertheless sending him away. If Septimus had not said what he planned for Trant or Tarceny, it was clear they would not include Aun.

Ulfin had been right. They were already beginning to move against each other. Whoever Septimus left to occupy Tarceny would be well placed. A widow who wanted to assert her position as landlord in Tarceny and Trant would need a powerful following, allies, and most probably a new husband. They all knew that. And if Septimus indeed intended that she should sit beside him on the throne in Tuscolo, and could find the right sort of men to hold Trant and Tarceny for him, why, he would be stronger than many a king in memory.

She felt very tired. And all at once she was angry. These half-people! Competent butchers of men! They were brave and spoke fairly, but in the end they shared all manner of Ulfin's faults without having an ounce of his knowledge or vision. And yet they would shape her future for her. She would be a piece on the board, loved and hated only for the advantages she might bring. How long before one of them remembered whose son Ambrose was? Septimus would abide by his word, but how many barons or counts might see themselves as kingmakers? She could not allow that to happen.

She wanted to leave, and find somewhere in all this house – her house – where she might rest. Yet there was one more thing.

'May I see the book, please?' she said. 'It will not take long.'

Aun passed it to her. He did not wait for Septimus's nod to do so.

It was heavy in her hands. She leafed through the pages of vellum, some blank, some written in Ulfin's flowing script, aware that the men were all looking at her. She could not be long, in case they started to think that she was researching some spell.

It was not a book of spells. It seemed to be more of a narrative. She turned the leaves. The first entry was headed 'PRINCE PAIGAN' and ran for pages, broken into short or long sections that recorded each meeting. Her eye fell on some sentences that contained the words 'King's Stone', but they told her no more than she had guessed. The next was headed 'PAIGAN' again.

The next entry was her own.

She was taking too long. The men were growing restless. Septimus was frowning, jerking his head slightly as if to indicate that Aun should take the book back. Aun remained impassive, waiting.

'A moment more,' she said.

Quickly her eye fell down the pages. Something in her cried out to stop, and weigh every word. There was no time. She skipped ruthlessly past Ulfin's impressions of a nine-year-old child by the pool, past their early encounters when the girl was learning not to jump and look round as the voice addressed her. Words such as 'wit' and 'lovely' rose from the page, and she ignored them.

. . . and I will whisper my wish upon the water and we shall taste it. For I have mourned enough, and it is time I loved again.

She wanted more than that. And there was more. There were lines that began with words like 'She understands quickly'; or 'She nurses a deep sadness that I cannot touch . . .' There was page after page of it.

But the room around her was thick with armed men and suspicion. The world was not safe, not safe for her to linger with the secrets of a man's love, to find if they were true.

'Thank you,' she said, and shut the book abruptly. 'Your Highness, I would have your leave to withdraw. It is late, and I am unused to such a day.'

Septimus nodded.

'There was something else in here,' said a bearded knight, as she returned the book to Aun. 'See, the cloth is marked.' He jabbed a stubby finger at the outlines left by

409

the box of white stones, and looked up at her, waiting for an explanation.

'I have no knowledge of that,' she said.

It cost her nothing to lie in that company.

XXIII

South Wind

nce more she was waiting for the dawn. The old moon was low above the horizon, the narrowest fingernail of yellow silver, with a whisper of the new moon in its arms. A ghostly light glowed upon the shadow to show the full disc against the sky.

She was at the window in the big room in Mistress Massey's house at Aclete. She had risen and dressed with Hera's help, quietly and with as little light as possible. Now Hera had gone. She was alone, turning memories in her mind.

What would the Angel write: upon Ulfin's page, and hers? Not revenge. Among the knights vengeance was justice. She did not feel vindicated or justified at the memory of his broken corpse, or of the others who had died that night; or of the widowed wives and fatherless children whom she knew.

The moon was rising, pregnant; and what she felt was loss.

So something had survived in her, when the foul priest had passed her the Cup that had set her free. Had she loved Ulfin from herself then, under all the effects of the

411

spell? Or was it that she had been so changed by the years of enchanted loving that no mere drink could restore her altogether? The secret is not to have fear, he had said. Perhaps the water had simply suppressed the fears that might have kept her from him: *think of your father; think of the power of your suitors; think of yourself.* And without such fear, love might have grown easily in the lonely girl during the long years when her best companion had been his voice, speaking from shadowed corners in the passages of Trant.

No one could tell her now. The Prince Under the Sky was her enemy. Ulfin was dead, and his book was beyond her reach. The words she had glimpsed on its pages had added to her knowledge, but not to her understanding. It was as fruitless to ask whether she had loved him as it was to ask if he had loved her.

He had betrayed Ambrose. Yet his very refusal to admit it to her, and his attempts to conceal it, showed that he had been ashamed. He had made some protection for his son, at some risk to himself. He had claimed that in the last resort he would have given his own life. What of that? Such a thing was easily said, before he knew who was listening. She did not accept it. But neither could she believe that the motives described by the Prince Under the Sky were all that had moved him. Ulfin had wanted the crown, and he had taken it. Yet, like a chess player, he had at the same time positioned himself so that he could make the sacrifice if it came to that. And would he have done so, if it had come? Probably not even Ulfin had known.

She watched the night greying, the headlands above Aclete beginning to take on distance. At last she smiled.

Footsteps, and a soft knock at her door. It was Hera, beckoning. Phaedra rose. Together they tiptoed along the corridor, past the room where Chawlin slept with his head still swilling from an evening's wine. Martin was waiting at the foot of the stairs, his head cocked towards the kitchen, where someone – Massey's housewoman – was chatting with the man who should have been on watch. He must have been lured indoors with the promise of a hot breakfast. The fellow would get trouble for this. Phaedra thought of leaving money to be smuggled into his purse. But that would only make it worse for him if it was discovered. She grimaced as she stepped from the door into the cold wind. In the world of iron, nothing could be done without causing hurt to someone.

Her escort had made no difficulties. They were guarding her on her way to Trant, and were to accompany her on to join Septimus at Tuscolo when the time came. They had taken it on trust that the ship would not sail until noon. Yet Chawlin knew that the prince and his counsellors expected the Lady of Tarceny to arrive safely for his coronation. And once at Tuscolo she would have no freedom at all until the ordering of the Kingdom, and her part in it, had been decided.

She would slip away now, and disappear on the face of Derewater.

Martin had fallen into step beside her, saying nothing. A few moments ahead was a parting that would last for many years. After this he would fade into the south of the country, for he alone of the party knew where Phaedra would go. It was a blow for him. He had given much for the chance to work on the mountain borders of the March.

413

But this part of the Kingdom would have a long memory of those involved in the lady's disappearance. And if they saw him in the valleys, they might begin to wonder if she had not gone that way too. It would be better for both of them if he were well away when Septimus, from Tuscolo, and Tancrem, from Tarceny, began to look for her.

They would not find her. Nor would Ulfin's followers (for whom she had obtained from Septimus their lives, if not their lands) when they came hunting for their revenge. She would stay only briefly within the bounds of the Kingdom, to gather Ambrose and supplies, and Eridi and Orani if they would still go with her. Then she would go into the mountains again. She had a duty to do.

'They are fell creatures,' Martin muttered at last. 'To have so little hurt from iron; and none at all, it seems, from my mouthings. Will you take care?'

Hearing his words, she smiled. 'Of course. But there is a simple answer. Do not fear for me.'

As they approached the jetty, she spoke again. 'I must take your miracle from you, Martin.'

'My lady?'

'The one who woke you in your camp, and brought you to find me . . .'

'Ah. Yes, I know.'

'You know who he was?'

'Remember, I saw him among those foul things a fortnight ago in Tarceny. And – it was not the first time.' He frowned, as if in thought.

'At Chatterfall?'

'Yes.'

'What happened?'

414

'It was a sore hour. I do not remember it gladly. He appeared and called on us to remove the stones. But diManey listened to his wife before his angel, and they did not come by us. You left your son in good hands. And so did I.'

So the priest had found the hiding place, and the people there that he had thought were his own. She shuddered. She had wanted to believe that Ambrose could remain hidden, even from him. She did not want to think that her son must live every day so close to capture. Yet Ambrose's defences – his defenders – had held. The ring had not been broken. Her friends had been true, and had not been deceived.

'Thank the Angels,' she said.

'Thank them indeed. For you have not robbed me of a miracle. Or if you have, they have given me another, and you as well. Did you hear how your husband spoke before they killed him? That was true prophesy, from the man who lied. I tell you, as we fought with those things, we heard the voice of Umbriel telling us what the end of this will be. I do not doubt that was what it was. And I think the one he spoke to knew it too.'

'Yes,' said Phaedra. 'I think he did.' For all his power, the priest had been in fear. Truly she could begin to believe in victory now.

There was a ship at the jetty, black against the greying water and the gilding sky. Its mast was stepped. It was rocking gently among the little wavelets that puckered the lake surface. There were men about it. Mistress Massey herself was waiting for them at the end of the quay.

'The master knows to steer north,' she said. 'Once you

are clear, you can tell him where to head. And my business will take him to Jent after this. He does not reckon to drop anchor in the March again for three weeks or more.'

Phaedra looked around at the harbour. Four other boats rocked at their moorings.

'And do you know, some rogue has been at my ships overnight?' said Elanor Massey. 'Every rope is cut – and the oars are hidden where it will surely take us all day to find them. That I should live to see this!'

Phaedra smiled. Almost the last of Tarceny's silver was in the purse at Mistress Massey's belt: a fair price for the trouble her people were going to. Aclete would benefit from the peace as well. Even so, she was proving a good friend, and one Phaedra wished she could have known better.

Farewells now on the jetty. Elanor Massey, with a smile and a slight bob. Hera, crying and trying not to. Martin, with a sudden energy in his handshake that said many things. She bowed her head and stepped aboard, unattended. The boatmen were lashing the last supplies and readying the oars. The captain was talking with Massey. Phaedra stood in the bow, feeling the gentle rock, tug, rock of the boat on the face of the water. Its soft urging spoke of a hurry to be gone. All that had happened here was memories. A new cycle was beginning.

Above her rose the bulk of Talifer's Knoll, its eastern face still deep in shadow. The curve of its brow was bare. She searched it for signs of some robed figure, or figures, looking down on the bay. There were none.

I know you now, Paigan, my enemy. I know what you meant when you spoke of truth and mirrors, up there. I

416

know what manner of creatures walked with you when you left us on the hilltop. You have worked all your living years to ruin the heirs of your brothers and bring each as low as is in your power – shamed, corrupted, condemned, even to the father who would kill his own son. I know how you trapped Ulfin; how you worked to trap me, and Martin, Adam and Evalia to be your pawns. Now we who are living have slipped you. And I am coming to wall you in.

It was simple, if not easy. The King's stone was the key. It lay where the brothers had felled it, in the mouth of the gap in the cliffs around the priest's pool. Raise it, and the ring the brothers had broken, the circle of white stones, would be complete. It would keep the things of the pool within, just as the pebbles that Calyn had cut from the monoliths had kept them out. She did not know how the stones had come there, or when. Perhaps the last of the High Kings had learned the source of the evil that was wasting his Kingdom, and had known how to confine it for a while. Perhaps they were ancient, the teeth of Capuu himself, and had risen and fallen many times at the hands of men.

The hillmen would help. She would need crowds of them, which would demand more gifts and goats, and the means to get them where they were wanted. She would need any aid that there was to be had at Chatterfall. They would wall Paigan and his creatures behind the King's stone. She would live in the ruined house, beyond the reach of counts and princes, watching over the ring. And Ambrose would run free on the mountainside; until one day she, or maybe he (if that was what the voice that had spoken from within Ulfin had meant), would find how to finish the monstrous prince within it.

The sun was rising. There was little movement in the town, and none from the escort, billeted for the most part at Ulfin's lodge. A sentry watched them idly from the doorway, uncomprehending. The sailors were waiting for their captain. They were squatting in the bottom of the boat, talking to one another in low voices. One had dug out a little reed flute and was nursing it on his knees. None looked her way. They must know who she was, and what she had done. Elanor Massey had chosen each one of them. They would do their part. And now the captain was stepping aboard. The sailors were pushing off, sitting to their oars and pulling the first short strokes. The strip of water between her and the jetty was already more than she could jump across.

Behind her the piper lifted his flute and struck into the ancient song of the lake-sailor, who calls on the winds to carry him home. She felt the rhythm of the boat alter. *Wash, wash, wash* went the oars, in time to the long notes. She waved a last farewell to the three figures on the quay, and turned to see the lake flooding with the sunrise.

Bright water, dark hill. The contrasts on the fringes of Tarceny were as the two faces of the moon. There had been a day, two years before, when she had stepped from one to the other. Even then her love had been corrupted by the waters of the undead prince. Perhaps all that had followed had already been inevitable.

But she had ridden up out of the lake at sunrise, on the arm of the man she loved. There was something perfect about that still. She could remember the mingled sense of wonder and disbelief, then and for a time after, as it had seemed that everything she had wanted and yet never known she had wanted was being given to her hour by hour. She had been more truly alive then than before, or than she ever would be again. That time belonged in her life. It shone clear like the arc of the new moon.

With it, there should have been other times, times with Ulfin unclouded by war or dark things, going on and on in the full disc of their lives. Maybe they would have been less bright – the face of the moon bore many marks and seas, as no doubt did many a marriage. They should have been there. And perhaps they were somehow, as the full moon was there beneath the shadow on its face. The shadow was terrible; darkening, corrupting. Yet in the ruin of her dreams she could imagine no other life that could have been meant for her.

Well, fancies coloured fact – the more so when she sought to justify what she had done. And it was done. Both brightness and the dark were part of her now. The months and years ahead would show her new perspectives.

But the sunset would bring her to Chatterfall: to Evalia, and Ambrose in her arms.

Also by John Dickinson

The WIDOW and the KING

★ "A delicately interconnected tale that gratifies on multiple levels. . . . [A] luminous and memorable high fantasy story."
　　　　—*The Bulletin of the Center for Children's Books,* Starred

"[A] compelling, thoughtful sequel. Dickinson creates an intricate, complex world with memorable characters and engrossing subplots that fantasy enthusiasts will thoroughly enjoy."　　　　　　　　　　　　　　—*Booklist*

"John Dickinson obviously has storytelling in his blood. He is a gifted writer, able to create a detailed fantasy with believable flesh-and-blood humans inhabiting a strange world."
　　　　　　　　　　　　　　　　　　—*KLIATT*

"An intelligent, literate sequel. . . . Its subtle depths demand careful attention that will reward any thoughtful devotee of speculative fiction."　　　　　　　　—*Kirkus Reviews*